The Amalfi Bride
by Ann Major

Damn it.
Why had he been born Principe
Don Nico Carlo Giovanni
Romano?

How could he watch her get on that plane and fly away?

She would marry someone else. Have his children.

But if he defied his mother and the rest of his family, marriage to her would be considered a disaster by everyone in his world. Especially by his mother.

His fist gripped a tangle of sheets as she continued to whisper love words in his ear. He wanted this night to last forever.

He caressed her hair and spoke Italian again, his heart making promises he could never keep.

Blackmailed into Bed
by Heidi Betts

ⓢ ✕ ⓔ

How did *she feel about Chase's offer?*

Her stomach jumped at the question, followed by a peculiar, almost traitorous warmth that spread through her.

Could she actually be attracted to Chase? On more than simply the detached level of a woman catching a glimpse of a good-looking man?

Could the attraction go deeper? Could she actually be considering saying yes to his proposition? To becoming his mistress?

A skittering of nerves joined the heat flowing through her bloodstream. She'd never been a man's mistress before, never been in a relationship based solely on sex. She and Chase had nothing in common other than her father's company. He wanted her for two reasons only – to look good on his arm at business gatherings and to satisfy him in bed.

And darned if that idea wasn't becoming more appealing by the minute.

Available in April 2008
from Mills & Boon® Desire™

His Forbidden Fiancée
by Christie Ridgway
&
The Royal Wedding Night
by Day Leclaire

ဖြစ်ပြုပြ

The Amalfi Bride
by Ann Major
&
Blackmailed into Bed
by Heidi Betts

ဖြစ်ပြုပြ

Bound by Marriage
by Nalini Singh
&
The Durango Affair
by Brenda Jackson

The Amalfi Bride
ANN MAJOR

Blackmailed into Bed
HEIDI BETTS

MILLS & BOON
Pure reading pleasure

First published in Great Britain 2008
by Harlequin Mills & Boon Limited,
Eton House, 18-24 Paradise Road, Richmond, Surrey TW9 1SR

The publisher acknowledges the copyright holders of the
individual works as follows:

The Amalfi Bride © Ann Major 2007
Blackmailed into Bed © Heidi Betts 2007

ISBN: 978 0 263 85898 3

51-0408

Printed and bound in Spain
by Litografía Rosés S.A., Barcelona

THE AMALFI BRIDE

by
Ann Major

Dear Reader,

I hope this story brings alive for you a place that is as beautiful and as mythical as a fairy tale – Ravello, Italy.

Stories often come in bits and pieces. I was inspired to write *The Amalfi Bride* on a trip I made with my husband to Italy last fall. While lunching in Rome at an open-air café, we met a darling couple. She was a burned-out lawyer from a foreign land, who'd come to Italy to reclaim her soul. He was a gorgeous fisherman she'd "discovered" on a beach in Positano at dawn. When the bill for their lunch came, he gallantly vanished, and she paid.

When Ted and I journeyed on to Ravello, which is on the Amalfi Coast near Positano, the stunning setting added a new dimension to the story that was already writing itself in my heart.

Enjoy,

Ann Major

ANN MAJOR

lives in Texas with her husband of many years and is the mother of three grown children. She has a master's degree from Texas A&M at Kingsville, Texas, and is a former English teacher. She is a founding board member of the Romance Writers of America and a frequent speaker at writers' groups.

Ann loves to write; she considers her ability to do so a gift. Her hobbies include hiking in the mountains, sailing, ocean kayaking, travelling and playing the piano. But most of all she enjoys her family.

This book is dedicated to Lady Jane Liddington, a dear childhood friend, now living in London, for suggesting we meet in Ravello.

I also dedicate this book to the marvellous staff of the Palazzo Sasso Hotel in Ravello, who taught me that paradise does exist on earth.

And to the Italian people, who were all so wonderful to me and my husband when we were in their country.

And last of all to the beautiful young woman from Australia and her Italian lover, whom I met in Rome at lunch, who shared their story and inspired me.

One

Amalfi, Italy

Her last few days in paradise…so many sights, so little time left to see them. So, what was she doing here…in a bar…wasting her valuable time…lacking the will to hike or to tour one more cathedral or villa? Flirting with a dangerous stranger?

Oh, my God! I'm not flirting with him.

It was late July and warm in the open-air bar, although not nearly as warm as it would be back in Texas. Regina Tomei grabbed her glass of chardonnay and sipped too much, too hastily, spilling a few drops on her chin and neck. Quickly she dabbed at the dribbles with her napkin.

Her lengthy list of cathedrals and the notes she'd written about the Greek ruins fell to the floor. She didn't bother to pick them up. Instead, she stole another quick glance at the tall, dark stranger leaning against the bar across the room.

Who had said, "I can resist anything but temptation?"

The man instantly stopped talking to his short, plump friend and lifted his bottle of beer in a mock salute to her.

Oh, my God! Not again!

He took a slow, long pull from the bottle. Then his gaze touched her throat and lips. She gasped. Involuntarily, her hand with the napkin went to her mouth and then to the hollow of her throat, where her pulse was racing.

The heat of her own fingertips made her imagine his big hands and his lips upon her flesh. She began to perspire, so she fanned herself with the damp napkin.

Then, realizing what she was doing, Regina seized the ornate golden cross around her neck and held on for dear life. She'd bought the necklace from Illusions, an opulent shop she'd discovered tucked away in an alley of charming Ravello near her hotel.

Sightseeing and shopping were her hobbies; not barhopping, not flirting with strange men in foreign lands.

Run!

The man took another pull on his bottle and then stared at the gardenia in her hair. Before she could stop herself, she grazed the velvet petals with a stray fingertip.

Do not touch, signorina, or the petals will turn brown.

Regina picked up her camera and set it on her little table. Agitated, her hands flew to her lap, where she clasped them and her napkin, but not for long.

She looked up again, straight at her Adonis. Was it only her imagination, or did his blue eyes blaze with the same intensity as the sapphire Gulf of Salerno behind him? Was she the cause of all that fire?

Heat washed over her and, at her blush, he smiled.

Mortified and yet thrilled, too, she picked up her camera and pretended she found her light meter fascinating.

His friend observed all with a raffish grin and then, as if bored, hugged Adonis goodbye.

Oh, my God! The short guy was leaving! He would have to pass by her table!

She buried her face in her hands to avoid conversation, and he chuckled as he passed.

Somehow, the friend's departure seemed significant.

Not wanting to think about that, she concentrated on the glittering rings of condensation on the ceramic table from her wineglass.

Rule number one: smart women traveling alone in foreign countries do not pick up strange men, no matter how handsome or friendly or desirable they seem. In particular, women don't pick them up in a bar, even one with whitewashed walls, cascading bougainvillea and lots of sunshine and tourists.

She told herself to grab her camera, get up and walk away! No! Run! She should run like she had last night. She had no idea what sort of person he was.

What if he was a gigolo or, worse, a serial killer?

Her mind returned to the G-word.

A gigolo? Was the blond fellow a pimp? Did gigolos even have pimps? She could write a brief on what she didn't know about gigolos and their business plans.

Regina frowned as she remembered the older woman with the platinum hair, loud makeup and trailing orange veils with whom she'd seen him yesterday in the red Maserati convertible. The woman had caught Regina's attention because she'd spotted the car in front of Illusions earlier.

The driver had been the same elderly shopkeeper who'd sold her the cross, the sentimental little painting of the black-haired boy playing in the sand, the scandalous pink-and-black lace underwear she was wearing now, her skimpy new dress and, of course, the darling white sandals to match.

Yesterday afternoon, when the older lady had dropped him off at the beach near the mooring of the immense white yacht called *Simonetta,* Regina hadn't thought much about her kissing his dark cheeks so many times. Nor had she wondered why the older lady had been so reluctant to let him go. When the woman had spotted Regina watching them, she'd recognized her and had waved, beaming. When he'd looked at Regina, he'd acted startled and had broken off the embrace.

Suddenly, the little scene took on a darker, more lurid meaning. A gigolo?

And what about that diamond the size of an ice cube on the finger of the regal, middle-aged woman in the black Ferrari with him today? She, too, had driven him to the same beach and had kissed his cheeks almost as ardently as the other, older woman. Only the second woman had had a more commanding air, summoning him back to the Ferrari twice.

Now, the stranger's eyes on Regina's bare skin felt like fire. She wished she'd put on something that was more *her.*

Regina's usual attire back in Austin, Texas, tended to be dull, predictable suits that covered her up, which were appropriate when a young woman was an attorney and made her living in courtrooms.

How ironic that his elderly mistress or client, or whoever the woman was, had sold Regina her revealing white sundress. The same woman had talked her into taking the clips out of her hair, too.

"You very lovely, *signorina.* With wavy hair down. You need flower in your hair. Special flower from magic bush. Then you get boyfriend for sure. Come. I show you."

Was it so obvious Regina had no lover? No boyfriend?

With orange veils trailing behind a body that was still voluptuous and hidden bells jingling, the woman had led Regina out of the shop down a cobblestone path to a courtyard with a marble statue of Cupid and a thick bush ablaze with gardenias.

"This bush blooms all year. Pick one every day you are here, if you like. And I promise, a miracle will happen. *Prometto.*" Her dark blue eyes had twinkled like a fairy godmother's.

Delighted, Regina had picked one yesterday. Then, this morning, she had gone back for another.

The gulf had a mirror finish; the sinking sun was turning to apricot the villas and hotels that perched precariously on the cliffs. Soon the coast would be magically suffused by the soft, slow twilight she'd come to love.

For as long as she could remember, Regina had wanted to visit the Amalfi Coast. Leaning down, she picked up her list of sights and notes. She should be admiring the mountains trembling steeply above the sea instead of devouring a man who could be a sexual professional.

You probably couldn't even afford him.

Oh, my God!

If he *was* a gigolo, *he* obviously thought she could afford him. Why else was he eating her up with his dark blue eyes?

Her throat went so dry that she gulped more chardonnay.

Gigolos were losers who preyed on older, lonely women; definitely not part of her life plan. She should be shocked to the core by her train of thought.

Afford him? She should indict him!

In Austin, she had a reputation for being prim and proper and…and well, bossy. Not that she was. Nobody, not even her family, understood how strongly she had to focus to accomplish her goals.

"You're a control freak and frigid!" Bobby had accused after she'd stunned them both, herself and him, by rejecting his marriage proposal.

"Please, let's don't get ugly," she'd said.

"Give me my ring!" He'd bruised her finger when he'd tried to pull it off. "Even though you chased me for a whole damn year, you probably did me a helluva favor."

"I chased you? I gave you my card at a party because I wanted to work for your father's firm."

"Just my luck! He hired you! You may be a good lawyer, but you're one lousy lay." He shoved his chair back and slammed out of the door of their favorite sushi restaurant, leaving her alone with a huge wooden serving dish filled with eels and shrimp and caviar, zero appetite, and the bill.

A lousy lay? Okay, so, yes, she had faked an orgasm or two. But only to make him happy.

What if a talented gigolo was able to teach a motivated student a few naughty tricks and make her sexier in bed?

Susana, her flaky, younger sister had tried to console her. "You're going after the wrong type. I never liked Bobby anyway.

Who wouldn't have to fake orgasms with a man who never thought about anything but billable hours? Just a word though, maybe you should try being more intuitive. And maybe you shouldn't boss guys around so much."

Susana, a housewife, who'd stolen Joe, the one man Regina had loved, had had the gall to give *her* advice. How had Susana, a college dropout, become the successful sister?

Hello! Susana had given their folks three darling grandchildren.

"I'm not *that* bossy."

"Well, don't let your boyfriends see all those lists you make."

"I just like to get things done," Regina grumbled aloud to the voices in her head as she crumpled another napkin and wiped the condensation rings on her table.

Intuitive?

She was sitting as far as she possibly could from the sexual professional, if that was indeed what he was. Too aware of his satiny black hair and flirty eyes, she tidied up her table, slipping a fresh napkin under her wineglass. Still, just knowing he was over there, alone now, had her pulse beating like a war drum.

Most of her girlfriends had shocked her by sleeping with strangers at least once, and then describing their sexual misadventures in vivid detail over long lunches. But that lifestyle hadn't been for Regina. She'd always known she'd wanted to love and marry a respectable professional man, and she'd accepted dates only from men who met her criteria. She had a long list of criteria.

But the instant she'd seen this stranger, who should be unappealing to her, her world had shifted. It was as if the real Regina had gone into hibernation, as if Austin were a remote planet on the other side of a galaxy far, far away.

Intuitive. Dangerous word.

If ever a man was the antithesis of the ambitious, Type-A individuals the real Regina always chased, this G-word guy was it.

Obviously, Adonis was all looks and no substance. Still, his broad-shouldered body seemed made of sculpted teak, with muscles that rivaled Michelangelo's *David.* What well-educated girl didn't appreciate a masterpiece? But could he read without moving his beautiful, carved lips?

Like all Italians, he wore clothes that fit perfectly. Hello! Why didn't she care whether or not he had a brain? A soul?

She was too entranced by the shallow stuff to dwell on deeper matters. His white shirt was open to his waist, revealing a lean, washboard abdomen. Some fierce mating instinct made her want to tear off his shirt and his ripped, faded jeans, to lick his warm, sun-caressed skin and have him do the same to her. *Yes!*

Despite the balmy July sea air, she thought of him naked. The idea of tasting him had her so hot she lifted her icy glass of chardonnay to her lips. Rethinking the more-alcohol move, she brought the cool glass to her warm cheek and then placed it against her forehead.

Would his babies be as gorgeous as he was?

Babies? The thought broadsided her. For a long moment she stared into her wineglass. Suddenly, dazzling golden images of a beautiful little boy and a darling little girl materialized, both with thick heads of shiny, black-satin hair, splashing in a backyard pool.

She swirled the wine in her glass so violently a few drops splashed her wrist. When he smiled, she blushed again.

A baby. His baby? No way!

What about E-321, which she'd learned about thanks to her friend Lucy? The sperm from a donor whose profile was so perfect Regina had bought the last eight vials of it from the sperm bank?

Hello, is the real Regina alive and well? The Regina who knows one doesn't buy sperm and then sleep around?

Okay, so she hadn't shown up on the day of her appointment for insemination.

But after Bobby, she had had a life-changing epiphany.

Baby first. Finding Mr. Right, second.

Time was running out for her to meet Mr. Right, date him, plan a wedding and get pregnant—in the proper order.

So, why not reverse the order of things?

Why not become a single mother of choice first and find her soul mate later?

So, how did one find the perfect father? Her best friend Lucy, who was now pregnant by sperm donor E-321, had been full of advice. After lots of research, Regina had decided E-321 was the right donor for her, too. Lucy and Regina's children would be half-siblings. Regina had told her family that she and Lucy and their babies would almost be a real family.

"You've got a real family!" her father had thundered. "This is your fault, Sabrina!" It was his habit to blame everything, good and bad, on Regina's mother. "You shouldn't have let her read all the time! Or run around with liberals like Lucy. I don't want to even think about those college loans I'm still paying off."

Although his temper hadn't won the day, he'd slumped into a scowling sulk and had remained glued to the television set whenever he was home over the next few days, refusing to speak to anybody, even his adored Sabrina.

Desperate, her mother had called an hour before Regina's insemination appointment.

"You're making Constantin unhappy. He's never gone quiet on me like this. Not in thirty years. It's summer. Take a vacation. When was the last time you took a vacation? Go to Italy. See your Nana before you do this crazy thing, eh, Cara."

Her mama always called her Cara, which was short for Carina, Regina's middle name.

"You can't control everything, Cara. In Italy, people let life happen. Susana fell in love. You will, too."

Yes, with Joe. I was in love with him! Susana stole him right out from under me. Why doesn't anybody, especially you, Mama, ever remember that Joe was mine first?

Regina covered her eyes for a long moment. Then she opened them to a line of ceramic pots overflowing and ablaze with geraniums, to terraces and umbrellas drenched in coppery light, and to him.

Two girls beside him were batting their lashes at him and looking winsome, but he had eyes only for Regina.

He looked at her with such longing, Regina felt a physical ache to simply get up and go to him, to press herself against him, to run her fingers through his hair, to touch him everywhere. To get to it. To do it somewhere nearby, any private place.

She wanted to lie under his lean, hard body on a soft mattress with sea breezes whispering over their glued-together, sweaty bodies. She wanted everything, all things, unnamable things, unimagined things from him.

I don't know his name. He hasn't even spoken to me and I want to make love to him like an animal.

Still, she knew his voice was low and deep and thick with amusement, because she'd heard him talking to the girls at the table next to his earlier.

In her real life across the Atlantic Ocean, she would have wanted to know where Adonis had gone to school, what were his life plans, who was his family. But this half-naked girl with the gardenia in her hair felt more than thought.

She was beginning to become a little scared. It was as if vital pieces of her being were rushing toward him and he was claiming all as his due. The hunger to be in his arms, to kiss him, to taste him, to know passion, real passion, maybe for the first time in her life, kept intensifying.

So, if he were a G-word guy, did that mean he could be hers…for a night? If she was willing to meet his price? Or did he just service a privileged few?

Blood rushed from her head.

But what about those eight precious vials of E-321's you-know-what stored at the sperm bank? What about E-321's picture and profile taped to her fridge? What about Lucy—brilliant, well-meaning Lucy—and their plan to raise their children together as siblings?

A sexy stranger was not for a health nut and control freak like Regina, either! She might catch something.

No. Something told her she wouldn't.

Maybe she'd gone without sex for too long. Maybe it was the voluptuous, naked statues dotting the landscape and decorating the palazzos all over Italy that had her hormones hot to conceive the old-fashioned way.

Regina believed sex was for committed relationships and marriage. Period.

What about for procreation? whispered the hormones. *You're thirty-three and single and nearly too old.*

You should be married, whispered another voice. All her life, Regina had been known for her brains, her old-fashioned morals, her perfectionism, her goal-setting abilities, and her quick decisions. What if she let herself go just this once?

Her lips parted. She nudged her skirt above her knee and waited for life to happen. How exactly did one go about hiring a gigolo anyway—*if he was a gigolo?*

Was there some secret signal? Should she lift her skirt even higher? Or maybe lower her lashes and wink seductively? Or should she walk over to the bar, open her purse and show him the money? Or should she just sit here and wait for him to make *the move,* whatever that was?

Last night he'd followed her into this same bar. Only, when he'd started to flirt, she'd run out and hidden behind some chestnut trees. He'd rushed outside and looked for her while she'd held her breath, frantic he'd find her. Finally, he'd given up and kayaked out to *Simonetta,* the mega yacht moored some distance from shore, where he must have spent the night.

With a woman? A client? The older lady in veils? Her thoughts made Regina feel slightly nauseated.

One moment, the object of her affections was leaning back against the bar, sipping his beer while studying the magnificent white yacht with a rather keen interest. The next, his gaze swept the room and fastened on her again.

She met his eyes. With a fingertip, she teased her skirt higher. Her lips parted. Spellbound, dry-throated, she did not look away.

His gold necklace flashed with the last of the sun's rays. A gift from a client? From the woman in the Ferrari? Or the one on the yacht? How many women were there? She had a prejudice against guys who wore gold necklaces.

Did one tip a gigolo? Would he tell her the rules? As an attorney, she had a natural interest in all contracts.

When he kept staring at her, the two girls giggled at the little table near his and then glanced at her, too knowingly. Doubtless, they were locals and knew his profession and read her intentions.

Was she that obvious?

When the girls frowned, Regina felt her cheeks heat and her pulse race.

Maybe she should rethink this. When she tried to stand up to leave, her legs felt too weak to hold her. She sagged against her table. Then her waiter scurried over with an icy flute of sparkling champagne. He said something in rapid, nasal Italian, which was beyond her minimal knowledge of the language and pointed to her admirer at the bar. When she looked over, Adonis shifted his weight onto his right leg and beamed.

Her heart sped up even faster, and her lacy pink panties trimmed in black lace began to feel damp. She should run out to the taxi stand and hire somebody to take her up to the palazzo where she was staying. She would take a cold shower or a long swim in the pool and then a sleeping pill. She needed to think this through, form a plan.

Instead, she touched the stem of the flute he'd sent over with a manicured fingertip. When she threw back her head, her long brown hair flowing down her back, and began to sip, his mouth curved again. She smiled back just as boldly.

Instantly, he uncoiled his long body and strode across the bar, causing a ripple of conversation, as well as bursts of giggles from the girls near the bar. When he pulled out a plastic chair at Regina's table, Regina gulped the last of her champagne.

"Do you mind if I sit down?" His voice was deep and dark, faintly accented, surprisingly cultured. It was as perfect as the rest of him.

A well-educated gigolo?

"I—I should say yes. I should go…really…."

"Probably you are right." He smiled. "But you're following a dangerous impulse." He paused. "Just as I am."

Her heart thundered.

Up close, his dense lashes seemed even longer and darker.

Why did God give guys eyelashes like those? It wasn't fair. But then, life wasn't fair, was it? Or she would be married and have children, and her father would still love her best.

Adonis's gorgeous, broad-shouldered body towered over Regina, making her feel even more vulnerable.

If you were to have a daughter by him, the lucky child would surely be movie-star beautiful, whispered her sex-starved hormones.

"I will go, if you want me to," he said.

When he turned, a savage pain tore her heart. "No."

Her throat went even drier. Her acute need threw her off balance. She licked her lips but could say no more.

He sank down beside her and signaled the waiter. Without asking, he ordered more champagne.

Did he expect her to pay? Was that part of the contract?

When the champagne came, she gulped it again, which seemed to amuse him. "Do I scare you?"

"I scare me. I've never done anything like this before."

"Good. That's reassuring." He laughed. "You're perfectly safe," he said. "I promise, we won't do anything you don't want to do."

Far too many needs and emotions were on fire inside her for such a comment to reassure her.

He held up his hand to order another drink, but she put her fingers over his. And instantly, at that light touch of fingertip to fingertip, a surge of syrupy heat flooded her. When the waiter looked over, she shook her head wildly.

Her admirer turned her fingers over and brushed the back of her hand with a callused fingertip. His touch was gentle; lighting hot sparks along every nerve in her body.

She felt weak, sexual, sizzling. All he'd done was caress her hand. When he fingered the cross at her throat, she pulled back, afraid he'd sense the rapid pulse that pounded beneath it.

She'd never experimented with drugs, because addiction hadn't been part of her plan for success. But now she suddenly understood the concept of mindless addiction at a profound level.

He was lethal.

No. He was just a professional. He knew what he was doing.

That was all. He was good at his job. This was what he got paid for. Everything was under control. He wouldn't do anything unless she decided to hire him. He was after money. Billable hours. Like Bobby. That she understood. *Too well.*

It wasn't as if he felt what she felt. She was in no danger. She was in control.

She felt hot, and the cool breezes gusting up from the sparkling gulf did little to cool her.

"I'm Nico. Nico Romano," he whispered against her ear, stroking her hand with that seductive fingertip.

The way he said his name warmed her blood almost as much as his touch.

But was it his real name? Did gigolos have stage names as actors did or pseudonyms as writers did?

"But then you probably know who I am…or at least *what* I am," he said, his expression almost apologetic.

So she was right—he *was* a gigolo.

She blushed, liking his discretion about avoiding the G-word.

"Yes." She glanced away.

"There's no reason to let it bother you. I'm a man, just an ordinary man."

"If you say so." She felt shy, unsure, out of her depth.

"And you are?" he continued.

"Carina," she said in a rush, choosing her middle name for protection, to put distance between them. "My mother calls me Cara. Everybody else calls me—" She stopped, realizing she was about to start babbling, something she did when she was nervous.

"Cara," he breathed. "In our country your name means *beloved.* It suits you."

The air between them seemed to grow even hotter, if that were possible. Or maybe it was only she who was ablaze.

He was good. But how much did someone of his caliber cost? Not in the mood to ask and discover his price excessive, she put the all-important question off.

"Are you hungry?" he murmured. "Or would you prefer to go straight to your hotel?"

Did having dinner with him cost more? And what would the staff of her palazzo think when they saw her with him in the restaurant? Did he go there often?

"I ate a late lunch," she said.

"So did I," he murmured.

He leaned closer. He slid one hand around her waist. His other hand lifted her fingertips to his sensually curved mouth, and he kissed each long nail and fingertip, lingering a little on the tips of her nails. Then he stared into her eyes. Everything he did was infinitely gentle. Somehow, nothing he did seemed faked or practiced, and long after he'd let her fingers go, the pit of her stomach felt hollow.

When she lowered her hand to the ceramic table again, she sighed. Good. She wasn't ready for the serious kissing to start. Not in public, anyway.

He leaned closer and traced her mouth with his fingertip, flooding her with more erotic heat. His eyes followed the path of his finger. He swallowed hard. So did she. The girls, who were watching, giggled again.

"Che bella," he whispered, scooting his chair back a little.

He wasn't subtle. But what had she expected? He was a gigolo. Not to mention Italian. This was a business relationship. She should applaud his talent and his professionalism. Instead, she was so caught up in what he was doing it was hard to remember this wasn't real.

He held up his hand for the check. Before she could rummage in her purse, he threw a wad of euros on the table, cupped her elbow and escorted her out of the bar. She was acutely aware that, when he'd stood up, everybody stopped talking. Even the music stopped. When he turned at the door to wave to the bartender, a final burst of girlish giggles saluted them.

He'd paid, no doubt, for appearances' sake.

He was one classy gigolo.

Remembering the Maserati, and the Ferrari and the yacht, *Simonetta,* where he'd spent the night, she began to wonder if she had enough cash in her purse.

If she didn't, would he take a credit card or at least escort her to the nearest ATM if they finished at a late hour?

Then she remembered he was one classy gigolo.

Of course, he would!

Two

Regina stepped out of the shower, dried herself with a warm towel and put on the hotel's thick, white fluffy robe as Nico had suggested. Her damp hair felt heavy and soft about her shoulders as she left the bathroom. Picking up her cell phone, she padded through the bedroom and then out onto her private belvedere to wait for Nico, who had left her suite to take a phone call.

Nico. She gulped in a breath of warm humid air. Trying not to think about him and what they were about to do, she looked down at the quaint town and its lush gardens. Nevertheless, her hands were shaking as she punched in her friend Lucy's number back in Austin.

Surely, heaven couldn't best Ravello. The jewel-like, medieval village seemed to hang suspended from its mountainside over the Amalfi Coast. The views from Regina's hotel, formerly a fourteenth-century palazzo with crumbling, vine-covered walls and Moorish arches, were breathtaking even now when the shadows were lengthening.

Flowers perfumed the balmy sea breezes. The bees were gone,

and the church bells were ringing. Cliffs and villas alike seemed to tumble to a dark, turquoise sea.

Not that she was all that interested in the white yachts or *Simonetta* or the sparkling water or even the palazzos. She was too consumed with excitement and fear.

"Pick up, Lucy," she whispered, tapping a bare foot with impatience on the sun-warmed stones. She could hardly stand feeling so alone and uncertain.

"Pick up!"

Pacing while she waited, she spotted Nico four floors beneath her. He was also striding back and forth on a terrace near the aqua pool, looking just as impatient and upset as she felt.

Did he want to be with her, or did he hate his work and dread the time he'd be spending with her? Or was it his conversation that had him on edge?

She wished his phone hadn't rung. She wished he'd look up and wave reassuringly, but his dark head was bent over the phone, and he seemed so absorbed she wondered if he'd forgotten her existence.

His cell phone had buzzed just after he'd ordered champagne, strawberries and an assortment of cheeses, and had suggested they get into the hotel's white, fluffy bathrobes and enjoy a drink on her balcony. When he'd recognized the caller's name in the little blue window on his phone, he'd frowned. Then he'd cupped Regina's chin, kissed her on the forehead, and apologized because the call was too important to ignore. He'd answered the phone with a smile and endearments in Italian and had excused himself, which had made Regina curious about the caller's identity, and a little jealous.

Was it a woman? A client? Whoever it was, the call was very important to him.

Just as Regina was worrying that her attraction to Nico might be heading toward an obsession—something she'd never experienced before in her orderly, controlled life—Lucy finally answered, her voice breathless.

"Hi!"

Lucy was pregnant by the sperm donor who she and her partner Beth had agreed was a perfect fit for them. They had pictures of him and his *children*, future half siblings to their own much-wanted child, posted all over their apartment.

"You'll never believe where I am," Regina began.

She went to the closet, pulled out the painting of the little boy playing in the sand, then returned with it to her balcony.

"Italy!" Lucy answered.

"I mean—" Regina stared down at Nico again "—where in Italy? And you'll never guess what I'm doing…."

The little boy's painted hair shone like black satin, exactly as Nico's did.

"You probably just got through jogging and are about to treat yourself to some tomatoes and fat-free mozzarella while you make long lists of must-see tourist attractions for tomorrow."

"Ravello! Which is *the* best place ever. I don't think anybody has ever heard of fat-free cheese over here, either. Are you familiar with Maxfield Parrish's paintings?"

"I'm not sure."

"Ravello is like those paintings." Regina lowered her voice. "I've met a man."

"Those are the four most dangerous words any other woman could say…especially if he's an Italian. But then you're you, so he's probably smart, ambitious…"

"He's not! But don't worry, this isn't serious. He's absolutely gorgeous, the most gorgeous man I've ever seen. *But…*"

"But what? With you, when it comes to your men, there always has to be a *but*."

For a long moment, Regina hesitated. She almost regretted calling Lucy.

"But? I'm waiting!"

"I—I think he might be a gigolo."

"You've got to be kidding."

Regina remained silent.

"That is such a cliché. And not a good one. Not for you! You've got to come home now! You've definitely been over there too long. You were supposed to relax, enjoy good food, art, pretty scenery, visit your grandmother in Tuscany…."

"I think the art may be part of the problem. The sculptures here are so erotic."

"Pay him and then drive straight to the airport," Lucy ordered.

"But he's so hot. I feel like I'm burning up."

"Did he slip something in your drink?"

"No!"

"Don't do it! This is all because Bobby said you were uptight and frigid and because you were pushing yourself at work way too hard. You don't have to prove you're a hottie in disguise. You don't! Now you know you called me because you wanted to hear the voice of reason."

No, Regina had called Lucy because she'd wanted to share something that felt important.

"I think I've been having doubts about E-321. I think Italy has made insemination just seem way too impersonal. I'm not *you*, you know. I can…be with a man."

"We talked about this, girlfriend. E-321 has gone through numerous screenings…. Use a condom with this Italian fellow if you don't come to your senses! What do you know about him except he's hot and that he charges gullible women like you a bundle for the pleasure of his body? I would think there would be plenty of free, horny Italians over there."

"Not like him."

Even three stories below her, Nico's tall, dark figure in jeans and a white shirt radiated power, assurance and masculinity. And something more.

When he looked up and smiled warmly, her breath caught in her throat.

She waved, as thrilled as a high-school girl with her first crush.

"I—I feel this weird, totally powerful connection to him."

"And you haven't even had your first orgasm! Not good. Run for your life! This is not a good thing."

"But it feels like a good thing."

"This is very, very bad."

Regina's cell phone began to beep. She saw Susana's name. Her flaky baby sister, who didn't have a digital gene in her body, never called her.

The name *Susana* flashed in bold blue.

"Oh, my God! Today's the day the twins are being christened. Susana's calling me! She's actually calling me—in Italy! I've gotta go! I totally forgot to call Susana!"

"One word! Airplane!"

"I'll call you right back."

"That sounds like a plan!"

Regina punched a button and took Susana's call. There was a loud wail on Susana's end, which meant either Regina's niece, Gina, who'd been named after her, or one of her twin nephews was unhappy.

"Hi, there," Regina said, feeling guilty. "How was the christening?"

"It's you! It's really you! Gina, she answered! I can't believe I really got you…on my fourth try even! All the way to Italy. Not that you know where that is, Gina, sweetie!"

"How's the christening going?"

"Everybody's here…except you."

Regina's guilt deepened.

"We're all out in the backyard. It's so hot. But you know Daddy. He had to grill. Mama's hovering to make sure he doesn't burn the steaks like he did last time. She keeps saying maybe you'll meet a man in Italy. She's still upset that you dumped Bobby. She hasn't given up on you meeting an Italian even though we all know that's not why you went. Don't tell her I told you, but she made me call you. She even dialed. She wants to know if the love bug has bitten."

Regina stared down at the extraordinarily good-looking man on the terrace and then swallowed. "Right."

"It has?"

"No!"

"She'll be so disappointed. She was sure Italy would do the trick."

Regina swallowed, her throat feeling extremely dry all of a sudden.

"Gosh, I miss you," Susana said. "Gina asks about you every single day. When are you coming home?"

"Three days."

"Gina's crying her head off. She wants you here. We all do. Especially since Daddy just said *the* most awful thing to her."

"What did he say?"

"I don't know what gets into him. I quote, 'Now that we've got two new cute baby boys, we don't need you anymore.'"

Oh! "He didn't! *Not again!*"

"Again?"

"Nothing."

Nothing…only…

Time whirled backward. Instantly, Regina was transported to the day when a darling, bald Susana had been brought home from the hospital in a flurry of parental excitement. Flushed with pride at being a big sister at last, three-year-old Regina had run to the baby carrier.

Her father had knelt, and she'd climbed into his lap and had thrown her arms around him.

They say you don't remember things when you're three, but they're wrong. His words had been like poisoned darts wounding her soul.

Now that I've got a new, cute daughter, I don't need you anymore.

Regina had backed away from him, and he'd picked up Susana. "Why don't we sing 'Rock-a-bye Baby'?"

Regina had raced to her own room and had hidden in her closet. Ever since, she'd been jealous of her sister and had doubted her father's love. Instead of abating with maturity, her dark feelings had grown more intense since Susana had married Joe and had given birth to her precious trio.

Her father didn't care about any of Regina's accomplishments. All he could talk about was Susana and the grandchildren. Not that Regina wasn't smitten by the children herself. Not that she didn't hate herself sometimes for feeling the way she did.

The green monster, especially when it involved a sister, had to be one of the most hatefully twisted feelings ever.

"Put Gina on," Regina whispered, biting her lips.

Gina's racking sobs got so loud Regina had to hold the phone away from her ear.

The poor, poor darling.

"Gina. It's Aunt Reggie. Listen to me, sweetheart. Papaw loves you. He was just teasing."

"I hate the baby brothers!"

Regina remembered all the times she'd felt as though she'd hated Susana just for being cute and petite and blond and adored, when Regina had been beanpole skinny in middle school. Not to mention flat-chested and too tall for all the boys.

"No, you're a good big sister. You love your little brothers. Dino and David need a good big sister. Papaw is being a bad Papaw! He does that sometimes. Everybody has a weak moment once in a while."

"Bad Papaw!"

"You're beautiful and adorable! Everybody loves you, darling. Especially me."

"And Pawpa?"

"And Pawpa," Regina said, even though she'd always secretly believed that once Susana had been born, he hadn't really needed his oldest daughter anymore.

"I love you, Aunt Reggie! Chocolate cake! Bye!"

"They're about to cut the cake," Susana said. "She's just like you when it comes to chocolate. Just like you in so many ways."

"You know I'm her biggest fan."

"I'm just glad I caught you."

"Me, too. Kiss all your darling children for me. I've missed them so much. I've bought two suitcases full of clothes and toys for them."

"Joe says hi."

Joe. Regina chewed on her bottom lip. What if Joe had married her? And she'd had children?

Susana hung up.

Her eyes misting, Regina couldn't stop thinking about her father and the hole he'd carved in her heart.

Now that I've got a new, cute daughter, I don't need you anymore.

For a long time, she stared at the dark gulf and the huge white yacht in the harbor.

Before Susana, her father had adored her. Regina had worked hard in an attempt to regain her number-one position in paradise. Always, always, she'd had to be a high-achiever, hoping against hope. But it hadn't worked.

Susana had been charming and flaky, *intuitive* as she put it, and so adorable that nobody minded her bad grades or lateness. They hadn't cared when she'd dropped out of college to marry Joe Hunt. Or even noticed that she'd stolen Joe from Regina, and Regina had been brokenhearted.

He'd been gifted, too. Law Review. Killer work ethic. He'd been *her* beloved boyfriend, but the moment he'd set eyes on Susana, the numerous things he'd had in common with Regina hadn't mattered anymore.

Too bad for Regina that Joe had been the only man she'd ever really loved.

Everybody in the family thought she was over him.

And she'd told herself constantly that she was. Just as she'd told herself that all her orgasms with Bobby had been real, too.

She didn't want to think about the fact that Nico was tall and dark and looked a little like Joe.

"Did you call Viola?"

Nico frowned. His mother, Principessa Donna Gloriana Lucia Romano—to mention only a few of her illustrious names and only one of her numerous titles—whose close friends called her Glory, was speaking Italian to him over his cell phone and quite rapidly, of course. Not that she liked Italian.

She'd been educated in Paris because her mother, Nico's grandmother, with whom Princess Gloriana was bitterly estranged, had had a French mother and had preferred all things French.

Both Nico's grandmother and mother loved the French language more than any other, but he preferred Italian or English, so his mother was humoring him. Because, as always, unlike Grand-mère, who wanted only his happiness, his ambitious mother wanted something from him.

"Not yet," he said.

"Nico, *tesorino,* why do you keep putting this off?"

"Maybe it's my gypsy blood."

She ignored his comment. She never liked being reminded that their original ancestor had been a gypsy king.

"You did promise to call the Principessa Donna Viola Eugenia di Frezano today when we lunched," she said. "You did say that you'd court her and that you'd ask for her hand in marriage as soon as possible."

"I did. And I will. You have instructed me as to my duty for my entire life. Have I ever failed in my duty?"

The silence between them was suddenly filled with tension.

"You know that the two families have already talked, that the marriage is practically arranged."

Of course, he knew. It would have already happened if he hadn't been dragging his feet—grieving. His heart was in the grave, as the saying went.

"You know that today marks…"

"I know," she said, trying to sound sympathetic. "But it's been two years."

His family and the family of his intended, Viola, were modern aristocrats with lineages dating back nearly a thousand years. Both families valued influence, power and money above all. Next, they counted culture, pedigree and tradition, not to mention titles—the grander and more illustrious, the better.

Nico's parents, who'd left much of his upbringing in the hands of countless nannies, tutors and chauffeurs, had taken the time to teach him and his sister that what really mattered was money, power and luxury, in that order. Personal wishes were to be sacrificed to strengthen the family.

A young man's dalliances with different types of women,

even actresses, were regarded as necessary, perhaps even a healthy diversion. Even after marriage, such playing around was tolerated, although not advisable.

But one did not marry just anyone.

"You're thirty-five," his mother reminded him again, just as she had this morning when they'd driven along the narrow roads high above the coastline. "It's time you settled down...again."

"I did settle down."

"She's dead. You're alive."

Was he? Every time the paparazzi caught him with another beautiful actress, the tabloids referred to him as the merry widower. But they didn't know about the guilt that tore at him over his treatment of Simonetta. How could they, when he'd been blind to what was in his heart until a month before Simonetta had died? At her death, love had overflowed inside him until he'd felt as though he were drowning.

"The *principessa* is very beautiful," his mother said.

"Like a jewel with icy fire."

"Without power and money, Nico, titles are meaningless. She has much to recommend her."

"So you've told me—countless times."

"You are a prince."

"A lamentable fact that overly complicates my life."

"With great privilege comes responsibility. You must marry well and behave responsibly to remain a prince. You must think of your children, of future generations. Our position has never been more fragile than it is in these modern times. Love, if one is lucky, comes after marriage. You loved Simonetta, didn't you?"

"I was lucky. Lightning will not strike twice in the same place." Annoyed by his mother, he drew a long breath. Somehow, he resisted the impulse to snap the phone shut. "Please, let's not talk about Simonetta."

"My poor *tesorino*."

His mother believed grief and all emotions were luxuries for people like them. After World War II, the Romanos had lost ten castles and nearly a million acres to the Russians. The family had prospered since the war by marrying well and diversifying their business interests. They had vast holdings in the Americas, many of which Nico managed.

Still, Viola's family had fared better in the past century and was much richer than his. His mother had begun courting Viola's parents at Simonetta's funeral.

"I understand that the match with Viola would be an exceedingly advantageous one for the family," he said. "But does everything really have to be about money?"

"Of course not, *tesorino*. But Viola is very beautiful, is she not? She is not an ogre. You will fall in love with her."

Nico frowned. As always, his mother had the worst possible timing. Because of Cara, he wished now he'd been more evasive on the subject of Viola when they'd lunched today at the family's summer palazzo.

He had no taste for marriage. It was too soon. Two hellish years ago he'd lost not only Simonetta but their unborn son, as well, when the brakes of her car had failed, and she and her chauffeur had plunged off the side of a cliff on the French Riviera.

His and Simonetta's marriage had been arranged, also, and because Nico had resented having to marry her, he hadn't realized he'd come to love her in the last months of her life.

Because of his willful stubbornness, their happiness had been too brief.

This time of year filled him with memories and regrets. He'd made her unhappy far longer than he'd made her happy. If only he could go back and make it up to her. But it was too late. His mother was right, in a way. Somehow, he had to find a way to move on.

Inadvertently, his gaze shot to the tall brunette standing high above him on her belvedere.

Guarda, che bella!

She was nothing like his shy, innocent Simonetta. Still, Cara was incredibly exciting. When Grand-mère, naughty Grand-mère, had dropped him off at the beach yesterday afternoon so he could take the tender out to his yacht, *Simonetta,* to brood, she'd pointed out the girl reading on the bench under the lemon trees. The instant Nico had seen Cara in that short sundress, she'd made him forget his grief. He'd changed his mind about going straight to his yacht.

Simonetta had been small and blond. Cara was tall, dark, more mature and self-assured. Or, at least, he'd thought so at first when she'd set down her book and taken off her glasses to study him.

He'd liked the way Cara's rich brown hair fell in glossy waves down her slim back. He'd liked the way her coffee-colored eyes burned him, even at a distance. The gardenia in her dark hair was more beautiful than a jewel.

She'd looked excited, as if she were mesmerized by him, too. Simonetta had been so shy in the beginning, so virginal in his bed that he'd found her sometimes childlike. Never had she looked at him with desire as blatant as Cara had shown, even in that first moment. Something told him he wouldn't have to waste time wooing this woman, that she was already his.

He'd imagined Cara had found out he was staying aboard *Simonetta* and had been waiting for him. He was used to being chased by celebrity hounds and aggressive fortune hunters, who were after his title and money and a few seconds of fame. Usually he avoided such women.

But Cara had made him forget, so he'd made an exception and had followed her into the bar when she'd run. He'd known he was right about her because she'd left her book on the bench for him to find and return, which he'd done. Then, much to his surprise, after smiling at him and blushing and taking her book, she'd run and vanished into thin air.

Now that he'd found her again, he was in no mood to dwell on his family responsibilities regarding Viola. He wanted to forget Simonetta and Viola. At least for tonight.

"Mother, I'll call you tomorrow," he said, aware that his voice lacked warmth.

"You won't forget to call Viola?"

"Ciao," he whispered, refusing to promise. He told her he loved her and hung up, even though he knew she would not be satisfied with that response.

Before she could call him back, he turned off his cell phone, slid it into his pocket and looked up at Cara again.

Her bright eyes touched his, lingering, her visual caress making him grow hot and hard. Even in her bulky robe, she looked full bosomed and slender hipped. Her dark hair swirled about her face. He'd always preferred blondes, but her rosy cheeks and the ripe lushness of her youthful, dark beauty made her look both innocent and as alluring to him as a siren singing from the fabled rocks.

Was she his siren? After all, this part of the coast was where Homer had placed the sirens whose songs lured men and made them forget their reason.

Was Cara naked underneath the robe? He guessed that she probably was. He looked at her and then looked some more. It was time to strip her of that bulky, unflattering garment and find out.

As he loped toward the elevator, Nico felt a wild stirring of desire. It alarmed him only a little that he was more powerfully attracted to her than he'd ever been to any other woman.

He was a prince. The blood of warriors who'd conquered lands, seizing anything and anyone they wanted, especially women, flowed in his veins. His ancestors had a history of discarding such prizes when they tired of them.

He wanted her. He would use her to forget the past and its sorrows, to forget the future, as well.

Tomorrow he would call his mother and promise to woo and wed the beautiful Viola.

Tonight belonged to Cara.

Three

Nico had a key, but he knocked before letting himself in. "Cara?"

His deep voice echoed in the tall-ceilinged bedroom. Then she ran in from the belvedere.

"Sorry about the call," he said, smiling because she was so lovely.

Cara hung back in the doorway. She was holding a rectangular frame, a painting, it appeared, which she set down on a chest. Flushing, she lashed the tie around her waist so that the robe fit more snugly.

"It's fine," she said. "I had a couple of calls to make, too." She pushed a long strand of brown hair behind her ear.

Oh, how adorable she was.

"I was out sightseeing all day and couldn't call my family earlier. I missed a christening."

When he saw the painting, his grandmother's painting, *his* painting, his brows shot together. Not for the first time, his grandmother had gone too far. With great effort he kept his face neutral.

"Christening?"

"My sister's twin boys."

He forced his attention from the painting. "So, how is Italy as a tourist destination?"

"Perfect." She swallowed. "I took an entire smart card full of pictures."

"Perfect. And soon to get better," he murmured, sliding a finger against the light switch, dimming the lights. "Good thing you can't take any more pictures."

"Oh, I have another smart card."

When she lingered by the French doors for a few more seconds, he regretted dimming the lights.

She was losing her nerve. He stepped soundlessly across the tile floor to her.

Her hesitation appealed to him. Aggressive women often annoyed him.

With the lights low, the room with its painted ceiling and gilt furniture was full of shadows. The last of the sunlight came from behind her, so he couldn't see her face clearly.

He didn't touch her at first, and neither of them spoke. But her dark eyes burned him and made him aware of the tension in his own body. He needed to take her to bed and make love to her as soon as possible.

Her eyes widened, and she scanned the room, as if seeking an avenue of escape. Afraid she might run, he gathered her into his arms.

"Mistake," she whispered, struggling to pull away. "This could be a huge mistake."

She was right. Especially for him.

What if she threatened to sell her story tomorrow about her night with the prince? He'd been blackmailed before. Not that the family hadn't hired people to deal with such matters.

"There's always a risk to everything, isn't there?" he asked, holding her tightly.

"I suppose. I'm not usually one for risks…with men."

"You miss a lot of good things, if you never take chances," he said, lowering his mouth to her cheek. When his lips nuzzled her hairline, she jumped as if his kiss shocked her.

"That's easy for you to say. The risk is mostly mine though. You do this all the time. With all kinds of women probably. It's what *you* do."

He tensed, not liking the reminder that she knew who he was and had had designs on him.

"You can't believe everything you read," he said, assuming she was referring to the tabloids. "My reputation has been wildly exaggerated."

She went still against him, and he was very aware of how her hips fit his, how the tips of her breasts touched his chest.

"Then you advertise…like an ordinary businessman?"

"Advertise?"

She squeezed her eyes shut and her hands were shaking. "I'm babbling. I do that when I'm nervous."

Clearly she was starstruck. He'd dealt with that before.

He needed to put her at ease. "I'm not really so different from you," he said. That wasn't entirely true, of course. A centuries-old lineage of privilege had a dulling effect on the human spirit. He was not allowed to surrender to his feelings all that often.

"But…"

He didn't want to argue. "I'm just man, and you're a woman. We find each other attractive." He feathered a kiss that was meant to reassure against her brow.

She jumped again.

"What could be more basic or more elemental or honest than a man and a woman and a night like this?" He kissed the tip of her nose, and she gasped.

"You know it's more complicated than that," she whispered.

He really didn't want to argue. Not when she was skittish and rigid in his arms.

He wanted to make love to her badly. She'd chased him and flirted with him for two evenings in a row. He'd thought about her last night for hours. He had to do something, so he kissed her full on the mouth.

She let out a sigh and then a harsh, uneven breath. Funny, how one taste of her was such a shock to his system.

When he deepened the kiss, she began to tremble, as if she were needy and ready, too. Good, she wasn't immune.

Still, after a kiss or two, she put her fists against his shoulders, and for a moment, he was afraid she intended to push him away. His mouth nibbled hers persuasively and she finally melted against him.

Slowly, ever so slowly, she relaxed her fingers and raised her arms around his neck. He felt wild with relief, and desire filled him when her mouth opened wider.

His tongue explored inside, teasing the tip of hers with his. When she let out another little sigh, sounding like a purr, he shuddered.

His heart sped up. She tasted sweet, and her skin was hot and soft, so hot he was mad, mad to have her. Had he ever been this mad for a woman? Still, remembering how nervous she was, he forced himself to hold her gently and to kiss her softly, lingeringly.

Her fingertips brushed the hair at his neck. "I've never done anything like this. I really don't know what's come over me. You see, I'm a planner."

"Me, too."

"And quite traditional."

"We have that in common, too," he whispered.

She smiled. "Are…are most of your women…regulars?"

"Regulars?" He didn't want to talk about other women.

"Women who are used to doing this sort of thing? Or are they like me? First-timers?"

"Why do you want to talk about other women?"

"Because I'm afraid," she admitted.

Suddenly, she seemed almost as shy and uncertain as Simonetta.

"Don't be."

"Let me go," she said suddenly.

He stroked her cheek, her throat, coaxing her with his lips and touch to stay in his arms. "As if I could—now. Cara…Cara…. *Tesorina. Ciccina.*"

Then he kissed her again, long and slowly, until she moaned.

Reluctantly, she pulled away. "So, do I get to be in charge? Do I get to tell you exactly what I want…if I decide to really do this?"

"What?"

What was going on here? One moment, she was as shy as a young doe. The next, she was the aggressor.

American women. They were taught to be so damned independent. Celebrity hound or not, he decided to humor her.

"I'm yours," he said in a light, teasing tone. "I'll do whatever you want."

"For how long?"

"All night," he said.

"What if I want you tomorrow, too?"

He thought about his mother and Viola. He could always say no to Cara tomorrow.

"That could be arranged."

"And the next day, too?"

He nodded even though he felt a strange, new tension building between them that he didn't understand.

"And the next? Both nights, too, of course?"

He was too hot for her to argue.

"I can pretty much clear my calendar. I might have to make a few phone calls though," he said, thinking of his mother. "Business obligations."

She blushed and grew thoughtful as her gaze raked him almost possessively. "I understand. Okay." The word came out like a small sigh, as if she'd been holding her breath. "It's a deal. And we'll stay in here for the most part, so people won't see us. I could see in the bar that you're well-known locally."

Not just locally, as surely she knew. "Whatever you want," he agreed.

"Then I'll do it. I can't believe I'm saying this!" Her coffee-colored gaze was intense. "Three nights. And two days. Then I fly home. So, we're settled on that?"

Again, he nodded, although he felt impatient with all this talk and ridiculous negotiating, not to mention a little concerned about how he would deal with his mother.

"And you'll really move in here, with me?"

"As I said—whatever you want."

"You're being most agreeable. I appreciate that."

"I try to please."

"I'm sure you do. I'm beginning to think I should have done something like this for myself a long time ago. I mean, most men are thinking about how a woman can please them…instead of the other way around."

Some painful emotion flickered in the depths of her dark eyes. She waited, as if she expected something more from him.

"How much?" she finally whispered.

He stared at her.

"I really would think you'd want to get that settled up front."

"How much what?" he asked, puzzled.

"Don't get me wrong. You are so sweet, so understanding about how difficult this is for me. And…and I like that. I like it a lot that you're so discreet and polite and you aren't pushy about the money. I mean, it's really sweet of you, especially since I'm a first-timer, and it makes me feel special or like we're almost friends or this is a real date or something sort of normal…instead of…what it really is. I mean, this is just one more thing about you that makes me feel so…so hot. In fact, I've never felt—" She stopped herself. "I'm sorry. I talk too much sometimes…when I'm nervous."

He'd never been so drawn to a woman, either. Why else was he being so patient with this endless, ridiculous, unfathomable conversation?

His lips barely moved. "Can't we talk later? If you feel hot and I feel hot, shouldn't we begin—"

"No. I really do have to know what you charge."

"Charge?"

For a moment longer he remained baffled, completely so, and then before she said anything else, the true meaning of her words slammed into him.

His grip on her waist tightened. "You think I'm a gigolo," he said softly.

"And, naturally, I want to know how much you charge for the sex?" Her whisper was raw, her face purple before she lowered her eyes.

She bit her lip savagely. "Do you charge by the hour?" She was fiddling with the sash of her thick robe like someone who was afraid she was in some sort of trouble. "Or do you charge for services? Do you take VISA or cash? I don't have all that much cash, so maybe we could go to an ATM later."

She was so embarrassed she couldn't meet his eyes, but when he couldn't think of any way to answer her, she continued fiddling with the sash. "I'm a lawyer, and I like to know what I'm getting into…I mean, when it comes to business."

An ATM!

"So the hell do I."

He let her go and then jerked away as if she'd slapped him. He strode to the minibar where he opened a little bottle and poured himself a Scotch and water. Studying the golden liquor in the lambent light, he opened a second bottle and splashed more Scotch into his glass. He didn't bother with ice.

She was watching him, shaken, her dark eyes wide and frightened.

"I didn't mean to insult you," she whispered. "I thought you'd want to talk about this."

"How exactly did you figure out…er…what I do for a living?"

"By watching you with those two older women. The ones who dropped you off. The way they kissed you."

His mother? His grandmother? His glance flew to the painting his grandmother had done of him when he'd been a child, visiting her for the first time. It was on the tip of his tongue to explain who the women actually were and who he was, when she went on.

"The Ferrari. The Maserati. Really, they gave it away. Not to mention the blonde's diamonds. I mean, her ring, it must be nine carats."

Ten. It had been in the family three hundred years.

He swirled the Scotch in his glass.

"The way they kissed you…like they adored you."

Did she know nothing about the Italian maternal instinct? He had always been his mother's favorite. His older sister had been pretty sweet about accepting that, most of the time. After all, he was her favorite, too.

"Your ragged clothes compared to hers."

He loved old, soft, worn clothes. They made him feel free, almost ordinary, not so burdened with who and what he was and all that was expected of him. Naturally, his mother wanted him in Armani.

"I see," he said. The Scotch burned his throat and set his stomach on fire. "And do you do this often—travel alone and hire gigolos?"

His gaze must have hardened, because she looked away. "No. I told you. Never. Never before! And probably never again! That's why I don't really know how to do this."

"Have you slept with other men in Italy? Men you met in your hotel or at restaurants?"

"No! I told you—you're the first."

The Scotch worked swiftly. He felt the beginnings of a much needed buzz. "So, you haven't read about me? You don't know who I…"

She studied him, her pretty face charmingly quizzical. "Maybe you do look a little familiar. Maybe I did see one of your ads or something, but magazines and papers are full of ads. I just look at the pictures in Italian magazines. Are you a really famous gigolo or something?"

He nearly choked on his Scotch. "You might be surprised at just how famous." He couldn't resist teasing her. "A gigolo to the stars."

God help him for what he was about to do, but he couldn't help himself.

"Then we definitely stay in my hotel."

"I could wear a disguise. I'm quite good at them, you know."

"I'm sure you have to be…in your line of work." She laughed nervously.

He smiled. He didn't want to play games, but this was obviously her fantasy and he wanted her more than ever. Maybe it was the Scotch, but her fantasy was beginning to turn him on, too. *A gigolo?* A professional who indulged a woman's secret desires?

"How much?" she said.

His lips tightened. Sober, he wouldn't have been able to endure this money talk or the fact that she thought he was a gigolo. But the liquor had mellowed him. Not to mention, he was hotter for her than ever.

"How much?"

"You are nothing if not persistent."

"I'm a lawyer."

He had a law degree and a business degree. "I know a thing or two about lawyers." They were pushy and bossy, traits he had not desired in his women—until her.

"Since it's so important to you, you decide," he said.

"I keep forgetting. You're the professional."

"Right." He eyed another little Scotch bottle and considered a third shot.

"Since you have all the experience, how could I possibly know what you're worth?"

"For you," he began, his voice deliberately husky as he stared into her eyes, "I'll make a special, one-time deal. Just for you. Pay whatever you feel like. The amount doesn't matter."

"Now? Or later?"

"Later. How will you know what I'm worth before you've sampled the merchandise?"

"You really are the sweetest gigolo ever."

"We are trained to please."

"You went to gigolo school?"

"Stop!" He really did have to have another drink to continue this idiotic conversation.

This time he threw ice cubes into his glass. Then he opened a third little bottle, poured the shot and downed it in a single gulp.

"One more thing—"

Hell. "What now?"

"I'm sort of a health nut…"

"You want me to use a condom? No problem."

"No…I…don't know how to say this."

"I'm sure you'll figure it out."

"I…I was wondering about Italy's health guidelines. I mean, for gigolos."

Oh, God.

Afraid he'd give himself away, he glanced out the window. "You may be assured…er…that I am extremely discerning about my women…er…I mean, my clients. Extremely discerning. I always use a condom. The very best grade, naturally. Then I go to the doctor every sixty days for a thorough examination. Blood tests. The works. I would go more often, if I thought it was necessary. My client list is extremely exclusive."

He set his glass down, determined to end this ridiculous conversation. "Do you need documents, or are you satisfied?"

"Not quite yet." She lowered her lashes and tried not to look at the bed. "But I'm sure I will be soon, now that we have all these obnoxious little business details out of the way."

"I've never had a complaint," he murmured drily.

Finally. He set down his glass and pulled her into his arms again. She closed her eyes.

Finally.

Four

Nico liked the way a faint tremor passed through Regina's body when his arm circled her shoulders and he cradled her close. He liked the way her pulse began to beat madly when he slipped his hand beneath her hair and pressed his mouth to her throat.

"I could still say no, pay you and call this crazy thing off," she whispered.

"But you don't want to do that, do you?"

"Not at all."

He lifted her fingers to his lips and kissed them one by one as he'd done at the bar. As he gently sucked their tips, she shuddered.

He slid a fingertip inside her robe and very slowly pushed it aside a fraction of an inch. "What do you want?" he murmured against her earlobe.

His hand coaxed the thick terry off her shoulder, and she gasped.

"You mean, I get to tell you what I want?"

"You hired me, remember. That was our agreement. I mean… er…bargain. Do you like it straight…or kinky?"

"Kinky? I...I...I'm not sure I know or want to know what you mean by that."

He laughed. "So what do you want?"

"I...I want you to undress me and then give me a massage and then maybe make love to me very, very slowly."

"I can't wait," he whispered.

He heard her breath catch even before his hand found the terry-cloth tie at her waist and he unthreaded it all the way. He slid the robe off her shoulders, and it tumbled in a heap to the tile floor.

"Pink bra, pink panties, edged with black lace," he murmured, cupping her breasts. "Nice."

"I bought them at Illusions," she said.

Grand-mère!

When his thumbs brushed her nipples through the black lace, her hands closed over him through his jeans.

"No, no," he murmured. "Let me do my job. After all, I am the..."

Again, he couldn't bring himself to use the graphic term for what she thought he was.

"Pleasure provider," she offered. Reluctantly her fingers, which had been seeking to fondle him through the soft denim, fell away.

Gathering her to him, he led her to the wall. "Pleasure provider?"

"Professional. Whatever term you prefer."

Her back was against the cool plaster as he knelt, at eye level with her belly. Using his hands, he spread her legs. Even before he began to kiss her navel, his tongue delving, she sighed. Then his callused palm began to stroke her from her waist to her ankle, gliding over her skin in slow caresses meant to tantalize.

"You're good," she gasped in a strangled tone.

"Thank you."

"Worth every penny."

On a low growl, his mouth followed the path of his rough palm, kissing her thighs, her calves, lifting her feet and sucking each bare toe. Then he did the same thing to the other leg. When he was done, his mouth lingered on her pink satin panties, on the area that covered the dark curls between her legs.

When a fingertip entered her, she clutched his head closer and let out a sob that made him groan.

"I want you so much," he said. Then he ripped her panties down and hauled her to bed.

As he settled himself on top of her, a knock sounded loudly against the outer door. "Room service," an impersonal voice called.

"Damn. Damn." He jerked free of her. "Who the hell ordered room service?"

"You." She giggled.

"Right."

"You said we had to have strawberries."

Sucking in a breath, he let her go. Then he picked up her robe and helped her into it.

"You stay here," he ordered.

"Tell him to add the tip to the bill."

"I think I can handle it."

She was still standing against the wall, clutching her robe to her body when he returned with the tray of food. His blue eyes were fierce and hot, his black curls damp against his brow.

"You look adorable," he said.

She bit her bottom lip. "Come back to bed."

"Sometimes it heightens pleasure to stop and start."

He carried the tray out to a shaded loggia and set it down. He plucked a bunch of purple grapes and went back to her. He nibbled half a grape and then shared the other half with her. It was sweet, yet tart.

"Did you really have a late lunch?" he murmured.

"No. I am…a little hungry, but I can wait."

"No, if you're hungry, let's eat now." He led her outside, pulled out her chair and seated her, placed a plate, napkin and silverware before her, and then opened a bottle of wine.

The evening was darkening rapidly. Birds settling in the nearby treetops twittered noisily. Delicate, fleecy clouds were lit up by the moon and the town's lights.

"We call clouds like that *pecorelle,* little sheep," he said.

"They look like they're on fire."

With another sigh, she breathed in the scent of the sea and flowers, as if she were, at last, relaxing in his presence.

"So, you're a lawyer?" he said.

"Yes."

"Do you like it?"

She seemed about to say yes and then stared at him, as if in wonder. "You know, I don't think I ever thought about how I feel about it until a couple of months ago. I just wanted to be successful."

"In what way?"

"Make A's in school. I wanted my parents to be proud of me. I wanted to live in the right neighborhood, have the right husband, and be acceptable to the right kind of people. So, I went to college and law school."

"I see."

"I suppose it's the same everywhere."

"And are you successful?"

"For a while, I thought so. I mean, I have everything I ever wanted. Only, it isn't like I thought it would be. My firm represents a lot of major corporations. Some of them do things I hate, such as pollute groundwater. I get paid handsomely to defend them. And even though I drive a nice car and have a nice house, lately I've been wondering if I'm still one of the good guys."

He nodded.

"Then there's my sister, who didn't even finish college. She's so happy. She's married, and she has three adorable children. My parents are prouder of her than they are of me, and maybe they should be. So, lately I've been wondering about my life, where it's going…where I want it to go."

"Do you want children?"

"Very much. I love my niece and nephews so much, you see."

"Boyfriend?"

"Not anymore."

He waited.

"What? You don't think I'd be here like this…I mean, with you…if I were serious about someone back home?"

"Some women come to Europe to play."

"I suppose you'd know about that."

He felt his mouth tighten.

"Sorry. I—I…" She drew a breath. "My last boyfriend, Bobby, asked me to marry him right before I came. I said no."

"Why?"

"Long story. I thought I wanted to marry him. But what I really wanted…" She stopped herself. "Why am I telling you, of all people, about my life?"

"Because I asked."

"Okay, I'm confused. Who isn't?"

He cut off a piece of cheese and placed it on a cracker. Then he offered it to her.

She bit into the cracker. "You know what's odd? I took two months off, which is unheard of at the firm, and came over here to think about my life. Only, this is the first time I've slowed down long enough to do it. Suddenly, I don't want to go home. I'm sick and tired of who I was there. It's like my real life is a weird dream that makes zero sense. I feel good, right now, right here, with you—which is crazy."

"I feel exactly the same way. It's incredibly easy being with you. Why is that, I wonder?"

He stared at her so long, she looked shyly away.

"I bet you tell that to all your clients."

Damn. "I don't," he said.

"I'm sorry," she whispered.

He sat back abruptly in his chair and took a long breath.

"Okay, I'm going to ask you a personal question," she said. "You don't have to answer. But in your real life, I mean, when you're not working as a gigolo…"

The word bit. He ran a hand through his hair.

"I mean…do gigolos ever fall in love?"

"Yes. I was married. I fell in love with my wife."

"Did you work while you were with her?"

"I was faithful to her in all ways, if that's what you're asking. Until she died."

"She died? Oh, I'm sorry."

"Two years ago today." He broke off, unable to go on.

When she reached for his hand, he gripped hers tightly.

"In a car wreck. She was pregnant. I didn't know about the baby until the doctor, who tried to save her, told me."

"I'm so, so very sorry," she whispered.

"We honeymooned in Ravello. I come here every year on the anniversary of her death. My grandmother lives here, so I visit her, too. She's been very worried about me. The rest of my family wants me to forget my wife, to think of the future."

"But you're not ready."

"My mother lost my father a few years ago. She didn't allow her grief to overwhelm her, so she doesn't understand me."

"I suppose everyone's different, or maybe it's different when you're younger. I guess when you're older, you've been through more. Hey, don't listen to me. I don't know what I'm talking about. Only, maybe you have a right to your feelings."

"I came here with my cousin to try to remember the good times. Only, my gra…er…my friend, my client, saw you and pointed you out to me."

He brought Regina's hand to his lips. "Your smile was so beautiful. For the first time since my wife's death, I feel almost at peace with the past, with her death. My mother keeps telling me that she's dead and I'm alive. I didn't really understand what she meant, until I saw you."

"I'm glad you're feeling better." She stroked his hand lightly. "Maybe you were lucky to have had her, even though her loss has been so painful. I'm almost jealous in a way. I don't think I've ever been truly in love. Not like that. In fact, before I came here, I was about to give up on men."

"I find that very difficult to believe."

"All my relationships, I mean the serious, real kind, not like this, always just fizzled out."

He continued to hold her hand, waiting.

"So that's why I'm here with you, I guess…a gigolo."

He felt a muscle tick along his jawline. "Do you have to keep harping on my…er…career?"

"I keep forgetting that it makes you uncomfortable."

The tension remained with him.

"I could never pay you enough for what you've done for me, and all we've done is talk," she said.

"They do say confession is good for the soul."

He got up and walked back into the bedroom. He stood before the chest where she'd propped the painting. Frowning, he lifted the picture.

"Do you like it?" she asked.

"Very much. It reminds me of a beach I once knew near my grandmother's house. It's always been quite wonderful being with her. She's been something of a black sheep and forbidden to me, by my mother. *Her* daughter. My mother is as proper as her mother was scandalous."

"Do they know that you're a gigolo?"

"No." He set the picture back down.

"Would they disapprove?"

"My grandmother approves of love, in all its many forms."

"You didn't include your mother in that last statement," Regina said.

"No."

They ate, and when they were done, Nico took her by the hand and led her to the bed. Slowly he removed her robe again. As it fell, her hand found the zipper of his jeans.

Suddenly she was tearing his clothes off and kissing him all over. He was huge. When he grew even larger, she laughed in delight.

"Cara, you're getting me so excited I can't remember your plan. Wasn't I supposed to massage you and make love to you slowly?"

"Forget my plan. I don't have a plan."

A rush of powerful feelings swept him. He took her in his arms and carried her to bed. Within seconds their bodies moved together in an ancient, timeless rhythm. When he entered her, he felt the most powerful, pleasurable connection to a woman in all his life.

For a long moment, he held her close, celebrating that first glorious wonder of being with her. Then his breath started coming in harsh, rapid gasps. He gripped her waist, pressing himself closer and plunged again and again.

"Faster," she murmured, her breathing as out of control as his. "Yes. Yes. Yes."

"I should slow down."

"No!" she whispered in a low, frantic tone. "Faster."

After they exploded together, she fell back against the bed, her body damp all over. He collapsed beside her, heavily exhausted.

"I'll never be able to stand or to walk again," she whispered. Then she began to laugh and to sob and to cling to him. "You're really, really good."

"You're incredible, *tesorina*."

"Does that mean we can do it again?"

Five

The thick black straps of the backpack cut into Regina's shoulders after their climb from the sea. The pack, which had felt light hours ago when they'd started their circuitous, uphill hike on a bougainvillea-shaded cobblestone path, felt as heavy as lead now. The dull pain throbbing in her lower back sharpened with every step.

Nico had offered to carry the pack. Why had she insisted on wearing it?

"Stop! I've got to rest." Her legs were shaking from the vertical climb, and she was gasping as she sank down against a low stone wall and stared at the breathtaking view of cliffs towering above the blue water. She pressed her hand into her spine.

"Didn't I tell you, you should let me carry this?" He lifted the backpack from her shoulders and set it on the dusty ground. "Do you want to go back to the hotel?"

"No." Not that going back to the hotel would be a bad thing.

After making love for hours and sleeping all night in each other's arms, she would surely have slept until noon if she hadn't heard him calling room service. After making the call, he'd rolled over and pulled her back into her arms, nuzzling her throat and lips with his mouth and tongue until she'd been fully awake.

"I can't let you waste your last few days and not tour the Amalfi Coast," he'd said.

"Waste?" She'd smiled up at him dreamily. "I'm not wasting them."

"Not if we hike. That was number one on your list."

"You read my list?"

"While you were sleeping." He'd smiled. "You'll never forgive yourself if you don't do what you came here to do."

"Oh, but I will. I assure you." She'd stroked his lower belly affectionately.

Room service had knocked just as he'd pulled her into his arms and had kicked off the sheets. He'd let her go, and they'd eaten and then dressed and prepared for this glorious if arduous hike.

"You were right," she said, speaking over the sudden barking of dogs in a village somewhere below them. "This is all so beautiful. Thank you. Thank you for making me come here."

"When you said you came here to hike the Sentieri degli Dei, I had no choice."

"The path of gods," she translated unnecessarily. "The guide book said it was steep, but the photographs were so extraordinary."

"Pictures can't really capture something like this, can they?" he said, his blue eyes on her face rather than the view. But then he'd seen it all before, she told herself. He lived here, didn't he? And gigolos probably weren't too keen on views.

Although she was deeply moved by the irresistible mountains and sea and had worked hard for this view, she couldn't stop staring at him. She pulled out her camera.

"So much beauty is dangerous," he murmured.

"Yes." She snapped a picture of him.

"You feel like you could fly into such a view and be part of it as you might in a dream." He brushed the tip of her nose with a fingertip and smiled.

Every moment with him had been perfect up to now. He'd served her breakfast in bed. He'd even sat on the bed, spoon-feeding her cereal with sugar and fresh raspberries. Never had she imagined that nibbling berries out of a man's hand could be such a sensual, magical experience.

The morning was sunny and picture-perfect, too. He'd organized everything—her, the hotel. He'd even told her what to wear and had bought her sunscreen in the gift shop. He'd had the hotel pack a huge lunch after their breakfast even though she'd protested that after two cups of raspberries—they had been too good to waste—she could never eat again.

Then with him directing her, rather bossily, she'd driven them to Nocelle, where they'd left her rented Fiat so that they could walk this trail that offered the most dramatic views of the rugged coastline.

She'd read that the walk to Praiano was four and a half hours and the return would be the same, so she'd protested when she'd realized his plan.

Nine hours of hiking.

Much as she liked to hike, she hadn't wanted to totally exhaust herself on the trail when they had so little time together.

"Don't worry." He'd placed the car keys under a rock behind the left, front tire. "A little genie will spirit your car to Praiano, so we can drive back from the end point of the trail."

"But my contract says I'm the only one who can drive."

"It will be okay." He'd lifted his cell phone to his ear.

"It will most definitely not be okay! The road was very narrow and windy. Your genie might wreck it."

"He is an excellent driver. Besides, this is Italy. He and I have many friends. Important people who will help. You understand, no?"

She would have argued, but he'd held up his hand. "*Scusa.* Massimo…" After that he'd turned away and had rattled incomprehensible Italian to this Massimo fellow.

Somehow, even though he was a gigolo, which meant technically she was the boss, she'd resisted the instinct to seize control. At the same time, she'd wondered if his many friends were rich women with important husbands, women who could pull strings for their gorgeous special pleasure provider, who made their pampered lives with dull husbands more bearable.

One night with him and Regina was feeling possessive of him, and as if she were losing control.

Not good.

Good thing she was leaving Ravello in a couple of days, or he might become a permanent addiction.

"Do you want some water?" he asked, still staring at her rather than the view, his question bringing her back to the present.

When she nodded, he uncapped his water bottle and offered it. When she was through sipping, he took the bottle and drank after her, as if their sharing the same bottle was the most natural thing in the world.

He slid the bottle into her backpack and lifted it onto his shoulders along with his own. He pulled out his camera and took a picture of her and the view. Then, of course, she had to take another one of him.

After that, they continued their walk and were rewarded with glimpses of ruins and an abandoned farmhouse and an ancient arch that once had led somewhere but now led nowhere. Of course, she had to photograph him again in front of the farmhouse and then the arch and had to have him photograph her in front of both settings, as well.

"You must send your pictures to me," he said, his manner so urgent and sincere she nodded.

She could almost believe this was a real date and that last night had been real, too; that they were beginning a genuine relationship that would be vitally important to both of them.

After they left the farmhouse, they came to an ancient convent filled with fading frescoes of saints. He charmed her by picking a bouquet of wild roses and olive branches. After giving her a rose, which she put in her hair, he knelt. His face grew serious as he said a silent prayer and left the saints the rest of the flowers as a humble offering.

When he stood again, he said, "If you are hungry, I know a perfect spot for a picnic."

"I could eat something."

"All right, then."

He led the way up another bougainvillea-shaded, cobblestone path that passed between the whitewashed buildings of a second deserted farmhouse, more charming than the first, and then through a lemon grove.

With every step the sun rose higher and became warmer on her back. The hike became more of a plod. She was breathless and perspiring long before they'd made their way up the hidden path and a nearly impassable cliff to a stone bench in the shade of an olive tree with stunning views of the mountains and sea.

"You're right. This is perfect," she said, still panting from the climb.

When she sank wearily down onto the bench, he came closer. Smiling down at her, he studied her so intently she almost stood up in the hopes that he might kiss her. But instead of doing as she wished, he lowered her backpack to the ground and rummaged in it.

Quickly, he got their boxed lunches out, sat down and spread their sandwiches, cheeses and wine between them on the stone bench. Then he deftly uncorked the wine bottle and poured two glasses of jewel-dark, red wine.

When he began to eat his sandwich in silence, she lifted a thick-crusted slab of bread to inspect hers. The mozzarella, grilled chicken, fresh basil and avocado smelled delicious.

Still, she was thirstier than she was hungry, so she sipped her wine rather too enthusiastically while he continued to eat his sandwich.

Their silence lengthened. The sun felt warmer. Not that his not talking felt the least bit awkward or the heat of the sun the least bit uncomfortable. No, it was one of those comfortable lulls that can happen between two people who are so completely at ease with each other that there is no need for idle conversation.

It was too perfect, being with him, both in bed and out of it.

He looked up at her and then at the view.

"Dolce color d'oriental zaffiro," he said.

"What?" She was beginning to love it when he spoke Italian.

"A gentle hue of Oriental sapphire." He smiled. "We Italians are quite attached to our *Divine Comedy*. I memorized big pieces of Dante's epic every year in school, and then again in university. We can all quote from it. Even my cousin, Massimo, can be quite eloquent."

"I'm afraid I read more *Cliff-Notes* than the *Divine Comedy* itself," she confessed.

"You missed something then. The great masters are usually worth reading."

A gigolo who quoted Dante and defended the great masters with passion?

"The line comes from 'Purgatory,' and it describes the sea-to-sky horizon when the Divine Poet emerged from the depths of Hell and came to the calm shores of Mount Purgatory."

"What can a girl who crammed for all her quizzes with *Cliff-Notes* possibly add to that?"

"Perhaps more than you think."

He smiled. Then he opened a sack of chips and offered them to her. Normally, she never ate chips. But the hotel had made these.

She took one and munched noisily as he grabbed one from the bag for himself.

The chip was pure grease and carb—and sinfully delicious. She glanced at his olive-toned hand holding his chip. Taking the hint, he fed her his chip.

Apparently, she was on a *sinfully-delicious* kick.

"How did you get started as a gigolo?"

He was swallowing a chip himself and choked so violently she began to pound his back.

He shot to his feet, and she began to beat on his shoulders. "I thought I made it clear I don't want to talk about my work." His manner was abrupt.

"Why are you so ashamed of it when you're so good at it?"

"Who wouldn't be?" he lashed. His eyes were hard and cold now.

"If you don't like it, why don't you stop? Do something else?"

"Believe me, I'm going to," he muttered. "The first chance I get."

"I could be your last customer."

"Believe me, you will be." He shot her a look filled with self-contempt. Then he knelt and began throwing things into his backpack. "Are you finished eating?"

She tried to swallow the last of her wine, but there was a painful lump in her throat. Was she so disgusting to him? Had he been acting last night? She remembered his passion, his tenderness. Closing her eyes, she fought tears.

For her, last night had been too wonderful to believe. Never had she felt so cherished or so special. Had it been awful for him? It must have been, and she couldn't bear the thought.

Obviously, gigolos had to be skilled actors to play the parts in whatever fantasy their clients demanded. If he'd been disgusted, his performance deserved an Oscar.

"I'm sorry if it was awful for you," she said in a broken whisper.

"Awful? What the hell are you talking about now?"

"Last night." She couldn't bear to look at him, so she was unaware of his expression. Pain cut her like a knife. "You found me disgusting."

Suddenly she felt his arms, tight and hard, pulling her against his muscular chest.

"Cara, Cara." His deep voice was infinitely soothing, his hands gentle now as he stroked her. His lips pressed lightly against her temple. "Disgusting? Last night was wonderful. I'm sorry I lost my temper. The last thing I ever want to do is make you unhappy."

"I feel the same way, even though you are a gigolo and I know you can't care about me as much as you act like you do."

"God!" He mashed her against his chest. "I hate this." He stroked her hair thoughtfully. "Cara, I…I'm afraid I haven't been entirely honest with you."

"How could you be? You were doing your job. But if your work is so repugnant, I relieve you from all obligations that we contracted for. I'll even pay you now for tonight, too, and for tomorrow, as well."

"I don't want your damn money."

"I refuse to take advantage of your generous—"

"Stop it, okay?"

For another long moment he held her close, his hands stroking her hair. He seemed to be struggling with something while she clung to him. Hating his anxiety and afraid of what he would say, she held on to him in a state of stupefied tension.

"I'm not a gigolo," he finally whispered, his low tone edgy.

She shook loose of his embrace and looked up at him. "You're not?"

"No. There. Now you know."

"You lied to me?"

"Yes. No!" He ran his hands through his hair. "Hell, I played along."

"Then who are you really?"

"Nico Romano."

"And your profession?"

"I'm…an international businessman."

"And those older women, who kissed you?"

He hesitated. "Relatives."

"That's it? You're telling the truth? The whole truth."

That muscle in his jawline quivered. He flushed. "Last night, I wanted you so much I think I would have said anything or done anything to have you. And nothing's changed. I still want you, maybe even more, if such a thing is possible."

"Me, too. Oh, me, too."

If she had an ounce of pride she would never have admitted her feelings to him so freely. Instead, she should have asked him about those older women in the fancy cars. Who exactly were they?

She'd slept with him. She had about a million questions, but when her gaze met his, his eyes burned with so much emotion she forgot everything except the simple joy of being with him now that she knew he hadn't been acting.

He hadn't been acting! She wasn't disgusting to him!

His arms tightened around her, and he buried his face in her hair. Soon she was lost, utterly lost to all reality. She wanted only this moment with him. Even before his lips claimed hers, she was aware of a wildly thrilling happiness.

When he began kissing her, the sinfully delicious chips and their sandwiches and wine were forgotten. Such passion could have only one ending. In the space of two kisses, they were both breathless.

"Farmhouse," he muttered on a ragged note.

She nodded as he began gathering their things, slinging them into his backpack, not caring that their sandwiches would be hopelessly crushed. Then he seized her hand. Together they ran stumbling, laughing back down the trail to the last deserted farmhouse.

Inside the musty-smelling building, he tossed their backpacks to the ground. Then he shoved her against the wall and leaned heavily into her. His mouth closed over hers again and devoured her lips.

Once again, the mysterious force that had drawn them together swept them up in its fierce tide. Their passion was like a wave that took charge of them, lifting them higher and higher and then shattering them against an unknown shore that was part of a strange, thrilling world they'd never known before and felt lost in.

The moist heat of his breath on her nipple through cotton made her heart skip. She was aching, dying for him as he pulled her T-shirt up and her jeans down. As eager as he was, she fumbled for his zipper. When she'd opened it and released him, her hand closed around him for a moment, every long inch of him, causing his breath to come ever more harshly. Then her hand fell away, and she stood on her tiptoes, arching herself toward him. He leaned closer, cupped her buttocks and plunged inside her.

Clinging to him, her nails dug into his back. He drove faster and faster until she began to weep. Then he shuddered and she quickly followed, and for a timeless moment they were joined in all ways, physically and emotionally.

Long seconds later, his black head slumped over hers. She felt herself falling back into herself, wondering once again what was happening to her. Sex had never been anything like this before.

"Cara, Cara…." His deep voice was infinitely tender. "If only…"

She was still gasping for every breath when he lowered his mouth to her throat and kissed the pulse beating madly there. Through her tears of exultation, she laughed a little, for she was so close to some edge, she was both happy and sad.

"I will never forget you." Clumsily, she wiped her eyes and then touched his cheek with her damp palm.

He pulled her close, kissed her tears away, then simply held her while the balmy sea breeze rustled the leaves of the lemon trees outside the farmhouse.

"Two days. That's all we have," he said in a tortured voice that indicated he never wanted to let her go.

"Two nights, too."

He began to kiss her throat again and then her lips, murmuring more Italian endearments that she didn't understand. And, as before, their desire built until the white heat of passion melted everything away once again, except the searing fact that they'd been made for each other.

Never again could she go to bed with another man without comparing him to Nico. Would she ever be able to fall in love again, to marry?

"And I wasn't even good at sex before," she said.

"I don't want to know about before," Nico said, his voice so harsh he would have frightened her if she had not felt exactly the same way.

Possessive.

Never before had she felt so completely possessive about a man. She wanted him to be hers, only hers, for the rest of her life.

But what good were such feelings when she was going home the day after tomorrow?

"I…I wish you were a gigolo!"

"No, you don't."

She pulled her jeans up and her shirt down. "Don't you see, I thought I was safe with you."

"Safe? With one of those guys?" He wasn't smiling as he arranged his own shirt and jeans.

"I couldn't possibly care about a gigolo. I just wanted…"

"Sex," he finished, his voice dark. "Something simple. I know, because all I wanted was to use you to forget my wife."

"But this is too much," she said.

"For me, too, but it is what it is."

His expression was growing gloomier by the second. She sensed in him a bleak determination to separate from the powerful force that had taken them both over, to separate from her. Forever. She half expected him to run down the trail.

Pain tore at her heart.

"Men always want to leave me," she said. "My sister says it's because I'm too bossy."

"Believe me, I'm used to bossy." When his lips curved in amusement, she wondered who had caused that smile. "I would never let you go if I had a choice."

"Are you engaged or something?"

He went still as death.

"Is that it?"

He didn't deny it.

"That's it. Oh, my God! You're engaged! And you're with me! You told me about your wife to win my sympathy. The real truth is that you're with me because you're having second thoughts about the woman you're about to marry."

"No!" But he looked away. *"Not exactly."*

"Yes."

"Listen to me. *I love you.*"

He looked so stunned by this admission, she almost believed him.

"No, you don't. So don't lie. You're going to marry somebody else."

The pain in his eyes cut her to the soul. "I didn't lie."

"You say you love me, but you're going to marry her? Is that the truth? Or not?"

He heaved in a breath. "Okay, if you'll let me explain, I'll tell you why."

"I don't need to hear any more!" She backed away from him, hating that, despite her anger, she still desired him. "You miserable, unholy skunk! You snake! And to think I was so touched by those flowers you left the saints." She yanked the flower he'd given her out of her hair and stomped on it. "What a miserable, insufferable piece of work you are. All men are skunks. Especially you!"

He stared at the mashed flower.

"How can you do that to *her?* She'll figure it out eventually. You'll break her heart. You know that, don't you?"

"No, I won't. Because she doesn't love me, either."

"Is she rich?"

His eyes narrowed.

Of course, she was rich. "So, you've got your cap set for a rich girl."

He didn't deny that, either.

"So that's it!"

He hung his head, his focus drifting toward the flower. "In a way you're right, I guess, although I wouldn't put it that way."

"Why not call a spade a spade?"

He reached for her. "Cara, it's not that simple."

"Sure it is! And don't ever touch me again! Don't you dare touch me, do you hear? Where's my Fiat? I want to go back to my hotel. Now!"

She would have run, but his hand snapped around her wrist. He caught her to him, his mouth closing over her. The power of her will was no match for his desire, and again, despite everything she'd learned about him, his kisses flooded her with warm, pleasurable sensations.

She yanked free of him, and then she stopped, realizing a way she could hurt him, too.

"Why shouldn't I have one more for the road? Correction— for the long flight home? I wanted a gigolo. You want to know something? You're not all that different from what I thought you were. Bottom line—you're selling yourself."

"Shut up." His expression was both tortured and wild. "You don't know anything about my life, and maybe it's best you don't."

"I want you—gigolo."

"Have it your way."

Before she could protest, he ripped her jeans and panties down and pushed her against the wall again. Then he knelt in front of her in an attitude of worship and spread her legs.

"No! What are you doing?" She felt too intimately exposed.

His broad brown hands locked around her waist. "I want to remember you and this day for the rest of my life."

When the tip of his tongue touched her outer lips and then slid upward and then down with slow, thrilling strokes, her mouth went dry. Heat from his lips poured into all her secret feminine places. Lava washed up her spine, flowed into every cell, drenching her in flames. Even her heart could not remain unaffected from such fire, and the cold place in its center melted, too.

When his tongue flicked deeply inside her and then went still, every pore in her being felt sexually charged. Instead of feeling ashamed, she forgot herself and clawed the wall.

He was what she wanted, what she'd always wanted. Without knowing who she was or what she did, she began to twist and writhe against his lips and tongue. Crying out his name, she wept.

Sensing how near she was to climaxing, he gripped her bottom and hauled her against his mouth. His tongue plunged inside her again and again until she screamed in ecstasy.

As the explosion ripped through her, she sank her fingers into his hair and dug her nails into his scalp. She held on to him, the chaos of her emotions tearing her apart as the shattering experience consumed her.

When it was over, he jerked his head back, and she sagged against the cool wall. Then her knees collapsed and she slid down beside him.

She wanted to hate him. At the same time she wanted his mouth to lick her intimately forever.

"Oh, Lord," she whispered. "What have I done?"

Her heart was pounding and her hair was dripping with perspiration. She was afraid because she'd lost all control. Because somehow, some way, against her will, in less than twenty-four hours, he'd made her his forever.

"I hate you," she vowed softly, "for what you just did."

"You only wish you did."

"Then I wish I'd never met you."

"So do I. So the hell do I."

He clasped her chin tightly, forcing her to stare into his tortured blue eyes. "What gives you the high moral ground? You're the one who wanted your own personal stud and hired a gigolo. Well, maybe you just got him, Cara."

She gasped. Then she bristled with all sorts of self-righteous indignation that he'd so aptly pointed out she had no right to feel.

"When the hell are you going to figure out neither one of us is in control here?" he said, his tone gentler, his eyes softer. "This thing has us."

When he pulled her close, she shuddered, willing herself to resist him. But, as always, she was weak and needy, so she let him hold her. At the thought of their impossible relationship, her mood grew unbearably sad—and angry, too.

This was all his fault! It had to be!

Or was it? Somehow her needs and emotions were all mixed up. How could this have happened in such a short time? She'd left Austin to sort out her life, not for confusion like this.

"You're a bastard," she whispered. "A royal bastard."

"You don't know how right you are," he muttered.

She'd been right to want to control things, too. Leaving him, even though she knew he was marrying another woman for money, was going to break her as nothing else ever had.

"You're a bastard!" she repeated. "How can you look so sick at heart when I know you're slime? I want you out of my life—gone! I don't want to ever think about you again!"

"You think you have all the answers, don't you? Well, you don't! Before you go back to Austin, there's something I've got to show you!"

"Nothing you could say or do or show me could change the way I feel about you!"

"We'll see then, won't we?"

Six

"You can't drive my car. You're not on the contract."

Regina was in *lawyer* mode. Translation: she was in the mood to argue about anything.

Nico shot her a look before he unlocked the passenger door for her.

She glared at him and refused to get in.

"Suit yourself," he said. "It's a long walk back to Ravello." He strode around the front of the Fiat.

"You can't just drive off in my car and leave me here."

"Watch me." He got in and slammed his door hard. "I'm a bastard, remember!"

When he started the car, she jumped in and slammed hers, too, harder.

He adjusted the mirror and the seat, so that he had more leg room. "The road is dangerous. I know it and you don't."

She was about to protest when he shifted into reverse. Tires whirred in the dirt, spitting gravel.

"You scared the hell out of me this morning when you backed

up and we nearly got rear-ended. And it was so early, the road was almost empty."

"I had to back up for that bus," she muttered.

"One bus. There'll be traffic now. Besides, like I said, even with the road empty, you scared the hell out of me."

She'd scared the hell out of herself. Was it her fault that the road was so narrow two cars couldn't really fit side by side, not to mention trucks and buses?

"Besides, you grind the gears," he said.

Without another word, she buckled her seat belt. If only they hadn't quarreled. If only she didn't feel achingly heart-broken, she might have enjoyed the lovely views and sparkling afternoon.

By the way he drove, she knew he was as enraged as she was. He ignored the scenery, whipped around hairpin curves, tires screaming. He passed a motorcycle with mere inches to spare on her side where a three-foot stone wall was the only thing separating them from a sheer drop to the sea.

Amber sunshine in the trees and deepening shadows made the mountainside a sparkling fairy wonderland. Not that she could enjoy it as cafés, trucks, villas and other cars raced by them at a sickening speed. Far below, fishing boats seemed as small as children's toys, bobbing in secluded coves.

She stole a glance at Nico's hard, silent profile. How could she have ever thought he was a gigolo? He looked more like a warrior.

"Stop! Now! And let me drive before you smash us into the mountain!" she cried.

"No."

"You're driving like a maniac."

"I know what I'm doing." He spoke between clenched teeth.

He did seem to be skirting danger closely, not recklessly seeking it. She decided he knew what he was doing.

"If you have a wreck, my insurance won't pay," she told him.

"I'll pay."

"Right. With your rich wife's money."

His eyes narrowed on the road. "You're wrong about that."

He slammed his foot on the accelerator and drove even faster. She covered her eyes with her hands when the whirl of mountains, blue sea, and their mad race on the winding drive carved on the verge of an abyss was more than she could bear. She was, however, peering through her fingers when he whipped past the sign that pointed to the high road that wound up to Ravello.

Forgetting her fear, she turned on him. "Where are we going?"

He said only, "You'll see," as the car left the main road, traveled through a wooded hillside and began to climb.

"I want to go to my hotel."

His glance was quick and unsmiling. "Later. I told you that I had to show you something."

The Fiat snarled up a steep hill lined with cypress trees and towering hot-pink oleanders on one side and dazzling views of the sapphire Gulf of Salerno on the other. Finally, they reached a tall golden gate that surely stood on the top of the mountain.

"Where are we?" she whispered.

He wrenched the Fiat to a stop and spoke blistering Italian into a little box on his side of the car.

No sooner had he said his name than the gates whooshed open, revealing an immense, opulent, late-Gothic palazzo with Moorish curlicues. The grand palazzo looked out on a park of lush lawns and bright flower beds that had been carved out of the craggy mountainside. Although not all that large, the palazzo was gorgeous. Somehow, Regina knew that men of taste and immense wealth had created it.

"Where are we?" she repeated, both her curiosity and wonder expanding.

Wordlessly, he drove her inside. When the gates clanged behind them, she felt a momentary frisson of panic, terrified she might be trapped in the wonderland forever.

Then she caught her breath because, on closer inspection, the palazzo standing in its sea of green with cliffs on one side and the sea on the other was *so* beautiful. She had never been anywhere so beautiful.

"Where are we?"

"This is the Palazzo Romano." He spoke in a low, dead voice. His blue eyes regarded her warily. "It is one of my family's *many* ancestral palazzos. A favorite, in fact, even though it is really only a small country home for us."

"Now you're telling me you're rich?"

She scanned the high, pink walls of the palazzo perched on its cliff top promontory and felt eyes, unseen and unfriendly, watching her. She stiffened at the thought that she was being judged inferior in some way and was unwelcome here.

"You mean this is your future wife's home," she exclaimed.

"The Palazzo Romano will be her home. Yes. But only when she marries me."

The Palazzo Romano? Hadn't she read about it in her guide-book?

What? Was he telling the truth? Surely not.

He got out of the Fiat and went around to Regina's side and opened her door. When he put his hand on her arm, she didn't resist his help getting out.

"Look," she said, glancing up at the windows again and feeling cold all over. "I see. It's beautiful. Impressive even."

"I think most people would be impressed," he replied, his tone oddly distant. "The paparazzi certainly are."

He took her hand and pulled her through the gardens, which were vast and well tended. They passed a pool with a pair of swans, countless fountains and statuary before they drew to a stop in an ancient cloister.

"This is my favorite part of the house," he said.

"It's quite charming."

"I used to play here with my sister when I was a little boy."

Was he telling her the truth?

"My family has a palace in Florence that is filled with four hundred years of fabulous art. We have extensive vineyards outside of Florence, as well. In the centuries when the Romanos really counted, they were known by nothing more than their surname, like the other great families of Florence."

She took a deep breath. The warm air was sweet with the scent of flowers.

"It was only when we started losing power that we gained our titles," he continued.

He hadn't missed a beat. He certainly had his little story, if that's what it was, down pat.

"You're good," she said.

"The Romanos were made marquises quite late in their history, in 1750, when the Dukes of Lorraine started handing out dignities to win the support of the town's patrician establishment. At first, the family scorned the titles. Not too long afterward, we were made princes."

When he took her arm and led her out of the cloisters, the tall parapets and towers looming above her seemed even bigger and more intimidating. Again, she had the distinct feeling that she was unwelcome.

There was a formality and a perfection to everything. There wasn't a single weed in any of the flower beds, nor a wilted petal on any of the roses. And yet, no gardeners could be seen.

"Very impressive," she repeated, wondering if he really was a Romano. More likely, he was a poor relation, or maybe the son of one of the absent gardeners.

"I understand that you want to live in a palace. Lots of people do…even in the States, which is why we have MacMansions…." She caught herself. She was babbling.

When they rounded a curve in the gravel path and she saw her Fiat, she said, "Just take me to my hotel."

He stopped. "Listen to me. This is only one of my homes. *Now. It is mine now. Before my marriage.* Or rather, it is one of my family's many homes. It might interest you to know that it has been in the family seven hundred years."

She stared at him. Was he serious?

"Do you work for these people or something?" she asked gently.

"Oh, most definitely." He smiled, but his eyes were wary and cold. "If we went inside, you would be greeted with dozens of gilded chambers hung with tapestries and baroque chandeliers, not to mention paintings by the great masters, as well as paintings of my ancestors—who resemble me."

"Really? I'm sure it's all very lovely."

"The older woman you saw in the Maserati is my grandmother. Only don't ever tell her I said she was old. The blonde you saw me with is my mother, the Principessa Donna Gloriana Romano. My father, Principe Don Livio Carlo Romano, died five years ago. My mother wants me, his heir, to do my duty and marry the Principessa Donna Viola Eugenia di Frezano. In fact, my mother is insisting upon it. Yesterday, I gave her my word that I would call Viola, whose family is as eager for the marriage as mine. The paparazzi, not that they know anything, say I'm the most eligible bachelor in Europe."

She stared at his dark, patrician brow which was knit, at his aquiline nose, at his magnificent warrior's physique and felt an unpleasant jolt of recognition. He looked tough and arrogant enough to be a conquering prince of old. And he did look a little familiar.

"You're a prince? You're really a prince?" Regina searched his incredibly handsome face for some sign of triumph or conceit. Humility was all she saw.

"I wish to hell I wasn't," he said. "I wish to hell I could change who I am and follow the path of my heart, which would be a life with you, *tesorina*."

Tall, dark and handsome…and an Italian prince to boot. If only she were a princess, too, maybe her life could be a fairy tale.

But Viola was the princess in this fairy tale.

"Thank you for bringing me here," Regina said grimly.

"You must understand—I cannot betray my family."

"I do understand." Her heart was thundering, threatening to explode. "What I don't understand is why you didn't tell me the truth in the beginning."

"I'm sorry."

"Not good enough!"

"I know."

"All those people in the bar knew who you were?"

"Yes."

"Including those girls who were flirting with you?"

"Yes."

"You deliberately made a fool of me!"

"No. At first, I thought you knew. Later, I played along with your fantasy."

Her feet crunched noisily in the gravel as she strode to her car. She opened the passenger side door for herself. He got in behind the wheel.

"Are you all right?" he asked.

"Just take me home."

He started the Fiat. "You could stay…indefinitely," he said.

"In Italy?"

"With me."

"Are you asking me to be your mistress?"

He was gracious enough not to restate his intent.

"We could sleep together while you courted and married your princess?" Regina let out a long sigh and then a little scream. She banged the dashboard with her fists just as she'd banged on so many tables in courtrooms. Then she turned to him again.

"Ohhh! You think I'd settle for that? How could you even ask me such a thing?"

"I love you. I want you. It might be the only way."

"Haven't you got any principles?"

"I thought I did, until I met you."

"Do people like you, princes who live in palazzos, I mean, get everything they want, just because they want it?"

"No. They follow the rules. They are taught that all that matters is influence, power and money. They are taught to marry one of their own kind, so that they can perpetuate their families' titles, pedigrees and traditions on the solid foundations of their wedded fortunes. It's all exceedingly dull."

"Poor little rich prince, who must try to get richer and richer. I'm not going to feel sorry for you, you know."

"I'm not asking you to. I just want you to understand my

future engagement. Viola's family is richer than mine. The tax man is vicious. For a thousand years my family has lived here and in palazzos grander than this."

"And they want to be in them for another thousand?"

"Aristocrats do tend to take the long view. Unfortunately, my father lost quite a lot of money, so the family's future rests on my shoulders."

"Which fortunately are quite wide." She paused. "Okay. I see. I understand. I wish you the best. Now, will you take me to my hotel?"

"Just so you understand what is expected of me and why. If I don't marry Donna Viola, I betray my family."

"I said I understood. But that's it. Don't pretend you're a good guy. Not when you lied to me."

Thankfully he didn't remind her she'd thought she'd been hiring a gigolo.

When he started the car, the gates opened as if by magic. Again, she was aware of unfriendly eyes watching her depart.

"Like I said, at first, I thought you knew who I was, that maybe you were a fortune hunter," he said.

"That's so lame."

"It's happened before."

"American tourists recognize you and chase you?"

"Yes. The paparazzi chase me, too."

"And do you always accommodate them as you did me? The other women, I mean?"

He muttered something under his breath. Then he lifted his chin and stared at the road coldly. He drove back to her hotel silently and slowly, but somehow his carefulness stung her like a deliberate insult.

"Well, do you accommodate them?" she goaded.

He flinched. Good. She'd gotten to him.

"No," he said, grinding the word between his teeth. "Damn it, no!"

"Then why did you decide to go slumming with me?"

He jerked the car into a driveway on the side of the narrow

road just as a bus whipped past them so fast their little car rattled violently. Then he turned and pulled her roughly into his arms.

"I wanted you. I had to have you. I didn't care about anything else. I'd felt so horrible for so long and there you were—so sweet and adorable. I thought we'd have one night."

"Why is this happening?"

"Hell if I know why. Hell if I know. Do you think I wanted it to? Damn it, now I want a lifetime. And I can't have it."

Before she could say anything, his mouth came down on hers, searing, punishing. His large hands spanned the back of her waist, his palms burning through her thin cotton T-shirt as he pressed her curves against the hard contours of his body.

At the first taste of his lips, her anger left her. So did her pride. Her heart thudded slowly, painfully. Then her arms climbed his neck and hung on for dear life.

Yes, for dear life because he was life itself. Because he was everything.

She had no idea how long they sat there on the side of the road while trucks and buses roared past them. Finally, he got control of himself again and gave a hard jerk out of her arms only to gaze back at her in shock.

She was as thoroughly shaken as he. She saw that his hands trembled as he started the Fiat. Somehow that made her feel a little better. So, he wasn't a total bastard after all.

When he reached the hotel, he cut the engine. Before he could get out and come around to her side, she flung her door open and raced to the hotel. She'd left her key at the desk, so Nico was able to catch up to her at the elevator.

"Cara…"

"Go! Just go! Marry your princess! Or principessa! Do whatever! Be happy!"

She punched a golden button on the wall and two gold elevator doors opened. She stepped inside.

"Cara!"

The doors closed.

She punched the number to her floor. When she got out, she

stepped onto a belvedere and saw him three stories below talking to the same short, plump man she'd seen him with that first night. His cousin, Massimo, she thought. His genie.

They looked up and saw her. Nico's blue eyes blazed. His dark brows lifted.

A single glance was enough to cut her heart in two.

To hell with him!

She gave a little cry and ran to her room.

Seven

Nico paced *Simonetta*'s deck with a vengeance. Massimo watched him with exasperation and amusement while sipping Pinot Grigio. Then Nico saw a flash of white on shore.

He grabbed his binoculars and ran to the railing to stare at the slim brunette in a white sundress with a flower in her hair. She had suddenly materialized on the seaside bench as if she were a supernatural being.

"It's Cara."

Massimo laughed. "Naturally. You two are like a pair of brainless magnets in heat."

"Don't laugh, Cousin."

"The paparazzi will love this."

"They haven't been around much since Simonetta's funeral. I've been too damn dull."

"Worse than dull. Dead."

Nico set down the binoculars and rushed to the stern of *Simonetta*. He hopped into his sleek, black tender and began throwing off the lines, which Massimo caught with one hand, careful not to spill his wine.

"Do you want a ride to shore?" Nico started the engine.

"No, thanks. She'll be gone in a day or two. I'll have you sulking and grieving all to myself soon enough."

"Don't remind me."

"So, enjoy and I'll kill the last of the Pinot."

Nico waved. Massimo held up his wineglass in a mock toast.

Two minutes later, Nico was striding up the beach. Cara saw him and got up slowly.

Again she was wearing a white gardenia, and the paleness of the flower made her dark hair and brows and wide, luminous eyes seem all the more dramatic. She looked so young, lovely, and vulnerable, he was thoroughly disconcerted.

"I'm weak," she said. "I couldn't bear my room alone, thinking that I would never see you again, knowing you were so near. I'm sorry about—"

"Don't." He took her hand, kissed her fingertips. "I understand completely. I'm just so glad you're here. I want to spend every free second I have with you."

For the rest of my life, he thought grimly.

"I don't want to think about the future," she said, her voice as desperate as his own emotions.

"Are you hungry?"

Her brilliant dark eyes lifted to his. "A cappuccino, maybe." He read her hunger for other things.

"I know the perfect place, and it has the best gelato in all of Italy."

"Really?" The excitement in her voice made his throat catch. She was looking at him, and it was easy to see her mind was not on sampling gelato.

"I'm something of a gelato addict," he murmured.

"I didn't know that. I'm glad to know that. Gelato, huh? That's all it takes to tempt you?" She squeezed his hand. "For me, it's chocolate."

He threaded his fingers through hers and led her to a nearby terrace restaurant on a cliff overlooking a tranquil cove. Under a canopy of dangling wisteria blossoms, he ordered cappuccinos and grilled calamari. Then more cappuccinos and a vanilla gelato for himself and a chocolate gelato for her, chocolate because she'd pointed to it and clapped like a child.

He liked watching her eat and drink while the gulls sailed above them and the wisteria stirred in the breeze.

"Would you like to go for a boat ride?" he asked as she licked the last bit of chocolate gelato off her spoon.

She stared at the blue water and then at him. "If you want to."

"I do."

"Okay then, yes." She laughed. "I want to. Very much."

Once they were in his tender and moving slowly away from the beach out into the glistening harbor, he said, "We can go fast or slow. Whatever you want."

"Fast," she said. "I want to fly."

"First, we see the yachts. Up close. They are quite impressive. But we have to go slow in the marina itself."

"Slow or fast. They're both good." She smiled, as delighted as a child with a new puppy, and he felt thrilled to be with her as they motored from yacht to yacht while he told her stories of the people who owned them.

When she pointed to villas and palazzos that dotted the hills, he told her their histories, as well. An hour or two sped by. The sun began to sink, the sky and sea exploding in brilliant color.

"People used to travel this coast only by boat," he said.

"After our nerve-racking drive, I can see why."

"Do you know how Amalfi got its name?" he asked.

"No."

"Hercules loved a nymph named Amalfi. When she died he buried her here because he thought this was the most beautiful place on earth. And then he named it after her."

"How romantic."

"I know a lovely sea cave that's even more romantic. We'll go there later. After the sun goes down."

Time seemed to evaporate when he was with her, and he felt complete. He cut the motor and they drifted on the slick gilded surface, holding each other tightly, until the sun sank and the light went out of the sky and sea.

As he stroked her hand, he thought about his family's palazzos that were filled with the portraits of generations of his ancestors.

"They remind us who we are and where we come from," his mother often said.

As a boy, Nico had stood under the massive gilt frames at length while his parents had told him about their ancestors' lives. "You resemble them," they'd said.

Outwardly, he resembled them. So why hadn't he ever felt he was one of them? Instead, he'd felt trapped by their traditions and their demands and most of all by their insatiable need for wealth.

Only with Cara, now in this little boat for the first time in his life, did he feel the easiness that comes when one is in tune with one's true self. Not even Simonetta had been able to free him of the life he'd been born to and its pressures.

He breathed in the sea air and pulled Cara closer. With her, he felt the possibility of discovery of a new kind of life. Which was absurd, of course.

He'd known from the first that their brief idyll couldn't last. He'd known his title and its responsibilities would be an insurmountable barrier. When the paparazzi discovered his yacht offshore, they'd start hounding him and thereby discover her, too.

Not wanting to dwell on the negatives, he motored to a sea cave where they removed their clothes and made love. Then he took her back to the marina. There he got his red Alpha Romeo, and they raced along a curving black ribbon of asphalt up to an exclusive nightclub on a mountaintop terrace, where he was known but would not be bothered. They danced and, in between dances, they held hands and sipped Pinot Grigio at a corner table in the moonlight.

"You can hear the traffic even up here," she marveled.

"Sound carries in the hills."

"You should have told me that when we were in that abandoned farmhouse."

Laughing, he caught her hand fiercely and kissed it. Under the big, quiet night at their private little table, they talked and talked, opening their souls and hearts so wide he wondered if he could ever close himself off to all emotion again.

"I could talk to you forever," he said.

"Why? Why is this happening?"

"You think everything happens for a reason? Not knowing the answer to that question is one of life's great mysteries."

She was a mystery he wanted to solve. He wanted to do everything with her in the short time they had left together. But of course, all too soon it was three in the morning and she was yawning.

"I'm boring you," he said.

"No, it's the wine. It makes me sleepy."

Taking her hand, he led her to the Alpha Romeo and drove her back to her hotel.

"I had a wonderful time," she said, as he helped her out of the car.

She seemed all right. Then a sob caught in her throat.

"What's wrong?" he whispered.

"Why do I need you so much?" she whispered.

His breath left his lungs on a shudder.

"I'm not usually such a crybaby." She brushed at her damp cheeks.

"Cara—"

Then she was in his arms. He had no idea how she got there, only that she belonged.

"I need to pack. But I—I need *you* more." She traced the shape of his face with loving fingertips. "How am I ever—"

When her hand trailed across his lips, he kissed them one by one.

She stared up at him for a long moment. Then she shut her eyes as if memorizing his features. He shut his eyes, too, and saw her lovely face behind his lids, every detail was perfect.

"I'm glad you took so many pictures," he said.

"Me, too." She spoke through more tears.

Even before she sprang forward a little and pressed her soft curves more tightly against his body, clinging to him, his arms clenched around her waist.

He remembered wishing he could bring Simonetta back to

life. Wishing for a second chance. Wishing that he could hold her just one more time.

How much harder would it be to let Cara go when he knew she was still alive in this world?

He pushed his hands under the straps of her sundress so violently a strap tore. He wanted to hold her, to bury himself in her warm flesh, to possess her so completely she could never bear to leave him.

"Not here," she pleaded in a soft, urgent voice.

His mouth found hers anyway.

"Someone might see," she insisted.

"Must you always take charge?" He kissed her hard.

She laughed a little. "You keep asking me that."

"And?" His own voice was rough.

"Only sometimes." She snuggled closer.

He buried his mouth against her breast and sucked at her nipple, tasting warm, salty-sweet woman, as well as wet, cotton sundress.

"Stop…before we can't," she pleaded. "Security might find us."

Or worse, the paparazzi.

Gulping in a savage breath, he set her aside. He raked his hair with his hands. Then he adjusted his collar and tucked his shirt back inside his jeans. He stepped back a few inches.

She straightened and stood a little stiffly, as if wary of him, too. When she turned and marched toward the hotel, her head held high, he tagged along behind her, his attention on the sexy sway of her cute butt.

When she went to the desk for her key, he waited by the elevator. She was coy and sedate and studiously proper in the lobby. When the elevator doors closed, whisking them upstairs, she stood as far from him as the small golden box with glass sides would allow. But when the doors opened on her floor, she gave a wild cry and chased him down the hall.

The moment they were inside her room, she shot the bolt and ran into his arms. Catching her, he cupped her chin and lifted her mouth to his.

In no mood for tenderness, she tore at his fly and then at the buttons of his shirt.

When a cool draft of air hit his naked chest, he laughed. Then he unzipped her sundress and watched it spill down her tiny waist and flaring hips to the glossy tiles. She kicked her sandals across the room. Then she sprang into his arms again, teasing him with her mouth and tongue, kissing his lips open, each hungry kiss promising and demanding more than her last.

Lifting her high, he let her slide down his body. She wrapped her legs around his waist, and he squeezed her tightly, holding her there for an infinite moment before carrying her to bed. It felt like long hours ago since he'd made love to her in the sea cave and had brought her to climax with his tongue.

She was slim and beautiful. Why did it keep amazing him that she felt perfect underneath him?

Her wide, dark eyes met his. When he smiled, her lips parted and those gorgeous eyes shone. She was like the moon and the sun, giving off light but reflecting his, too.

With his lips he touched her smooth forehead, her silken hair, her eyebrows, even her eyelashes. He wanted her babies, and the thought that he'd been born to a complicated life and couldn't have her or those babies caused a visceral pain near his heart.

She was leaving in little more than twenty-four hours. Suddenly, the urge to possess her now, this minute, forever, over-powered him.

"Cara. Oh, Cara." Forgetting himself, the love words he used as his hands roamed her body were Italian. He cupped her breasts, caressed her waist and thighs. Then he slid a finger inside and stroked her there, too. When he had her quivering and her breath almost stopped, his pulse raced out of control.

His mouth found her lips again, teasing her tongue with the tip of his, playing and sucking until her nails dug deep into his shoulders. Until she moaned.

"I want you so much," she murmured as she crawled under him. Her skin felt feverishly hot as her arms locked around his neck. He was on his knees, and her sleek body was open and ready beneath him. When his heavy sex touched her entrance, she gasped and then licked her lips. Without more foreplay, he plunged inside her. Buried to the hilt, he went still, his blood pounding in his temple. He wanted this moment to last forever.

She was slick, tight, wet. And hot, so hot.

And then she moved, and he went wild.

"Oh, Nico… Nico…"

He slammed into her again and again. Soon, he was driving faster and faster until she was screaming and he was out of control, fighting himself as he hurtled over the edge.

"Don't stop. Just take me with you."

Then she was crying and shuddering, too. He pounded into her two more times before he exploded.

They held on to each other. He caressed her hair and spoke Italian again, his heart making promises he could never keep while she said his name over and over again in the sweetest, throatiest whisper he'd ever heard.

When their heartbeats finally slowed, she ran her fingers through his damp hair.

He heard her muffled sob.

"I never cry," she said.

"You keep saying that."

"Only with you."

He clasped her fiercely. Damn it. Why had he been born Principe Don Nico Carlo Giovanni Romano? How could he watch her get on a plane and fly away?

She would marry someone else. Have another man's children.

But if he defied his mother and the rest of his family, and married Cara, such a union would be considered a disaster by everyone in his world—especially his mother.

His fist gripped a tangle of sheets as Cara continued to whisper love words in his ear. He wanted this night to last forever.

Their damp, hot bodies still joined, he fell asleep with her arms wrapping him loosely.

Eight

When Regina woke up hours later in Nico's arms, the damp sea air smelled of gardenia and felt cool against her skin. Silver moonlight washed the bed and him. She knew the exact moment his long lashes lifted drowsily and his eyes caught the light.

"Cara?" he whispered, nuzzling closer.

She fingered the ornate cross on her throat. "I'm right here, darling."

"Are you all right?"

"Better than all right." She touched his sex. "You're so big."

"They say size doesn't matter."

"*They* don't always know everything. Besides, that's hearsay."

When she sighed in contentment, he took her hands and kissed her fingers. She felt delicious, satiated, complete.

So, this was what love felt like. At least now she knew. Some people never found this kind of easiness or passion ever, although her happiness was made bittersweet by the knowledge that she had to leave him.

At least I have him now.

She touched his large maleness gently, just enough to make contact. She smiled possessively, and then yawned because his warmth had made her sleepy again. She went limp against him and soon was asleep once more. The next time she awoke, the sun had tinged the bedroom with slanting, pink radiance. Nico was already awake beside her, his expression tender, his dark eyes shining as he watched her.

Never had she felt more protected or cherished.

"How long have you been awake?" she whispered, feeling a little shy.

"A while. You're so beautiful."

"So are you," she said, running her hand down from his throat over his magnificent brown chest.

The sheet wrapped her waist, leaving her breasts exposed. She couldn't believe that lying naked beside him, even after all the sex, could feel so right, so easy.

"You don't seem all that grand. Shouldn't a prince be cruel and haughty?"

"You're right. I command you to make love to me all over again."

"I have to take a shower first."

"We could take one together," he whispered.

"All right." Using her knuckles, she stroked his rough, shadowed chin. "Why did I have to meet you the last two days I was here? Life isn't fair."

"Life never is." He closed his eyes, but not before she saw his pain.

She squeezed her eyes shut, too.

"I came to Italy to find myself. And I have. Only now when I go back…"

"What?"

Biting her lip, she shook her head, not ready to admit to him that she would be leaving a big piece of herself behind.

"Maybe this is better," she said brightly. "I'll always think I found the perfect love. I'll remember how passionate you were, yet gentle, and I'll compare you to all other men."

"Damn it. Do you think I want to hear about other men?"

"I'll never get annoyed with you for forgetting my birthday or our anniversary."

"As if I would. I plug important dates into my digital assistant. Which reminds me, what's your cell number?"

When she told him, he wrote it down on the hotel notepad by the telephone. He ripped off the page and then scribbled something on the next sheet.

"This is my private cell number…just in case you ever need me for anything."

"You'll never get impatient with me for keeping you waiting because I can't decide what earrings I should wear or because I've lost my keys. Did I ever tell you I lose my keys all the time? We won't fuss because I spend too much money on clothes or furniture. I like to shop—I think I told you that. I buy the most atrocious things at flea markets and garage sales—horrible purple sofas for a dollar with the stuffing coming out."

"Shut up."

"We can always imagine our children would have been perfect, dark-haired angels with enchanting dispositions, little prodigies who potty trained at one. And our sons will be…virile, athletic and great scholars."

He put a fingertip against her lips, and she stopped herself at last.

"Sorry, I'm babbling."

"How could your babies be anything other than darling little prodigies or our sons anything but pint-size studs?"

"You don't know what I was like as a kid," she teased.

"I was a bit of a handful myself. Two nannies were assigned to me."

"High-maintenance?"

"I'm an aristocrat. It comes with the territory."

"From having that supersize appendage?"

"Would you stop it with that? I was always scaling the castle walls, flying kites off them. After I nearly dived off a parapet to reach one kite I lost, I was confined to the nurseries and the gardens with my two nannies or with Tiberio."

"Tiberio?"

"I owe my life to my family's majordomo, Tiberio Abruzzi. I was awfully hard on all the antiques, too. By the time I was eighteen, every time I sat down, priceless brocade tore and fourteenth-century gilt wood shattered. Pieces were constantly having to be restored."

"I really had better take that shower."

"With me, remember?"

When she raced into the bath and turned on the hot water, he followed her inside the steamy, white-tiled cubicle.

When he closed the door, her nipples brushed his arm. She giggled because of the tightness of the space and the immense size of his dark body.

"There's no way to move without touching you."

He cupped her breasts, and she shivered.

"Exactly," he whispered, lowering his mouth and sucking each nipple until they were as hard as berries.

"You keep accusing me of being bossy. Now I have to live up to that. Stand against the wall, Your Highness."

When he stayed where he was, she placed her hand squarely against his chest and pushed him backward.

"Hell, nobody calls me that," he muttered.

"Spread your legs, Your Highness!"

When his legs moved apart, she sank to her knees and looked up at the coils of dark hair and at his other, impressive stuff, playfully, as warm water streamed over her head. Without a word, her hand circled his huge, erect organ.

"Definitely, it's Your Highness," she said.

He growled low in his throat.

"Maybe we should call you Your Bigness," she said as she buried her face against his groin. "Or Your Hugeness."

"I'm almost beginning to like Your Highness."

Then she began to lick him, up and down and all around. With every delicate stroke, he grew harder and tighter and bigger until, finally, he burst in her mouth.

He began to whisper to her in Italian.

"How I love it when you speak Italian."

"How I love it when you do the things you do."

Very tenderly he lifted her up. Encircling her with his arms, he held her close against his chest for a long time.

"Good thing the hotel is five star." He turned off the faucets and opened the shower door.

"What?" She felt as limp as a noodle as he toweled her off.

"The hot water never gets cold."

"I wouldn't think you, being a prince, would know anything about running out of hot water."

"Four-hundred-year-old castles leave a lot to be desired."

She brushed her teeth while he watched, which was kind of nice and almost as intimate as the sex. He observed her darken her brow with a pencil and put on mascara, too.

She opened her lipstick and whirled on him. "I'm going to mess up if you don't go."

When he didn't budge, she couldn't stop staring at His Bigness, which caused prickles of heat to climb her spine.

"I like knowing what you do in the morning to put yourself together," he said.

"I want you to think I'm a natural beauty."

He leaned against the doorjamb.

"Would you just go? Or at least put on a towel. My hand is shaking."

"Hot for me again?"

She forced her attention away from His Bigness.

"No! What I am is starved…for breakfast." And she was. Much to her surprise, she really was.

"So, you worked up an appetite."

"Why don't you be a good boy, *Your Highness,* and call room service? I want some of those delicious strawberries again and an omelet and more of those fabulous croissants with the gooey chocolate inside them. Can you see if they have hot chocolate, too?"

"*Bossy.* It's getting harder and harder to remember who's the blue blood."

He grabbed a towel off the rack, whipped it around his waist and wandered off to do her bidding, so that, at last, she could put on her lipstick and dress in peace.

She smiled when she heard his deep voice on the phone ordering coffee, omelets, berries, fresh orange juice and croissants.

"You're forgetting the hot chocolate," she yelled.

He laughed and ordered it for her.

How easy it was to imagine he would be with her every morning for the rest of her life.

The next few moments were filled with bliss and peace. He asked her what she wanted to do for the day. She handed him one of the long lists she'd made of the various possibilities.

He laughed. "We'd need two weeks."

"You pick," she whispered.

"I see you listed a sightseeing boat to view the coast. I'll take you out on *Simonetta*. You'll save money, and I'll have you all to myself."

She put a new smart card in her camera and snapped dozens of pictures of him wearing only a towel, and then, when he was dressed, more shots of him out on her balcony with the gulf and the mountains behind him.

He stole her camera and photographed her, too. Then she set the camera up on the railing and made the necessary adjustments so that it would photograph them together. But every time she tried to pose or get him to pose for the camera, he'd cup her breast or buttock and kiss her lips in such a way that the picture probably looked like she was swallowing his tongue.

"I'm not going to be able to show anyone my X-rated pictures."

"I want you to remember me." His mouth stretched lazily into a grin. "Like this!"

The flash went off as he put his mouth to her breast again.

When the expected knock sounded at the door, she jumped away from him like a startled wild thing. Not wanting the hotel waiter to see her erect nipple or the telltale damp spot on her sundress, she turned and began to rearrange her hair and the folds of her full skirt and let Nico stride to the door.

When he threw it open, she heard men, yelling questions.

"Prince Nico, who is she—"

When she turned, a dozen flashes whitened Nico's chiseled, tanned face.

He swore vividly in Italian or, at least, she imagined the harsh, rapid-fire bursts to be colorful curses.

With a little cry, she ran to him, hoping to protect him from the horde and their cameras, not realizing that her sudden appearance would energize the demons.

Like a spark set to gasoline, their roar was an explosion.

"Signorina—"

"Get back, you little fool!" Jumping in front of her, Nico slammed the door.

"Are you all right?" he demanded distractedly.

"F-fine."

She placed her hand gently on his arm.

Furious, he jerked free of her and strode to the phone and rang security.

"Paparazzi! Get someone up here! Fast! Get rid of them!"

Nine

The hot chocolate and omelets never came and were forgotten. Regina had lost her appetite, so what did it matter? Nothing mattered except that the paparazzi had found them and that Nico was upset.

If only he would stop pacing back and forth.

"Grab your things. I've got to get you out of here before these jackals swarm the gates."

"Haven't they already?"

"This is nothing," he said.

Too agitated to fold clothes and pack them with tissue, she opened drawers and dumped the contents into her suitcase.

"No," he said, pausing in the middle of the room. "On second thought, I'll send Massimo up to do this. We need to get you out of this mess, if we can."

When she tried to pick up one small suitcase, his hand covered hers, and he forced her to put it down.

"But—"

"Trust me. I'll take care of you. Massimo is on the family payroll."

Nico rang someone and rattled more high-speed, impatient Italian. She could catch only a word here and there, but she surmised, by his friendlier tone, that he'd called his cousin Massimo.

What had happened to the romantic mood after their shower? Suddenly her beloved Nico was not only a prince but a furious stranger.

She'd known him—what? All of two days.

He was an Italian prince who'd been indiscreet with a young woman. This probably wasn't the first time.

Why hadn't she thought of this before? What she felt for him was a once-in-a-lifetime experience. But how many times had this happened to him? How many other women had lost their hearts to him?

Who wouldn't fall for him? His looks, his manners, his elegance, his abilities in bed and on the dance floor; not to mention the title, the yacht and the palazzos. Or *his size*. For centuries, his kind had been groomed from birth to charm, rule and seduce.

He would forget her in a week, and then he would court and marry his princess and make blue-blooded babies with oversize ding-dongs. If Regina were wise, she would look at their little adventure as a unique vacation experience, something to chat about with her friend Lucy or her sister Susana over a lingering lunch. Maybe she could even brag a little about *the appendage*.

Regina bit her lip and swallowed hard. The day that had dawned like a golden dream now felt cold and empty.

Nico set the phone in its cradle. "I've arranged for a car and a driver. We leave by a private entrance in five minutes."

In less time than that, the phone rang again. When he hung up, he took her arm to lead the way. At the door, she stopped. Then she ran back and seized the painting of the little boy playing in the sand.

"Leave it," he said.

"I'll carry it on the plane."

Regina scanned the tapestries, paintings and antiques and tried to act as if she wasn't the least bit intimidated by the opulent grandeur of the beautiful salon. In truth, she felt like a naughty little girl who'd run away from a paid tour and had gotten lost in the grand palazzo and would be found and scolded for such mischief.

Where was Nico? Why didn't he come? Had he forgotten she even existed?

His regal mother in her silk designer suit and exquisite pearls had gone through the motions of behaving graciously to Regina, greeting the limousine with a frozen smile. She'd even extended an icy hand to Regina and had offered tea, which Regina had desired but politely refused, not wanting to put the princess to more trouble. The princess had pursed her lips. The next moment, Regina had been asked if she would be a dear and wait while the princess and Nico discussed "the situation" alone. When Regina had nodded, a tall, imperious man in a stiff, black suit that emphasized his height and gauntness, introduced to her as Tiberio Abruzzi, had whisked her out of the way and escorted her here.

Glancing at her watch every five seconds, Regina tried to sit as still as one of the marble statues. She really tried, but the brocade chair was stiff and she'd been here nearly an hour. And she didn't have a clue about what was going on.

Every time she turned toward the door, her gaze met Abruzzi's forbidding black eyes. His face was shaped like a skull, his skin white as a cadaver. Was he as old as the castle, or rather, the palazzo?

Definitely, he'd been ordered to watch her. Thus, she'd sat as still as she could for as long as she could with her hands folded neatly across her lap.

Then like a toddler restrained too long, she burst out of her chair. The ancient chair groaned, and when she began to pace the parquet floor, Abruzzi's brooding gaze followed her as it seemed the painted eyes of Nico's ancestors did, as well. Feeling self-conscious, she walked the length of the golden oak-and-porcelain-filled Gothic sitting room and then retraced her steps.

She stopped in front of a portrait of a staid, elderly man in red velvet, who had a particularly disquieting stare. A cardinal? One of Nico's predecessors? Had he been painted by one of the old masters? When she moved closer to inspect the artist's signature, Abruzzi stepped closer.

Warned, she jumped back from the painting, and like a shadow, he receded to his former place. Afraid that the glittering antique glass-and-gem-studded snuff boxes on all the little tables were worth a fortune, Regina steered clear of them as she continued walking.

Feeling trapped and out of place in such dazzling surroundings, she stepped to a tall window and looked out at the lush, sloping lawns. Two white swans gliding serenely on a dark pool caught her attention.

How she envied them their beautiful garden. Was it only yesterday that Nico had brought her here and told her who he really was and all that was expected of him?

Not wanting to dwell on any of that, she went back to her chair and sank down again onto the hard little cushion. No sooner had the spindly wooden legs made a cracking sound again than she wanted to spring to her feet once more.

Instead, she tilted her head back and stared up at the ornate ceiling, where a profusion of angels swirled in colorful, painted robes.

When had it been painted? What story had been in the artist's mind? Beneath the ceiling, a chandelier from a later period blazed like ten thousand diamonds. Not that she had the slightest idea what period that might be.

Nico had probably been taught from birth the value of all these items. No doubt he appreciated their artistic worth. He was accustomed to fine things, fine homes. He knew famous people.

The Nico she knew saluted girls in bars with his beer bottle, went dancing on mountaintops at midnight, made love in dark sea caves. That Nico laughed and was tender, and she thought he had shown her something of his secret, innermost self. But his real life, the ordinary, methodic rhythm of his days, was spent here.

His tall, reed-thin mother hadn't said a word about how unsuitable Regina was. She'd simply left her in this room with its priceless furniture and jeweled snuff boxes, and the room had spoken volumes.

Regina thought of her parents' cluttered, three-bedroom tract house with its framed prints and recliners. She was from ordinary, middle-class, all-American stock, and more fortunate than most. But an accident of birth had thrown Nico into an extraordinarily exalted position that she could never belong to or begin to understand.

Impossible relationships. My specialty, she thought.

Measured footsteps rang faintly from the hall. Hoping for Nico, Regina sprang to her feet just as his tall, sharp-featured mother glided inside. Regina tried to smile, but her lips wouldn't move. His mother, obviously more practiced than Regina, managed a tight little pursing at the edges of her mouth.

"I didn't do this on purpose," Regina stammered.

A draft of icy air gusted between them in the ensuing silence.

His mother's lips moved. "Still, I'm sure you must understand how difficult this is for the family."

"I'm sorry."

"Well, we'll have to carry on the best way we know how," the Principessa Donna Gloriana Lucia Romano said. "This, too, shall pass, as they say." Again the rigid lifting at the corners of her mouth. "At least the press doesn't know who you are, and if you don't tell them—"

Where was Nico?

"Surely you don't think that I would—"

The Principessa Donna Gloriana arched her brows. "Of course not," she said softly.

Clearly, Gloriana saw Regina as the enemy.

"Massimo has arranged a new airline ticket for you. First class. Tonight."

So, she was to be bought off with a first-class ticket.

"Thank you."

Gloriana nodded, her decorum flawless. Did Regina only

imagine that she had a keen talent for using her careful manners and her regal bearing as weapons? Never had Regina felt more common and uncouth, nor so entirely inappropriate for Nico.

"Where's Nico?" Regina asked, in a crushed voice she barely recognized.

"Right here," rang his deep, cold voice from the doorway. "Did my mother tell you that everything has been arranged?"

Feeling even more chilled by the coldness in his tone, Regina nodded.

"Mother, we'd better go," he said.

With a look of resignation, the *principessa* joined him in the doorway.

Regina wanted to run past both of them and make her escape, but, of course, some reporter would probably find her. Then she would only make more trouble.

With a little shrug, she forced herself to walk slowly toward them. Thrusting her chin upward, she imitated his mother's haughty carriage so exactly Nico smiled. As Regina's heels clicked on the parquet, like fingers tapping a keyboard, his mother frowned.

Unable to maintain her regal act, Regina laughed nervously and ran into Nico's arms. Even though his body felt stiff and wary, he hugged her tightly. His mother's expression grew arctic.

Inside the limousine, Regina slumped against the leather seat. When Nico got in after another lengthy conversation with his mother, he wrapped his arms around Regina.

"I thought it went fairly well," he said. "You held your own with her."

Had she? "My luggage?"

"In the boot."

The chauffeur slammed doors and started the engine.

"And Massimo?"

"He's driven on ahead. He'll meet us. I'm afraid he'll have to escort you inside once we arrive at your terminal."

"I understand." Of course, she didn't. She was merely trying to sound brave and act sophisticated.

"The last thing I want is for you to be hurt because you became caught up in my life and family's position and all its complications. I don't want your name dragged through the mud."

"I'll be fine. It could never have worked out. We come from different worlds. This only proves—"

"Cara. Oh, Cara… Sometimes I wonder if all the things that separate us aren't rather shallow in these modern times. If we simply pursued this relationship, wouldn't the fuss die down? I've been lucky at making money. So what if you don't have a title or a fortune?"

"And your mother? Would she move on?"

"It wouldn't be easy for her, not in the beginning, but then she wouldn't have a choice, would she? She has too many responsibilities to dwell on a single disappointment."

Regina tried to imagine sharing Christmases and Easters with such a formidable mother-in-law. What would they talk about or do together? What sort of grandmother would she make? What sort of expectations for her grandchildren would she impose on their mother, the commoner?

Nico held her while the big black car sped along the Amalfi Drive. The limousine swept past spectacular views of mountains and sea. Normally, Regina would have had her nose pressed against the glass window like a puppy. Today, she was too aware of Nico and the short time she had left with him. Burying her head against his shoulder, she snuggled closer. She loved him so much she ached.

"I just wish we'd had today to make more memories together," she said aloud.

"We have the backseat of the limousine."

She focused on the square shape of the driver's head and cap. "But the chauffeur…"

"For a lawyer, you don't get around much."

"I'm in Italy."

"That's not what I meant."

Nico pressed a button, and a little wall went up between them and the driver. Door locks snapped.

"The windows are tinted," Nico said. "Our privacy is complete, *tesorina*."

The next thing she knew she was flat on her back and naked beneath him, and, as always, the sex was much more than sex. Oh, the gifts to her soul he bestowed with every kiss.

Once they reached the airport, she would never see him again. To say they made the most of what little time they had left would not be saying nearly enough.

Ten

Massimo walked Regina through the airport and helped her with her electronic ticket and bags. On their way to security, they passed a newsstand. A close-up of Nico's angry face, his hands raised to shield Regina from the cameras leaped out at her. His name was splashed across the front pages of two tabloids in two-inch headlines.

Regina's heart sank. She approached a counter to buy a paper, but Massimo laid a warning hand on her shoulder. "Let me," he said.

After she'd boarded the plane, alone with her hoard of newsprint, she devoured the photographs of all the beautiful women with whom Nico's name had been linked. So many women. Then Regina read the articles, and each story chipped away at her self-confidence. Had she really been so special to him?

In the past, she'd read about celebrities, but reading about Nico and seeing her own blurred picture was entirely different. If Nico's mother had made her feel totally unsuitable, the lurid coverage of his numerous romances reinforced that point for her on a deeper level. His other women were so beautiful, so famous.

Could she, who was so bad at love, possibly have held his attention for much longer?

Fame, status and glamour are supposed to bring status and happiness, not to threaten or diminish it. Regina's hands shook as she closed and refolded the newspapers.

The flight attendant came up and asked her if she would like a drink.

She shook her head and wiped at her eyes. "No, thank you."

"He's so darling, no?" the woman said, her gaze on Nico's picture. "Every woman in Italy…we all love him, and they say he has a big heart…." She leaned closer. "And a big *you-know-what* to love all the women in Italy, no? A flight attendant I know says she spent three days in Portofino with him once. And they never leave her hotel. They eat strawberries and chocolate and they drink champagne."

"Three days…lucky girl." Regina turned away. Her throat worked as she swallowed.

She wasn't crying.

She wasn't.

Nico sat with Viola, or rather as far as possible from her as he could, in the west wing of the palazzo, and thought that he'd never liked this grand room because the long French windows let in more shadow than sun. He looked past Viola's lovely blond head, past all the precious furniture and tapestries, to the simple glass door that led to the marble staircase, a dramatic and rather terrible renovation in the eighteenth century.

He had only to arise from the crescent-shaped sofa and fly to that door and then down those pale, stone stairs to escape this impossible interview that his mother had insisted upon as soon as he'd returned from Rome. He imagined streaking back to Rome on the autostrada in his red Alpha Romeo. He would be willing to fly any way he could, even coach, just so long as it got him to the States. To Austin, Texas.

His mother cleared her throat, and the sound snapped him back to his reality. For one final second, he saw Cara's face in his mind's eye, her dark hair, her dark, glistening eyes when he'd told her goodbye. At the vision, a jolt of white-hot pain hit him.

With an effort, Nico forced his attention to Viola.

Viola. Beautiful Viola. Marriage. Duty.

She was flushed and golden, but her beauty did not move him. Yes, she was as exquisitely formed as any of the cold marble masterpieces that graced the palazzo. When they married, heads would turn. The world would applaud them as a glittering, fairy-tale couple.

Viola smiled at him, a shy, uncertain smile. So, she was human after all. Too bad for her. Too bad for him. He did not want to hurt another woman.

His wife?

Dear God.

The mother of his children, his all-important heirs? He remembered Cara's perspiring, satiated body beneath his in the limousine, her shining eyes adoring him.

The shadows in the room darkened. He got up and strode to the windows, where he watched a pair of swans swimming together on their distant pool.

Swans mated for life. He found he could not tear his gaze from them.

His mother's chair creaked. She got up and led Viola to him.

Like a robot, he forced himself to turn and smile politely at the two women, to take Viola's hand. But instead of bringing the slender hand to his lips as he'd intended, he dropped it and turned back to watch the swans.

The glass door opened, and Tiberio announced that the photographers had arrived. His mother had told Nico earlier that pictures of him with Viola were necessary to quell the rumors about his mysterious romance.

"We must give the masses their fairy tale," she had said, the corner of her lips lifting. She didn't like the media, but she was not above manipulating the press any time it suited her interests.

Nico took Viola's hand in his again. "Shall we go?"

Watching, his mother smiled.

* * *

With a frown, Regina closed the file on her antique desk, then looked out the window of her lavish suite in the offices of Merrit, Riley & Whitt, her mind a world away. Seven stories beneath her, white diamonds danced on the emerald surface of Town Lake and flickered like silver medallions in the pecan trees. She saw a tall dark man on the red jogging trail, holding hands with a slim brunette who seemed to be looking up at him lovingly.

Regina squeezed her eyes shut and tried hard not to think about Nico.

She'd buried herself in work ever since she'd returned from Italy, her goal to forget Nico. But visions of his mouth, eyes and handsome dark face wouldn't vanish at her command. Now, she returned to her computer keyboard and saw that she'd received fifty-two e-mails in the two hours she'd spent reading the Hewit complaint. Most of them were from Black Boar.

Frowning again, she picked up the Hewit file. The complaint against Black Boar, an immense oil and gas drilling company that Regina's firm had represented on numerous previous occasions, seemed too legitimate to discard.

Rebecca Hewit had worked for Black Boar for twelve years. A methodical person, she'd carefully collected dozens of memos and documents that proved Black Boar was recklessly pouring carcinogenic toxins into a municipal water supply. While still on the job, Rebecca Hewit had told management to change its ways or she'd blow the whistle.

Black Boar had fired her. When Hewit didn't disappear quietly, Black Boar's corporate attorneys had made threatening calls. Rebecca Hewit had recorded them all. She'd spent the past six years collecting incriminating evidence, keeping a detailed diary, and printing and saving damaging e-mails.

Regina flipped through the formal complaint slowly. She even replayed one of the taped copies of a telephone threat. Black Boar's henchmen sounded rough, scary. Rebecca had grit. Maybe because her little girl had leukemia.

Just yesterday, Regina had watched her niece, Gina, play in her backyard kiddie pool, immersed in gallons of water.

Nobody except Black Boar executives and a few corrupt, local officials probably had any idea what Black Boar was up to.

Black Boar had to be stopped.

Not your job, sweetheart. You're on the other side. You're one of the bad guys.

Ever since middle school, Regina had known where she wanted to go. She'd made a plan, and she'd stuck to it. Valedictorian, National Merit Scholarship, Rice University, University of Texas Law School, Law Review. And those weren't all her honors.

Landing this job at Merrit, Riley & Whitt, the hottest firm in Austin, a year ago had been sweet. And she was still here, climbing the ladder, even dreaming that someday, maybe even before she was forty, she'd make partner.

The Hewit file burned her hand, and she dropped it.

Her plan didn't matter. None of the ambitions that had driven her so long mattered. She simply couldn't do this.

Why? What was wrong with her?

She was shaking when she picked up the file again, but when her hand finally steadied, she charged out of her office and down the hall to talk to Robert Riley, Sr., the man she'd once believed would be her father-in-law.

"I can't make Rebecca Hewit go away. I can't represent Black Boar."

Robert didn't open the file when she thrust it at him. He did listen patiently, at least, for nearly a full minute, before smiling paternally, indulgently.

"I don't like the way Italy affected you. You're different."

"Read the file."

"I don't need to. But you need to take a long lunch and think this over. Very carefully."

Not good.

She barged ahead with the rest of her speech anyway.

* * *

The sky was still ablaze in a magical way, as was the sea. But long shadows were creeping across the Amalfi shore.

Nico strode past the kiosk selling tabloids that ran front-page stories about his developing romance with Viola and saw only the beach and the empty bench under the lemon tree.

He stopped. He'd had a long day at the office, and he was tired and in no mood to see Viola.

He was still staring at Regina's bench when a woman in veils driving a red Maserati much too fast screeched to a stop behind him. She tapped her horn mischievously just to startle him.

"Damn." Nico spun on his heel. "Someday you'll give me a heart attack doing that."

"You won't be the first man. But never with a car." She winked at him. "Nico. My precious little love."

As always, his grandmother spoke to him in French. Since her mother had been French, it was her favorite language.

"Grand-mère," he said, smiling when he saw that the veils blowing about her papery, blue-veined skin were pink. "Aren't you too old for pink?"

She smiled wickedly, her face crinkling in all sorts of places it shouldn't have.

"Old. Awful word. Someday you'll know just how cruel it is. All my life people have tried to tell me how to live."

"Tried and failed."

"Thank goodness." She laughed. "I did listen to them when I was too young to know better…as you are now trying. And I failed. I think you have my genes."

How beautiful she still was, he thought, even if her skin, which had seen too much of the Mediterranean sun and had known the caresses of so many younger lovers, was as dry as parchment. Like a faded movie star, she had the painted brows and lips of another age, but beneath the makeup, her eyes were young and bright and shone with all the love for him that filled her generous heart.

"Get in," she commanded. "I've been trying to call you. Of

course, all your mother's dreadful people told me you weren't in. Gloriana even came to the phone and told me herself."

His mother, *her* daughter, did not approve of his relationship with his scandalous grandmother, the artist who'd divorced her royal prince, but doing so only after she'd done her duty and had produced heirs.

"So, my magic gardenia failed, and you gave up the beautiful American girl," she said as she sped along the narrow road, her focus on him instead of the traffic.

His eyes on the oncoming bus that was taking more than half of the road, he said nothing.

Fortunately, the bus stopped. *Grand-mère* swerved at the last second, too, missing it on her side and missing the low rock wall on his, but by mere inches. "I was hoping you wouldn't give her up," she said, not the least bit perturbed.

As soon as the danger was past, she was whipping around the curves again, tailgating within a millimeter, oblivious to everything except their conversation, as usual.

"*Grand-mère,* you should let me drive."

Her hands tightened possessively on the wheel. "I'll drive. Back to your girl…."

He made a silent vow to never get in *Grand-mère's* red death trap again unless he could drive. But he'd fight that battle on some other day.

"You know what my life is, what is expected," he said.

"Other people's expectations."

"The life I lead would have made her miserable."

"And you think she is happy without you?"

"Happier," he said. "Why did you sell her that painting of me, the painting you'd always promised me, and then point her out to me and tell me what you'd done? If you hadn't pointed her out—"

"A wicked little voice told me to do it, the same voice that tells me what to paint, what to buy for my shop, and who to love next. I am a slave to *the voice.*"

"It was wrong of you to meddle. Very wrong."

"Are you sure, my precious little love?"

"You've made us both unhappy. Viola, too."

"We make our own happiness in this world. The choice is yours, my love."

"No. I have a duty—"

"But are you suited to your duties and to this life any better than I was? I have watched you suffer these past two years. I only wanted you to be happy again. You don't have to give in to your mother. She was an extremely difficult child, you know. Quite dull. Never took to painting or anything the least bit interesting. Just sat in her corner and put beautiful clothes on her dolls. She isn't like you, you know. Do you remember how wild you were when you were little? You are meant to know grand passion, as I have. You will make Viola miserable."

"You shouldn't have meddled. It was a wicked voice."

"But I did. What is done is done. And cannot be undone. If it weren't for the wicked, life would be very dull, indeed."

She'd made a loop, and they were back at the beach and the lemon trees where she'd picked him up. She said goodbye and kissed him many times. He got out of the Maserati and strode toward his tender and tried to forget what she'd said.

A minute later, he was motoring toward his yacht. He secured the tender and jumped aboard *Simonetta*.

When he looked back at the beach, he remembered the night he'd brought Cara here.

Would she haunt him forever?

In his stateroom, he chose a bottle of his finest whiskey and poured himself half a glass. As he lifted the glass, his cell phone materialized in his other hand.

Who the hell did he intend to call? Massimo? No. Viola?

As he gulped from the glass, savoring its fire, he found Cara's saved number on his phone. Then he punched a button.

Not knowing what he'd say if she answered, only knowing that he had to hear her voice, he waited.

"Hello." Her voice, pure and sweet.

What the hell was all that background noise?

Babies were crying. Then a high-pitched, energetic voice chirped loudly, "Can I have another cookie, Aunt Reggie? Pl-e-e-e-e-z!"

He'd read somewhere that one three-year-old could make more noise than two hundred civilized adults.

"Just a minute, sweetheart. Sorry. So sorry about that! Hello! Hello!"

Even though she sounded like she was next door, he felt the ocean and all the distance between them.

"It's me. Nico. I had to know if you arrived home safely."

"I called Massimo weeks ago. Didn't he tell you?"

"Yes. I wanted to hear it from you."

"I'm okay." She sounded a little lost. "Working hard. Baby-sitting for my sister today. It's Saturday, you know."

Babies screamed. Then a toddler shouted, "Aunt Reggie. Aunt Reggie!"

"Oops! Oh, no! Not the whole plate of cookies, sweetheart! You will turn into a Teletubby if you eat all that! Nico, it's a circus here. Could you hang on a sec? I've got to go!"

Nico heard more noise and what sounded like a crash.

"Hello!" a little girl yelled merrily.

He heard telephone buttons being punched, no doubt by a stubby-fingered, little hand. Then the line went dead. The toddler had hung up on him.

Maybe it was for the best. Cara had her life. He had his.

He clenched a fist. Feeling bleak and empty, he lifted his glass and drained it. Lucky for him, the whiskey was real, its effects strong.

Or maybe not so lucky.

With his guard down, memories of Cara's face, body and smiles consumed him. He thought of the recent nights when he'd awakened stiff, hard and throbbing because of his hot, lascivious dreams in which she writhed beneath him or licked him all over with her tongue.

He stared at his phone, but instead of reaching for it again, he got up and poured a second shot of whiskey.

Eleven

David and Dino were both yelling at full volume from their cribs. Regina felt close to tears herself when Gina, who had grabbed the phone away from her to say hi to Nico, snapped it shut.

Was it only yesterday that Robert Riley, Sr., had echoed Donald Trump's favorite phrase?

You're fired!

What had Rebecca thought would happen when she'd sashayed into Robert Sr.'s office and tossed the Hewit complaint on his desk? After she'd insisted on voicing all of her reservations and objections about the case, he'd ordered coffee. As he stirred in sugar and cream, he'd *explained,* in the careful, softly modulated tones that one would use with a child, exactly how many hours the firm billed each year to Black Boar.

When she hadn't backed down, he'd fired her. Just like that. For the first time in her life, she had no plan.

What she did have was a large credit card bill from her trip to Italy and stacks of unpaid bills on her desk. She'd spent half the night on her computer, tweaking her résumé. But she was clueless about what kind of job she might want. What she did know was that as soon as she was near a pay phone, she'd make an anonymous call to Rebecca and recommend a more gifted attorney than the one she had now.

"Gina, why'd you hang up on him?"

Gina's eyes gleamed with mischief. Then she frowned, her chubby face twisting in innocence and confusion. When she cocked her head playfully, her rhinestone tiara toppled to one side.

She was wearing her blue satin princess costume, and Regina's dark Ray-Bans. Only the overlarge shades were upside down and hovering on the tip of her nose, about to fall off as the child bit off another chunk of chocolate chip cookie.

The babies' cries turned to screams in their cribs.

"You shouldn't have grabbed the phone. My friend will think I hung up on him."

Gina shrugged and chomped off more cookie. "We can call him back!" She threw up her hands.

"And no more cookies, young lady, for either one of us."

Clutching the remnants of her cookie, Gina raced to a far corner. When it came to chocolate chip cookies, Gina did not have a stop button.

The babies were still yelling and Regina was leaning down to pick up the tray and all the spilled cookies, when the doorbell rang.

Regina ran for the door and peeped through the window shade. "Lucy!"

Regina flung the door open and hugged her radiant pregnant friend before allowing her to waddle across the threshold.

"Chocolate chip! My favorite!"

"Join the club."

Lucy plucked a cookie off the tray. "What's all the ruckus?"

"Thank goodness, you're here. I'm pretty overwhelmed. Watch Gina while I change the babies."

Lucy ran a hand through her short, spiky red hair. "There was an accident on Lamar. The traffic was horrible."

Gina smiled coyly at Lucy from her corner.

"What have you got there, Princess?"

Tina opened her mouth, displaying her tongue and chewed-up cookie.

"Are you a princess today?"

"Cinderella."

"My favorite fairy tale. Do you want me to read it to you?"

"I can read it myself."

Ten minutes later, each woman had a baby guzzling a bottle in her lap while Gina sat on the floor at their feet with her dolls and books, waiting to be read a story.

"I can't wait for mine to be born," Lucy said. "Babies are so sweet."

"But trouble. Lots of trouble."

"They're worth it." Lucy petted Dino's dark head. "Aren't you a cutie-pie?"

Now that the children were temporarily under control, Regina remembered Nico's aborted call and wondered if he was okay. She'd bought all the tabloids that had stories about his romance with Viola. Prince and princess: they sounded perfect for each other.

Why had he called her?

Don't think about him.

I can't help it.

Yes, you can. You can do anything you want to do.

You should start dating again.

Not until I find a new job.

She should never have risked her position by speaking so recklessly without another job. Just thinking about that depressed her. If only she had a plan.

Forget Nico. Get a job. Pay your bills. That's a plan.

"We've hardly talked since you got back from Italy," Lucy said.

"I've been busy.... Work." Technically, Regina was still earning a salary since she'd been given two weeks' severance.

"You never told me about the gigolo."

"He wasn't a gigolo."

"He was a real guy, huh? And you had a real date?"

"It's over."

"So-o?"

"I—I can't talk about him right now."

"That good, huh?"

"I hate the way you think you can see straight through me."

"The way I think…ha!"

"It was a dream. I woke up. I'm here, and he's there, and that's the end of it."

Lucy's eyebrows flew together. "I don't mean to criticize, but sometimes your devious lawyer mind is too smart for your britches."

"Quit!"

"Are you in love with him?"

"I said quit!"

Lucy wouldn't stop looking at her, so, of course, she saw Regina's telltale blush.

"That's it!"

"It wouldn't have worked. He's Italian."

"And what are you? Italian-American!"

"We're completely different, okay? Not possible!"

"Nothing is impossible," Lucy said. "Look at me. I finally got pregnant."

"You, you're a walking miracle."

"Your turn will come. So, if the gigolo-guy's a no-go, have you thought any more about E-321 and maybe having that little half brother or sister for my baby?"

Regina shook her head. "I'm not ready. Neither is my family. I've got some bills. Italy…" She thought about Nico and blurted, "I'm just not ready to have anyone else's baby."

"Anyone else's…? Hey!"

"I didn't mean that. I didn't mean what it sounded like."

Lucy lifted Dino to her shoulder to burp him. "Why won't you talk about this guy?"

"I just can't."

"You seem different somehow. I mean, after Italy. Was it *him*?"

"I wish people would stop saying that. People change. Maybe I matured."

Lucy shook her head.

Closing her eyes, Regina told herself she had to quit thinking about Nico all the time. She was home, back in her real world. Someday soon she had to rethink the E-321 issue. Her biological clock hadn't stopped ticking just because she'd chosen the wrong man.

Why had he called? Had he missed her a little? Was the gorgeous Viola as icy as his mother? Regina bit her lips. She hoped so.

No. If she truly loved him, she should want him to be happy. But she was human, okay? And humans aren't perfect, right? Nobody expected her to be a saint filled with noble virtues, did they?

Still, when she'd first come home, she'd buried herself in work to avoid her dark, selfish feelings.

Having finished eating every single cookie crumb off the floor, Gina ran to her and patted baby David with her chocolate-smeared fingertips.

"Gently," Regina cautioned. "And why don't you lick your fingers?"

When Gina bent over her fingers, her tiara fell off. Leaning down, Regina picked it up.

Gina snatched it and put it on and whirled, clapping and giggling, making Lucy and Regina laugh.

"When I grow up, can I be a real princess?"

"Of course you can, my darling," Regina whispered, her voice choked. "Come here, darling, so I can straighten your tiara again. All that twirling, it's hanging on your ear."

"Are you all right?" Lucy asked as Regina brushed at her eyes.

Like Regina's sister Susana, Lucy was too intuitive sometimes. "I'm fine."

She didn't feel all that well, actually. The sweet baby smell was getting to her. Regina set David's bottle on the floor. Holding him close, intending to put him in his swing, she was instantly too dizzy to take a step.

Lucy's red hair and freckled face whirled amidst flashes of brilliance. Then the room became bright white and suffocatingly hot. Beads of perspiration popped out on her face. A band of iron circled her chest. Clutching David, she sank weakly back into her chair.

"Are you okay?" Lucy whispered, her low tone urgent.

The white flashes were still swirling as Gina ran to Regina and tugged at her arm. "What's the matter, Aunt Reggie?"

"I—I'm fine."

"You're as white as that wall behind you," Lucy said. "What's wrong?"

"I just feel a little faint. That's all. Busy week. I guess I stood up too quickly."

"Maybe you should see a doctor."

"I said I'm fine."

But later that night when Regina was eating warmed-over pizza while she further revised her résumé at her computer, the black font blurred sickeningly. Her head began to feel thick and funny, and her pulse sped up.

She spit out her pizza and pushed her white wine away. The pizza was spicy, the way she usually liked it, but much too spicy tonight. And the chilled wine, Nico's favorite, was so dry her mouth felt like cotton after one sip.

When bile climbed her throat, she ran to the kitchen and drank ice water.

Still queasy, she fell onto her bed without removing her jeans. Not that she could sleep. The next morning she woke up with raccoon circles under her eyes. Her skin was pale and clammy, and when she even thought about cooking oatmeal, she felt so sick again she had to lie back down.

As she lay on her back, she grabbed one of the celebrity magazines off her nightstand and studied Nico's picture and then Viola's. Bold headlines screamed. Prince and His Princess. Fairy-tale Marriage.

Their gorgeous faces began to spin.

Regina threw the magazine at the wall.

Suddenly overcome with an urge to retch, she got up and raced to the toilet, where she threw up disgusting chunks of undigested pizza. Her head was still over the bowl, when a life-changing thought occurred to her.

She hadn't had her period.

Not since Italy.

The phone rang. Still feeling weak, she crawled back to her bed, grabbed the receiver and flung herself on her rumpled sheets, belly up.

"Hi. You there? It's your mother. Say something, Cara, so I'll know you're alive!"

"M-Ma! Hi."

"It's Sunday. I'm calling about lunch. Joe's out of town, but Susana and the kids will be there."

Sunday lunch was a longstanding tradition.

"I'm sorry. I don't think so. I—I don't feel well. Nausea."

"Maybe you should see a doctor. You haven't been yourself. Not since Italy. Maybe you caught something over there."

Twelve

Pregnant.

A shocked Regina sat in the doctor's waiting room with her right hand cupped over her mouth. Her left hand was clutching the armrest of her chair as if it were a life preserver. Her stomach tightened, and she looked down at it and was surprised that it was still so flat.

Nico had used a condom every time, but the doctor had confirmed the results of the pregnancy test Regina had taken at home with more tests and a physical exam.

Nico. How would he react when she told him? And she *had* to tell him. Would he be pleased?

Was she pleased?

Yes. Or, at least, she would be when the shock wore off. For another long moment, unsure about whether or not she could stand, much less walk out to her car and drive, she simply sat there, adjusting to her new reality.

Pregnant. Nico's baby.

Baby first. Husband second.

Her plan.

Only she'd hadn't planned *this*. For one thing, a job had been a given. How could she raise a baby without a job?

And Nico. She thought about the lovely Viola and his plans to marry her as soon as possible. He had to be told immediately.

Biting her lips, Regina stared up at the ceiling. A baby. Nico's precious baby, but no job and no husband. And no Nico.

"Thank you," she whispered, even as she began to shake and feel scared at the same time. "Thank you. With your help, I can do this." *Somehow.*

When she finally felt strong enough to drive and was behind the wheel, her thoughts strayed back to Nico. She hated upsetting him, hated telling him over the phone. But this problem wasn't going away.

When she got to her house, she flipped on the television to CNN, muted the volume and then pulled her cell phone out of her purse. At the thought of calling Nico, what little confidence she had leaked out of her.

Sinking onto her couch in a daze, she punched in his number. Her heart began to beat faster with each ring.

"Ciao," he mumbled in a cranky, groggy voice.

"Oh, my God! *The time!*" She looked at her watch in horror. "Nico, I'm sorry. It's five-thirty in the afternoon in Texas! I totally forgot it's twelve-thirty your time! I'm sorry! Sorry, sorry!"

She was still babbling when he said, "Viola?" And then louder, "Cara? Cara! Is it really you, *tesorina?*"

Did she only imagine that his deep voice had softened?

Viola's picture flashed on her television screen and was followed with a clip of Nico dining with her at a posh restaurant in Rome, holding her hand, smiling. There was a shot of them on his yacht.

Regina closed her eyes. Did he suck her fingertips, too? They did look perfect together.

"It's Regina."

"Regina?"

Her stomach knotted. He didn't even know her name.

"I mean Cara. Regina's my real name. I—I shouldn't have called. I'll call back at a better time."

"Cara! Wait!"

"I'll call back. Sleep well." She hung up. She shut her eyes again. "Sleep well, my darling."

Viola? He'd expected Viola.

How quickly we forget.

Wide-awake now and in a hellish mood because Cara had sounded so lost, Nico rang her back as fast as he could. When he got her voice mail, he cursed vividly.

She'd called him. Then she'd turned off her phone.

Women.

But she'd sounded scared. He had to talk to her, so he left a message, demanding that she call him at once.

He held the phone in his palm for an hour. When she didn't call, he began to feel crazed as the uncertainty in her tone grew in his mind. Something was wrong.

He called her again and again, leaving more messages demanding that she call him. Then he paced his gilded bedroom until two like a caged cat.

Her voice had sounded strange. He had to find out what was wrong, as soon as possible. Despite the late hour, he rang Massimo.

"Can this possibly wait? I'm in a bar. With the most gorgeous *signorina.*"

"Sorry to disturb you. You have to help me check up on Cara."

"Cara!" Massimo groaned.

"She called and hung up on me. Now she won't take my calls. I'm worried about her."

"She's fine," Massimo said, sounding bored and distracted. There was a lot of music and laughter in the background.

"I have to know that for sure."

"It's the middle of the night, and the *signorina* is touching me in places I won't discuss on a cell phone."

"It's not the middle of the night in Texas. Hire detectives.

Keep me and the family's name out of it. No scandal, but do whatever it takes."

"If she doesn't want to talk to you—"

"I don't give a damn about that. Call me as soon as you know something."

Nico hung up. Not that he'd quit trying to call her himself.

Not that she didn't consume his every thought that night and throughout the next day.

"When are you going to announce your engagement?"

Nico dropped his fork, looked up from his omelet and frowned at the regal woman sitting beneath her peach-colored umbrella just outside the pink walls of her favorite palazzo. His favorite, too.

He felt like he was in a prison, and his mother and the generations before her were his jailers. Her black silk suit fit her exquisite figure like a glove; her perfectly groomed hair gleamed like spun gold. Now that things were going her way she looked young and lovely and quite serene.

He wanted to stand up, seize control of his destiny and tell her what to do, which was the way he always acted in business. And in that arena, in the space of a decade, he'd made his family richer than they'd ever imagined. He'd done so by working hard and by following his gut instinct.

Why was it that, when it came to marriage and lineage, he let her run him?

Maybe because she had a thousand years of tradition on her side.

"Can't you think of something besides my marriage?" Nico said, his tone clipped.

He hadn't touched his omelet. Usually he ate a huge breakfast. Now he had no appetite.

He stood up and tossed his napkin down. "I have an early appointment."

"But, Nico, darling, you didn't eat anything."

When he saw the hurt on her face, he felt guilty. She was only doing what she'd been taught was the right thing to do, what the generations before her had believed to be right. Modern ideas of democracy and romantic love meant nothing to her.

"I apologize," he said. Then he stalked off the terrace and into the palazzo.

Later, at his office, he regretted his rudeness to her, but the mounting pressure about his romance with Viola, his mother's stubborn ambition for him in all arenas, and his genuine concern about Cara had him feeling disturbed.

He'd thought he could give her up. Damn it, he'd tried.

As the hours passed and he attended to his routine business duties and appointments with no further word from Massimo, he grew even edgier, snapping out commands, hanging up too abruptly on important people, even a French financial minister, whom he had to ring back with an apology.

At eleven that night, when he was beside himself, pacing in his bedroom, Massimo finally rang.

"You're not going to like this," his cousin said.

"Is Cara all right?"

Nico splashed Scotch into a crystal glass, waiting for an answer that didn't come.

"Damn it, Massimo? Is she?"

"Yes. And no."

Nico ground his teeth. "And?" He gulped the Scotch.

"She's pregnant. Saw the doctor yesterday."

Pregnant?

"Pregnant?" He began to cough and spit Scotch.

"Who's the lucky father?" His strangled voice was barely audible.

"Not sure. Apparently, before she met you, she told everybody she wanted to have a baby on her own, to be a single mother of choice."

"What the hell is that?"

"Some crazy American-women idea. Her parents weren't for it. Her father went into quite a sulk when he found out she'd bought eight vials of sperm from a sperm bank. So, she broke her appointment to be inseminated, took a leave of absence, and flew to Italy."

And tried to seduce a gigolo.

A hard band closed around Nico's lungs.

"Did she get pregnant in Italy? Or after Italy? How far along is she?"

"The detective couldn't say. He's happy to keep digging though. Likes the money. It was getting late, so I thought I should call—"

"Thanks. I'll let you know," Nico mumbled a few more questions. Then he jotted Cara's full name and address and all her phone numbers in a little black notebook and slammed his phone shut.

For a long moment, he stared at the phone numbers, not really seeing them as he considered calling one of them on the long shot she'd answer.

No, she was a lawyer. Better to show up without giving her any warning. That way she wouldn't have time to build up her defense.

Pregnant? Vials of sperm?

Had she known who he was and set him up?

He went to the tall window of his bedroom. In the moonlight, he could see the swans gliding peacefully together on their glimmering pond.

Was he the father? Why had she called him yesterday? To inform him? To blackmail him?

Had her parents pressured her into giving up on the sperm-donor idea? Had they talked her into getting pregnant the old-fashioned way? Had that been the real purpose of her vacation? Her real purpose in that bar?

How many men had she slept with before him?

He stared at the swans, his emotions tearing at him. How could he have let himself believe that at least for a short space of time, she'd cared about him for himself alone, cared enough to sacrifice her own feelings for the higher good of his family?

Hell. What a fool he was to have thought she might love him.

Wearily, he turned away from the swans. Their loyalty made him angry somehow. He had to banish all softness, all notions of enduring love and romance. He had a duty to his family. He also had a duty to his unborn child—if he had one.

Bottom line: was he the father?

He felt betrayal and something even worse.

Damn her to hell and back.

If Cara had manipulated him, if she intended to use this pregnancy to hurt his family, to use their child for financial gain…

He'd see her in Dante's inferno first.

Thirteen

*P*regnant.

Regina smiled. She would have a baby to love, a baby who would be just hers, someone who couldn't abandon her, someone who would need her for a long, long time.

Nico had called her back, too. Again and again. But he'd sounded so urgent and upset she hadn't been able to force herself to return his calls.

She would; she even wanted to.

She'd been trying to work up her nerve to do just that. She sat on the couch listening to his messages again, each one colder than the last, while her lifelong feelings of abandonment resurfaced to make her think that perhaps he'd never really truly cared for her in the first place. She decided that maybe a nice, long bath would relax her and make calling him easier.

Pregnant. Nico's baby.

In her bathroom, she stripped and studied her breasts and stomach with a critical eye. Although she wasn't showing, she felt so totally changed. Already she loved this baby so much. And yet…

All her life she'd tried to be strong and independent. Now she felt just the opposite—one big reason she dreaded telling Nico about the baby. She didn't want him to think she expected anything from him, and still…

Truly, she wanted to reassure him that she was perfectly able to raise their child alone even though the very thought of doing so alarmed her.

He was her baby's father. And she loved him. And the baby would love him. It was stupid, idiotic, hormonal, whatever. But she felt a strange, new, wonderful vulnerability and at the same time, a crushing sense of dependency.

Their baby needed a mother *and* a father.

Hello! This is the modern world. What happened to the idea of being a single mother by choice?

Nico owed his family. There was no room in his complicated life for her. She knew that. Just as she knew she couldn't fit into his world any more than he could fit into hers.

But hormones don't listen to reason. Their siren song is more ancient and truer than any new social idea.

So, a conflicted Regina, the modern woman and the ancient, ran her tub full of water and then lay down to soak and hoped she'd relax.

Like a child, she batted at the bubbles floating on top of the water. Then she sang, as she always did, off-key. Finally, when she was hoarse, she soaped a leg and lifted her razor.

An hour later, the water was cold, her bubbles were gone, and she was still without a single solution to her life's riddles.

Suddenly, a loud banging at her front door shook her out of her reverie. Terrified, she leaped out of the bathtub. When the banging persisted, she sat back down and turned on the hot water full blast.

"Stubborn idiot!" she whispered. "Go away!"

The knocking stopped, and she sighed in relief until her cell phone began to ring.

She sat up again.

So much for peace and relaxation.

Her cell phone stopped and then her home phone burst to life.

What was going on?

Her family! She was filled with panic at the thought of a car crash or a heart attack. Then she imagined Joe, backing out of the driveway in his van and running over Gina, who was never where she was supposed to be. Regina shot out of the tub and toweled herself dry.

She put on her thick, terry-cloth robe and ran into the kitchen to find her phone.

"Answer your damned door," Nico yelled.

Nico? Here?

Oh, my God!

She'd left her garage door open, so, of course, he'd seen her car. He'd probably heard her run into the kitchen, too.

Heart racing, she tiptoed to the front door and cracked her shade, gasping when she saw a white stretch limousine gleaming in her driveway.

Although Nico wore a charcoal suit and tie that probably cost a small fortune, he looked as fierce and frightening as a warrior prince from another age on a rampage.

Nico? Nico!

Frantic, she let go of her shade. When it crashed noisily against the window, she screamed.

When big brown knuckles rapped on the windowpane so vigorously she was afraid the glass would shatter, she jumped away. Then, gathering her courage, she clutched her robe tighter and yanked her shade back up again.

Nico crossed his muscular arms, leaned against the door frame and glared at her through the glass. His huge body in that perfectly cut suit was so tense she knew he was barely restraining himself. His blue eyes burned like lasers. A wild thread of fear knotted itself around her heart and pulled tight.

She was naked underneath her robe, but if she took the time to dress, she knew it would try his patience to the extreme, so she unlocked the door.

He blew past her into the foyer, slamming the door so hard the whole house shook.

She'd hung the painting of the little boy playing in the sand in her foyer. When he saw it, he stopped cold and stared at it for long seconds, his frown deepening.

Then, as if it offended him, he turned his back on the painting.

"Why did you call me and then not call me back?" With each word, a blue vein pulsed savagely in his temple.

She let out a strangled cry and sagged against the wall. "I was—"

"Trying to drive me crazy? Because if that was your intent, you damn sure succeeded!"

With her face scrubbed clean of makeup and her hair in wet tangles, she imagined he compared her to the beautiful Viola and found her pathetic.

He strode past her into the kitchen, where he opened and closed drawers, sifting through their contents.

"What are you doing?" she cried. "What are you looking for?"

"Who the hell are you?"

Next he began gazing at all the photographs on her refrigerator. She wanted to scream that he had no right to go through her things, but she watched him, mute, afraid.

Mostly the photographs were of Gina and David and Dino; of Susana and the rest of her family. She'd pinned up a few she'd taken of various sights in Italy.

He lifted them one by one, reading the back of the pictures, as well. It was her habit to methodically jot the names of the people, the location and the time.

"I see there are no pictures of me," he said. "Did you delete them?"

No. No. No. They were on her computer, and she looked at them every night.

When his hand touched E-321's profile, she ran over to the refrigerator to distract him.

He turned, his intense blue eyes cool and calculating now. "Why did you call me and then not call me back? What are you up to? What do you want?"

She couldn't tear her gaze from his dark hand, which rested on E-321's profile.

When he wouldn't stop staring at her, either, her skin grew hot and clammy. Suddenly bile crawled up her throat and her mouth went dry.

Oh, no! No. No!

Cupping her lips, she rushed to the sink and was sick.

When she could lift her head and breathe again, she felt his hard, critical gaze boring into the small of her back. She straightened to her full height and turned slowly to face him.

"You're as white as a sheet," he said without a trace of sympathy. "No makeup."

He opened a cabinet and got out a glass. Then he went to the refrigerator and poured her a glass of icy water.

He gave her the glass, and she sipped the cool liquid gratefully.

She should tell him about the baby now. But she couldn't. Not like this. Not when he was so angry.

"Why are you here? Why are you so upset?" she whispered.

He turned back to the refrigerator and yanked off E-321's profile with a vengeance. *"Why am I here?"*

He wadded up the profile and threw it at her.

When it bounced at her feet, she jumped.

"You're pregnant. That's why."

She sucked in a breath. "You knew even before I was sick. *You knew!"*

"You're hardly in a position to accuse me."

Cornered, her legal mind went on full attack. "That's privileged, private information. I haven't even told my mother yet. You have no right—"

"No right?" Like a predator closing in for the kill, he stalked her.

She skittered backward until her butt hit the cabinets and his tall, muscular body in designer charcoal loomed over her, blocking her escape.

"Who the hell's the father, damn it?"

She looked up at him, and her tongue froze against the roof of her mouth.

He gripped her shoulders so tightly she felt each finger bruising her flesh.

"Is it mine? Or is it the damn sperm donor's? Or some other man's? Did you call me to blackmail me?" The fingers mashed harder, cutting her.

"Blackmail? No! No! No. How can you think…"

She felt as if she were dying inside. She didn't want him here. Not like this.

"Then who's the father?"

She knew she should lie. If he thought she was as low as he was accusing her of being, she should definitely lie. She was a lawyer. Surely she should be able to make up a plausible story that would rid her of him forever.

"Why don't you just tell me the truth for once?" he said.

"You aren't going to like this."

His hands dug even deeper. *"Is it mine?"*

Aware of those rough fingers and of the muscle ticking along his hard jawline, she fought for every breath.

"Nobody has to know," she whispered.

"What? *Nobody has to know?* That's your answer?"

If she'd struck him, he couldn't have looked more stunned. *"I know,"* he said. "I know."

"I wasn't planning to blackmail you. I just wanted to tell you. That's all. I swear."

"Why?"

"I—I…" She broke off. "Because it's yours."

There was no trace of tenderness or even humanity in Nico's face. She'd seen such cold implacability in the courtroom many times. It always spelled doom. No matter what she said, he wasn't going to believe her.

"I'm telling you the truth. That's the only reason I called."

His eyes narrowed until all she could see was glittering blue slits of fire behind his black lashes. "Well, you're not blackmailing anybody because you're going to marry me, you little fool."

"Impossible. You told me we could never be together."

"That was before you became pregnant with my child."

My child, too! she wanted to scream.

"What about Viola? Your family? Your mother?"

"They will have to accept it, as I have to accept it. A higher duty calls."

"You're a prince. I want you to marry Viola. You have to marry her."

"And have my child grow up a bastard in America, raised solely by a woman like you, never knowing him and all the while knowing he'll always feel abandoned by me, his father, knowing, as well, you could use him and threaten to sell your story for your own gain. No! What would that do to him, to have his father abandon him to a mother like you?"

Stung, she almost wept. "I would never do that!"

He stared at her for a long moment. "Did you know who I was that first day? Did you do this deliberately?"

"I don't need you or your title or your money. I'm an attorney. I have my career—"

He laughed. "Some career. You were fired from Merrit, Riley & Whitt. Two days ago."

"How do you know that?"

"Money buys a lot of answers. Being a lawyer, *you* should know that."

"I'll have you know there are privacy laws in this country."

"There should be laws against what you did to me. All your miserable life, you've been out to prove you were somebody."

"How do you know—"

"Is that why you ditched the sperm-donor plan, why you wanted to catch a prince?"

"I—I want you to leave! Now! I—I called you because I thought you were a reasonable person and I wanted to tell you, just to let you know. But now I know who you really are—a total, arrogant bastard."

"As I know who you really are."

"But I'm not what you think and you are what I—"

"All your life, you've felt like an outsider. Your sister was the one everybody loved. You've fought and scraped to climb out of some imaginary gutter. You didn't care who you hurt."

Who had talked to him?

"I don't need you. I can raise my baby without you or anybody else."

"But you're not going to because I won't allow it. You're going to marry me. *For a year.* So I can stake my legal claim to my son."

"I hate you."

His eyes flashed with equal passion. "Surely we can stand each other for a year."

"Are you out of your mind?"

"Yes, and it's your fault." His tone was low and was so maddeningly calm she wanted to slap him, wanted to yank tufts of his thick black hair from his scalp. "After the year is over, you can do what you want."

"My life is here."

"Not for the next year. No child of *mine* is going to be a bastard."

"*My* child, too!"

"If you don't agree to marriage on my terms, I'll fight you for custody. My family is very powerful. Don't force me to lean on you. Believe me, it will not be a pleasant experience."

She tried to swallow. She'd been the legal lackey representing wealthy people and corporations too long not to know the power of big money. He was right. He could crush her.

"So, you will marry me, and fast," he said. "You can seek a divorce when our child is three months old. After our divorce, I will want to see *him* as often as possible."

"*Him?* How can you keep saying *our* baby is a boy?"

Our baby. The phrase echoed in her heart.

"Or her," he corrected.

"If you think I'm going to let you take over my life and my unborn child's life…even for a year…"

"This isn't my fault, you know. You're the one who hired me to be your stud."

"I most certainly did not!"

"You bought that dress, wore that flower, acted like a sad, lonely American woman in need of a gigolo."

The awful G-word gonged like a rusty bell. "I did not!"

"I felt sorry for you," he finished brutally.

"Sorry for me?" She drew a sharp, horrified breath.

"And all the time, you had this plan because you're so damned insecure."

"I did not! I am not!"

"I don't believe you, Miss Tomei. As I said before, your entire life has been about climbing some imaginary ladder." He picked up her phone and began to read aloud from a little black notebook. "Five-five-five, six-four-five…"

He punched in the familiar-sounding string of numbers and waited.

Suddenly, she realized he'd dialed her parents' number and listened in horror when he smiled and said, "Mr. Tomei?"

"Don't you dare!" she screamed. "He doesn't know about any of this!"

"Excuse me, sir." Nico put his hand over the phone. "Then it's time he found out. From what I hear, he's crazy about his other grandchildren."

"You can't just barge in here—"

"Mr. Tomei…"

She took a deep breath to steady herself. Somehow, Nico knew that she'd always wanted her father to think she was special, and that she'd failed, and tonight Nico was determined to destroy her and make her father hate her forever.

"It is a pleasure to meet you, even over the telephone. I am Prince Nico Romano." He said all of his numerous names, which Regina knew she would never be able to remember, even if she stayed married to him for a whole damned year. "Yes, a *real* prince. Yes, we do own a castle. More than one, actually."

Her father, an avid golf fan, who didn't keep up with the lives of celebrities, didn't have a clue who Nico was, no matter how much had been written about him in the tabloids. Nico's voice was low and respectful as he explained who he was, but with every word Regina felt an immense pressure building inside her head until she was nearly sure invisible flames had to be spewing out of her mouth and ears. Otherwise, she would have exploded.

He was going to tell her father! He was determined to ruin her life forever!

"I have only recently learned that your daughter is pregnant with my child."

Oh, my God! He'd said the P-word! Daddy!

I will be the bad daughter forever now! Thanks to you, Prince… no…Principe Don Nico Carlo Giovanni Romano! Even if I do become Principessa Donna Regina Carina Romano di Tomei!

How had she remembered all those names?

Rage must have sharpened her memory.

Time spun backward. Regina was suddenly three years old again. She'd just dropped a jar of peanut butter her father had forbidden her to touch onto the floor. The shattering glass had awakened Susana in her crib, and she'd started crying. Her father had gone to get the baby before returning to the kitchen. Then, as he'd cradled Susana lovingly in his arms, he'd called Regina all sorts of horrid names. Or, in her shame, she'd imagined that he had.

Regina shut her eyes against the awful memory and sagged against the wall. Prince Nico paused and shot her a significant look. Not wanting him to see her vulnerability, she stood up taller and straighter and drew in a calming breath. And then another.

"No, I'm not a sperm donor. I met your daughter in Italy. Love at first sight."

Love. For a second, all she registered was Nico's chiseled male beauty and the intense blue of his eyes. Her entire being blazed. Some incredibly stupid part of her almost believed he was telling the truth, that he'd truly found something rare and beautiful in their brief affair, as she had.

No, she hadn't! And it was impossible that he had, either! He was furious with her. As she was with him—due to his absolutely despicable, totally unforgivable, arrogant behavior of the past five minutes. He was manipulating her and her father. She couldn't possibly ever love such a man!

"You know how it is when something like that catches you by surprise." Nico's white smile flashed.

Why had the devil given him the sexiest smile in the universe?

She squeezed her eyes shut and fought against the memory of their passion. Surely that had been the devil's work, as well.

"Yes, sir. It was like being hit with a thunderbolt."

It had been exactly like that. Was he mocking her?

"Yes, I would like to meet Susana and the children."

Regina's throat tightened with grief and rage and some wild, unnamed emotion that made her feel faint and lost, almost sick again. Nico's sweet lies had exposed that awful, barren place that would be her heart if he really hated her forever.

How humiliating to still want him! To still love him!

With a choked cry, Regina ran to her bedroom, locked her door, tore off her robe and began yanking clothing out of her closet in an attempt to find something to wear.

Through the thin walls, she heard the rest of the conversation.

"I would like to meet all of you as I hope to ask you formally for her hand in marriage."

"Bastard," she breathed. Then she threw a hanger at the wall.

Then Nico hung up, strode to the door and yelled through it. "You'd better hurry. Your father has most graciously invited us to dinner."

"Damn you," she muttered in a low, inaudible voice.

"Tonight. Seven o'clock. I told him I'd buy wine. You have fifteen minutes. Do you need any help?"

Like a child having a tantrum, she tossed the outfits she didn't want to wear into a heap on the floor. Then she stomped up and down on them.

"Fifteen minutes," he repeated. "If you're not dressed, you'll go naked. Your choice."

One glance in the mirror at her nude body and her pale un-made-up face had her gulping in air at a frantic pace. For one second, she entertained the notion of marching into the living room stark naked.

What if she kissed him? Or grabbed his big member? Would his arrogant fury explode into something entirely different? If she threw her arms around him, would he pick her up and carry her to the bedroom? Would sex burn away the hate and open the door to love?

But what if he turned away in disgust?

Shaking, she sank down on the little velvet stool in front of her vanity to apply her makeup.

Why couldn't she have been dressed and gorgeous when he'd arrived instead of being pale and wet headed and wearing her oldest robe? With an effort, she began to concentrate on making the most of her limited time. She even curled her lashes and was pleased with her reflection when she twirled in front of her mirror after he knocked on her door ten minutes later.

Not that wanting to be especially beautiful tonight meant anything. It didn't. But when she opened her door and waltzed into the hall in her low-cut swirly green dress and heels, with her shining hair curling about her face, it pleased her no end when his eyes stalled on her red mouth and then again her breasts. She heard the sharp intake of his breath and fought the urge to smile.

For a long time, she couldn't breathe, either.

Slowly he raised his eyes, but the power of speech had left him, too.

"Ready?" she managed, feeling almost as beautiful as the exquisite Principessa Donna Viola.

Fourteen

Regina's triumph was short-lived. Her beauty, indeed everything about her, seemed to annoy the hell out of him. His face was colder than ever as he stomped out of her house and led her to the car.

She was pregnant, and, therefore, he felt trapped. Her thoughts began to circle around and around, buzzing in a negative loop. By the time she latched her seat belt in the limo, her mood was blacker than his. Nor did being whisked, against her will, through the darkening streets in his luxurious car toward her parents' house improve her mood.

Her family! Why did he have to compound this disaster by dragging them into it?

Nico stopped to buy wine, and, at first, she felt relief at being able to wander through the aisles while he was occupied at the cash register with the clerk. Then she passed a row of brightly colored labels of Italian wines. Instantly, the familiar names and pictures of the wineries took her back to Tuscany where she'd visited her grandmother and then to the Amalfi Coast, which, because of him, had been a dream.

Images of mountains and sea, the cypress-lined roads, the cerulean skies, the flavor of lush dark olives and the sweetness of winter pears in *vino noble* seared her. Most of all, she remembered *him* in that sunlit bar, him on *Simonetta*. Last of all, she remembered her desolation at the airport after she'd made love to him for hours.

Massimo had led her away and, with every step, she'd thought, *Why am I leaving this perfect place and this perfect man?*

For an instant longer, she remained in that lost dream. Again, she felt the cold, stone wall of the deserted farmhouse against her body and Nico's hard warmth surging against hers; his mouth and tongue all over her, and then her own wild abandon as he'd brought her to climax. Sex with other men had never come close. It was as if she were able to be with him on levels that were not possible with anyone else.

And he hated her for trapping him. She didn't want to beg for anyone's love ever again as she'd begged for her father's.

On a strangled sob she ran out of the wine shop and flung herself back into the car. She sank down onto the soft leather, hugging herself in the dark. Much to her surprise, Nico came at once and found her huddled there, feeling as desperate and needy as the lost child she'd once been.

"Are you all right?"

No! I'm not all right! How can you even ask?

"I'm fine."

"Fine? You look unhappy."

"Are you happy? Are you?"

When she looked away, he leaned close enough for her to smell his tangy aftershave. *Lemons.* She remembered the lemon grove outside the farmhouse.

Then his knuckles brushed her cheekbone, causing her heart to race, causing her to hope.

"Are you going to be sick again?" His voice was gentle.

Startled by his concern and even more by his nearness and touch, she jumped away to a far corner of the limo.

"No! I'm not sick! I told you I'm fine. I'm perfectly happy.

Perfectly, perfectly happy, you big, domineering idiot! What could possibly be wrong? I love being forced into a marriage of convenience by a man who feels superior to me, a man who hates me and will hate me forever. Whose entire family will hate me forever." She put her hands over her face and began to sob wildly.

Even to her own ears, her words and tears sounded a bit over the top. But drama-queenery ran in her blood on both sides of her family. The trait had come in handy more times than not in the courtroom although she had been chastised by more than one judge. Not that she was faking this. She felt frightened, wild.

The bleakness that flared in his eyes tore at her heart and instantly stopped her weeping.

"I don't hate you," he said, his tone so low and broken she squeezed her lashes tightly against her cheeks for fear she might burst into tears and humiliate herself all over again.

Was he unhappy, too? Did he grieve for what they had lost, as she did?

Absurd thought.

A wistful moan escaped her lips. For one crazy moment, she wanted to throw herself into his arms and beg his forgiveness. She wanted to trace her fingers through his inky hair and comfort him, to press herself against his wide chest and to find solace herself. She wanted to kiss his brow, his eyelids, his lips. Almost, she could taste him, she wanted him so much.

The last thing she'd ever wanted to do was make him unhappy.

But doubt made her certain he would reject her. So, instead of embracing him or even touching his face as he'd touched hers, or lifting her lips, she turned away, sitting as stiff and rigid as a flagpole, her body language conveying unforgivness.

"I'll be right back," he muttered, his low tone weary now.

The door closed gently. She was aware of him standing there for a moment, as if he were puzzled or worried, but when she finally looked at him, she was disappointed to see his tall, broad-shouldered body striding purposefully through the shop's doors to complete his purchase.

When he returned, he placed the wine bottles on their sides

on the opposite seat. She felt his eyes on her face, but her emotions were still so raw she refused to look at him. She was glad at first that he did not attempt conversation. Then, perversely, she wanted him to say something, anything. Maybe then she could find a way to apologize for the scene she had just made. If he didn't begin, she couldn't. She was so overwrought, she lacked the wisdom to know where or how to start. Once again, an increasingly awkward silence built between them while she sat wrapped in her own misery, and acutely aware of his. If only she could think of something to alter their unhappy state, but she couldn't.

When the limousine braked, and they walked up to the front door, her heart drummed double-time with dread at the prospect of the evening ahead of them.

When Nico rang the bell, he turned. With an effort, he forced himself to speak. "This will be easier if you smile and act happy."

"Easier for you, you mean! Aristocrats spend their lives putting on a show for the world. That's what you do! Well, maybe it's not what I do!"

No sooner had she finished speaking than she wanted to bite her tongue off.

"You're a bride, remember. Your family will only be hurt and worried if they know the whole truth. Is that really what you want? I thought you wanted to please your father."

Her father! Oh, God! What did Nico care about her family or her relationship with her father? Still, she caught something in his controlled tone that made her heart beat even faster.

What if he did care a little?

Suddenly she longed to be back in Italy, skimming across the water in his tender as he pointed out the palazzos and villas and told her stories about his friends and fabled ancestors who lived or had lived in them. She wanted to cling to him again as they entered that secret, hidden, pirate grotto.

She'd asked him to play like a pirate and ravage her.

"I want to make love to you. Will that count? I don't want to hurt you or ravage you."

But he'd held her down as she'd secretly wished. Only he'd made love to her as if he'd cherished her.

"If only happiness was like a switch that one could turn on and off at will," she said, remembering the dark sea cave where he'd dropped the anchor and how silent it had been when he'd cut the engine. She remembered lying with him in the darkness, wrapped in his arms while the boat rocked them like a cradle.

"If only." His tight voice was even gloomier than hers.

"I feel like I'm being kidnapped by a man I don't even know."

"I feel trapped, too."

"I never wanted to make you so—"

She swallowed the word *unhappy,* because at that exact moment, her father threw open the door, extended his arms and hugged Nico fiercely. Then he embraced her and kissed her on each cheek, which was his usual greeting for Susana.

Behind her father, the house was brilliantly lit and redolent with the sweetness of cut flowers and chopped basil from her mother's flower beds. Gina's piping voice could be heard in the backyard.

Her father shook Nico's hand and pulled him inside. Constantin Tomei didn't really understand who Nico was or who his family was or the vastness in social rank and position that separated them. He did not act the least bit awed by the expensive bottles of wine or by the fact that Nico was a prince. Being Italian, he took the wine, appreciated the gift for what it was, a sharing of the vine rooted in an ancient communion between guest and host.

Not that Nico wasn't perceived as a guest of honor.

All the usual clutter, her father's newspapers, her mother's photograph albums and cookbooks had vanished into hiding places, into laundry baskets in the garage probably. The kitchen floor even looked freshly waxed. Regina could smell olive oil and tomatoes and cheeses bubbling on the stove. A screen door banged. She heard her mother and Susana and the children laughing in the kitchen.

Wreathed in smiles, her mother took off her apron and came to the door. Since she never read celebrity magazines and mostly watched cooking shows on those rare occasions when she found the time to watch television, she treated Nico as if he were her equal, too. With many more gracious thank-yous, she accepted the wines Nico had selected when Constantin handed them to her, one for each course, before scurrying back to her domain to stir her pots.

Her mother wasn't a measurer. She simply bought the best available ingredients or grew them and then let them guide her. Much of what she cooked was too simple to be a recipe, but infinitely superior because of her talents.

"Well, he's a catch. No doubt about that," her father said, plucking a halved fig off a platter and nibbling on it when he caught her alone. He and Nico had drunk wine together alone in the den behind closed doors for half an hour by that time and were already great friends, or at least, amiable companions.

"He has a fine mind. We discussed golf and the war."

"The war?"

"World War II. Told me all about what Hitler did to his family. He lost a lot of castles. Then we discussed the wedding."

"The wedding?"

"Yours. He insists his family must pay for it. He says it has to be a very private affair, managed by his staff. He's going to send a jet for us so that we can attend your wedding. He wants me to console your mother because she won't be allowed to plan it. That won't be easy. You know how she is."

All this, *her* wedding, he'd discussed with *her* father. Instead of her.

"Well, you're a sly one. Sperm donor! Gave me a few more gray hairs! Blamed your mother for spoiling you! Ha! Then you went to Italy and snagged yourself a real prince. Well, you had us all worried there for a while." His tone was affectionate, indulgent even.

"I did not snag him."

"You did well, daughter. He's a good man, and I think he's strong enough to deal with you."

Strong enough? As if she were a problem?

"I can't believe…"

Her father swallowed the last of his fig and beamed jovially as he patted her on the waist, the way he often patted Susana, who found them like that when she came in to tell them dinner was on the table.

"I'm going to marry a prince, too," Gina announced when everybody had gathered around the table and were serving themselves.

You could have heard a pin drop as the little girl picked up a piece of ricotta cheese with her fingers, placed it squarely in the middle of her spoon and then, smiling brightly, lifted the utensil with the poorly balanced food to her mouth.

Regina was holding her breath when the cheese toppled onto the floor.

Gina was about to dive for it when her grandmother grabbed her tiara and said, "Leave it there, darling."

Gina looked at her grandmother and then wisely grabbed her tiara and placed it back on her head. She picked up her fork and stabbed a piece of cheese.

"When she heard a prince was coming, she had to wear her blue princess costume," Susana said, smiling at Nico as if she recognized him.

Susana read the tabloids occasionally. If she was in the grocery store and a lurid headline caught her attention, she would thumb through the magazine. If she failed to find the story and read it before the checker finished, she would often buy it.

"Aunt Reggie gave me my princess costume!" Gina piped as the ricotta fell off the fork onto her plate.

"Since you're so much like your aunt, I'm sure you'll marry a prince, too," Nico said, "if you decide you want to."

Regina stiffened.

"I've never cooked for a prince before," Sabrina said. "You probably have a chef."

"More than one. When you come to the palazzo for our wedding, you must give them all lessons." Nico took Regina's hand and squeezed it, but when her furious gaze rose to his, he looked down at the table, his inky lashes sweeping his dark cheeks.

Smooth. He was too smooth, too sure of his charm. And he should be. He had the carved profile of an ancient emperor. He was probably related to emperors. He'd won her when he'd stared at her on that bench, and he'd won her family in less than an hour.

He was probably kin to emperors. This shouldn't be happening! Their worlds were too different. She remembered his palazzo with its gilded antique furnishings.

He'd invaded her family's simple home and had conquered them. Regina was suddenly so mad at the power he had over her that she tried to kick him under the table. When her toe struck the table leg between them, she gasped and bit back a cry of anguish.

He glanced her way, his blue gaze tender.

Pretend tenderness, she thought.

Noting Nico's concern and his daughter's flushed cheeks, Constantin smiled indulgently at them both. "Ah, young love." He met his wife's eyes. "The baked peppers with ricotta and basil are delicious."

"So are the fried zucchini flowers and lemon chicken," Nico said. "You're not eating, darling? More morning sickness?" Again his eyes were ablaze with a disturbing tenderness that could unravel her.

Why did he have to be so good at faking it?

"No! I'm fine!" Her voice was so harsh Susana and Sabrina frowned and shot warning glances her way.

"Try to eat then, dear," her mother said. "For the baby. Try the cheese."

Regina stabbed a chunk of ricotta and lifted it to her lips. Satisfied, her mother got up to see about dessert.

When everybody had finished their meal, Regina jumped up and was about to clear the table when her mother raised her hand. "Before we do that, why don't you tell us how you two met."

"We—I…" Regina sat back down, unable to find the words.

"On the beach in Amalfi," Nico said, his eyes softening every time he looked at Regina. "My grandmother owns a shop in Ravello and she met Cara first…and was charmed by her. She'd sold her a dress, a most fetching dress. So, later, when she saw Cara under a lemon tree, she waved at her. I looked over and when Cara looked at me, I couldn't look away. It was as if—"

He stopped. Somehow his silence was riveting. "Nothing like that had ever happened to me before."

"How romantic," Susana gushed.

"It was, actually," he said, looking tenderly at Regina, whose hand lay on the table near him.

When his own larger hand covered hers, she felt a rush of unwanted excitement.

Lacing his fingers through her tense fingers, he brought her hand to his lips. While everyone watched, he kissed her fingertips as he had the first time in the bar. He was very still, his eyes on her face, his earnest gaze a pledge in front of her family.

Regina swallowed, but the sudden lump in her throat refused to go down.

"She swept me off my feet," he continued, turning her hand and blowing a scorching kiss against her slender blue-veined wrist, a kiss so hot it made the icicles around her heart melt.

The rat! He was only pretending!

Flushing, Regina yanked her hand free. "Everyone finished? Can I take your plates?" Wild with panic, she pushed back from the table and started stacking the plates much too noisily. Nico stood, too, and began to gather the silverware. Susana and Sabrina were about to protest when Dino and David started to howl.

"Bottle time," Susana said, as mother and grandmother galloped toward the cribs.

Thus, Nico and Regina were left to do the honors of clearing the table and preparing the final course. He made a pot of coffee while she ladled mascarpone custard over sliced pears on crystal plates.

"You probably never did anything like this in your life," she said.

"I'll ignore that and carry the desserts to the table."

"Okay, I'll be blunt," she said when he returned for the last two plates. "I want you out of this kitchen and out of my life."

"You're going to have to get used to me, you know."

She was so angry she wanted to scream. When she picked up a spatula, he grabbed it and set it down on the counter.

"You can't just take over somebody's life," she said.

"Then why did you deliberately become pregnant with my child?"

"I didn't."

He stared into her eyes longer than she could bear it.

"I swear I didn't! And you don't have to marry me!"

Without saying anything, he picked up the last two plates. With a sinking heart, she watched him walk into the dining room, sit down and begin joking with her family as if their exchange had never occurred, as if this were a normal evening.

Normal? His being here, his ordinariness with her family, their acceptance of him was driving her crazy.

Did he intend to win them and break their hearts? Was he that cruel? Or was he just being a man and insensitive and blind as a result?

Except for Regina's nervous tension, the dessert and coffee went as smoothly as dinner. If she grew increasingly silent, everybody was too thrilled by him and the thought of a wedding in a castle to care.

Conversation flowed on all sides of her without the least difficulty. Her mother graciously accepted the fact that she would not be allowed to plan her daughter's wedding. It was almost as if Regina's family had been expecting her pregnancy and this marriage and were overjoyed by them.

Who were these people? She'd never mentioned Nico to any of them. How could he just pop into their lives without any warning, take over, and be so totally accepted?

Why couldn't they have ever accepted her this easily? Who she was? Why had she had to work so hard for the slightest praise? When she felt her thoughts heading into one of those negative loops, she put on the brakes. Her family and Nico either loved one another or they deserved Oscars, and that was just the way it was.

Later, when they were all laughing together in the living room while she stood in a dark corner, feeling left out, Nico got up, put his arms around her and led her to the couch, where he pulled her down beside him, so that she was in the heart of the family circle. He took her hand in his again and held on tight, ignoring her every attempt to pull free. And the truth was, under different circumstances, she might have enjoyed herself.

Regina leaned over and whispered in his ear. "Can't we go now?"

Before he could answer, Gina brought a storybook and laid it on his lap.

He laughed. "How can I resist your niece?"

"Read!" Gina commanded.

"Oh, dear, she's got your bossiness," he whispered into Regina's ear. Aloud, he said, "Why don't I read to her while you help your mother clean up in the kitchen?"

"I can do that later," Sabrina said.

But Nico insisted on playing with the children while Regina helped Sabrina in the kitchen, and, thereby, he won her sister and her mother even more completely. Although he did not go so far as to change a diaper, he did feed each twin part of a bottle, and he burped them, too.

"Can you believe it?" Susana said in the kitchen as Sabrina hand-washed and Regina and Susana dried. "He can tell the twins apart. He even called them by their names. Nobody else has ever been able to do that. I can't believe he's a famous prince. I even saw him on television."

"Then you should know he was about to announce his engagement to a princess," Regina whispered. "Only I got pregnant and ruined his life."

"Don't do that! Why do you always do that?"

"Always do what?"

"Doubt yourself. Overthink stuff."

"I don't always doubt myself," Regina snapped.

"Okay. You're right, as always. You're a lawyer. Everything's got to be logical and go along with some plan or list you've made. I learned a long time ago not to argue with you when you're in lawyer mode. But this man loves you."

Susana spoke with all-knowing, completely exasperating confidence.

"You couldn't possibly know that."

"Maybe you made straight A's, but I was the one who was good with men...and feelings."

Ouch. Regina remembered how deftly Susana had stolen Joe right out from under her. Suddenly she was glad Susana had.

"Trust me," Susana said. "Trust him. Trust yourself. And your feelings. For once. He loves you. Sometimes feelings can be smarter than you are."

Susana should know. That's the way she'd always operated.

And everybody loves her, said a little voice.

By the time the dishes were finished, Nico had read Gina several fairy tales about princesses while she'd stared up at him with big, awed eyes.

"Read *Cinderella* again," Gina begged when the women came out of the kitchen.

"He's already read it three times," her father said.

"Then that's enough," Susana said. "He has to take Regina home. She's going to have a baby, and she needs her rest."

Three whole times? He'd read *Cinderella* three whole times.

"We do have to go," Regina agreed, trying to act like she wasn't the least bit impressed with his talent with children or jealous if he happened to smile at Susana.

"I was having so much fun I didn't realize how late it was," Nico said. "I hope we didn't overstay our welcome."

"Oh, no! No! We loved having you!" her parents and sister gushed.

"I'm going to marry a prince—just like you!" Gina cried. "And live in a castle!"

"Big hug," Nico whispered, kneeling, and the little girl ran into his arms. "When you're all grown-up, I'll introduce you to lots of princes."

When Gina finally released him, he stood up and put his arm around Regina, and for a moment it seemed almost possible that he would be at her side always, that they would have a real marriage.

When he headed toward the door, her family followed them down the sidewalk. Their goodbyes were so warm, her fantasy that they could be a real couple and have a real future persisted a little longer.

At the limousine, her daddy embraced her and wouldn't let her go for several long moments. "I'm so happy for you," he said. "So proud of you."

They smiled at each other in the silvery dark. For the first time since Susana's birth, Regina felt a closeness to him that was almost a completeness.

And she had Nico to thank! Nico, of all people—the enemy!

The two men shook hands. Her mother kissed Nico's cheek.

It was so wrong.

They're all so happy and I'm so happy! But this marriage isn't real! I should tell them now! Tonight! That it won't last a year. I really should tell them!

But, of course, she didn't because she didn't want to, and all too soon she was alone with Nico in the dark, silent limousine again.

Fifteen

"I thought that went well," Nico said a few minutes later as the long car slipped through the silent dark.

"Doesn't it bother you at all that you'll break their hearts?"

"I don't intend to break anybody's heart. That's your specialty."

"I don't want to break anybody's heart," she whispered.

To that he said nothing.

"You didn't have to be *so* nice to them, you know. Especially *so* nice to the children."

"Was that so bad? Do you really think everything I do is to hurt you?"

"After tonight, they'll never understand how awful you are. They'll always be on your side."

"Stop being a lawyer. What if there aren't any sides?"

"There are always sides."

"No. Not always. Two people can become one."

"Not us," she whispered.

As though he were very tired, he leaned back and shut his eyes, seemingly weary of fighting her.

Was he right? Did there always have to be sides? Could two people as different as they were, two families as different as theirs were, live in harmony for the rest of their lives?

She remembered the golden, hazy perfection of Ravello. The pink sunsets, the sea breezes.

What if *they* could? What if…

When she glanced at him and saw the blue-black highlights gleaming in the lock of hair that fell over his brow, she felt a dangerous softening in her heart.

Chiseled profile, olive skin, black hair, sensual lips. Did he have to be *so* incredibly handsome? To act *so* nice, at least, when he wasn't furious? She marveled at his patience, reading *Cinderella* to Gina three times.

Suddenly, Regina wondered where he was staying tonight. The intoxicating memory of him standing naked and as glorious as a well-endowed god or Michelangelo's *David* in her hotel room came back to her.

When the limousine stopped, he let her out and walked her to her front porch. Without a word, he took her key and deftly unlocked her door. She crossed her threshold and then stopped without inviting him in. She was surprised and disappointed when he didn't assume he had the right to follow her inside. Hesitating, she flipped on the light in her foyer and noted the deep shadows under his eyes.

"You look tired," she said, her voice gentle.

"I am. A little."

"Do you want to—" she nodded shyly "—come in?"

He stepped inside and shut the door, and then they both stood there, aware of each other and yet unsure of each other, as well.

Suddenly, she realized how much she wanted to be alone with him, had wanted it all night during the long, drawn-out dinner. Only she hadn't wanted to admit it. And now that she had him all to herself, she didn't know what to do or say. Or even what to think.

What if she simply slipped out of her dress and ran naked into his arms?

Her hand went to the zipper at the back of her dress. Watching her and perhaps reading her intent, he turned on his heel and strode into the kitchen. Cabinet doors banged open and closed until he found her liquor supply. Quickly, he poured himself a double shot of Scotch.

With an acute ache in her heart, she watched him go to her living room and sink into the soft cushions of her deep couch, his dark head falling backward across the navy cushions. His shoulders slumped as he stretched out his long legs and tore his tie loose. She turned a light off. But not before she saw the lines and the gray shadows beneath his eyes again.

He'd flown all the way from Rome. He was probably jet-lagged and utterly exhausted from dealing with her.

"You could sleep here if you wanted," she offered. "I have a spare bedroom. Two, in fact."

His brows lifted in wary surprise. For a long, unnerving moment it seemed to Regina that the word *bedroom* hung heavily in the air.

She didn't know what else she could say or do, so she stood motionless and silent.

"Thank you." He drained his Scotch. "For the offer."

Feeling awkward and yet rejected when he didn't move or state his intentions, she fled down the hall to her own bedroom. Deliberately leaving her door unlocked, she undressed. As she slipped into her sheerest nightgown and washed her face, even as she brushed her teeth, she tried not to think about Nico sprawled on her couch in the living room.

Despite attempts to busy herself in her bathroom by straightening her towel on its towel rack and scrubbing out an immaculate soap dish, all she could think about was him.

Did he still want her? Or was theirs to be only a marriage of convenience? Every time a board creaked in the house, she would glance toward her door, hoping he'd be there.

All of a sudden, nothing mattered except that she was having his baby and he was going to marry her. If they lived together as man and wife, maybe there was still a chance.

She'd forgotten her own anger and all his harsh words and

accusations and even the domineering way he'd proposed. He'd been sweet to the children and considerate of her family, considerate of her, too, at least, around them.

There was no logic to explain the reason her desire for him began to feel like a pulsing, all-consuming need. The simple truth was she could not be around him for long without loving him and wanting him, even when knowing he could be as bad tempered as an angry skunk.

She thought about going in to check on him, hoping he'd notice her in her sheer nightgown. Instead, she pulled back the sheets and climbed into bed, her heart beating faster and faster.

She turned out the light and waited breathlessly. The little clock on her bedside table ticked and ticked and ticked, and in the dark she began to count those maddening passing seconds. Finally, crazed, she grabbed the clock and stuffed it under a pillow.

Should she go to him? Should she try to explain again? Her mind whirled, caught in one of those tangled loops.

Hours later, when she was only half awake, she started at what she thought were heavy footsteps in the hall. Her heart thudding, her mind blurred with exhaustion, she looked up and saw a shadowy, wide-shouldered figure looming in her doorway.

Nico.

Her eyes snapped open. Her heart thundered.

"Sorry. I didn't mean to scare you." He leaned against the doorjamb and combed his thick hair with his fingers. "The Scotch must have hit me pretty hard. I fell asleep. I'll be going to my hotel now." His husky voice sounded infinitely weary.

"I know you must have had a long day. You don't have—"

"I'll call you. First thing tomorrow."

His manner was cool, businesslike. *Final*. Abruptly, he turned on his heel.

She heard her front door close softly and the limousine drive away.

"It already is…tomorrow."

Filled with conflict and doubts, she lay tossing and turning. Would he come back? Or was he finished with her?

She was still awake when the sky turned rosy and the phone rang.

"I've chartered a jet," Nico said. "We leave after lunch. I spoke to my mother an hour ago."

Again his voice was cool and deliberately businesslike.

When he hung up, Regina lay against her pillows, feeling more mixed up than ever, but pleased that he'd called and so early. As if he were impatient.

How quickly time brings, if not happiness exactly, acceptance and hope.

All of a sudden, her sleepless night hit her. Pulling her little clock out from under the pillow, she set the alarm to go off in two hours. When she lay down again, she fell instantly and blissfully asleep.

She dreamed of Italy. Again she was lying with Nico in the bottom of his tender in that cool, dark cave that smelled of dank sea things. The water was lapping against the sides of the boat as rhythmically as his warm body drove into hers. And all she knew was that she wanted to be with him forever.

Sixteen

Even though the rain had slowed to a drizzle, the wipers were still slashing the windshield at their highest setting. Nico drove through the tall gates. As he braked the Alpha Romeo in front of the palazzo, Regina sat up straighter.

As if on cue, a horde of whispering servants rushed out of the beautiful pink house.

"Who are they?"

"I told Mother no fuss," Nico said.

A single glance from Abruzzi, the same gaunt, balding gentleman who'd stood guard over Regina not so long ago, soon had everybody lined up in the rain. Each stood as stiffly as a martinet on either side of the granite stairs.

"Oh, no! Why is he making them do that? They'll be soaked!"

Sudden queasiness climbed her throat. Gasping for air, she rolled down her window. There'd been too many long miles, too many narrow, winding roads. And now this.

After she'd gulped in a few breaths and managed a smile, Nico cupped her chin, lifting it.

"Are you all right?" His face was creased with worry.

"I think so."

Harried-looking men and women in black business attire, obviously secretaries, accountants and administrators, rushed out and stood above the maids and cooks, housemen and chauffeurs.

"I'm sorry, but maybe it's for the best," he said. "You had to meet them sometime. The rain will be our excuse for cutting the introductions short."

"My mother doesn't even have a maid. My father mows the lawn."

Nico got out quickly and ran around the front of the car to help her out.

Bone weary from the overnight flight and the long drive from Rome, Regina clung to him throughout the introductions.

Their plane had touched down at Fumichino at ten in the morning in black skies and heavy rain. Due to bad traffic and more storms, not to mention several accidents on the autostrada, they hadn't reached the Amalfi Coast until five.

No sooner had they greeted the staff, and everyone was inside drying themselves off, than Massimo appeared, his plump, tanned face wreathed in smiles. He greeted them warmly, embracing Regina even, before leading them down an elaborately appointed gallery to Gloriana's high-ceilinged, ornate study.

Looking formidable in royal-blue silk and huge diamonds, the princess neither smiled nor rose from her Louis XIV desk when they entered. Her calm blue eyes passed over Regina as if she were a ghost and totally invisible.

With a little pucker between her painted brows the princess focused entirely on Nico. "I need to talk to you. Alone. It's most pressing."

"Mother—"

"Tiberio and Massimo will show Miss Tomei to her suite, the red rooms, so that she can rest. The poor dear looks exhausted."

So, she had seen the ghost, her future daughter-in-law, after all.

Tiberio Abruzzi materialized as if by magic. The princess

nodded at Massimo, who rushed toward the man. Abruzzi turned to Regina, his stern glance ordering her to follow—at once.

Regina seized Nico's hand and clung.

He squeezed her fingers and then released them. "You'll be all right. I won't be long. I promise. I will come for you shortly before dinner, which is at seven."

Feeling abandoned somehow and overwhelmed by the palazzo again, she lifted her cheek, hoping for some scrap of affection. When his lips brushed her cheek, a wild, tumultuous heat flooded her.

Slowly she lifted her chin. Then she followed Massimo, who walked with her a short way and then turned her over to Abruzzi. After that, she had to race to keep up with the tall servant as he sped silently through the many halls and galleries to the red rooms.

An hour later, she was still alone trying to feel at home in the gorgeous, gilded bedroom that had been assigned to her. She forced herself to study the furniture, the crystal, the brocade curtains, and each of the old masters hanging on the red-satin wallpaper. If she were to live here, she must grow used to the beauty of these delightful rooms and objects; she must learn to take them as her due.

She tried to tilt her chin higher so that she could study the ornate ceiling where splashes of turquoise had been combined with crimson and gold. But suddenly her neck hurt, and she realized she'd been awake for many hours and that all she wanted to do was lie down and wait for Nico.

First, she went to the window and opened it, so that she could smell the cool sweetness of the lightly falling rain. Then loosening the buttons of her dress, she went to the bed and pushed the heavy satin spread back and sank tiredly onto the mattress.

Two months ago, it would not have been dark at this hour. Oh, but how nice it was to stretch out horizontally between cool, clean sheets while the rain tap-danced on the balcony and balustrade outside. Her head ached with exhaustion as she strained to hear Nico's footsteps.

Soon he would come. She tried to stay awake, but slowly, the rain was music that lulled her. And a black curtain came down. And she was gone.

When Nico knocked at the door of the red rooms and called her name, she didn't answer, so he slipped inside.

The silent room was shrouded in darkness.

"Cara?"

Above the patter of the rain, he heard her sweet sigh from the bed. He turned just as the moon peeped through the clouds, bathing the bed and her with its silvery light.

She looked like an enchanted princess. *His* princess.

Her lovely face was as pale as alabaster; her hair gleamed like dark satin against her pillows. Her chest, sculpted by the white sheets, moved up and down. Her lips were cherry red and he was eager to wake her and kiss her. But she looked so peaceful asleep; so adorable, almost happy.

His heart swelled with desire and with something even more powerful that he refused to consider. She had not looked like this since he'd dropped her at Fumichino two months ago after they'd made love the whole way to Rome. How her eyes had glimmered with tears at their parting. How she'd clung to him, kissing his cheeks and lips and then burying her face deep into his chest. And only after she'd walked away with Massimo and he'd watched the exact spot where she'd vanished for more than half an hour, the longest thirty minutes in his life, had he even begun to realize how deeply he might need her.

Who was she really? A cynical opportunist who'd used him? Or the gentle, passionate woman he'd fallen in love with?

He didn't care. Whoever she was, he wanted her. Something had begun that he was powerless to stop. From the first, when she'd waved at *Grand-mère* from the bench under the lemon tree, he'd wanted her more than he'd ever wanted any woman. And the wanting had only grown more fierce.

Why? Why her?

Did why ever matter? Some things just were. From the

beginning, he'd been in over his head, his passion having assumed a life of its own.

Love. War. Birth. Death. Human beings thought they could control such matters, but they were an arrogant, doomed species whose passions ruled them.

He stood over her for an hour, his shadow falling across her pale face. The dinner hour came and went, and yet he felt compelled to stay and watch over her. At least, when she was asleep, he could protect her from the forces in this house, in his world, even from the forces within himself that resented and threatened her.

Finally, he leaned down and kissed her lips gently. She stirred and smiled. When she whispered his name, he wanted to kiss her again and again. But he knew that if he did so, he would not stop.

The first thing Regina noticed when she awakened at dawn was the pink sun streaming through the long windows, filling the beautiful room with soft feathers of early light. She felt the pillow beside her and realized she was alone.

Nico had not come.

Seventeen

At eight o'clock sharp, a young maid with creamy skin and a white apron announced to Regina in a beautiful Polish accent that breakfast was to be served on the north terrace at nine and that she would be back to fetch her.

"Where's Nico? I mean, Prince Nico?"

The pretty maid looked confused. "Sorry, *signorina*. Princess Gloriana told me to come. That's all I know."

She curtsied and was about to go when Regina called her back.

"I've been up and dressed for hours. I would like to walk in the garden. Could you show me the way and then come find me there?"

"As you wish, madame."

Nico had not come. With a sickening feeling of abandonment, she followed the girl outside to the pool where the swans made ripples across its dark, glassy surface. Birds were singing in the cypress trees. Exotic blossoms bloomed in the flower beds even though it was autumn.

Some variety of flower must bloom all year here in this centuries-old paradise. But where was Nico? She glanced up at the palazzo and thought she saw a tall, dark man and a blond woman at a long window watching her. Then they vanished, and she wondered if they'd seen her or if she'd merely imagined them.

She began to walk along the intricate gravel paths that wound through the beautiful garden overhanging the sea, this garden that seemed more fantasy than reality. At first, she tried to concentrate on the crunching sound her feet made so that she wouldn't dwell on Nico or the multitude of questions that tortured her heart.

Then she began to enjoy the glories of the garden with its mountains that climbed to the sky on one side and the blue sea that stretched forever on the other.

Her verdant surroundings were so beautiful that soon her walk took over. Her mood became meditative, and she opened her heart to infinite possibilities.

She was here. She was to marry Nico. All her life she'd thought she could plan and that her ambitions and work would take her where she wanted. But she'd lost touch with herself. She'd done things she wasn't proud of. She'd wanted more than her career, more than marriage to a respected professional. Only, she hadn't known what *more* was until now. No man had ever felt so right as Nico, who was from this extravagant world that she had never even imagined.

Life was so much more mysterious than she'd bargained for. One never knew what the next moment would be or bring. As she stared at the palazzo, she couldn't begin to imagine what her life would be like as his wife.

The maid came as she'd promised, startling Regina out of her reverie and then leading her back inside. Regina followed through what seemed like miles of galleries and sitting rooms, all filled with rococo, neoclassical and Louis XVI furnishings. Through the centuries, Romanos must have collected these beautiful things and designed rooms to display them advantageously. As always, the beauty of the palazzo dazzled and overwhelmed her as the garden and its simple pleasures had not.

Suddenly, a door opened, and a slim blond woman, a younger version of Nico's mother, emerged into the hall. Then, as if to catch her breath or regain her composure after some unfortunate encounter, the woman stopped and stood outside the door for a long moment. Then lifting her chin, she turned and headed straight for Regina.

She had fine, delicate features; soft, light-colored hair and luminous violet eyes. Her complexion glowed. She was exquisite and so perfectly made that, except for her stricken expression, she seemed more like a doll than a human.

Principessa Donna Viola Eugenia di Frezano.

Regina gasped in awe and then compassion swept her.

Viola had frozen, too. Then without a word, the princess turned and fled, but not before Regina had seen that her cheeks were streaked with tears.

No servant needed to lead Viola through the maze of gilded rooms. Clearly, even blinded by tears, she knew this maze of ornate rooms by heart.

When Regina looked inside the door from which Viola had come, she saw a grim-faced Nico staring out a tall window. Was it the same window where she'd seen the couple watching her?

"Nico?"

He turned, his expression dazed. For a long moment, it was as if she weren't there.

Was he brokenhearted over having lost Viola?

"Cara?" His dark face registered surprise. He stood up straighter. "Did you sleep well?" His tone was polite, formal.

Regina found his perfect manners, so like his mother's, unendurable. Were they to be man and wife and yet strangers, never to talk about what mattered?

"You said you'd come for me."

"You were asleep."

"I just saw Viola," she whispered.

"For the first and last time."

"You broke your engagement with her?"

"I explained the situation to her. She was very understanding."

"But upset?"

"Yes."

"She looked hurt, devastated."

"I never told her about us, you see. Her staff will speak to the press later today."

"And what will she say?"

"Whatever she wants to say. She will have to move on. As we all will."

"I'm sorry for all the trouble. If you love her, if you prefer her…"

"It is done." He crossed the space that separated them, and yet he felt as far away as ever. "Shall we go down to breakfast together?"

He took her hand. His palm felt cold, and she noticed that he did not bring her fingers to his lips.

"My mother is expecting us."

Would they eat with her every morning? Would they never be alone like a normal couple? Share their own private confidences? Have their own lives? Were they always to live here, with his family?

If only they could have eaten alone this morning.

The Principessa Gloriana was already at a table shaded by a melon-colored umbrella. As they walked up to her, hand in hand, she sipped coffee, patted her lipstick with her napkin, and then gave Nico a chilly smile. Again, she treated Regina as if she didn't exist.

Maybe that was for the best.

"Isn't it a lovely morning," Gloriana said to Nico. "All the dark clouds gone and our glorious Amalfi sun shining so brightly."

"Yes." Regina nodded even though she knew she had not been addressed. "The terrace has such breathtaking views of the water and cliffs."

"It does indeed," Gloriana said. "How lovely to see you again, my dear." Her words were polite, but her blue eyes, so like her son's, were colder than polar ice chips. "I do hope the flight wasn't too tiring and that you rested well. For the baby's sake."

Regina's throat went dry.

Nerves, she hoped. Not morning sickness.

Hot bile climbed her throat. Near panic, she fought to swallow.

Feeling more miserable by the second, she forced a smile. When her mouth twisted, Nico's hand closed over hers.

Then a manservant brought a cart brimming with fruit and cheeses and all kinds of breads including buttery, rich croissants, Regina's favorite. Tiberio Abruzzi, who was standing behind the man and his cart, stared down his nose at her and asked in a lofty tone what the *signorina* would like.

Regina's gaze flicked across luscious thick white lumps of buffalo mozzarella, to raw eggs, omelet makings and then to thick slabs of ham.

"I—I'm not hungry." Clammy with sweat, she sank back in her chair as the awful stuff in her throat bubbled higher.

Terrified of embarrassing herself before Nico, she tried to swallow. But it was hopeless.

Her chair scraped the table as she stood up. Not knowing where a restroom was, she bolted. Behind her, china shattered and the principessa gasped. Regina barely made it to the nearest hedge before she was on the ground losing the contents of whatever she'd managed to eat on the plane.

"Cara—"

She flung herself toward the palazzo, desperate to escape them all, even Nico. A violent cramp shot through her stomach, and she realized she was going to be sick again. There would be no escape. Weakly she stumbled back to the hedge and fell to her knees a second time.

Even before she finished, she felt strong arms around her, supporting her and then Nico was lifting her, holding her tightly because her knees were so rubbery she couldn't stand.

"I'm sorry," she whispered.

"Don't apologize. Don't ever apologize," Nico said.

She caught the citrusy tang of his aftershave, usually a pleasant scent. She swallowed again because she so longed to stay in his arms, but that faint fruity odor ruined it.

"Your aftershave…lemons…awful. I'm sorry." Feeling fuzzy, she fell to her knees again. Only this time, her stomach was empty, so she only had the dry heaves.

Nico's face was lined and grim as he led her back to her room.

"I don't want to make you unhappy," she whispered when she

was sitting down on a little chair in the shade of her balcony as Nico applied a cold towel to her face. Abruzzi stood just inside the door, awaiting further instructions.

"You don't want to marry me," she whispered. "You must let me go. For both our sakes. For your mother's sake. For the baby's sake."

"Hush. Hush. When you feel better, we'll talk. Abruzzi suggested crackers and bananas and some cottage cheese. He said that's all his wife could eat when she was pregnant. Do you think you could eat that?"

She nodded, not wanting to displease him or the terrifying Abruzzi. Then she shook her head miserably.

"No. No crackers."

Abruzzi's stern face fell.

"Ice cream," she said, craving it suddenly. "Chocolate ice cream. Lots of chocolate ice cream…please."

Abruzzi beamed with delight. "Gelato, chocolate, *signorina,* for the baby!" His black eyes came alive as he raced away to do her bidding.

When he brought two heaping bowls, she began eat small spoonfuls. Nico asked if he could leave her briefly to shower.

"So you won't keep wrinkling your nose and rushing to the nearest bush because I smell like lemons."

"Don't even say the word."

He laughed and was gone. When he returned, the bowls of ice cream were gone, and she was feeling much better.

"It's not too late, to change your mind about marrying me," she whispered when he sat down beside her on her balcony.

"I want to marry you."

"But ours won't be a real marriage, if we're already planning to divorce."

His brows shot together. "Cara, nobody must know this isn't a real marriage. Nobody. We who live here say the palazzo has ears in every wall. Rumors start so easily, and, if the media hears even a hint of such things, they can cause great unhappiness. Even my family, Massimo especially, has difficulty keeping secrets. We Italians are extroverts. All we do is talk. I don't want our child's birth surrounded by unnecessary scandal. Do you understand?"

"Yes. You're telling me we'll live a lie, that we'll pretend we love each other. I guess I can at least try, since you're only asking me to do that for a year."

"Damn it." His face dark, his voice held a steely note she hated.

"What do you want me to say then?" she asked.

"Kiss me and pretend you mean it."

She froze. "All right."

She stood up. So did he. She lifted her lips, standing stiffly, regally.

His eyes narrowed as if something about this whole situation displeased him. Then he leaned forward and caressed her shoulders. Her eyes drifted shut as she waited. Then his mouth found hers and even though his lips barely touched hers, her passion flared to life.

She rose onto her tiptoes and threw her arms around his neck. Then she pressed herself closer, closer, until she could feel his heat and hear the drumbeat of his heart.

He deepened the kiss, and she leaned farther into him, offering herself, offering everything.

He drew back, smiling at her, really smiling at her, for the first time in days. Playfully he kissed the tip of her nose.

"You're very good at pretending," he said.

"So are you."

Eager for more, she pulled his head down to hers again and lost herself in more kisses. He began to say soft, caressing things to her in Italian.

"I love it when you do that."

"What?"

"Speak Italian."

He smiled. "I love the language…which melts like kisses and sounds as if it has been writ on satin…syllables which breathe… er…" He struggled for the rest of the line. "Passion."

"Why, that's beautiful."

"Lord Byron, or rather a jumble of Lord Byron. I'm afraid I don't remember the entire poem."

"I like it that you can quote poetry. Dante."

"Memorization is not the loftiest of mental gifts, you know."

"Don't belittle yourself," she said.

"Kissing you is fun. Maybe we should pretend we love each other again," he said, bringing his mouth closer to hers again.

As he gazed down at her, her heart began to flutter nervously. She wet her lips in anticipation.

Then his mouth found hers again, and his tongue came inside her lips. He groaned. She moved her body against his, rubbing her breasts against his massive chest, wanting to be nearer, nearer, aching to be consumed utterly by him.

"Nico, my darling, darling."

When more Italian burst from him, her whole body burned with desire.

Was he saying he loved her, or was he only pretending? He took her hand and was leading her into the bedroom, when there was a sound at the door.

Who knows what might have happened next, if his mother hadn't chosen that moment to appear. As always, she was perfectly groomed and as dazzling as a rare jewel in an absolutely exquisite pink silk suit. Parisian runway, no doubt.

Apologizing politely and lifting her arched brows, she said there was a crisis that needed Nico's attention immediately.

"Can't it wait?" he said in a low, irritable tone.

She shook her head and swept from the room, her footsteps growing fainter in the hall.

"Sorry, darling." There was only a faint echo of passion in his voice. He squeezed Regina's hand and kissed her lightly on the cheek.

Then he was gone, too, and she was left alone on her stone parapet with only her beautiful view for companionship.

Juliet without her Romeo.

Hugging herself, she leaned against the balustrade, shuddering in frustration. She needed a job, something to do, *anything*.

But what? What could she do today? She began to pace the balcony. What did a future princess do to amuse herself all day *in paradise?*

The garden beckoned beneath her. The sunlight was brilliant in the trees. There was an ineffable sweetness of flowers mingling with the scent of the sea.

She dashed out of the red rooms. She would take a walk among the flowers again, a long meditative walk in the garden. She would watch the swans.

When she grew bored with the big white birds, who were content with each other and their placid pond and paid no attention to her, she meandered along the gravel paths until she grew tired of the garden, too. She felt confined, lost.

As she was about to turn back toward the palazzo, she discovered a little gate shrouded with ancient grape vines. A gardener was weeding nearby, so she asked him where the path led.

Yanking an earphone out of his ear, the man stood up. He was dark and thick around the middle. His white shirt was caked with black dirt; his silver curls wet with sweat. His English was as terrible as her Italian, but somehow he managed to make her understand with many smiles and much wild gesticulating that the vine and the path were pre-Roman, that the trail had been used for centuries by the shepherds and their flocks.

How wonderful. She opened the gate and wandered like a child in a land of enchantment for an hour or more, forgetting her restlessness and feeling that she was useless, as she explored the terraced gardens and ochre-colored villas that dotted the cliffs above the sea.

Only when she became thoroughly lost did she notice the time. She sat down on a low rock and pulled out her cell phone, which she must have switched off. When she turned it on, she saw that Nico had called her at least five or six times.

When she rang him, his voice was terse and cold. "Where are you?"

"I don't know. I was walking in the garden. I found a little gate and a shepherd's trail that led down the cliffs. I didn't think. I'm afraid I'm lost."

For a long moment he didn't speak. "I've been worried sick." He asked her to describe her whereabouts.

Five minutes later, he was loping down the steep path toward her. When he saw her, he stopped and sucked in air.

She took three faltering steps up the mountain toward him.

"I thought you'd left me," he said.

"I'm sorry if I worried you."

A long silence followed her statement. He stood very still. How lonely he looked, she suddenly thought, her heart going to him. Did he need her then, just a little?

Or was she only imagining that he did?

Who was he really, this prince she was marrying?

This handsome stranger?

Eighteen

A dazed Princess Donna Regina Carina Tomei di Romano sat in the red rooms alone staring at the glittering band of diamonds on her left hand. She still wore the simple white suit she'd been married in, as well as the little hat with its short veil.

She had married a man she hardly knew.

The private ceremony in the magnificent Salon d'Or with her family and Nico's royal mother watching had been awful, simply awful, at least for her. Because of her morning sickness, Regina's voice had been inaudible to all but Nico, who'd leaned close to hear.

Well, now he was trapped, and so was she. And the whole world was watching, waiting for the first sign of a crack in one of her glass slippers.

The palazzo had notified the press immediately after the ceremony. A trusted journalist, who'd agreed to allow Gloriana final approval of his article, wanted to write Regina's "Cinderella story." Gloriana had personally granted him a private interview with Regina on the terrace.

Unfortunately, his first two questions had made Regina too sick to complete the interview.

Question number one: "Was Prince Nico's 'good friend' Princess Viola on the guest list?"

"The ceremony was small and private. We simply couldn't invite everybody," she'd whispered, wondering why she had to do this on her wedding day.

"And quite sudden, I understand." He'd leaned closer, scribbling furiously.

"I—I… Yes. I suppose it seemed sudden."

"Why the hurry?" When his eyes bored into her, Regina's stomach had rolled.

"I—I don't feel—" She'd arisen and run. Now, she was terrified that she'd given away her secret pregnancy.

Her wedding ring and the red wallpaper blurred. Feeling dreadful about her first failure with a journalist, she walked to her balcony and watched the swans on their placid pool.

Well, at least the ceremony was over.

For Regina, the hasty preparations, the wedding, her family's joyous arrival, which had infected the palazzo with gaiety, had all passed as if in a dream.

Only yesterday, Princess Viola's staff had announced that there was nothing to the rumors of marriage regarding herself and Prince Nico Romano, that they had always been and would continue to be just "good friends." When Nico had been asked to comment, he'd been unavailable.

Nico's "good friend" had not attended the marriage of Prince Nico Romano to *Signorina* Regina Carina Tomei, which had taken place in the magnificent Salon d'Or in the midst of a sea of lilies, roses and orchids.

To Regina, the civil ceremony had felt cold and rushed. Nico's mother hadn't smiled during the ceremony nor during the celebratory reception afterward for one hundred people.

Nico's mood had been equally severe during both events. He'd said all the right words, slipped the ring on her finger, but his lips had felt stiff and cool after doing so.

Only little Gina, and Regina's father and Nico's grandmother, who'd enjoyed causing a stir by upsetting her daughter, had acted happy. Seconds before the wedding, the old lady had arrived unannounced in green veils and wearing so much gold she'd looked like a Gypsy.

Regina's father had been flushed with pride as he'd led her down the grand staircase. He hadn't been the least bit intimidated by the palazzo or by Nico's mother or even by his older sister, Principessa Carolina, who'd flown in from Madrid, demanding to know why she hadn't been told about the wedding sooner.

Maybe it was the morning sickness blurring her senses, but the whole, horrible affair didn't seem real to Regina now.

I'll wake up, she thought, *back in Texas...where I belong.*

She heard a sound and turned. Gloriana, in the same smartly tailored white suit she'd worn to the wedding, stood there.

Wasn't there some rule that a mother-in-law's outfit should not compete with the bride's?

Her blue eyes were huge and luminous and filled with profound grief. She couldn't have looked sadder if she'd buried Nico.

"People are asking where you are. You're upsetting Nico." As always, her voice was pleasant and well modulated.

"How long will it take me to learn that appearances are everything?"

"I should think you would want to be at the reception in your moment of triumph."

"You would think that."

"You caught him when he was weak, grief stricken."

So that was what she thought.

"He is not in love with you. When he comes to his senses, he'll hate you. This marriage is a huge step down for him. You're not even from a princely family, much less a royal one, as he is. You are not even rich. Who are you? An attorney, who was fired for incompetency? How many languages do you speak?"

"I love him."

"I hope, for his sake, that you do."

"We both love him. At least we have that in common."

"No, I *love* him. Someday, soon, you'll know how deep a mother's love is. I want what's best for him." She drew a deep breath. "All I ask is that you at least pretend you love him. Don't hurt him any more than you already have."

"You must teach me how to pretend."

Where this conversation would have gone would always be a mystery because Nico appeared. His mother whirled, her lovely face instantly serene.

"I will leave you to enjoy your bride," she said in a sweet, false tone.

"No time for that—yet. I was looking for both of you. More pictures need to be taken."

"So many pictures? I feel a little like a movie star," Regina said, wishing only to be alone with him.

"These are for the newspapers and television. They won't take long."

After more photographs, Regina stood beside Nico on a balcony and watched a fireworks display in their honor while flashbulbs flickered constantly beneath them.

"The media circus has begun." Nico turned. "Smile at me, *tesorina,* they want the fairy tale."

So do I.

She smiled up at him and he brought her hand to his lips.

"Why so fast?" the reporters demanded of anyone who would answer questions.

"Who is this *Signorina* Regina Carina Tomei?"

"Where did she come from?"

"How did they meet?"

"Why did he marry her?"

Lucy left frantic messages for Regina. Reporters were camped outside her door, demanding to know every intimate detail of her friend's recent vacation in Italy.

"Tell me what to tell them!" Lucy cried in her final message. "I get contractions every time the phone rings!"

So, this is my life. I'm a princess now. Regina felt wonder as she watched streamers of orange fire blossom against a black sky and drizzle bits of gold to earth in her honor.

Nico leaned closer and grasped her hand tightly in his. "You were a planner. Of all the men in the world, why did you pick me? Why me?" His voice was dark and urgent.

"I didn't pick you. I just…" *I just couldn't resist you.*

Ribbons of white curled against the sky.

"You knew who I was, didn't you?" he persisted.

She shook her head.

"I've always been wanted because I'm a Romano and the heir to all this."

"I didn't know who you were."

"But you're a plotter and a planner."

"What if you could believe that I didn't plan any of this?" she said. "That it simply happened, like you once told me?"

"What if?" he whispered, his eyes devouring her.

"I didn't know who you were. I swear."

Regina was wearing a filmy nightgown and a transparent robe that she'd bought in Portofino for her wedding night. Every time she glanced at the great bed and its red satin spread, she trembled.

"I will leave you to wait for him alone if you want me to," Susana said. "Maybe he knows I'm with you. Maybe that's why he hasn't come."

Susana headed toward the door.

"No! Stay! There's something I must tell you—a secret."

Susana ran to her. "This is like a fairy tale."

"No. I can't bear for you to think that." Regina hesitated. "He didn't want to marry me. He wanted to marry Viola. He plans to divorce me in a year."

"Don't do this. Don't always do this. He loves you," Susana whispered. "I know he does. I told you, I can tell."

"You are so naive. Look at this room. Do we…do I belong here?"

"You could. I could if Joe had grown up here. Why are you

always so cynical, so ready to believe nobody can love you? Why? When you are so gifted and talented?"

"Why is loving so easy for you?"

"Maybe because I always had you to protect me and to look up to. I felt safe and happy, protected. Trust me on this. It will work out, even here, in this place, if you love him, too. Do you love him?"

"Yes. But I have always been unlucky in love."

"The past doesn't matter. Not if this is true love. If you really love him and commit, you will do whatever it takes to make him happy, and he will do the same for you. You'll see."

"I wish I could believe you. Daddy was so proud today."

"Yes. He was great until he drank all that champagne and had to go to bed with a headache. Mama is very upset to have missed the dancing."

"And it's all based on a lie."

"Don't say that. Don't even think it."

"I can't help myself. I'm so afraid. Where is Nico? It's late."

Susana glanced at her watch. "Oh! You're right! I need to go check on the twins and Gina and see how Daddy's doing. But I hate to leave you like this. I know how your mind works when you get in a mood like this."

"I'll be fine."

"You're sure?"

Trembling all over, Regina nodded bravely.

They hugged. Susana let her go and then looked up at her, giggling. "My big sister, the princess!"

Alone in the red rooms again, anxiety swept Regina. She began to pace. One minute she felt on fire. In the next, the blood drained from her face and hands, and she was freezing. Then she caught fire all over again.

Terrified, she ran out onto the balcony. When her eyes grew accustomed to the gloom, she saw a tall, dark figure in the moon-light, staring up at her.

She leaned over the railing. "Nico?"

Was he as frightened as she was?

He turned away, and she cried his name again. "Nico! Come to me!"

When he turned back, she slid the transparent robe off her shoulders and let it fall in a swish of silk to the stone floor.

"No!" he yelled. "Don't!"

"You'd better come up here then before I strip for the whole world to see! Even the paparazzi!"

He was running toward the palazzo even before she tore off her nightgown and flung it at him.

Nineteen

Nico raced toward the red rooms like a wild man.

What had she thought? Tearing off that filmy thing with the light behind her? Anyone could have seen her. Photographed her. Why didn't she care that the paparazzi were everywhere?

The mere memory of her slim body, so clearly revealed, made his heart pound faster. He felt like a beast, driven by a savage hunger.

When he banged on the doors to the red suite, and she didn't answer, he kicked the door open and strode inside. Alone in the silent, dark room, all he heard was the harsh rasping of his own breathing.

Then she glided out of the shadows into the moonlight. Except for the gardenia in her hair, she was naked. Slim and curvaceous, she was more beautiful than a goddess from some ancient myth.

He closed his eyes, clenched his fists, fighting the all-consuming fire burning inside him.

"Nico?" she said softly. "I wanted you to come. I waited and waited."

"Were you going to show yourself to the whole world? You're mine. Only mine."

He moved toward her with the swiftness of a jungle beast. Seizing her, he picked her up and carried her to the bed.

"Mine," he said fiercely.

"Always and forever, Nico, *my* darling."

Her eyes were blazing as he stripped, flinging his formal clothes to the floor without a care.

"You win."

She was staring at his erection. "I know."

She smiled up at him. Then she tried to speak again, but his mouth covered hers in a hard, punishing kiss. His hands and lips roamed her silky limbs. Then her body began to twist and writhe beneath his, and nothing mattered, not even his anger. Nothing mattered except being inside her, claiming her for all time.

He made love to her in different positions, in the bed, on the floor, against the wall. And every time, she gave herself to him utterly, and her sweetness and eagerness obliterated every dark emotion and left only love.

Who was she really? The upstart his mother believed her to be, the American who'd ensnared him with her sexual powers because she preferred a prince to a sperm donor? Did he care?

When he had rested, she crawled on top of him and began to eat him with her tongue. He hadn't thought things could get any wilder or any sweeter than the first time, but they did.

Sex was like death, he would think later, when he could think. He couldn't sleep with her and remain whole. Every time he exploded inside her, she stole another piece of his soul. Soon there would be nothing left of him that wasn't hers.

A year. He'd told the upstart he'd believed her to be she had to stay a year. He'd been furious at her in Austin; out of his mind with rage, totally unreasonable and unable to listen to what she'd said in her own defense.

No matter who she was, or what she was, he wanted her forever.

But he loved her too much to force her to stay.

He rolled off the bed and stood up, feeling weary, despising himself for having forced her to marry him.

He dressed hurriedly and walked out onto her balcony.

* * *

Regina didn't know what to do when she woke up and Nico was gone. She couldn't believe she'd done the things she'd done, and yet she could. She'd wanted him so much.

Still, she felt hot with embarrassment every time she thought about it. Was he disgusted with the commoner he'd married? It was terrible of her, but thinking about how her tongue and lips had made love to him, especially that huge part, only made her begin to tremble with fresh need.

Where was he? Why had he left her? Had she totally displeased him?

Oh, why had she flung off her robe outside? He probably found that cheap and low-class. Was he angry about it or ashamed of her?

She arose from the bed and, when she couldn't find her nightgown in the dark, she dragged the heavy satin spread around herself. Trailing red, she was on her way to the bathroom when she saw him slumped on the chair outside, his face white as he stared at the moonlit garden.

"Nico?"

He jumped at the sound of her voice but didn't turn.

Did he hate her that much?

"I'm sorry," he said, his low tone filled with loathing.

Suddenly she was truly afraid. "I don't understand."

"I was out of control. Not myself. I never meant for all that to happen."

"You didn't want to make love to me?"

"I didn't say that."

"Things have a way of getting out of hand with you and me," she whispered, her own heart pounding in fright. "I'm sorry, too."

"I don't want you to be sorry any longer. I was crazy in Austin to say you had to stay a year. I arrogantly thought you wanted me because of who I was. Because I'm a prince, you see. That hurt. I was angry, furious, and concerned about the baby. I wasn't thinking."

"What are you saying?"

"You're not that person. I can't force you. I won't force you. It's not fair to you or the baby."

"Do you mean you want me to go?"

She continued to stare at him, unable to think because of the emotions tearing at her.

He wanted out. As fast as possible. That's all she heard.

"All right then," she said, when he didn't answer. "I understand. Thank you. I'll leave tomorrow with my family. I don't know what I'll say to them. They thought we loved each other."

"You were right. I should never have involved them. I never wanted to hurt them. Or you. I'm sorry. I'm sorry for what will be written in the papers."

"I don't care about the damn papers," she whispered, but so softly he didn't hear her. "I love you, just you, you big idiot."

"I never meant to hurt you," he repeated, his voice low and dull.

She strangled on a wild sob.

But you did. Because you made me believe, for one stupid, glorious moment that you loved me, that I was lovable and special and that you were satisfied with just me.

What a silly fool she was. Nobody had ever loved her like that. She wasn't Susana.

The limousine raced around a curve and Regina saw the beach and the lemon trees and the dazzling blue water where *Simonetta* was moored.

"Stop!" Regina cried. "Stop the car!"

Dino and David were yelling in the limo while Gina sang the seven dwarves' song from *Snow White,* about whistling while you work, so the driver didn't hear Regina.

Frantic, she pounded on his window. "Stop!"

When he did, she said, "This will just take a minute."

His expression glazed, her father nodded. He had a bit of a hangover. He and her mother had been in shock ever since she'd told them she was leaving Nico and going home with them. Susana, who'd ordered her to quit being her usual bullheaded self and make up with Nico, wasn't speaking to her because Regina had said that wasn't possible.

Slowly, as if in a dream, Regina walked toward the lemon trees and the bench where she'd been sitting when she'd first seen Nico. She sat down and stared at the blue water that was so beautiful it hurt. Why did it have to be the exact shade of Nico's eyes?

Simonetta blurred. Tears, tears that she didn't feel any shame for or try to brush away, leaked out of her eyes and streaked her face.

Everything was the same, but nothing was. She fingered the ornate cross at her throat. She'd felt so much love here. She wondered if such emotions lingered in a place and made it magical for others. Had ancient lovers been here before them? Would someone else find true love in this exact spot?

She buried her face in her hands and sobbed, praying such lovers would be luckier than she was.

"Cara?"

She was sobbing so violently she didn't hear him at first.

"Cara, darling. *Tesorina.*" Then in a deep, dark voice he began to caress her in Italian. "Your sister came to me earlier."

"Nico?" She stood. She couldn't believe he was really here. Then his arms came around her from behind, and she felt his heat against her hips and spine as he molded her against his body.

"Why are you crying, my love?" He stroked her back and her hair.

"Oh, Nico. I know I don't deserve you. I'm not nearly good enough."

"You are perfect in every way."

"Your mother wouldn't want me underfoot all the time."

"My mother has her own household, her own homes, you know."

"I thought you lived with her."

"No. My main residence is outside Florence."

"Why are we talking about houses?" she whispered.

"Maybe because we're afraid of what we feel, of how much we care."

She whirled, half-blind with tears. "Then why did you send me away?"

His dark face was a blur.

"Is that what you thought? You broke my heart when you left."

"Are we both crazy?"

"Crazy in love. All lovers are a little crazy."

When her sobs subsided, she wanted to kiss him. She wanted to kiss him so badly.

"Not here," he said, his eyes scanning their surroundings for cameras.

He took her hand. Then they were running toward his tender and speeding across the blue water to *Simonetta*.

Once they were safely inside his stateroom, she threw her arms around him, and he kissed her.

"I love you," he said, many torrid kisses later.

"I love you, too. Always."

"That, too," he murmured tenderly. *"Always."*

He lifted her hand and began sucking her fingertips. He was tugging her down onto the floor when she remembered.

"Oh, my God!" She ran to a window and stared at Amalfi.

"What?"

"I forgot all about my family. They're in that limousine—still waiting for me."

He pulled out his cell phone and snapped it open. When he hung up, he smiled and said, "Susana said she wanted you to call her as soon as you can. She takes full credit for this happy ending."

Regina grinned. "That may be a while."

"Yes, she's on her way to the States."

"I have a feeling we'll be pretty busy, too," she murmured.

"It's more than a feeling. It's a certainty."

Then they were on the priceless Persian carpet, and she was staring up at him in fascination as he tore off his jeans and then his shirt. He was lean and brown and gorgeous, not to mention, swollen with desire.

Yes—to mention. And he was huge. And all hers.

He loved her. She was loved for herself, just like Susana. She didn't have to be *more* or perfect or even an attorney. She could just be herself. And that was enough.

Then he was disrobing her, kissing each part of her as he removed an item of clothing. Soon, with his lips pressed against intimate, secret flesh, she had no time for thoughts. Only for love.

When he kissed her on the mouth again and began to murmur in Italian, her whole being caught fire.

"Will you marry me for more than a year?"

"Forever," she whispered. "Forever. I love you."

"Then show me."

"With pleasure."

And being a commoner, she did.

* * * * *

BLACKMAILED
INTO BED
by
Heidi Betts

Dear Reader,

As soon as I started writing my Desire™ title, *Bedded Then Wed*, I knew that the hero's brother would have to get his own story. With a name like Chase Ramsey, how could I resist?

I wasn't sure just what kind of trouble he should find himself in, though. Then it hit me – blackmail. I'd never done a revenge book before, and it sounded like great fun to me. And what could be better – or sexier – than being *Blackmailed into Bed*? Needless to say, I quite enjoyed writing Chase and Elena's story, and I hope you'll enjoy them, too.

Watch for Elena's sister's story, too, which will be out soon. Because a woman like Alandra Sanchez deserves a very special hero.

All my best!

Heidi Betts

PS Don't forget to visit www.heidibetts.com for information about all my books.

HEIDI BETTS

An avid romance reader since junior school, Heidi knew early on that she wanted to write these wonderful stories of love and adventure. It wasn't until her first year of college, however, when she spent the entire night reading a romance novel instead of studying for finals, that she decided to take the road less travelled and follow her dream. In addition to reading and writing romance, she is the founder of her local Romance Writers of America chapter and has a tendency to take injured and homeless animals of every species into her Central Pennsylvania home.

Heidi loves to hear from readers. You can write to her at PO Box 99, Kylertown, PA 16847, USA (an SAE with return postage is appreciated, but not necessary) or e-mail heidi@heidibetts.com. And be sure to visit www.heidibetts.com for news and information about upcoming books.

To my wonderful readers, who are
– without question – the greatest in the world. So
many of you, so sweet and supportive.
Thank you for your letters and e-mails and kind
words of encouragement when I see you in person.
You remind me on a daily basis of why I love my
job so much, and keep me going on those long,
dreary days when the words won't seem to come.
This one's for you!

One

Elena Sanchez looked up and down the long hallway, her heels clicking on the expensively tiled floor as she moved. There was no one behind the desk where she assumed a receptionist would normally sit, but then, it was lunch time. Even she had sneaked away from the office to come over here.

She glanced at the doors as she passed, searching for the one she needed, for the name of the man she had to see, whether she wanted to or not. And she really didn't want to. If her father wasn't desperate—if she wasn't desperate on her father's behalf—she probably would have gone the rest of her life without bumping into Chase Ramsey.

She certainly wouldn't have made a point of tracking him down.

When she saw his name printed in black block letters

on the gold door plate at the end of the hall, her stomach jumped and she had the sudden urge to turn and run. But she'd made up her mind to do this, so she would.

Raising a hand, she knocked, and then wiped her damp palms on the sides of her red linen, knee-length skirt so he wouldn't realize how nervous she was if he shook her hand.

She heard mumbling from the other side, perhaps even a curse, followed by a grumbled, "Come in."

Twisting the knob, she pushed the dark wooden door open and stepped inside.

His office was huge, encompassing three large plate glass windows that overlooked downtown Austin. An oriental rug and two dark green overstuffed leather armchairs filled the space in front of his wide cherrywood desk.

Behind that desk, Chase Ramsey sat scribbling notes while he held the phone to his ear and carried on a somewhat heated conversation with whoever was on the other end of the line. He didn't bother looking up, even though she knew he must have heard her enter.

Not presumptuous enough to take a seat until invited, Elena stayed where she was, standing just inside the office door, clenching and unclenching her fingers around the strap of her purse that hung at her side.

He was as handsome as she remembered. Darn it. But in a darker, much more mature way—she hadn't seen him since they were teenagers.

His hair was as black as midnight, cut short, with just a hint of curl that fell over his forehead. And from what she could see above the desk, he filled his dark gray, expensive, tailored suit to perfection. Broad shoulders, expansive chest, tanned hands that looked strong enough to lift a small building.

Or stroke across a woman's thigh.

Oh, Lord. Where had that come from? She clutched the strap of her handbag more tightly and fought the urge to fan her face. Butterflies were flying in rapid formation through her stomach, making her weak in the knees.

So he had big hands. Big, dark, impressive hands. The fact that she'd noticed—and was apparently quite distracted by them—meant nothing. Except perhaps that it had been awhile since she'd had any decent, attractive male company. Even longer since a man had been near her thighs—with his hands or anything else.

She heard a click and blinked, raising her gaze back to the man behind the desk. While she'd been fantasizing about long, masculine fingers sliding beneath the hem of her skirt, Chase Ramsey had apparently finished his conversation and was now staring at her with an impatient, annoyed glint in his sharp blue eyes.

"Can I help you with something?" he asked.

Taking a deep breath and steeling her nerves, she stepped forward to stand between the two guest chairs angled in front of his desk.

"Yes, actually," she said, brushing a lock of hair behind her ear before resting her palm on the high back of one of the chairs. "My name is Elena Sanchez, and I'd like to talk to you about your interest in Sanchez Restaurant Supply Company."

She knew the exact moment he recognized her. Not just the name of her father's company as one he was in the process of taking over, but recognized *her*. Her name and possibly her features, if he remembered anything about her from all those years ago.

His eyes turned hard and dark, his mouth tightening to a thin, flat line. He dropped the pen in his right hand on top of the papers he'd been working on and leaned back in his chair, resting his elbows on the padded arms and steepling his fingers in front of him as he rocked back and forth, back and forth.

Inwardly, she cringed. Judging by his reaction to her presence, his memory was as impressive as his physical attributes.

And his disdain was justified, she knew. Two decades ago, she'd been a spoiled, high-strung teenager, and had treated a lot of people badly, Chase included.

Not that her youth could be used as an excuse. Everyone makes mistakes when they're kids, and sometimes those mistakes have to be paid for or made right.

This, Elena decided, was her punishment for having had a lousy attitude as an adolescent—coming face-to-face with Chase Ramsey again, and essentially having to grovel in an attempt to help her father save the family business.

It might not be easy, but she would step up and take her lumps like the mature adult she'd grown into.

A phone rang out in the hallway, but Chase ignored it. He just kept rocking in his high-priced leather desk chair, staring at her as though he could see straight through to her soul.

And maybe he could. She felt exposed down to the bone. She might as well have been standing in the middle of his office stark naked, instead of in one of her most professional dress suits.

The red linen skirt and matching jacket over a low-cut

white blouse always made her feel powerful and in control. She'd worn it purposely this morning, knowing she would be facing the lion in his den.

But now she realized her choice of clothing made absolutely no difference. She could have been wearing a suit of armor and would be no less nervous about standing in front of Chase Ramsey, waiting for him to strip a few layers of skin off her hide or order her out of his office without even letting her explain her reason for being there.

Instead, he lifted one black eyebrow and sat forward again, the corners of his mouth twisting in the grim mockery of a smile.

"Elena Sanchez," he murmured coldly, pushing slowly to his feet and moving around his desk. "Now, there's a name I never thought I'd hear again. Can't say I ever expected you to saunter into my office, either."

He paused directly in front of her, with fewer than three feet of space between them. The air was thick and tense, and Elena found her lungs straining for breath with him standing in such close proximity.

Leaning back against the edge of the desk, he crossed his arms over his chest and pierced her with that glacial blue glare.

"I take it you're here to beg me not to buy out your daddy's business," he said, his tone only a notch above patronizing. "Sorry, sweetheart, but I didn't build Ramsey Corporation into a multimillion dollar company by falling for long lashes and a nice pair of legs."

He let his gaze travel blatantly down her body, past her breasts, her waist, her hips, until they caught and held on the expanse of leg left visible below the hem of her skirt, which fell just above her knees.

"No matter how shapely they might be," he added before dragging his eyes reluctantly back to her face.

It was her turn to raise a brow. She dropped her purse on the seat of one of the guest chairs and took a more defensive stance.

"I'm not here to *beg* you for anything. I came to *speak* with you about a business issue that's important to my family. And whether or not you find my eyelashes and legs attractive is completely inconsequential. We're both adults; we should be able to sit down and talk in a calm, professional manner without you ogling me like a parolee on his first visit to a strip club after twenty years in solitary confinement."

The muscles in Chase's cheeks twitched, and it took all of his willpower to keep from letting that twitch spread into a full-blown grin.

It had been almost twenty years since he'd seen or spoken to Elena Sanchez. Frankly, he'd never given a damn if he ever saw or spoke to her again. She was one of those painful memories from childhood that still oozed and bled if he let down his guard long enough to peel back the curtain between present and past.

Thankfully, he didn't do that very often. He hadn't thought about Elena in years. Not even, surprisingly, when he'd begun the process of buying out her father's restaurant supply company. To Chase, it was just another smart business move; the kind that had transformed him from a modest rancher's son to a millionaire and CEO of his own self-named corporation at the age of thirty-five.

Kicking away from the desk, he smoothed a hand over his tie and once again rounded his desk.

"By all means," he told her, waving toward one of the chairs on either side of her body, which she was holding nearly as still and rigid as a statue, "have a seat and we'll talk. Like adults. About business."

For a moment she didn't move, almost as though she expected his offer to be some sort of trap. Then her muscles began to relax and she took a sideways step to her left, perching on the edge of the chair that didn't hold her little red handbag.

Knees together, spine straight, she held her folded hands on her lap, looking every inch the debutante she'd been raised to be.

The image wasn't a pleasant one for Chase. It reminded him too sharply of the girl she'd been at fourteen. The same girl who'd bruised his heart and trampled all over it with the sharp little heels of her open-toed shoes.

Pushing aside those old hurts and the feelings they evoked, he met her eyes and tried to regard her just as he would any other business associate.

"All right," he said, leaning his forearms on the top of his desk, "I'm listening. What is it you need to speak with me about?"

"You're trying to buy out my father's—my family's—company, Sanchez Restaurant Supply," she said.

"I'm *going* to buy out your father's company," he corrected.

To her credit, his comment didn't upset her or cause her to back down.

"I'm here to ask you to reconsider your decision," she

continued without flinching. "Or at the very least, to give my father a bit more time to come up with the money and resources necessary to save SRS."

"Does he think he can do that?" Chase asked, always interested in any new information that might help him get the upper hand or finalize a deal. "Come up with the financial backing, I mean."

"Yes."

She glanced away for just a split second, telling him she wasn't as confident as she was pretending to be.

"He thinks, given enough time, that he could get the company up and running successfully again. And I'm here to ask you to give him the time he needs because I'm worried about what will become of him if he loses SRS."

Her green eyes, surrounded by full black lashes that matched her long, flowing black hair, met his, wordlessly begging for his understanding and compassion.

Something warm began to unfurl low in his belly, but he clamped his jaw on his fist, and bit down on it. He'd been roped in by her soft eyes and sultry features before, and gotten kicked in the teeth for his trouble. He wouldn't let her lull him again.

"The company is his life," Elena went on. "He built it from the ground up, when he had nothing. It's the cornerstone of our family. After my mother died, he let things slide—he knows that—but he's trying now to set things right and get SRS back to where it belongs."

It was a pretty story, one no doubt designed to pull at his heartstrings. Little did she know he didn't have any heartstrings.

"What does that have to do with me?" he asked bluntly.

Those green eyes flashed for a brief moment before she seemed to remember he held her life and future—or at the very least, her father's—in his hands.

"You want to buy Sanchez Restaurant Supply and break it into pieces, selling it off to the highest bidder. I realize it would make a tidy profit for you, but I'm asking you to consider the blood, sweat and tears that went into building SRS. Consider the emotional impact losing the company will have on a good man and his family."

"Emotions have no place in business. Buying out SRS is a sound financial decision, and you're right—I stand to make a tidy sum on the deal. I can't worry about how the previous owner is going to feel about the takeover or what he did to put the company at risk to begin with."

Chase waited for that hint of fire to burn in her eyes once again, but it never came. Instead, she inclined her head once, slowly, before making one last, desperate pitch.

"I thought that's what you would say. I even understand your position. But will a few more weeks really hurt you? There have to be other companies out there that can net you just as much profit. Can't you give my father just a few more weeks, maybe a month, to see if there's something he can do to save the business? If he can't, all you've lost is a little time." She paused for a beat, looking him straight in the eye and lifting both brows. "Unless there's some *personal* reason you would be averse to helping me or my family."

She put just enough emphasis on the remark to let him know she remembered that night twenty years ago as well as he did, although he doubted her reaction was anything close to his own. He felt a spiral of shame and embarrassment begin low in his gut and he tamped it down, refusing to be controlled by memories…childhood ones, at that.

Elena Sanchez hadn't changed a bit since he'd last seen her. Oh, she'd grown into a beautiful, breathtaking woman, but then, she'd been a pretty girl.

Where it really counted, though, she was exactly the same. She still expected her feminine wiles and her family's wealth and reputation to get her whatever she desired.

Sanchez Restaurant Supply was apparently in enough trouble for her to feel compelled to try to help her father, instead of her usual attitude of letting daddy solve *her* problems. It was obvious she expected Chase to see the situation from her perspective and be mesmerized enough by the bit of skin she was flashing below the hem of her skirt and between the vee of her blouse to give her what she wanted.

Too bad for her that Chase Ramsey was not a man to be led around by the nose…or any other part of his anatomy.

"I told you," he said, with very little warmth to his words, "even if I had feelings about your family one way or the other, I wouldn't let them interfere with a business decision."

"Well, then," she said shortly, getting to her feet and retrieving her purse from the seat of the other chair, "I guess I'm wasting my time and yours. Thank you for seeing me. I'll let you get back to your work."

He watched the rigid set of her shoulders and the sensual sway of her hips as she walked away, having the uncontrollable urge to call her back.

Why should he want to keep her with him a few minutes longer, when up until today his fondest wish had been never to lay eyes on her again?

His brain was in chaos, struggling to process the conflicting feelings, while at the same time, he was kicking himself for still finding her even moderately attractive. He was like a man with split personalities: a part of him wanted to help her and part of him wanted to punish her.

"Wait," he called out, just as her long, red-tipped fingers curled around the knob of his office door.

Slowly, with obvious reluctance, she turned to face him.

"I've got a proposition for you," he told her, pushing away from his desk and moving closer, stopping before his actions could be considered intimidating.

"I happen to be in need of a female companion. A beautiful woman to accompany me on business trips and to related dinners and events."

He straightened his tie and smoothed the lines of his jacket. His statement was at least half true. He might not *need* a companion, but it certainly would be convenient to have one at his disposal. He just couldn't figure out why he felt compelled to offer the position to this particular woman.

But it didn't keep him from pressing forward, even though she had yet to respond.

"If you agree to be available to me whenever I need you, I'll agree to give your father the same amount of time to do what he can to save SRS. A day, a week, a month—it's entirely up to you."

Her lips twitched, as though she was about to speak, but before she could utter a word, he held up a hand to stop her. "You should know, before making a decision, that there will be sex involved. I'll expect you to share my bed, if that's something I require."

Elena's eyes widened and she barely stopped herself

from reaching out to slap him. What kind of woman did he think she was?

"Aren't there women you can hire for that sort of thing?" she snapped. "I'm not a prostitute."

"I never said you were. I'm simply telling you what it is that I need, and what you can do to help your father save his business."

"So you're asking me to be your mistress. Where you want me to be, when you want me to be there—a living doll you can take out of its box to look pretty and satisfy your physical needs, then put back when you're finished."

He shrugged and stuffed his hands into the front pockets of his slacks, causing the sides of his suit jacket to bunch.

"That's not exactly how I would have put it, but yes. I need a mistress and you need to buy time for your father to save his company. That's the deal, take it or leave it."

"You bastard," she muttered with a breathless laugh that was anything but amused.

"Quite possibly," he said. "But you're the one who came to me. And you should consider yourself lucky I'm making you any sort of offer at all. I could have just as easily given you a firm no and sent you on your way."

She wished she could argue, but knew he was absolutely right. Coming here had been a long shot, and the fact that he was suggesting any compromise at all was a blessing.

The question was: did she have a choice?

If she turned him down, she would have to go home and watch her father lose the business he loved, the company that essentially defined her family and made their name so well-known across Texas and the surrounding states.

But becoming Chase Ramsey's mistress… Sleeping

with a virtual stranger was a difficult concept to swallow, but she was pretty sure this particular near stranger hated her with every fiber of his being. It was probably the driving force behind his proposition, since she couldn't picture him sitting across from any other woman who came to his office to discuss business and announcing that he would give her more time if she agreed to go to bed with him.

She took a deep breath, letting the fresh oxygen fill her lungs and pump through her bloodstream. Her fingertips turned numb from the death grip she had on her handbag.

"Can I have some time to think it over?" she asked, making sure to keep her voice strong and steady. "Or do you need an answer right this minute?"

Instead of responding, he pulled his hands from his pockets and returned to his desk. Still standing, he grabbed a sheet of memo paper and a pen, then leaned over to scribble a quick note. Marching back in her direction, he handed it to her.

When she glanced down, she found a date, time and the name of the local airport. Below that, he'd added the gate number for a flight to Las Vegas.

"I'll give you until Thursday. If you show up, I'll take it to mean you agree to my terms, and your father will get the chance to try to save his company. If not—" He tipped his head and raised a brow. "I'll continue with my plans to buy out SRS."

She heard the underlying threat loud and clear, and left his office with the butterflies in her stomach flapping even harder than when she'd arrived.

Two

When Elena arrived home later that evening, she was both physically and emotionally exhausted. After her fateful meeting with Chase Ramsey, she'd gone back to her office and tried, to no avail, to focus on the appointments and paperwork involved in her job as a social worker. Thankfully, she didn't have any home visits to make and could go over her notes again later, when she was feeling more herself and less…distracted, drained, overwhelmed.

All day she had heard only four words playing over and over in her head. Chase's deep, seductive voice saying, *I need a mistress.*

I need a mistress…
I need a mistress…
I need a mistress…

And what bothered her most, what sent her mind careening into confusing, dangerous territory, was that every time those words rumbled through her brain, vivid images were quick to follow.

She could picture him stripped of that expensive suit, all tanned skin and rippling, corded muscles. Hovering over her as she lay stretched across satin sheets, naked and panting for his touch.

He was an attractive man—a handsome, virile, mouth-watering man—and she was a flesh and blood woman. No one could blame her for entertaining a fantasy or two about him, especially after he'd invited her to share his bed not five hours before.

What frightened her was that, instead of being outraged as she was initially, she was now seriously considering it.

Dropping her briefcase at the base of the coatrack just inside the front door, she kicked off her shoes and gave a sigh of relief as she wiggled her toes in freedom. She didn't usually wear such high heels to work, but the red sling-backs went best with her favorite power outfit, and she'd needed all the self-confidence she could muster to make her way to Ramsey Corporation to face Chase Ramsey himself.

In her stocking feet, she padded across the highly waxed parquet floor of the wide foyer, pausing for a moment to flip through the pile of mail on the table at the base of the steps.

She'd lived in this house in Gabriel's Crossing all her life, but lately had begun to feel uncomfortable and out of place. Maybe because it wasn't so much a house as a mansion, looking like something out of *Gone with the Wind*. There were giant Ionic columns out front; a wide, curved staircase directly across from the front door leading to the second-story; and balconies at the back overlooking several acres of beautiful Texas landscape.

Her father had had it built when Sanchez Restaurant Supply first began to turn a decent profit, and Elena had long suspected the ostentatious design was in part the home her parents had always dreamed of living in, and part proof to anyone who doubted that a first-generation Mexican-American could not only do well for himself and his family, but do *extremely* well.

And until a few years ago, she'd loved it here. As a teenager, she'd considered it another status symbol to impress her friends, and she'd taken every opportunity to have sleepovers or pool parties.

Now, though, without her mother to fill the house with her own brand of love and laughter, the house felt somewhat empty and much too large.

It was time, Elena knew, to start thinking about moving out. She should have done so years ago, but first her mother had been sick, and then her father had needed her.

Her sister, Alandra, had stuck around for the same reason.

Pulling out the letters and magazines with her name on them, Elena started up the stairs and headed for her room. All she wanted was to climb out of her clothes and sink into a nice hot bubble bath. She would light a few candles, turn on some soft classical music, and maybe even pour a glass of wine to sip while she floated away and did her best to forget Chase's troubling proposition.

Halfway down the hall, Elena knew it might be awhile before she could be alone with her exhaustion and jumbled thoughts. Her sister's choice of music—loud, blaring rock and roll—vibrated through her closed bedroom door, and Elena could hear Alandra's voice singing along.

She was about to pad by, sneak into her own room a few doors down and attempt to block out the thrumming beat of drums and a bass guitar, when Alandra's door opened and she stepped out in nothing more than a pale pink chemise-style slip and black stockings.

Both women jumped slightly in surprise, then Alandra threw her arms wide and rolled her eyes in relief.

"Oh, Elena," she called over the volume of the music, which was even louder with the door open, "I'm so glad you're home. I was about to go downstairs and ask Connie what she thinks of my outfit, but I value your opinion more."

She waved a hand, inviting Elena in, as she moved across the lushly carpeted floor and turned off the stereo. The sudden silence was almost deafening, but Elena appreciated the gesture; her sister knew how much the loud music bothered her. At a lower volume, it was almost tolerable.

"I've got a dinner in an hour. We're trying to raise money for a battered women's shelter. I'm not in charge this time, thank heavens, but I still want to look good."

While Elena perched on the end of her sister's canopied princess bed, Alandra went to the closet and pulled out two dresses on padded hangers.

"Which of these do you like best?" she asked, holding one and then the other in front of her tall, slim body.

Alandra Sanchez was, quite simply, gorgeous. Olive skin, as clear and smooth as a baby's bottom, and an hourglass figure were her shining glories. But she'd also been blessed with a pair of traffic-stopping dark brown, almond-shape eyes.

Elena's only consolation to being the less attractive sister was that everyone said they looked so much alike, she knew she wasn't exactly an ugly duckling herself.

It also helped that Alandra was as beautiful on the inside as she was on the outside. There was nothing she wouldn't do for someone, and the more they needed, the more she was willing to give. Personally, financially, it didn't matter.

She attended four or five fund-raising dinners a week, just like the one she was getting ready for now, and just as many lunches. She belonged to every "good cause" organization in the state, a few across the country, and a few more internationally: battered women and kids, underprivileged children, life-saving medical research, save the whales, save the wild mustangs, save shelter cats and dogs from euthanasia.

Alandra's greatest talent was in convincing others to give both time and money to her many worthy causes. Just being around her seemed to make everyone else care more—and sometimes feel the slightest bit guilty for not feeling so before she cornered them.

One side of Elena's mouth curved with pride. Her little sister could charm the scales off a snake and have the naked reptile thanking her afterward.

"This one?" Alandra asked, breaking into Elena's thoughts and holding up a sleek black tube dress for her perusal. Then she switched hands and held up one in pale pink with black trim, reminiscent of the Jackie O era.

In the black one, Alandra would be a knockout. Men would be drooling and falling at her feet. In the pink one, she'd still get more than her fair share of male attention, but those men would at least stand a chance of paying attention to the dinner speakers and getting interested in the cause.

"The pink one," Elena said. "Definitely."

Alandra nodded and stuck the black sheath back in the closet. "That's what I thought, but I needed a second opinion. I'll save the black one for next week when I need to raise funds for the no-kill animal shelter."

She grinned, telling Elena she was well aware of the devastating effect she would have in the other dress.

With a sigh, Elena pushed to her feet, planning to head to her own room while her sister finished getting dressed.

"Elena, wait."

She turned to find Alandra with her arms in the air, her head only half peeking through the neck of the pink and black dress. The tops of her thighs were visible, showing old-fashioned stockings held up by a sexy black garter belt.

Her sister gave a little shimmy and the dress slipped the rest of the way down. She sauntered over, turned her back to Elena, and held up the long fall of her straight black hair.

"Zip me up, and then we'll talk about what's bothering you."

Elena pulled the zipper up. "Nothing's bothering me. I'm just tired."

Alandra shook her head. "*Uh-uh.* That might work on Pop, but it won't work on me. I'm your sister; I can read you like a book."

She spun around and dragged Elena back to the bed, taking a minute to slip her feet into high-heeled black pumps before crossing her legs and perching beside her.

"All right, spill," Alandra said, sounding entirely too

chipper for the headache that was beginning to throb at Elena's temples.

"Did you do it?" she asked, lowering her voice a fraction. "Did you talk to Chase Ramsey?"

From the moment she'd first thought of going to the CEO of the Ramsey Corporation for help in saving her father's business, Elena had confided her plan to her sister. They had been best friends and confidantes since childhood, and shared just about everything with each other. Elena trusted Alandra not only to keep her secrets, but to act as a sounding board to let her know if her ideas were logical or bordering on insane.

And while Alandra had agreed that speaking with Chase Ramsey was a good idea, neither of them had breathed a word of their intentions to Victor Sanchez. Their father was a proud man and wouldn't appreciate anyone—least of all his daughters—interfering in his business or coming to his rescue.

They would only tell him, they decided, if things worked out to their benefit. Otherwise, he need never know what Elena had done.

Elena nodded, her mind flashing back to every tense, *in*tense minute of her meeting with Chase.

Alandra's eyes glittered with interest. "And how did it go? Is he going to help us?"

"That depends."

"On what?"

Elena met her sister's gaze and murmured in a voice lacking all emotion, "On whether I sleep with him."

Her sister's screech of outrage was comforting, but Elena quickly hushed her for fear their conversation would be overheard. She didn't think Pop was home yet, but Connie, their longtime housekeeper, could often be found in the hallways dusting or doing other chores.

Once Alandra had calmed down, Elena filled her in on the details of her face-to-face with Chase Ramsey, recounting every word and facial expression from the time she entered his office.

"And then he told me that he'd give Pop extra time to try to save SRS if I agreed to be his mistress. He wants me to meet him at the airport for a trip to Vegas if I'm willing to go through with it."

From her jacket pocket she pulled the slip of paper Chase had given her, and handed it to her sister. Alandra studied the scrawl before refolding the note and giving it back.

"What are you going to do?" she asked.

"I don't know." Elena released a pent-up breath and shook her head, still racked with indecision.

"Do you want me to do it?"

Elena gave a bark of laughter, then caught the flat look in her sister's eyes.

"Are you serious?" she asked. "You'd do that for me?"

Alandra shrugged. "For you, for Pop, for the family business. It wouldn't be that much of a hardship. You did say he was cute, right?"

She hadn't, and "cute" wasn't even close to the word she would use to describe Chase Ramsey's strong features, fathomless blue eyes and attractive physique.

"It's not like I have that much going on in the boudoir these days, anyway," Alandra continued with a small eye roll when Elena didn't respond. "And if this guy just wants to get laid, then he probably won't care which sister he's with."

Elena laughed again, this time in amusement. She threw her arms around Alandra and hugged her tight. "Oh, Alandra, I love you."

"I love you, too. And I'm more than willing to take this bullet for you, if you want me to."

Elena could just imagine that. The only problem was that when she pictured her sister in bed with Chase instead of herself, she felt a stab of inexplicable jealousy.

How could that be? How could she be jealous of her own sister, who was willing to sleep with a complete stranger just to save Elena and the family business? And how could she suddenly feel territorial about a man who had made her such a disrespectful offer? Primarily, she suspected, as an act of revenge for what she'd done to him as a teenager.

"No," she said, drawing a deep, cleansing breath. "I'm the one who came up with the idea of going to him in the first place. And I'm the one with a past relationship with him."

"All right," Alandra acquiesced, "then how do *you* feel about Ramsey's offer?"

Her stomach jumped at the question, followed by a peculiar, almost traitorous warmth that spread through her breasts and between her legs.

Lord, could she actually be attracted to Chase? On more than simply the detached level of a woman catching a glimpse of a good-looking man.

Could the attraction go deeper? Could she actually be considering saying yes to his proposition? To becoming his mistress?

A skittering of nerves joined the heat flowing through her bloodstream. She'd never been a man's mistress before, never been in a relationship based solely on sex. She'd dated a good number of men, and even slept with a few of them, but those relationships had always moved slowly and been based on other things, like friendship, mutual attraction, similar occupational interests.

Chase had no interest in getting to know her, and she doubted they had a single thing in common other than her father's company. He wanted her for two reasons only— to look good on his arm at business gatherings and to satisfy him in bed.

And darned if that idea wasn't becoming more appealing by the minute.

Squeezing Alandra's fingers, she felt tears prickle at the back of her eyes as she met her sister's gaze. "Is it terrible that I'm thinking of going through with it? And not entirely to help out Pop?"

Alandra gave a soft chuckle, pushing a strand of hair back from Elena's face and tucking it behind her ear. "Of course not. You're allowed to think a guy is hot and want to roll around with him for a while, with or without ulterior motives. I'd be more worried if you thought Chase Ramsey was a dog, but were still willing to sacrifice yourself and your body for SRS. The important question, I think, is how you'll feel about yourself afterward. Can you chalk it up to one of life's many adventures while remaining emotionally detached, or are you going to feel guilty or ashamed when it's all over?"

Her sister was right, but Elena knew she wasn't going to make a decision tonight. She had a couple of days before Chase left for Las Vegas, and she was going to take every one of them to make up her mind.

* * *

Chase wished he could say he was unconcerned and un-interested in whether Elena Sanchez showed up today. But in truth, he'd gotten to the airport an hour earlier than he normally would, just in case.

He'd positioned himself in one of the chairs facing the main area of the airport so he could see everyone who passed by and watch for her.

Just in case.

He'd dug out his laptop and was trying to work, making sure he had a clear view over the top of the monitor.

Just in case.

Part of him hoped she wouldn't take him up on his offer. It had been a totally spontaneous, reckless sugges-tion, and he still wasn't sure why he'd made it.

Maybe because he'd always wanted the chance to knock her down a few pegs. Maybe because it had been obvious that day in his office that she wasn't quite the high and mighty princess she'd been in high school, with a father wealthy enough to buy and sell Chase's own modest, hard working family and every acre of land they possessed.

Or maybe because, despite his better judgment and the gut instincts that screamed for him to back away, keep his distance and not get sucked in again by her sparkling emerald eyes, he wanted her on a purely primal, carnal level.

He'd spent the last few days kicking himself for letting his libido run rampant and make decisions for him. He wasn't a randy youth anymore, and was more than capable of ignoring and overriding his lust.

Unfortunately, all that had seemed to fly out the

window after one glimpse of her long black hair, olive skin and full, kissable lips. The shape of her breasts and flared hips in that tight red suit hadn't hurt, either.

Just the memory of her slim figure and musky perfume caused his body to stir. He shifted restlessly on the uncomfortable airport seat and tried to focus once again on the spreadsheet on the monitor in front of him.

A second later, something tall and green entered his peripheral vision. He glanced up to find Elena standing before him, and his heart skipped a beat. In surprise and sexual longing, he was sure. Not for any other reason.

Reaching out with one hand, he slowly lowered the lid of the laptop and set the computer aside, then took a minute to soak up her appearance.

She wore forest green dress pants and a blouse that matched her eyes, with a narrow slit down the front and brightly colored sequins and beads on either side as decoration. Her hair was pulled up at the sides and held in place with matching copper combs. Dangling earrings made of copper, gold and silver circles glittered at her ears. And on her feet were a pair of tan heels that looked somewhat out of place for travel and added to her height a couple of inches that she didn't need to showcase her other more-than-adequate attributes. In her hand, she held the straps of a matching handbag and at her feet was a somewhat lumpy, overstuffed carry-on bag.

Making a concerted effort not to swallow past the lump of longing in his throat, he offered a small smile and patted the seat of the empty chair to his left.

"You came. I have to say, I'm surprised."

"You didn't give me much choice. It was either this or

watch my father lose his business, with no chance of at least trying to rescue it from certain doom."

Although her little speech was dramatic and heartfelt, he refused to feel so much as a niggling of guilt. She was a big girl, capable of making her own decisions.

It was true that he'd backed her into a corner with his unusual bargain, but it was also true that anyone else would have been sent from his office with a firm and absolute no. He didn't negotiate outside of the boardroom, and even there it often wasn't necessary since he did his homework and knew how to get exactly what he wanted with a minimum of fuss and muss.

"Well, consider your sacrifice a worthwhile one." Retrieving his cell phone from one of the outside pockets of his soft leather expandable briefcase, he flipped open the top and hit the speed dial number for his office.

"Nancy," he said when his personal assistant picked up on the other end. "Do me a favor and put a hold on everything pertaining to the Sanchez Restaurant Supply takeover. I want to give the deal a bit more thought before we go any further. Thanks," he said after her affirmative response, and hung up.

"There you go," he told Elena, shifting to face her more fully and drape his arm along the back of her chair. "Whatever your father thinks he can do to pull his company out of its downward spiral, now he has the time to do it." Reaching into his jacket, he pulled out two first-class tickets to Las Vegas and held out hers.

She took it and studied her name printed in bold black ink at the top.

"You must have been pretty confident that I'd show up to buy me a ticket."

He shrugged and cocked his head to one side. "It was a calculated risk. I couldn't very well have you show up and *not* have a ticket for you, now could I? But I did make sure it was transferable, so if you hadn't shown, I could have used it for another trip later."

For the first time since she'd arrived, a ghost of a smile started to steal across her face. She raised green eyes to his, a twinkle of amusement playing behind her long, dark lashes.

"You're a very cocky man," she told him, her voice haughty but with a hint of warmth that hadn't been there earlier or in their previous meeting. "Are you ever *not* completely sure of yourself?"

Only when Elena Sanchez is in the room, he thought sourly. She was the only person who still had the ability to make him feel gawky and gangly and sixteen years old.

He would work that out of his system this week, though. Or die trying.

But aloud, for her benefit, he said, "Nope. It's been a long time since junior high," he added pointedly.

He knew his comment had hit home when her lips turned down in a frown and she glanced away.

"Yes," she said simply. "It has."

Several beats passed in uncomfortable silence before Chase let out a huff of breath and decided he probably shouldn't have needled the woman he hoped to seduce shortly after touching down in Las Vegas.

He didn't fool himself into believing her agreement to sleep with him was a done deal. Yes, she was here, which he assumed meant she had every intention of sharing his bed. But if she changed her mind at the last minute or got cold feet, he wasn't going to force her. He'd never forced any woman, and he wasn't going to start with Elena Sanchez.

Of course, she didn't know that. As far as she was concerned, flying to Las Vegas constituted her first act as his mistress, and he planned to go with that for as long as he could, hoping everything worked out just as he'd been fantasizing since she'd walked into—and out of—his office.

"Relax, Elena." He touched her arm with his free hand and rubbed the bare flesh with the side of his thumb. "We have the whole week to get to know each other better. And I promise not to jump your bones until after we've checked into the hotel."

Three

The short flight to Nevada was comfortable in first class, and quite uneventful. Chase kept his word, barely touching her the entire time and keeping their conversation to benign, unimportant topics.

But that didn't keep the nerves from skittering up and down her spine. In fact, the closer they got to the hotel, the worse her anxiety became.

He'd said he wouldn't "jump her" until after they arrived at the hotel. Did that mean the minute they hit the lobby? Would he accost her in the elevator, or as soon as they were inside the room?

She knew she was being irrational. In all the time she'd spent with Chase so far, she hadn't seen him do anything the least bit impulsive. For some reason, she simply couldn't picture him being so overcome with lust that he'd

corner her in the hallway or participate in some passionate public display of affection. He was entirely too somber,
too controlled.

Not that any of that kept her mind from wandering
down a dozen confusing, carnal alleyways. Her body felt
like a tightly strung bow, waiting for the moment he
would touch her, kiss her, demand she fulfill their bargain
between the sheets.

And she cursed herself for the anticipation building
like a tornado at her center. For wanting him to do just that
when she should be despising him for forcing her into an
unacceptable situation.

A spacious black town car met them at the airport and
took them directly to their hotel. The Wynn was one of
the luxury hotels directly on The Strip, with marble
floors, chandeliers and lots of gold and dark, polished
wood. There was a casino off to the side, but it was
obvious this particular establishment was meant for
wealthier visitors to the city, rather than those who
might come in for a weekend of fun and debauchery.

Little did the owners of the hotel know that their rich
patrons could be just as interested in debauchery as those
with limited funds; they were simply better at hiding their
true intentions.

A bellman dressed in a maroon uniform trimmed with
gold accompanied Chase and Elena to their suite. He
opened the door, ushered them inside, then transferred their
luggage from the wheeled cart to the bedroom.

The suite was made up of a large sitting area, a kitchenette, bathroom, and through a wide double doorway, the
bedroom and a second, more private bath.

Elena had grown up with money and stayed in her fair share of luxury hotels, but even she found the opulence of this particular suite to be somewhat overwhelming.

A king-size bed filled the center of the bedroom, surrounded by ornately carved dressers and a wall of mirrors that hid the long closet space. The bathroom had a shower stall and a separate, deep Jacuzzi, both big enough, she thought, to hold three or four people.

She was standing in the doorway, admiring the almost spa-quality equipment, when Chase came up behind her and whispered in her ear.

"We have more than an hour before we need to be downstairs for dinner. Would you like to take a nap, or unpack, or…something else?"

Although he wasn't touching her at all, his voice poured over her like warm honey, his hinted suggestion sending off fireworks low in her belly. Her breathing grew choppy and she had to blink several times to stave off the sudden bout of lightheadedness that assailed her.

She wasn't ready. Not yet. She knew the moment would come when she couldn't put it off any longer, but for now he'd given her other options, and she grabbed at them like a drowning victim reaching for a life raft.

"I think we should unpack," she said a bit too loudly and a bit too brightly, spinning on her heel and slipping past him before he could protest or—worse—try to stop her.

Not waiting for a reply, she hurried to where their bags had been left and hoisted her suitcase onto the mattress. There was a luggage rack off to the side, but she decided that if the bed was covered with clothes and such, it couldn't be used for…other things.

Without a word, Chase joined her and they unpacked in silence, filling the drawers and closets, and cluttering the counter around the bathroom sinks.

When they were finished, Chase suggested they start getting ready for dinner and politely left her alone to change. She hurried with her hair and makeup, and shrugged into one of the half dozen cocktail dresses she'd brought along, knowing Chase would need time in the bedroom and bathroom to get ready himself.

Stepping into the sitting area, she found Chase standing at the bank of tall windows, staring out at the bright lights and bustling activity that made up the heart of Sin City. Though the thick, lush carpeting absorbed the sound of her footsteps, he seemed to sense her presence and turned as she rounded the end of the floral-patterned sofa.

His eyes softened when he saw her, and a gentle smile curved his lips as he skimmed her appearance, from the upswept knot of hair that left her neck and shoulders visible, to the strapless royal blue dress with its lace overlay that hugged her every curve and left her legs seductively bare. She shifted slightly and toyed with the sapphire pendant at her throat, uncomfortable with his thorough perusal.

He strode forward, taking his time and keeping his gaze firmly locked with her own.

"Nice," he murmured as he passed, careful to leave just enough space between their bodies that her skin prickled in awareness, but they never actually touched.

"I won't be long," he added before disappearing into the bedroom and closing the connecting door behind him.

* * *

Dinner, Elena was relieved to admit, passed much more enjoyably and with a lot less stress than expected. Chase had introduced her to his business associates by name, with no further explanation, rather than referring to her as his girlfriend or mistress or some other label she'd been concerned he might use. And though she'd made small talk with the other women at the table, she mostly remained silent and allowed Chase to conduct his business.

He even asked her to dance at one point, and held her close while the orchestra played a slow, romantic song. After a couple glasses of wine and the lulling atmosphere seeping into her bones, she let herself lean against the strong wall of his chest and absorb the heat of his fingers where they rested at the small of her back.

She hadn't forgotten their agreement or her reason for being here—both to help her father and become Chase's lover—but since the outcome of her decision was inevitable, she started to relax and live for the moment rather than obsess over what might come next.

They said goodnight to the others and made their way through the lobby to the bank of elevators, their footsteps slow, her arm wrapped around his and their hips brushing.

"You were great tonight," Chase said as they stepped into the empty elevator car. "Finklestein and Rogers loved you. And I think their wives were glad to have another woman at the table. My unattached state usually causes them to spend the entire meal going through a list of single young ladies they think might suit me."

Elena offered a small smile, but didn't reply.

"Bringing you along was definitely one of my better ideas."

When the elevator stopped at their floor, he led her to the suite, opened the door with his keycard and waved her inside ahead of him.

They'd left a lamp on at the far side of the room, so the suite was bathed in pale yellow light. The closed curtains kept the neon sparkle of The Strip from intruding.

"Would you like something to drink?"

Elena turned to find Chase standing near the entrance to the kitchenette, but shook her head. "I already had too much wine with dinner. Any more and I'll probably pass out and sleep for a week."

"We can't have that," he replied, his voice a low rumble.

Moving closer, he stroked the pads of his fingers down her bare arm, raising goose bumps all along her skin. His gaze held hers and she swallowed hard to keep from shivering.

When he reached her wrist, he unhooked her gold and diamond watch, setting it aside on the kitchenette counter. From the next wrist, he loosened her dangle bracelet, then slipped the rings off her fingers, adding them to the growing pile. Next came her earrings and necklace, until she stood free of accessories.

"Did I tell you how beautiful you look tonight?"

To her great embarrassment, the only reply she could manage when she opened her mouth was a strangled sort of sound. Chase grinned, his blue eyes turning storm gray and twinkling devilishly.

His hands lifted to her hair and slowly, one by one, he removed the pins holding the long locks in place. When he was finished, he drove his fingers into the twisted strands and combed them down to hang to her waist. A second later, she felt him tugging at the zipper of her dress, and then the fabric slipped from her body.

She didn't fight it, didn't grab for the garment before it hit the floor. She simply stood there and let him strip her down to her bra and panties, garter belt, stockings and high heeled shoes.

He took a small step back, just a millimeter to allow him to look his fill. "Lovely."

"They were my sister's idea." The words popped out without conscious thought and she was rewarded for her senseless muttering by his warm, lopsided smile.

"What was?"

"The garter and stockings. She told me they were sexier than pantyhose, and that you'd appreciate the difference."

His grin widened and turned even more wicked, his gaze locked on the lace edging at the tops of her thighs and the thin straps holding them up. "Your sister was right. Remind me to send her a thank-you note when we get back. And maybe a box of chocolates or some flowers."

Elena nodded absently, her insides going both weak and hot at the same time.

With one hand on her hip, the other trailing up and down the length of her arm, Chase leaned in and blew on the shell of her ear.

"Tell me, Elena," he whispered, sending shockwaves through her system, "will you come to bed with me? Now? Tonight?"

Her eyes drifted closed, the lids too heavy to keep open. Her blood felt like syrup slogging slowly through her veins.

If she'd known he was going to have this effect on her,

she probably wouldn't have come. He was too handsome, too charming and obviously had too much power over her. The power to make her weak in the knees and cloud her senses. The power to make her not only willing to sleep with a man she barely knew, but be on the verge of begging for his touch.

He had to know she was putty in his hands, had to know she was his for the taking. And yet he'd asked permission to make love to her, and was still waiting for her answer.

As much as she'd agonized over her decision to come here with him, the decision to go through with sharing his bed was easy. She wanted him, and regardless of his reasons for wanting her, there was only one response she could give.

Her lashes fluttered, and she opened her eyes to see him watching her closely, his expression intense and strained.

"Yes," she said finally.

She felt the tension seep from his body, saw the lines in his face vanish. Then, before she could form another thought, he scooped her into his arms, his long strides eating up the distance to the bedroom.

Once inside, he laid her gently on the made bed, then stepped back to divest himself of clothing. Raising up on her elbows, she watched him kick off his shoes, undo his cuff links, shed his jacket, tie, shirt and slacks. He came back to her in all his naked glory, so magnificent he made her mouth go dry.

Sitting on the edge of the bed, he opened a drawer in the nightstand and removed a box of condoms, setting them on one of the pillows in easy reach. And then he turned his attention back to her, undivided, focused. The need swirling in her belly began to build and spread outward.

He traced the line of pale flesh above the scalloped cup of her black bra, never taking his eyes from hers. Leaning in, he used his teeth to nibble and bite at her bottom lip. She opened to him, wanting more, wanting everything. And he gave it to her, covering her mouth, molding their bodies together, kissing her until she was limp and gasping for air.

When they parted, Chase grabbed her by the waist and dragged her more to the center of the bed. Then he sat back and lifted her leg until the sole of her satin pump rested flat against his bare chest.

He reached past her bent knee, letting his callused palms run up and down her thigh. His fingers caught one of the garter fasteners and deftly released it. The strap, once pulled taut, snapped back, stinging the delicate flesh of her abdomen. She gave a gasp of surprise and Chase chuckled, covering the spot with his thumb and rubbing gently.

"Sorry. I'm not used to garter belts. I'll be more careful next time."

Proving he was as good as his word, he reached around to the second clip and carefully unhooked it from the stocking.

When he began to roll the silky material down, Elena almost wished he'd snapped her again. The tiny, biting pain had to be better than the slow agony he was creating now, the heaving, writhing lust monster coming to life in her belly and between her legs. It had fangs and claws and was tearing at her insides, making her shiver and moan.

And she could tell by the simmering, possessive look in his eyes that he knew exactly what he was doing to her.

"Patience," he murmured, slipping off her shoe and the

rumpled stocking, and pressing a kiss to the inside of her bare ankle.

She made a sound deep in her throat, a cross between annoyance and a whimper. Which only seemed to amuse him all the more.

He switched to her other leg, following the same process, causing perspiration to break out along her upper lip, inside her elbows, behind her knees. When he finished, he took hold of her panties and the garter belt in both fists and slid them over her hips, down the length of her legs, and off, tossing them to the floor. Next, he reached behind her and deftly undid her bra, pitching the strapless garment in the same direction as her other lingerie.

"Now, that's what I'm talking about," Chase said, sitting back to admire his handiwork.

She fought the urge to hide her nudity with her hands or reach for a corner of the bedspread, reminding herself that she'd chosen this.

And Chase Ramsey wasn't exactly the first man to see her naked. He was merely the first in a while—as well as the most handsome and masterful.

She couldn't remember another man ever making her want him with just one look, ever making her mouth water or her body vibrate so strongly with unleashed desire.

If he was doing this to get back at her for what she'd done to him in high school, then more power to him. She felt like throwing out her arms and screaming, "Take me. Use me. Make me pay." His form of revenge was her idea of pure ecstasy.

He moved to cover her body with his own, taking her mouth in a slow, bone-melting kiss. His broad chest, with its sprinkling of dark, springy hair, flattened her breasts and rubbed against her nipples. His erection, hard and hot, nudged her stomach.

Digging her nails into his slick shoulders and back, she tipped her hips, trying to get closer, urging him to slip inside, where she needed him most.

But his exercise in torture wasn't over yet. He finished with her mouth, trailing his lips along her chin, down the column of her throat, across her collarbone and the swell of her right breast.

His tongue swept across the beaded peak and she groaned, arching upward. He continued to lick, nip, suckle and drive all sensible thought from her head.

She dug her fingers into his hair, trying to tug him away even as her back bowed into his magician's touch. A whimper slipped past her lips, and she fully expected to expire on the spot. If she survived long enough to regain the use of her limbs and brain cells, she fully intended to exact a bit of her own sweet revenge.

He lifted his head and a cocky, satisfied grin spread across his face. But the smoldering heat in his eyes belied the lighter lift of his lips.

"I want to do more," he said in a tight, gravelly voice, holding her gaze. "I want to kiss you from head to toe. Taste every inch of your skin, then come back for seconds."

He crawled up a few inches until their eyes and mouths and naughty parts aligned. Threading one hand through the hair at her temple, he reached past her and grabbed the box of condoms, struggling to open it one-handed.

"I want to," he repeated, "but I can't. I don't have that much self-control."

When he had a single square packet free, he tore the end off with his teeth and spat the plastic aside. It took him less than a second to sheath himself and settle more fully between her legs, which she had wrapped loosely around his hips.

He took her mouth, speaking between wet, breath-stealing kisses. "Later, all right? I'll lick you all over later. I promise."

With one smooth, powerful motion, he was inside her, stretching her, filling her, setting her nerve endings on fire. Air hissed through his clenched teeth as he held himself perfectly still above her, the muscles in his throat roped and taut.

She knew he was waiting for her, giving her time to adjust to his invasion, the size and hardness of his impressive length.

But she didn't need time. She only needed him.

From the moment he'd entered her, everything about this encounter had felt right. And now all she wanted was for him to move, to fill her even more fully and send her flying over the abyss that hovered just out of reach.

Twining her arms around his neck to match the twist of her legs at his hips, she drew him closer. "Don't stop now," she whispered a split second before their mouths met.

He groaned, the sound vibrating against her lips, through her torso and limbs and into her soul.

His hands tightened on her waist, lifting her slightly as he pulled back. She started to whimper at the friction he created and the sudden loss of his heat, but before the noise could work its way up from her diaphragm, he thrust forward again.

Slowly, methodically, he moved in and out. Smooth motions at first, then building in speed and intensity.

Her breathing increased, her lungs contracting to absorb less and less oxygen with each breath. She raised her legs higher, gripping him about the waist, doing everything she could to pull him deeper.

It wasn't enough. He was pounding into her now, his fingers digging into the flesh of her buttocks, but still she wanted more. She wanted harder, faster, stronger... *More, more, more.*

Even as she thought it, the words tumbled from her lips. Broken and disjointed, but directly into Chase's ear.

He heard, agreed, obeyed, taking her higher and faster until she was gasping. Her body strained for him, strained for release.

And then it hit with the impact of a bullet, making her cry out and claw at his back with her nails. Her inner muscles spasmed around him, and she moaned in wonder as he took her climbing again.

The second climax was as strong as the first, rocking her to her very core. And this time, he came with her, grinding his mouth to hers as he pumped one last time, then went rigid above her.

For several long minutes, they lay there, tangled and still, their ragged breathing the only sound in the otherwise silent room. Elena couldn't move, her bones weak, her will nonexistent.

She hadn't ever experienced an orgasm even close to that in her adult life, not to mention the level of sensuality, passion, eroticism and intensity he'd shown her.

If she'd ever suspected sex with Chase Ramsey would be half as satisfying as what they'd just done, she'd have been tempted to look him up long ago...or seduce him back in high school.

She might even have to thank him for blackmailing her

into this situation, because so far, being his mistress was turning out to have some incredible perks.

With a reluctant groan, he rolled aside. The air in the room washed over her naked, damp body, making her shiver. But a second later, he'd pulled back the bedspread and was dragging her toward the headboard. He tucked her under the covers, propped a pillow beneath her head and then slipped an arm around her shoulders and hugged her close.

"Go to sleep," he whispered, pressing a kiss to the side of her head.

As pillow talk went, it was somewhat lacking, but she was too tired and too satisfied to care. Curling into him, she closed her eyes and let herself drift off, only vaguely aware of the smile stretched across her face.

Four

Elena awoke the next morning to a gentle clinking and the heavenly smell of scrambled eggs and fresh-brewed coffee. She rolled to her back, inhaling deeply and stretching her arms high above her head before forcing her eyes open.

The room was still dark, the bed so soft and warm and comfortable, she never wanted to leave it. But the scent of breakfast and sounds of someone moving around in the other room drove her to throw back the covers and sit up.

It took her a moment to realize she was stark naked, the cream-colored satin sheets soft against her bare skin. And then she remembered the events of last evening, a bright flush heating her from her toes to her hairline. She couldn't decide if she was embarrassed or sorry Chase wasn't still in bed beside her so they could once again do everything they'd done last night—and more.

Padding across the soft plush carpet, she found a robe and nightie set in one of the dresser drawers and put them on, then took a few minutes to brush her teeth and wash her face before moving to the open doorway between the bedroom and sitting room.

Chase was already dressed in a charcoal-gray suit, white shirt, and seafoam tie, his black hair neatly combed and styled. He sat at the round mahogany table arranged in front of the wide open windows, sipping hot coffee and reading the morning paper.

Running her fingers through her still sleep-tousled hair, she cleared her throat and started forward.

He lifted his head when he noticed her approach and gave her a small smile. "Morning. Did you sleep well?"

She nodded, taking the seat across from him and reaching for the coffee carafe to pour herself a cup.

"I didn't know what you'd like for breakfast, so I ordered a little of everything," he told her, reaching for the room service cart a few inches away and removing the silver lids from several platters.

There were pancakes, scrambled eggs, crisp bacon and sausage links and a wide array of fresh, seasonal fruit. It looked delicious, and she wasted no time filling her plate. She added cream and sugar to her coffee and poured a bit of syrup over her pancakes before digging in.

A second later, she lifted her head and glanced at Chase. "Aren't you eating?" she asked.

He shook his head and lifted his cup to his lips. "Coffee's all I need in the morning."

Having him watch her eat what amounted to a truckload of food while he merely sipped his black coffee made her feel like a glutton. Not that it would stop her, she thought, popping a bite of honeydew melon in her mouth.

After she swallowed, she waved her fork at him, distracting him once again from the business section of the *Las Vegas Review-Journal.*

"It's not healthy to skip breakfast, you know," she told him, breaking a slice of bacon into smaller pieces and nibbling them one at a time. "It's the most important meal of the day."

One side of his mouth lifted indulgently before he returned his attention to the paper without a word.

She ate in silence awhile longer, enjoying the sunny view out the bank of tall windows, but not her current company. Finally, she put down her fork and grabbed a second plate, filling it with small portions of the same items on her own.

"Here," she said, pushing the paper aside with a rattle and placing the plate in front of him. "You're driving me crazy. You have to eat something."

He stared at her for a long minute, brows knit in a frown. "I don't need anything to eat."

He started to open his paper again and straighten the page she'd wrinkled. With a sigh, she half-stood and took the paper from his hands. Before he could grab it back, she returned to her seat and leaned far enough away that he couldn't reach her unless he got up and came around the table.

"How about if I read the paper to you while you eat?" she offered brightly.

His frown turned into a full-blown scowl. "Elena," he murmured, lacing her name with dire warning. "I didn't bring you along to mother me or tell me what to do. I'm thirty-five years old and already set in my ways. I have a routine and I like to stick to it. Now give me back my paper."

She tipped her head. "Indulge me. Please? You've got a busy day ahead of you, and we expended quite a bit of energy last night. You need to keep your strength up or you'll be of absolutely no use to me in bed tonight."

She felt her cheeks heat at her own audacity, but forced herself not to squirm under his intense regard. He studied her for several long seconds while her insides turned to jelly.

And then he let out a bark of laughter and picked up his fork.

"Fine," he said. "You read, I'll eat. And don't worry," he added with a pointed, just-shy-of-boiling glance, "I'll have plenty of energy for anything you might have in mind tonight."

Opening the paper to hide any more bright color that might suffuse her face, she swallowed hard and began reading where she thought he'd left off. The information was boring enough to counteract the caffeine already coursing through her bloodstream, but she didn't stop until she'd reached the last page. She even recapped the comics for him one by one.

When she was finished, she folded the paper and set it aside, delighted to see that he'd cleaned his plate and even poured himself a small glass of orange juice.

"I've changed my mind," he said. "From now on, I'm going to have a huge, four-course breakfast…and I'll leave the reading of the morning paper to you. Aloud, and in that amazingly sultry voice of yours."

Sultry? She'd never thought of her voice as sultry before. A little low and raspy at times, but never sultry.

"You have a touch of your father's accent, did you know that? Like a hint of Mexico just beneath the Texas twang."

Considering his own Texas drawl was as thick, if not thicker, than her own, she didn't think he had much room to talk. But still, the compliment—and she did take it as a compliment—washed over her, warming her from the inside out.

"Maybe you could read to me again tonight," he continued. "In bed. Something sexy and a little naughty."

Nerves jangled in her stomach, unexpected desire skating down her spine like an Olympic hopeful going for the gold.

"Do you have any sexy or naughty reading material?" she asked, surprised when the words came out strong and surprisingly sensual. For the first time, she heard the sultriness he'd spoken of, as well as an unspoken, almost unintentional invitation.

And from the look in his eyes, she knew he heard it, too.

"Not here," he said, his voice tight and graveled with lust. "But I'll find something by this evening even if I have to buy up every book and magazine publisher on the West Coast."

He held her gaze and it was all she could do not to wiggle in her seat, both from nerves and a growing sense of longing. How he could have such an effect on her after such a short amount of time, she didn't know. But it was there, strong and powerful and alive.

"Unfortunately," he went on, dragging his gaze away from her to check his watch, his voice returning to normal, "I have to get going or I'll be late for my first meeting."

Pushing his chair away from the table, he stood and dug
out his billfold. "I'll be busy pretty much all day, so I'm afraid
you'll have to find something to keep yourself occupied.
Here, take these." He handed her a gold card and a stack of
crisp bills in large denominations. "Go shopping, do lunch,
have fun. I'll see you back here around four. We have another
business dinner I'll want you to be ready for, all right?"

She took the cash and credit card, even though she
didn't like it. Being handed money to "keep herself
occupied" made her feel cheap, entirely too much like a
paid companion. But then, she supposed that was just part
of the job when one agreed to become a man's mistress.

Throwing back the last swallows of his coffee, he crossed
the room for his briefcase, then headed for the door. With
his hand on the knob, he tossed an already distracted "See
you later" over his shoulder before disappearing into the hall.

The door clicked closed behind him, leaving Elena
alone in the sprawling suite. She glanced down at the wad
of bills in one hand and the credit card in the other.

Well, that had gone from interesting to disappointing
in the blink of an eye, she thought. But this wasn't a
vacation; it was a work week for Chase, and the fulfillment
of a business agreement for her.

So she would find something to fill her day like a good
mistress, and be back in time to get ready for her next
dinner performance.

Where the hell was she?

Chase stood in front of the bedroom bureau, straightening his tie in the mirror for what had to be the fifth or
sixth time.

He was showered, dressed and ready for the dinner meeting. The only thing missing was his date.

He glanced at his watch again, even though only a minute had passed since the last time he'd checked, and muttered a colorful oath.

She was almost an hour late. He'd told her to be back in the room by four o'clock, and here it was going on five.

She was probably busy burning up his credit card with dozens of clothes, shoes and expensive trinket purchases. What more could he expect of a spoiled, selfish debutante like Elena Sanchez?

The problem was, she hadn't acted spoiled or selfish since meeting him at the airport. He hadn't even seen any signs of the shallow girl she used to be—her bossiness at breakfast that morning notwithstanding.

He'd actually found her strong-arm tactics during that little incident amusing…followed by highly erotic when she'd agreed to use that husky, arousing voice of hers to read to him in bed.

Of course, now he knew the last day and a half was more of a fluke than anything else. He'd given her his gold card and a stack of cash in fairly large bills, and she'd apparently found a way to blow through it all. Enough so that she was still busy shopping.

Which didn't surprise him in the least. Truth be known, he'd given her such a long lead line to prove—to himself, if no one else—exactly what he knew deep down in his bones. Elena Sanchez hadn't changed. She was still indulgent, self-involved, too beautiful for her own good, and she put her own comforts and desires above the feelings or well-being of others.

The pointed reminder was worth paying a few thousand dollars to his credit card company.

But if she didn't get back soon, if she made him late for this very important business dinner, he would not only make her pay the charge bill herself, but he'd put her on the first plane back to Gabriel's Crossing and have her father's company bought out and in his portfolio by morning.

He swore again and was just turning his wrist to check his watch for the ten millionth time when he heard the door to the suite click open.

"Finally," he breathed, following that by another grumbled curse.

"Where the hell have you been?" he charged, turning on his heel and marching into the other room.

He expected to find her grinning from ear to ear, her hands full of boutique bags, her arms piled high with ribboned boxes. She'd probably want to show him everything he'd bought her, maybe model some designer dresses and sexy new lingerie.

He might even be willing to sit through a lingerie fashion show…later, after they got back from dinner and he wasn't in such a foul mood.

"Sorry," she apologized, rounding the corner of the kitchenette.

She looked rumpled and windblown, her simple, sleeveless cotton blouse and denim skirt wrinkled, her hair starting to fall out of its now-crooked ponytail. Her face and shoulders rosy from the glaring Las Vegas sun.

As far as he could see, there wasn't a single bag or box anywhere near her.

He paused in mid-step, momentarily confused.

Maybe she was having everything delivered. But just to be sure, he walked the rest of the way across the room and glanced toward the door.

Nothing.

She didn't look overly happy or bubbly or excited, either, the way most women would after what amounted to a carte blanche shopping spree.

"You're late," he pointed out, uncomfortable with the knowledge that she'd knocked him off his guard, managed to sidetrack him from his focus on her whereabouts and their dinner schedule.

"I said I was sorry," she told him, not the least intimidated by his accusatory tone or thunderous expression. "But I won't take long to get ready, I promise."

Pulling the ponytail holder from her hair, she started for the bedroom, already unbuttoning her blouse. "I'll only be twenty minutes."

She left the connecting doors open and he could hear her moving around. Shedding clothes. Opening dresser drawers and closet doors. Stepping into the bathroom, out, then in again. The bathroom door closed and he heard the shower turn on.

Regardless of what she said, he fully expected her to take at least an hour to change and do her hair and makeup. He didn't know any woman who wouldn't.

A quick glance at his watch showed that if she took an hour—an hour, and not one minute more—they could still make it down to the hotel restaurant on time. Barely, but they would make it.

Strolling into the bedroom, he moved to the dresser where he'd abandoned his cufflinks when he'd heard her come in, trying not to imagine Elena's wet, soapy, naked body in the generous shower stall. A space large enough to fit two comfortably…in any number of creative positions.

Clearing his throat, he turned his attention back to attaching the gold and diamond studs at his wrists. Just because he was annoyed at her tardiness didn't mean he didn't still want her. If they weren't already running late, he'd leave a trail of clothing behind on the walk to the bathroom and join her for a long, enjoyable steam— among other things.

Afraid that he would give in to temptation if he stayed this close to her for much longer, he turned. As it was, he ran the risk of spending the rest of the evening trying to hide an embarrassing arousal.

But before he went a step, his gaze caught on two items on the dresser top. His credit card and the pile of cash he'd handed Elena earlier.

Ignoring the card, he picked up the bills and counted them out. Only twenty-odd dollars missing, from the hundreds he'd given her.

Well, that wasn't so surprising, he decided. She'd probably charged just about everything all day. The cash could have been used solely for tips or some such.

In the bathroom, the water shut off and he quickly replaced the cash beside the card. He didn't want her to know he'd fanned through it. And since he would probably have supplied her with the same again tomorrow, he might as well leave them where she'd put them.

But just out of curiosity…

He quickly glanced at the phone number on the back of the credit card, memorizing it, then slipping quietly from the room before she emerged from the bathroom. Closing the door silently behind him, he crossed to the phone on the desk in the far corner.

It took a few minutes to get through to an operator and verify his identity, then a second more to make his request and wait for the answer. Had there been any charges on his account today, and if so, how much did it total?

He thanked the woman on the other end of the line and returned the handset to its cradle, a deep frown marring his brow and tugging his mouth down at the sides.

Zero. Zero charges. His balance was the same as it had been before, and the last purchase was one he'd made himself.

Now he was even more confused than before. She'd been gone all day, on his dime, presumably shopping, yet hadn't spent more than thirty dollars.

He didn't know any woman who could shop all day and only spend thirty bucks.

So if she hadn't been shopping, where had she been and what had she been up to?

Before he could devise a list of possibilities, the bedroom door opened and she stepped out, looking like every man's fantasy come to life. Her hair was swept up into an artful twist. Her long black gown glittered with silver in the lamplight. A slit ran from her ankles to very high on her thigh, and the front was cut low, fastening around her neck with a single strap, leaving the front of her neck, shoulders and back bare.

She wore minimal jewelry—a couple of rings, a pair of silver string earrings and a small charm on a thin silver necklace that matched the bracelet on her wrist—and three-inch spike heels that caused his blood to thicken and slog through his veins.

"Twenty minutes, as promised," she said, making a small pirouette where she stood.

The gown showed off her womanly shape as though she were naked, and he suddenly wanted to keep her inside the room with him rather than take her out, so no one else could see her.

"What do you think?"

He thought way too many things, none of them suitable for delicate ears or pre-dinner conversation. After dinner, though…that was a whole different story.

"Good. Good. You look good." His tongue felt like an old gym sock in his mouth, and even though he knew he wasn't making much sense, he was content to be able to form words at all. The synapse in his brain was barely firing, cells washing away to join all the others in his body south of the equator.

To buy a few much-needed moments to recover his senses, he cleared his throat and checked his watch. She was right; she'd only taken a little over twenty minutes to get ready, from the time she'd disappeared into the bedroom…twenty-five counting the time he'd wasted standing there feeling speechless and steamrolled.

"Okay. Well, then…" He tugged at his cuffs, straightened his tie and somehow managed to step forward, offering his arm. "Are we ready to go?"

She nodded, meeting him halfway. He noticed the shawl in her other hand and took it from her, draping the long-fringed lace around her shoulders.

"You look amazing," he said, perhaps belatedly.

"Thank you."

He pulled open the door, holding it until she'd passed into the hall, then hooked her arm around his elbow again and guided her to the elevator. Their reflection shimmered back at them in the polished golden doors, and he couldn't help noticing how good she looked standing beside him. Tall, glamorous, gorgeous.

He'd known she was beautiful when he'd suggested this arrangement—a man would have to be blind not to, and even then, any man worth his salt would have a pretty good idea of her charms just from her voice and the way she handled herself.

He'd also known she would make a good impression on his associates. She was funny and charismatic and knew when to put in a few words or hold her tongue while business was being discussed. And there was no arguing she was easy on the eyes.

What he hadn't counted on was the force of his attraction to her.

Beautiful women were nothing new to Chase Ramsey. He was wealthy, a self-made multimillionaire, which happened to be an attribute that a lot of women apparently found irresistible.

And he'd enjoyed his fair share of them. Some might say he used them, asking them out only when he needed a date for one event or another, and then taking them to bed—a place they were always more than willing to go.

But the way he saw it, any using was mutual. They wanted to be with him because he had money, wanted to be seen with him because of his power and prestige.

And most of them, whether they were blatant about it

or not, harbored hopes of finagling a wedding ring out of him and snagging themselves a rich husband.

Elena, however, was in an entirely different category.

She didn't seem impressed by his wealth at all. Yes, her family had money of their own, but so did the families of a lot of women he dated. That never kept them from wheedling for or accepting expensive gifts. Permission to use his credit card for the day would have had most of them squealing like a litter of hungry piglets.

She didn't take forever in the bathroom or fuss obsessively over her appearance, and once she was ready, she was ready. She carried herself with confidence and seemed comfortable with whatever she was wearing instead of fidgeting with every little thing.

It was that confidence, her silent assurance, that turned him on almost as much as her shapely body and passionate nature.

Aside from that, he also found her simply fascinating. She never did what he expected, never reacted to things quite the way he thought she would.

And she hadn't charged a single damn thing to his credit card, which he had to admit was driving him positively crazy. He wanted to know where she'd been all day, what she'd been up to.

He *needed* to know.

"So," he murmured as the elevator doors whooshed open and they stepped inside the plush compartment. "What did you do today?"

Five

Elena raised the back of her hand to her mouth to stifle a yawn. It had been a long day, and she was suddenly feeling every minute of it. The two Manhattans she'd sipped through dinner probably hadn't helped, either.

"Sleepy?" Chase asked, brushing a loose tendril of hair away from her face.

She offered a small smile and leaned into his touch as the same elevator that had taken them down to the lobby a few hours before now took them back up to their floor.

It was amazing how comfortable she felt with him after such a short time, and it worried her. She'd expected their relationship to be cold, businesslike. Intimate, but functional.

Instead, things between them had been warm and friendly. She liked it, and that bothered her most—that she liked it maybe a bit too much.

"I'm a little tired," she answered.

His hand slid from the lobe of her ear to the nape of her neck, where he gently kneaded the taut muscles with his calloused fingertips.

"You must have had a busy day."

It wasn't the first time he'd tried to find out how she'd spent the afternoon. But so far, she'd avoided giving him a straight answer. It wasn't that her activities were that much of a secret, just that she didn't feel like sharing.

He'd handed her a wad of cash and a credit card, and basically told her to keep herself occupied while he worked. Well, she had—without spending more than twenty-five or thirty dollars of his money, either. Since she hadn't let him foot the bill for more than a short cab ride and a salad for lunch, it was no one's business but her own how she'd stayed busy.

When it became apparent she wasn't going to answer, he went on.

"When we get back to the room, I'll help you slip out of these clothes, then turn down the covers and we'll crawl into bed."

"Just to sleep?" she teased.

"Just to sleep," he assured her. And then his lips curved and a devilish glint sparkled in his blue eyes. "Unless you're interested in something else."

A slow heat began to unfurl low in her belly. That was another thing she found surprising about this situation…that making love with him didn't feel like a chore she had to subject herself to in order to help her father save his company. She *liked* being with him, and was already looking forward to spending the night in his arms. Just the thought made warmth pour through her system and put her nerve endings on red alert.

"What did you have in mind?" she asked as the elevator doors opened and they stepped into the hallway, any drowsiness quickly morphing into arousal and anticipation.

"Oh, I don't know," he drawled, his arm twined with hers as they strolled slowly toward their suite. "We didn't have dessert with dinner so maybe we should order something sweet from room service."

They stopped in front of their door and he fitted the key card into the lock, waiting for the light to flash green.

"Strawberries and champagne?" he suggested, holding the door open for her. "I could nibble juice from your chin and trickle champagne into your navel. Or hot fudge sundaes. I understand chocolate sauce tastes even better licked off a beautiful woman's naked flesh."

If she hadn't been turned on before, the mental images he was creating certainly aroused her. She shivered as she thought of his tongue scraping along her skin, of chocolate and ice cream mixing with passion in her mouth as he kissed her after cleaning them from her body.

"So what will it be?" he asked when she was halfway across the room. "Dessert or straight to bed?"

His voice sounded farther away than she'd expected, and she turned to find him leaning against the wall, just a few steps past the closed and locked door. His arms were crossed over his chest, one leg cocked over the other at the ankle.

One glimpse of him standing there, looking so casually relaxed yet so intensely masculine, and she knew there was no way she'd be sleeping tonight. At least not anytime soon.

But that didn't mean she couldn't have a little fun with him first.

"I'd like to go straight to bed," she said, feigning a yawn that a few minutes ago would have been real. Reaching up to remove the pins from her hair, she watched the air of confidence seep from his expression, the cockiness disappear from the firm set of his stance. His reaction amused her, but she didn't tease him for long.

Shaking her head and letting the long strands of her hair fall to the middle of her back, she added, "With the strawberries, champagne *and* a hot fudge sundae. With nuts on top, please."

She turned on her heel and sashayed toward the bedroom, but not before she saw the wide, positively predatory grin that spread across his face. It wouldn't have surprised her if he'd pushed away from the wall and sprung on her like some sleek jungle beast. A part of her even wished he'd do just that.

They would fall to the floor right where she was standing in a tangle of limbs, his heavy frame pinning her down. Clothes would be torn off, tossed away or left in tatters. Mouths and hands would be everywhere. They would come together fast, hot, frantically, the carpet leaving them scraped and raw.

And it would all be worth it.

She almost whimpered at the very idea, moist heat pooling between her legs, making her weak in the knees. She bit her lip, wondering what she might do to make it happen.

But in the end, she couldn't think of anything that felt right. She wasn't used to seducing handsome men, let alone devising a plan to get one to attack her.

So she settled for simply lifting her hands to the back of her neck and unhooking the single strap of her dress. The two pieces of material fell, an arm across her breasts the only thing keeping her from being completely bare.

"You will bring everything into the bedroom when it gets here, won't you?" she asked as seductively as she could manage. Then, without waiting for an answer, she stepped into the other room and closed the door behind her.

Her heart was beating a mile a minute. She'd never done anything like that before—taunted a man, tried to work him into a lather and lure him into bed.

And now she would have to deliver. At the speed of light, she raced around the room, undressing. She kicked her shoes off so they each flew in different directions. Her dress fell to the floor and she opened the closet door to kick it inside. It was no way to treat an obscenely expensive designer gown, but at the moment she couldn't care less.

Hopping from foot to foot, she made her way to the bathroom while working to undo her garter belt and roll off her black stockings. She left them in a ball on the floor, along with her matching black panties.

Naked, she stood at the sink, in front of the huge wall-to-wall mirror, and quickly brushed her teeth, washed her face, ran a comb through her hair. She reapplied a dab of perfume behind each ear and at the pulse points of her wrists, then hurried back to the bed.

Sweeping back the covers, she leaped onto the ivory satin sheets, plumped a couple pillows behind her back and tried to adopt a sexy, alluring pose. Marilyn Monroe, Jane Russell, Anna Nicole Smith…she thought of every pinup girl she could remember and tried to channel their spirits.

She pulled the sheet up to her waist, then over her breasts, then threw it off again. Bent her legs to the left, then the right. Threw an arm over her head, then scooted down and laid spread-eagle across the bed like the smorgasbord she hoped he would use her as.

When she heard the rattle of the doorknob, she startled, swallowed a panicked squeak and froze in the best position she could come up with at the last minute. She let the muscles in her face go lax and half-closed her eyes, hoping he wouldn't notice she was a nervous wreck. She wanted him to think she'd just been lounging on the bed, waiting for him to serve her.

The bedroom door opened and he strolled in, dragging a room service cart behind him. This time it held a bowl of strawberries, a magnum of champagne on ice, two glasses and a very large, decadent, already melting ice cream sundae.

Normally, her stomach would have rumbled at such delicious-looking fare. But at the moment, it was her other four senses and her raging libido that were starving for attention.

Chase turned, his gaze soaking her in, slowly skimming from head to toe. From the hardening of his jaw and the steam rising behind his sea-blue eyes, she thought he must like what he saw.

A thrill rolled through her and she sat up straight, careful to act sleepy and nonchalant.

"Mmm," she murmured. "It looks good."

"Yes," he said slowly, still staring intently at her. "It does."

After a few tense seconds when she thought he might forget the food altogether and simply lunge at her, he picked up the bottle of Roederer Cristal, dried the bottom with a cloth napkin and popped the cork. He poured the champagne into both flutes, then handed one to her, followed by the bowl of strawberries.

She took a plump, bright red berry and bit into the tip before taking a sip of champagne.

"Good?" he asked, sampling a piece of fruit on his own.

"Delicious."

Taking a long swallow of champagne, he set his glass and the bowl of strawberries aside and began shrugging out of his clothes. Suit jacket, tie, shoes…they all evaporated as though they were made of smoke.

As naked as she, he turned back to the wheeled cart, grabbed the dripping sundae and a spoon and climbed onto the wide mattress beside her.

"*This* is what I'm hungry for," he said.

He lowered her gently until she fell back against the pillows. Before she'd even had a chance to get comfortable or wonder what he might do next, he dropped a dollop of whipped cream right in the center of her belly button.

She gave a little yelp and nearly came up off the bed, her first instinct to get the chilly substance off her bare skin. But the clicking of his tongue and the shimmering heat in his glance reminded her of the game they were playing.

Taking a deep breath, she relaxed her body and sank farther into the pillows and glossy sheets, ready to let him do what he wished with his sweet, sticky dessert and her naked, vulnerable body.

He grinned, flashing straight white teeth at her capitulation and digging once again into the sundae.

It took all of her control, all of her concentration not to squirm and shiver as he decorated her nipples, left dribbles of hot fudge sauce along her chest, midsection and inner thighs. Plucking the bright red maraschino cherry off the top by its stem, he placed it on top of the whipped cream on her navel.

"There," he announced, setting the remainder of the sundae on the nightstand and sitting back to admire his handiwork. "Perfect."

She chuckled, a brittle, throaty sound working its way up from her diaphragm. A trickle of vanilla ice cream was melting between her tightly closed legs, heading in a direction where she wanted only warmth—preferably created by Chase. "It's cold."

"Hmm," he hummed, shifting closer. "Let me see what I can do to heat things up."

His low tone and the determined look in his eyes sent a ripple of anticipation skating down her spine, taking precedence over the goose bumps breaking out along her skin.

He leaned in, covering a smear of chocolate with his tongue, then dragging upward to the underside of her breast. The action caused her nipples to bead beneath the fluffy white clouds he'd deposited there.

She writhed beneath him, her back arching, her arms lifting automatically to reach for him.

"Ah, ah, ah," he warned without moving his lips from her skin. The words vibrated through her. "No touching from you. Not yet."

His hands closed around her wrists, pushing her arms up over her head. "Lie back and enjoy."

Easier said than done, she thought. At the moment, his idea of enjoyment bordered on torment—and he was just getting started.

He licked the whipped cream crowning one breast, tiny flickers like a cat lapping at a bowl of milk, until her nipple was bare.

Elena bit down hard on her bottom lip to keep from crying out as he switched to her other breast. This time he gave a low growl and engulfed the tip all at once. No small nibbles to draw out the agony, but that didn't make the pleasure any less sharp.

Her hands clutched the pillow behind her head, her heels dug into the mattress. Already, her inner muscles were tightening, begging for release. "Chase, please."

"Soon," he whispered, kissing his way back down her stomach, picking up stray hot fudge as he went. "Very soon."

He slurped the whipped topping from her belly button, working around the cherry, leaving it to fill the indent of her navel. Sliding down, hands skimming her hips, he parted her thighs and began to nuzzle ice cream from between them.

But he didn't stop there. Even though she was sure the ice cream hadn't dripped any deeper, he lifted her legs to his shoulders and began to explore. He nibbled, licked, stroked her moist folds until she couldn't help but clutch at his hair—to pull him away or hold him close, she didn't know.

When he concentrated his efforts on the hidden bud of her desire, her blood pressure skyrocketed and she climaxed against his mouth almost without warning. Tremors racked her body and she gasped for breath, arms falling to her sides as her bones and muscles turned the consistency of watery oatmeal.

With a feral grin, Chase raised his head and lifted himself on all fours to hover over her. He started to crawl forward, pausing only long enough to close his teeth on the stem of the cherry in her navel and carry it with him to her mouth. Her lips were already parted, her lungs still straining for oxygen.

"No. No more," she panted, letting her eyes fall closed. "I can't take any more."

"Sure you can." His words were slightly muted as he talked through his teeth, still holding the cherry by its stem. "Open."

With a sigh that was part exhaustion, part reluctant anticipation, she opened her mouth and let him drop the cherry inside.

"Now close."

She did, and he tugged, breaking the stem away from the plump, sweet fruit.

"Chew," he ordered.

Maraschino cherries were one of her favorites and she gave a little moan of enjoyment as the tart juices played over her taste buds and ran down her throat.

In a much softer, huskier voice, Chase said, "Now open again."

When she did, he meshed his mouth with hers, kissing her deeply, passionately, thoroughly. To her great surprise she found her strength coming back and her arms snaking up to wrap around his shoulders.

He pulled back slightly, his lips curled up at the corners as he hummed with pleasure. "That is the best hot fudge sundae I've ever tasted. I never want to eat one with just a spoon again."

Elena gave a shuddery chuckle. She didn't know if she could live through another session like that, but she was absolutely sure she would never see sundaes in quite the same way. She would never be able to look at one without remembering this night and the wicked things Chase Ramsey could do with a bit of whipped cream, chocolate sauce and his tongue.

Oh, that tongue!

"But we aren't finished yet," he said.

Scraping his teeth along her jaw and biting her earlobe, he reached into the nightstand drawer for a condom. He tore open the packet and sheathed himself, all without taking his focus from her neck and shoulder. Settling more fully into the cradle of her thighs, he found her feminine opening and sank inside in one long, sleek movement.

She was already wet and more than ready for his entry. Only moments ago, she'd thought herself ruined for ever again experiencing an ounce of pleasure. But she'd underestimated the power of Chase's mode of persuasion.

He was ruthless, taking no prisoners. There was no slow buildup this time around, no teasing or tantalizing. He filled her to overflowing and began to pound into her like a piston.

His fingers dug into the flesh of her buttocks, pulling her closer to meet him on each thrust.

Harder, faster, he drove the air from her lungs, his own breaths coming rapidly. She tightened her legs around his waist, her nails raking his sweat-slick back.

"Chase," she moaned.

"Elena," he groaned in return before burying his face in the curve of her neck and biting gently on the taut line of muscle that ran across to her shoulder.

The orgasm, when it came, rocked her, made the room feel like it was spinning around them and spilled through her like a tidal wave. She gasped…then stopped breathing altogether. Above her, Chase gave one deep, final thrust and shouted with completion.

A second later, he collapsed, his weight pressing her into the mattress. Instead of being uncomfortable, she smiled at the boneless, total relaxation taking over his body. She could feel his heart racing in his chest, in tandem with her own, his breath stirring her hair.

Sooner than she'd have liked, he groaned and rolled away. He lay flat on his back, arms and legs spread wide, while he continued to breathe heavily.

"You'll be the death of me, Elena," he said with a heartfelt sigh, rolling his head to the side so he could look at her. He grinned. "But I'll die a happy man."

Before she could respond, he pushed up from the bed and walked stark naked to the bathroom, closing the door behind him. Suddenly conscious of her blatant nudity and the fact that she was sprawled like a rag doll in a less-than-attractive position, she hopped up and hurried to the dresser for a nightgown.

Slipping it on, she glanced at her reflection in the mirror. Her cheeks were rosy, the rest of her skin aglow. Her lips looked puffy, reminding her of that old term, "bee-stung."

She'd never had bee-stung lips before. But then, she'd never been kissed quite as senseless, quite as passionately before, either.

Since her hair was a tousled mess, she ran her fingers through to untangle the long strands, turning just as the bathroom door opened. Chase stood there, still blessedly naked, his hands braced on either side of the doorjamb. Just the sight of him made her pulse pick up and the slippery fabric of the nightie feel rough against her bare skin.

"You didn't have to get dressed on my account," he quipped.

She smiled somewhat nervously, curling her painted toes into the soft, thick carpeting. "I'm not used to lying around in the altogether."

"Too bad," he said, striding forward and stopping directly in front of her. Using the knuckle of his index finger, he tipped her head up until she had no choice but to meet his crystal blue eyes. "That's something I'd pay money to see. Besides, we weren't entirely finished with our dessert. We still have champagne and quite a few strawberries to get through."

"Well…" she said slowly, butterflies flapping sensuously in her belly, her courage growing in direct proportion to the longing heating up his gaze. Hooking her thumbs under the thin spaghetti straps at her shoulders, she slowly began to peel them down her arms. "It's just a teeny, tiny scrap of satin. You could get it off again in no time, if you really wanted to."

Desire flashed across his face, followed by the wicked lift of one dark brow. "Really?"

He replaced her thumbs with his own fingers and finished the job of sliding the top of the nightgown down, uncovering her chest, then her breasts and ribcage. As soon as the straps were free of her arms, he released them, letting the garment drop to the floor where it pooled around her feet.

"Well, will you look at that," he murmured in mock astonishment. "You're naked again. Just the way I like you."

She squealed in surprise when he wrapped his hands around her waist and bent slightly to lift her onto one shoulder.

"Chase! What are you doing?"

"Turning caveman," he responded without apology.

Stalking to the bed, he flipped her over and dropped her unceremoniously in the middle of the king-size mattress. She bounced on the tight springs and giggled as she couldn't remember doing since she was a little girl.

Taking two steps to the side, Chase grabbed the bottle of Cristal by its long neck and then hopped on top of her, pinning her in place.

"This time," he said, his tone leaving no question of his intent, "I want to see how champagne tastes when I sip it from your belly button."

"All right," she agreed, stretching out, ready to once again be a part of this man's dessert. "As long as I can do the same to you."

Six

The next morning Chase got up even earlier than usual, slipping out of the bedroom while Elena was still asleep. He closed the connecting doors so nothing he said would be overheard, then set about rescheduling his appointments for the day. It wasn't an easy task, considering most of the meetings had been set up weeks in advance and it was earlier than most of his associates' offices opened.

But by the time Elena made an appearance—once again wearing the short, sexy green nightie and matching robe that accentuated the emerald of her eyes—his day was clear and he was ready to put his plan into motion.

Although he was chomping at the bit to get going, he tried his best to act normal. He sipped his coffee and read the paper. When she pressed him to eat breakfast, he grumbled, but managed to down a couple of sausage patties and half of the western omelet she transferred from her plate to his.

An hour later, he rose from the table and repeated his speech from the day before, telling her he would be busy until dinnertime and that she should go out and have fun, at his expense. He handed her the same gold card and pile of cash she'd left on the dresser yesterday.

Out in the hall, he took the elevator to the lobby, but instead of leaving the hotel the way he normally would, he found a spot behind a bank of slot machines where he could keep an eye on the entrance without being seen.

He waited longer than he'd expected, checking his watch every few minutes. It took more than an hour for Elena to finally step off the elevator and head for the revolving doors leading outside.

She wore brown chunky heels, loose linen slacks the color of sunflowers and a form-fitting top with renaissance sleeves. Dark-tinted sunglasses were perched atop her head, and she carried a good size tan tote on one shoulder.

Hopping up from his stool, Chase followed her, staying a fair distance behind so she wouldn't spot him. She stopped on the sidewalk, pulling the sunglasses down to shade her eyes from the bright mid-morning sun as she glanced in both directions, then started walking.

It seemed to Chase that they strolled down the street for an awfully long time. The sidewalks were already crowded, tourists flooding in and out of casinos and storefronts. Perspiration beaded his brow and pooled inside his thousand-dollar designer suit.

He was no stranger to working up a sweat, having

grown up on a working ranch in Texas, where it could get just as hot as Nevada. Even though he'd chosen a different path and had more money than Croesus, he still enjoyed spending the day helping his parents or brother on their connecting properties. Currying horses, shucking hay, fixing fences… He just didn't usually do any of those things in a fine Italian suit that cost more than his brother's favorite saddle.

If Elena didn't get to where she was going soon, he was going to give up and flag down a taxi to take him back to the Wynn.

Almost as soon as he thought it, she turned into a storefront. He stayed outside, trying to catch a glimpse of her through the giant plate glass windows.

So she was shopping, after all, he thought. The confusing part was that it wasn't a fancy boutique, didn't carry shoes or jewelry or designer clothes. It was a candy and toy store, full of fun, colorful products that would have had any child squealing with joy.

Elena strolled up and down the aisles, studying the bins of candy and chocolate, the racks of water pistols, action figures and plastic princess jewelry. When a clerk came up to her, she smiled and started pointing at certain items, nodding when the woman seemed to understand what she was interested in.

What the heck was she doing? Chase wondered. He adjusted his own sunglasses and tried to get a better look without being tagged as a stalker.

He watched as she stacked toys on the checkout counter, the other woman filling bags with assorted candies at Elena's instruction. By the time they finished, her pile would have put Willy Wonka and his legendary Chocolate Factory to shame.

The clerk scanned everything, rang up the total and Elena handed over a credit card. But it wasn't a gold one, so it obviously wasn't his.

Rather than take plastic bags with the store's logo on them, she put everything into her own tan tote, thanked the woman behind the counter with a wave and headed back toward the street.

Chase whipped around and hurried to the storefront right next door. This time, she flagged down a cab, and he suffered a moment of panic worrying he might lose her. Then, when he caught a taxi of his own, he felt like the headliner of a bad action movie, ordering the driver, "Follow that car!" The hundred-dollar bill Chase flashed kept the driver from commenting or looking at him as though he had a few screws loose.

Several minutes later, they pulled up in front of a large gray brick building surrounded by a tall chain-link fence. Chase watched from half a block away as Elena got out of her cab and slipped through the closed gate. He asked his driver to wait, then hurried along to see just what she was up to.

He didn't have to go far. She hadn't actually gone into the building after passing through the gate, but was seated on the bench seat of a red plastic picnic table at the edge of what looked like a school's play yard.

Staying back, he watched kids of all ages crowding around her, and she was smiling and laughing, making a point of reaching out to touch each one on the head, the cheek, the arm.

Something lurched deep in his gut at the sight of her looking so happy. She was talking, teasing, her hands moving a mile a minute, then reaching into her bag for the things she'd bought at the store.

It took him a moment to realize the children weren't as noisy as he would have expected, and that Elena's animated hand motions weren't simply a side effect of her exuberant mood.

She was speaking in sign language. The children bustling around her couldn't hear. Chase looked around and his eyes lit on the sign on the front of the building that labeled it a school for the deaf. Yet Elena was interacting with them as easily as she would anyone else... perhaps better.

Oh, no, he didn't want to see this. Didn't even want to know about it.

He spun around, glancing at the taxi waiting for him at the curb, then turned back.

The kids loved her, loved the goodies she'd brought them, loved the attention.

And he hated it, because the entire situation was living, breathing proof that Elena wasn't the same shallow, vapid girl he'd known nearly twenty years ago.

His mind in turmoil, he whirled around again and stormed to the cab, ordering the driver to take him back to the hotel. He fumed the whole way, stopping just short of ranting to himself and removing any doubt from the cabbie's mind that he was a few quarters short of a roll.

He didn't want to deal with any of this, didn't want to see Elena as a sweet, thoughtful woman who knew sign language and would choose to spend her days in Las

Vegas entertaining a group of differently-abled children rather than shopping and running up his credit card bill.

Had he ever met another woman who would do the same? His mother and sister-in-law, maybe, but they didn't count.

What was he going to say to Elena when she got back tonight? He didn't think he could look at her the same as he had that morning. Or touch her without remembering the sight of her with those children.

Because Chase had been so upset the day before when she'd returned a little late from her outing, Elena made a point of getting back early this time. She was hot and sticky and looking forward to taking a quick shower before she needed to start getting ready for dinner.

To her surprise, the suite was empty when she got there. She'd expected to find Chase at the desk, clacking away at his laptop, or in the bedroom getting dressed. Instead, as she checked each room and even called for him, he was nowhere to be found. And he hadn't left a note to let her know where he was or when he'd be back…at least none she could find.

Well, maybe he was still working or one of his appointments had run long.

She dropped her tote in a corner, left her sunglasses on the narrow kitchenette countertop and headed for the bathroom.

Half an hour later, she emerged fresh and clean, with one towel wrapped around her wet hair and another tucked above her breasts. She was humming, off in her own little world, and didn't realize Chase was in the room until she glanced up and saw him standing on the other side of the wide, neatly made bed.

She jumped, pressing a hand to her heart. "Good Lord, you scared me," she said with a light laugh.

A little thrill went through her at the sight of him. He looked more handsome than any man had a right to be in his navy suit, his dark hair smoothly styled, a splash of color spilling down his chest from his tie. She was even getting used to his intense blue eyes and unsmiling mouth.

"You should have knocked on the bathroom door or given a yell when you got back so I'd know you were here." Moving to the dresser, she started opening and closing drawers, pulling out an assortment of under-clothes. "I won't be long. I was just about to get ready."

"Don't bother."

His words, as well as the coldness in his tone, gave her pause. She stopped what she was doing, a pair of dia-phanous black, French-cut panties dangling from her fingertips.

"Excuse me?" she said, telling herself not to let her imagination run away with her.

Chase Ramsey wasn't exactly the warmest person she'd ever met—he might have had a bad meeting and was taking his lousy mood out on her.

"We have another dinner tonight, right? Don't you want me to dress to the nines and impress all your business associates?" She grinned and twitched her hips seductively.

His expression didn't change. He still looked like he was contemplating something particularly unsavory.

"*I* have a dinner meeting," he finally replied, his voice like a splash of ice water on her already wet and chilled body. "Your presence isn't required."

He rounded the bed, leaving enough space for a tractor trailer to park between them as he passed. "I'll be back in a few hours."

She stood where she was, stunned by his announcement and abrupt departure. From the other room, she heard the door of the suite open and then slam shut, and knew she was alone.

Why in heaven's name would Chase suddenly decide that he didn't need her with him, when that was his sole reason for blackmailing her and bringing her along?

And what was with his attitude? He could be a hard man, distant and cruel at times. At least with her; she didn't know how he acted with his family or friends. But she also knew why he treated her that way, and that—in his mind—she deserved it.

But lately, since they'd been here in Las Vegas, sharing this enormous, lavish suite, he'd been different. She'd thought that he was beginning to soften toward her, that they were beginning to connect.

And, she admitted, she'd begun to develop feelings for him.

She wouldn't go so far as to say she was in love with him, since she wasn't sure it was possible to be in love with a man whose mind was set on revenge against her. But she had started to be kind of glad he'd manipulated her into becoming his lover. She doubted they ever would have gotten together otherwise, and now that she'd spent so much time alone with him, she realized she wouldn't be opposed to a relationship with him.

Chase apparently had other ideas. From the way he'd treated her just now, it seemed he not only didn't want her to accompany him to dinner, but might not want her around anymore at all.

Swallowing hard, she let the barely-there panties fall back in the drawer and slammed it closed. Then she marched into the bathroom, dropped the towels from her hair and chest and shrugged into one of the big, fluffy terry cloth robes the hotel provided.

She'd never worn one of them before, opting instead for the sexier sleep sets she'd brought along. Everything she'd packed was sexy, because that was what she'd thought Chase would want.

Well, to hell with him. From now on, she would go for comfort, wear what she wanted, without a thought to his likes or dislikes.

It's not as though he would be touching her again, anyway. If he so much as tried, she'd break his wrist and kick him where it hurt.

Stalking into the sitting room, she grabbed the room service menu, found about twelve things that sounded appetizing, and ordered them all. Ha! She might not have used the credit card he gave her, but she sure would run up his room charges.

She spent the rest of the evening curled up on the over-stuffed sofa, stuffing her face and flipping through channels on the television. Nothing seemed to catch her interest, and no amount of food seemed to fill the hole burning in her gut.

It was close to nine o'clock when she heard the scraping of the key card on the other side of the door. Her stomach lurched and every muscle in her body tensed as she prepared herself to face Chase.

It was the last thing she wanted. For a brief second, she considered running for the bathroom and locking herself in. But that would be the coward's way out, and she didn't want to be a coward. She just didn't want to deal with him again any time in the near future.

The door opened, then closed, and she heard him moving across the carpeted room in her direction. It took all of her willpower not to turn her head and scowl at him, but she kept her attention on the TV, pretending to be deeply absorbed in the crime drama playing on the screen.

The closer Chase got to the sofa, the more her skin tingled, every hair standing on end. And still she refused to acknowledge him.

"Elena," he said after a moment.

His voice was tight and clipped, but she refused to respond.

"Elena," he repeated, more softly this time. "Won't you at least look at me?"

She clenched her teeth to keep from saying something truly scathing, and instead punched the remote control to turn up the volume a couple more notches.

"Dammit, Elena." Chase leaned down, entering her vision for the first time, and snatched the remote from her hand. He tossed it onto the seat of a nearby chair, well out of her reach.

Barely managing to hold on to her temper, she slid her folded legs off the couch and stood, moving away from him to skirt the low coffee table. She made it just a few feet from the bedroom door before he stopped her by grabbing her arm.

She opened her mouth to give him a piece of her mind,

only to have him spin her around, pin her to the nearest wall with his imposing bulk and mash his lips to hers.

With a moan of outrage, she pushed at his shoulders, turned from side to side trying to wiggle away. He merely tightened his hold until his hard chest pressed against the growing tautness of her nipples, his strong thighs trapping hers.

And then the pressure of his mouth changed. Lightening, growing more cajoling than demanding. She moaned again, this time in surrender.

Her nails dug into his shoulders, pulling him closer rather than attempting to push him away, and her leg snaked up to wrap around one of his. His hands spanned her waist as he tore his mouth away, his lips moving to her chin, her throat, the curve of her ear.

"I'm sorry," he panted, the words vibrating over her skin and into her bones. "I acted like an ass earlier. I was in a bad mood and took it out on you. I shouldn't have, and I'm sorry."

Her brain was turning to liquid, as was the rest of her body. She could barely remember what he'd said to her all those hours ago, let alone how upset she'd been with him afterward.

"Forgive me?"

His fingers fumbled with the thick belt of her robe, getting it open and pushing apart the edges of the heavy terry cloth. She was naked beneath and the cool air of the suite washed over her rapidly heating flesh. He fastened his mouth on the straining tip of one breast and she whimpered, digging her fingers into his hair to hold him in place.

How could she deny him when he made her blood flow like molten lava and drove every rational thought from her head?

"Yes," she said breathlessly. "Yes, yes."

He moved to her other breast and she gasped, letting her head fall back against the wall as sensation after sensation washed over her. Reaching between them, he quickly undid his pants and lifted her legs around his waist, filling her in one long, strong stroke.

Biting her bottom lip to keep from crying out, Elena crossed her ankles behind his back, arched her back in an attempt to get even closer to him and let the ripples of pleasure wash over her.

He was so powerful. So confident and masculine and…incredible. No one had ever had such a profound effect on her before. And she doubted anyone ever would again.

Chase's breathing sounded in her ear, heavy and harsh to match her own. It took only moments for the intensity to build, for the desire spiraling in her belly to grow almost unbearable and for her to shatter into a million little pieces, taking Chase over the precipice with her into ecstasy.

They clung to each other, gasping for air, then slowly slid down the wall to the floor in a tangle of limbs and disheveled clothes.

Several minutes later, his chest rumbled with a low chuckle. He shifted slightly, moving into a more comfortable position and bringing her with him to rest in the crook of his arm. "Guess I understand now why make-up sex has such a stellar reputation. Maybe later, we can get into another fight and do that again."

She gave an exhausted, wheezing laugh, positive she would never have enough energy to argue *or* make love with quite that much exuberance again. She'd be surprised if she could even manage to walk on her own two legs before early next week.

Seven

Standing in the corner of the huge, crowded ballroom, Chase buried his hands in his pants pockets and scuffed his booted foot on the highly polished floor. Adults were milling all over, drinking, laughing, nibbling on little finger sandwiches and chunks of cheese speared with fancy toothpicks.

At least that's what he thought they were eating. When they'd first come in, he'd taken a good look at some of the trays the waiters were carrying around and decided there was nothing on them he'd be putting in his mouth.

The big, expensive house was decorated for Christmas within an inch of its life. Santas, reindeer, holly boughs, snowflakes, bells, angels, mistletoe…if it had anything to do with Christmas, it was stuffed somewhere in this mausoleum.

He hated this sort of thing. If his mom and dad hadn't made him come to this stupid party, at this stupid old mansion, he would be home right now, watching TV or doing chores in the barn with his brother.

But from some of the whispered conversations he'd over-heard between his parents, things hadn't been great with their family lately, financially speaking. Victor Sanchez had hired his dad to do some work with his horses and paid him well for his expertise, so when the man invited the Ramseys to his home for a huge holiday celebration, it would have been rude—according to Chase's mother—not to accept.

But he still didn't see why he and Mitch had had to come along. If his parents wanted to schmooze and make a good impression, fine, but this was nothing but a waste of time for him.

There were hardly any other teenagers in attendance and those who were looked to be stuck-up snobs. He rec-ognized a few of them from school, all part of the "in" crowd—while he and his brother definitely weren't.

Not that he was complaining. He liked his life, liked living on a horse and cattle ranch and helping his father out every chance he got. If he had his way, he'd drop out of school altogether and spend his days working with the animals and riding his favorite gelding, Skywalker.

And he'd never have to dress up in a ridiculous suit, with a tie just about strangling him to death. He tugged at his shirt collar, trying again to loosen the darn thing before it cut off his air supply.

There was only one person here he was even kind of interested in being around, and that was Mr. Sanchez's daughter, Elena. She was a year or two younger than Chase, and he saw her around school once in a while, but they definitely didn't run in the same crowd.

The Sanchezes were rich.

The Ramseys weren't.

Elena Sanchez was gorgeous and popular.

Chase didn't exactly look like he'd been hit in the face with a brick, but girls like her didn't hang around boys who wore faded jeans, dusty boots and beat-up cowboy hats.

Of course, that didn't mean boys in faded jeans and Stetsons didn't enjoy watching pretty girls in their pricey clothes.

And Chase had watched Elena plenty. Not that he'd admit to such a fact, even if his brother put him in a headlock and threatened to dunk him in the disgusting, algae-covered water trough he hadn't gotten around to cleaning yet.

Chase huffed a nervous, indecisive breath and tapped the heel of his boot a couple more times on the floor. He'd never have the courage to go up to her at school, with so many other kids around, but maybe here he could.

This was a Christmas party. Everyone was in a festive and possibly more receptive mood than usual.

So maybe…

Glancing around, he took a couple tentative steps away from his post against the wall. His mother and father were chatting with another couple on the far side of the room. His brother was dancing with some older, attractive girl, smiling and swinging her around in the center of the area designated for just that purpose. An eight-piece orchestra was playing high-brow music, interspersed with the occasional holiday instrumental.

And over by the punch bowl stood Elena with a few of her friends. They looked familiar, too. He thought their first names were Tisha, Leslie, Stephanie and Candy, but wasn't sure of their last names. Not that the specifics mattered; they were all part of the country club set.

He took the long way around, skirting the crowd, scuffling his feet when he should have been taking long, confident strides. But his brother was the smooth one with girls. Chase liked them well enough, and most of the time, they liked him back, but they also tended to be the tomboy type and were more friends than girlfriends.

Elena definitely wasn't the tomboy type, but she would be the first girl he'd asked to dance...if he ever got around to it.

He was at the edge of the buffet table now, only a yard or two away from her. A man walked past, bumping into Chase without apologizing or even acknowledging the slight. Typical of this crowd, Chase thought. If you weren't one of their own—namely rich and powerful—then you might as well not exist.

Shaking off the thought, he took a deep breath, pulled his hands from his pockets and stepped forward.

It took a moment for Elena to notice him. She was dressed in a pretty red velvet dress with white lace trim. One side of her long black hair was pulled up and pinned in place with a sprig of live holly.

Her friends, however, noticed him right away. The four of them fixed him with cold, snooty stares, as though he'd just tromped in from the cow barn, covered head to toe in manure.

He ignored them, keeping his attention firmly locked on Elena.

"Hey," he said, sliding his hands back into the front pockets of his dress pants, bunching up the bottom of his matching jacket.

She glanced at him, then at her friends, then back to him. "Hello."

Her response could have been warmer, but it wasn't exactly glacial, either. He pressed on.

"Um... are you having fun?"

Another shifted look to her friends. Her expression remained impassive, not terribly interested, but also not as offended as the others in her little clique.

"Yes."

Dragging his hands from his pockets, he straightened his suit coat and wiped his palms on the sides of his slacks.

"So, do you want to dance?" he asked on a rush, feeling his face heat and resisting the urge to yank at his tie.

Her brows rose and she slanted a sideways glance at her girlfriends, who now had their arms crossed over their chests and were scowling at him. One of them threw her head back and laughed.

Chase almost told her she sounded like one of his father's mares when she whinnied, but at the moment he was more concerned with Elena's answer to his question.

Elena gave a snort, crossing her arms and hitching a hip in a perfect replication of her friends' poses. "I don't think so," she told him in a snotty, highfalutin tone.

Her green eyes flitted down to the floor, taking in the pair of cowboy boots he was wearing. They were his best pair, black and polished to a shine, but they were still boots instead of leather dress shoes.

She lifted her head, once again meeting his gaze. "Why don't you go dance with one of your horses?"

Her friends burst into hoots of laughter, huddling

together to share their amusement at his audacity in daring to approach one of their own.

Chase felt as though he'd been doused with a bucket of ice water. His cheeks heated and his stomach lurched sickeningly.

Without another word, he turned and shouldered his way through the crowd, rushing outside into the chilly night air. Even in Texas, the nights could get cold, especially in December.

But he didn't care; he wasn't going back inside. He would sit in the car and wait for his parents and brother to decide to leave the party, but no matter how cold or hungry he might get, he wasn't going back in that big house—or anywhere near Elena Sanchez ever again.

Hours after their frantic, explosive coupling against the sitting room wall, Chase and Elena were wrapped around each other in the center of the king-size bed, sheets tangled about their naked bodies. The muted noises of the outside world mingled with their breathing to lull them both to sleep.

Chase honestly hadn't thought his legs would ever work again, never mind other parts of his anatomy. He'd thought he'd expire right there on the carpeted floor—sweaty, drained, clothes askew, with Elena sprawled half on top and half beneath him.

But within the hour, he'd somehow found the strength to climb to his feet and help Elena to hers, too.

He hadn't intended to do anything more than get her into bed, but then he'd caught a glimpse of her flushed skin and her half-exposed breasts through the opening of her fluffy white robe, and he'd realized that where Elena

Sanchez was concerned, there was no such thing as being completely exhausted—or completely sated.

He'd started kissing her in the doorway of the bedroom, and before they'd crossed the threshold, they were tearing their clothes off the rest of the way and stumbling for the bed.

Now they were once again pleasantly worn out, and—for the moment, anyway—satisfied. She was tucked along his side, her head on his shoulder, one leg thrown across his thigh. Her breathing was shallow and even, and her long, midnight hair fell over his arm like an expensive silk scarf.

She was probably sleeping. After everything he'd put her through this evening, he wouldn't blame her if she slept straight through the rest of their time in Vegas.

And he sort of hoped she was, because after what he'd seen earlier that day, and all the old memories that had been assaulting him ever since, he couldn't seem to stop himself from saying, "I saw you this afternoon."

He felt her inhale sharply in startlement, then shift closer, her chin rubbing absently against the top of his chest.

"Hmm?"

He held his breath, waiting to see if she would wake up or slip back into unconsciousness, and didn't know which he wished for more.

She continued to wiggle around, making it hard for him to remember that they'd already made love twice that night. And then she lifted her head, blinking like an owl as she struggled toward wakefulness.

"I'm sorry," she said, covering a yawn with her hand. "What did you say?"

In for a penny, in for a pound, he thought.

"I saw you this afternoon," he repeated, careful to keep his tone flat, indifferent. "In the school yard."

A beat passed while he watched emotions play over her face. Shock, guilt, uncertainty. It only lasted a second, though, before her features settled back to their usual calm.

"I thought you were in meetings all day," she said by way of response. Pulling the covers up to her neck, she settled more comfortably, still snug at his side.

"I was supposed to be. But I wanted to see where you went."

"Why?"

She didn't sound angry or annoyed, simply curious. Which allowed him to admit the truth without feeling self-conscious.

"You didn't use my money or charge anything to my credit card yesterday." He shrugged. "I wanted to know what you were doing with your time in Sin City without spending a dime."

"I spent a dime," she corrected. "Quite a few of them. It just happened to be my money instead of yours."

She slid around, straightening her leg to rest between both of his and splaying herself more fully across his chest. Propping her chin on top of her hands, she met his gaze and said, "Although, I did use some of your cash for a cab and a bit of lunch yesterday. Hope you don't mind."

A flicker of annoyance flashed through his system. She was being purposely obtuse.

"I don't care about the money. I wouldn't have given it to you if I did. I want to know what you were doing at a school for deaf children, when most women with an unlimited line of someone else's credit would have cleared out every boutique in a ten-mile radius."

One corner of her mouth twisted up in a mocking grin. "What kind of girl do you take me for?"

"A spoiled, self-absorbed debutante," he replied, not even needing to think about it. Pain flickered across her eyes, but he wouldn't let himself be moved by the reaction.

With a sigh, she pushed away from him and sat up, taking the satin sheet with her.

"You're right. That's exactly what I was. Maybe I still am, I don't know."

He watched her cross her legs and fold the sheet more fully around her body, moving just far enough on the wide, firm mattress that they were no longer touching. Using his forearms, he pushed himself into a sitting position, stuffing an extra pillow behind his back so he could recline against the headboard.

"You're a social worker. You know sign language. And you somehow managed to find probably the only special-needs school within the city limits on your first day in town. None of those are things I ever would have expected from the girl I knew in junior high."

"Well, to be honest, I've known about the school for years. A friend of mine used to teach there, and even though she doesn't live in Nevada anymore, I still like to drop by and spend time with the kids whenever I'm in the area."

She clutched the sheet tighter against her breasts and readjusted her legs. The fire engine-red polish on her toenails peeked out briefly before disappearing again.

"And a lot has happened since we were teenagers. A lot has changed."

Enough to turn a cruel, selfish brat into a kind, selfless woman? He wasn't sure he believed such a drastic shift in personality was possible.

"I know this is almost twenty years too late," she said softly, "but I'm sorry for the way I treated you at that Christmas party when we were kids. You're right—I was spoiled and selfish and every other nasty word you can think of. My parents had money and were important in the community, and I thought that made me rich and important, too." Her usually bright eyes darkened, and for a moment, she wouldn't meet his gaze. "But it only made me a bitch."

Since that was exactly what he'd always thought of her, he didn't bother trying to correct her or make her feel better. It was only slightly gratifying to hear her admit the same.

"What I said to you that night…it was cruel and unnecessary and unforgivable. And even though I know it can't make up for the pain and humiliation I caused you, I am sorry."

Chase gritted his teeth, his hands fisting unconsciously at his sides. Moisture played along her lashes, adding sincerity to her already heartfelt words. But he'd be damned if he'd let a few tears and a long overdue apology convince him that she'd turned over a new leaf and no longer possessed any of those negative, stuck-up teenage traits.

"So what happened to bring about this remarkable transformation?" he asked, his voice sounding acerbic even to his own ears.

Her answer, when it came, was short and without embellishment—and immediately made him feel like a first-class heel.

"My mother died."

Lips thinning, he muttered a curse. "I'm sorry."

"Thank you," she murmured quietly. The long curtain of her hair hid her face as she turned her gaze to her lap, toying with a corner of the sheet.

"She was sick for quite a while, and that sort of experience changes a person. One minute, I was a carefree prima donna, and the next my whole world was falling apart. That's when I realized the whole world didn't revolve around my wants and needs, and that there are more important things in life than money or social status."

He wasn't sure he agreed with that sentiment. He'd spent his entire adult life working to make money and build his social status in an attempt to prove to the Elenas of the world that he wasn't just a poor rancher's son. He was an industrious businessman, who—in recent years, at least—had become one of the wealthiest men in Texas.

It was no small coincidence that the Ramsey Corporation happened to be the company poised to overtake Sanchez Restaurant Supply. Chase had been keeping an eye on Elena's family for years, not only so he would know when he'd surpassed them financially, but in hopes that just such an opportunity would present itself.

He wanted nothing more than to thumb his nose at them—at Elena—and show them all what he'd become. Not just a stinking rich tycoon in his own right, but a man to be respected and admired.

Which didn't explain why he was suddenly feeling pangs of guilt over his plans for revenge against this woman.

So she'd suffered a loss. Didn't everyone at some point in their lives?

So he found her irresistible in bed. What red-blooded American male wouldn't?

It didn't make her a saint, and it didn't make him a bad guy.

"The things I'd always thought were so important," she continued, "weren't anymore. And no amount of my father's wealth or prestige could make my mother better. She had the best medical care money could buy and still it wasn't enough."

"So you became a social worker," he said, tamping down on the sympathies threatening to overwhelm his better senses. "To try to save the world in other ways?"

"Not save the world," she said softly. "But I did want to help people. Our family has more than enough money to get by. Even if we lost the business—which I don't want us to do because of how important it is to my father—" she added with a meaningful glance, "we'd still be okay financially. I wanted to do something with my life that made a difference."

"And I'll bet you do. Make a difference, I mean."

A small smile played over her face. "I try. There are so many kids in trouble out there, so many families with problems. I just do what I can—and what the law allows—to make things a little better for them."

"And you don't turn down awkward teenage boys when they ask you to dance, just because their parents aren't as rich as yours?"

She flushed, her cheeks turning pink with embarrassment. "I'm not sure how many teenage boys would ask me to dance these days, but no. I wouldn't turn anyone down based on their upbringing or bank account. Especially you."

"But I've got money now," he pointed out, arching a brow. "Doesn't that make me more acceptable?"

"No more and no less. I don't judge people that way anymore and I never should have to begin with."

Wiggling around the bed, she pulled the sheet with her as she once again took up position along his side, one leg draped over his thigh, her breasts pressing into his chest.

"At the risk of making you even angrier about that night," she told him, turning her head to rest on his shoulder, "I really did think you were cute back then. If it hadn't been for my friends and my fear of what they might say, I probably would have danced with you—and enjoyed every minute of it."

He didn't reply; instead he let the room fall into silence and her words sink deep into his bones. Beside him, Elena's breathing turned deep and even, and he knew she'd fallen asleep.

But Chase couldn't sleep; his mind wouldn't let him. Into the wee hours of the night, he stayed awake, trying to make sense of what she'd told him, of the thoughts and feelings ricocheting through him like a pinball in an arcade game. No matter how hard he tried, he couldn't seem to reconcile this "new" Elena with the memories he had of her and the woman he'd expected her to be.

All he knew was that the emotions *this* Elena was churning up inside him made him distinctly uncomfortable.

Eight

The next few days in Las Vegas passed easily. Chase spent his days in business meetings, while Elena made one more trip to play with the children at the hearing-impaired school, then did a bit of window shopping. She sent postcards to some friends, even knowing she'd likely be home before they arrived. And she bought a pair of silver and amethyst swing earrings for Alandra from a boutique in the Wynn.

In the evenings she would accompany Chase to any dinner functions he needed to attend. Once or twice, they even ordered in, eating from the room service cart while they sat in front of the television in nightgown and boxer shorts.

And at night, they made love.

There was no more talk of that Christmas dance at her parents' house nearly twenty years ago, or the type of person she'd been as a teen. Chase seemed satisfied with the answers she'd given him about her mother's death and her change of heart. At least for the moment.

Elena didn't try to fool herself into believing that the past was entirely dead and buried, of course. She was afraid the hurt she'd caused him by turning him down so rudely in front of her friends ran too deeply to be forgiven overnight. But she was happy to go on the way things were running now. Spending time with him, sharing less volatile memories of their school days and mutual acquaintances, sleeping each night in his arms.

It was the last one that caused her the most turmoil. Because she was just a bit *too* comfortable with him. Enjoyed making love with him a bit *too* much. Found herself forgetting the exact details of their arrangement a bit *too* often.

It was just so easy to pretend they were a normal couple, spending a week together out of town and getting to know each other better. No deals or arrangements involved. No blackmail to get her there, no guilt driving her to do whatever she could to save her father's business.

A big part of her *wanted* to be there. And worse, she wished it were real.

How could this have happened? How could she have gone from resenting him for blackmailing her to share his bed, to wondering how she was going to feel when their arrangement was over?

It wouldn't be easy. Already, her chest felt tight and her eyes stung whenever she thought about the time when they would go their separate ways.

That moment was closing in fast.

She finished folding a knit dress and tucked it into her suitcase, trying not to think about what would happen next.

Chase was at his last meeting of the week in Las Vegas. He'd packed his things earlier, then left her behind in the room to do the same. Their flight back to Texas was scheduled for after lunch.

And that, she thought, was when it would all be over.

She took a deep breath, patting her clothes down before heading to the bathroom for her toiletries.

If, in the week she'd been gone, her father had managed to get enough money together to save SRS, then there would be no reason for her relationship with Chase to continue. He would have nothing to hold over her head and no leverage to demand she remain his mistress.

How pathetic was it that the prospect saddened her? That she actually *wanted* her father to be having trouble getting his finances and backers together so she could have an excuse to remain with Chase just a bit longer.

Her sister would have a fit if she knew what Elena was thinking. Alandra would put her hands on her hips and shake her head, then launch into a lengthy lecture about Elena standing up for herself and not letting a man dictate her moods. If she wanted to be with Chase Ramsey, then she should simply tell him that she didn't want their relationship to end once her father managed to save SRS. She should tell him she wanted to be more than just his mistress. How much more, she wasn't sure, but she would at least like the time and opportunity to see where things led.

But, oh, wouldn't Chase love that. His feelings for her were already bitter enough; all he needed to send them right into pure hatred was to have her announce that she might be falling in love with him and didn't want to let him go after their deal was done.

She released a brittle chuckle as she dumped bottles of lotions and shampoos into her suitcase, closed the lid and zipped it shut.

Oh, yes, he'd just love that. The woman he'd blackmailed into being his mistress suddenly got too attached and wanted more. Wouldn't that just shoot his plan for revenge all to hell.

From the other room, she heard the door to the suite click open and then close. She took a deep breath and blinked a few times, fighting to get her emotions under control before he came in and noticed how close she was to falling apart.

"Hey," he said, tossing the key card on the dresser.

Smiling a bit too widely, Elena turned to greet him. "Hey."

"You all packed?"

"I just finished," she said, patting one of her bags.

"Good. If you want, we can have the bags taken down, then get some lunch before we head for the airport."

She nodded. "Fine with me."

She started to pull her bags and suitcase off the bed, moving them closer to the doorway, where he was leaning against the jamb.

"One other thing before we go," he murmured, taking the handle of the wheeled case, the larger of the two bags, from her. Turning, he headed for the main door and propped her luggage with his own.

"Yes?" she asked distractedly, hitching the strap of her purse on her shoulder as she followed along behind and set her smaller carry-on bag next to the rest. She straightened to find him watching her intently, his blue eyes shining like crystals behind dark lashes.

He took her arm, his fingers banding firmly just above her elbow. "When we get back," he told her slowly, "if your father hasn't come up with the resources necessary to pull SRS out of the fire, I'll expect you to continue with our agreement. Unless, of course, you're no longer concerned with helping Victor save the family business."

The latter seemed to be half apology, half threat. Elena thought she should probably be offended, or at least act outraged that he would dictate her actions once they returned home to Gabriel's Crossing.

Instead, she felt almost elated. Ten days wasn't very long to collect the kind of money her father needed to stave off the Ramsey Corporation, which meant the chances were pretty good that they *would* need to buy more time. Time she'd be required to remain with Chase.

That had been the deal, after all. She would play the part of his mistress for as long as it took for her father to raise the funds to save SRS. Just because they would no longer be a practically anonymous couple in the bright lights of Las Vegas didn't mean she could go back on her word.

Taking a deep breath, she met his gaze and nodded. "Of course. I only ask that we be discreet. My family and the rest of world don't need to know the details of why we'll suddenly be spending so much time together."

He inclined his head, his fingers dropping from her arm. "Agreed."

With that, he turned to open the door and she felt a wave of relief wash through her. She would be spending more time with Chase, after all, rather than being tossed aside like an old pair of gym socks as soon as their plane landed in Texas.

And if she also felt more than a small jab of guilt at hoping it took her father awhile longer to move the family back into the black, she would deal with that later.

They'd been home nearly a week when Chase called Elena at work. She hadn't spoken to him since he'd dropped her off at the house she shared with her father and sister the afternoon they'd returned from Las Vegas.

She'd wondered about him, caught herself jumping whenever the phone rang, half hoping he was calling to demand she spend the night with him. Or even that she accompany him to some dinner or another.

But he hadn't, and since she hadn't given him her work number, she'd never expected him to call her there. Of course, she should have known that a man like Chase Ramsey could find her wherever she was, if he put his mind to it.

As always, he got right to the point.

"My mother invited me to dinner tonight. My brother is going to be there with his wife and daughter and I thought you might like to go and meet everyone." Before she could respond, he went on. "No problem if you already have other plans. I'll just tell Mom I'm in the middle of an important business deal and will be working all evening."

For a minute, Elena didn't know what to say. She clutched the phone to her ear, her mouth hanging open in surprise.

He wanted her to meet his family? And if she said no, he wasn't going to go at all?

What did that mean? Was he simply being polite, or did he have a more personal, hidden agenda?

Her mind was spinning, her heart racing a mile a minute.

"U-um," she stuttered before quickly shaking herself. "Yes, of course. I'd love to go."

"You're sure?" he asked, sounding almost sorry he'd called. "Because—"

"I'm sure. My evening is wide open."

It hadn't been, but it would be now. Her sister would understand. They had only been going to the mall, anyway. Something about looking for toys for the children at one of Alandra's charities.

"What time will you be picking me up? Or would you rather I met you there?"

"No, I'll pick you up. Let's say…six o'clock?"

"Six it is. I'll see you then."

"Good. Great. See you then."

The line went dead, leaving Elena to listen to the hum of the dial tone. Slowly, she lowered her arm to hang up, leaving her fingers curled around the earpiece. A second later, she put the phone back to her ear and jabbed out a number she knew by heart.

"Hello?" her sister answered after only two rings.

Elena spoke only one word: "Help."

What should a girl wear to dinner to meet her lover's parents and brother? Especially when they were only lovers because he'd blackmailed her into bed.

That might not be the full reason she was staying in his bed, but it was certainly how he'd gotten her there to begin with.

Thankfully, she had a sister who was much more savvy about this sort of thing and knew the answers to these kinds of questions. As soon as Elena had called Alandra's cell phone with her semi-desperate plea, her sister had dropped everything and met her at home for a full sweep of both their closets.

It was only dinner at his parents' house, so nothing fancy was required. Instead, she needed something casual but elegant. Attractive and becoming without looking as though she'd worked at it.

Formal would have been easier, she soon realized. If she were attending a black-tie affair, she would simply have had to throw on something long and sequined with a pair of high heels. But dressing for dinner with Chase's family bordered on cruel and unusual punishment.

They immediately crossed blue jeans off the list for being too casual. And a dress of any type for being too fancy. Skirts were borderline, depending on the style and design.

Finally, after two or three hours of feeling like the mannequin for a window designer with multiple personality disorder, Elena held her arms up while Alandra pulled yet another top over her head, then stood back to study her latest creation.

"I think we've got it," her sister announced, grinning as she pointed at the mirror for Elena to see for herself.

Elena sighed in relief as she saw that she looked almost perfect. Maybe a little overdressed, but not by much. Especially if Chase came straight from the office and was still wearing his usual suit and tie.

Alandra had decided on a pair of wide-legged black slacks, with one-inch plain black pumps and a periwinkle blue sweater set trimmed with red, white, and black embroidered flowers.

"Are you sure?" she asked, tugging at the hem of the sweater and turning left and right to view the full effect.

"Absolutely. You look gorgeous, but not like you're trying to impress anyone. If I were meeting my new boyfriend's parents for the first time, I'd wear that exact outfit."

Elena's heart shuddered at her sister's words. "He's not my boyfriend," she said softly, her mouth gone dry as she turned away from the mirror. She couldn't quite bring herself to meet Alandra's gaze, so she moved to the bed, busying herself with putting earlier discarded garments back on their hangers.

"You're right," her sister readily agreed. "He's way too cute to be just a 'boyfriend.' He's your red-hot secret lover."

Face flaming, she whirled in Alandra's direction, waving a hand and glancing frantically toward the open bedroom door.

"Shhh," she hissed, marching past her sister to shut the door to hopefully provide them with a bit more privacy. Just in case. "No one is supposed to know, remember? And it won't be a secret much longer if you keep talking about it at full volume."

She turned back in time to see Alandra roll her eyes toward the ceiling. "You're going to have to tell people eventually if you keep spending so much time with the man."

"I haven't spent any time with him. This is the first time he's called me all week."

"Yes, but you flew to Vegas with him and stayed there almost a week."

Elena crossed her arms beneath her breasts and tapped her foot on the carpeted floor in agitation. "I flew to Vegas on *business,*" she corrected. "No one knows I went with Chase or what we did while we were there."

"*I* know," Alandra murmured pointedly, crossing her arms in a mirror image of her sister's pose.

Elena raised a brow. "What are you saying? That you're going to blackmail me, too?"

Honestly, was she giving off pheromones to signal that she was ripe for the picking? She'd gone thirty-three years without being bribed or strong-armed into anything, and now she was about to be manipulated twice in the same month. And once by her sister, no less!

But Alandra quickly put the quash on any concerns about that.

"Of course not! What kind of sister do you think I am?"

Dropping her arms, she stalked forward and took Elena's hand, tugging her to the set of pastel-striped arm-chairs by the window.

When they were both seated, Alandra said, "I'm worried about you, Elena. First you tell me you're being coerced into sleeping with this guy to help Pop save the company. And I understood your reasons for going through with it, really I did. I'd have probably done the same thing. But now you're standing here nervous about meeting the man's parents and worrying over what to wear when you do. Do you realize what that means?"

Elena blinked. It meant she was nervous about meeting Chase's parents, and that she wasn't the ever self-assured fashion plate her sister was, didn't it?

"It means you care," Alandra informed her gently. "If this were just a business arrangement, you wouldn't care how you looked tonight. You'd have probably gone in the same outfit you wore to work today and not given it a second thought."

"That's not true. I care how I look," Elena protested, but the words came out with so little confidence, even she didn't believe it.

"Of course you do. But you looked fine in what you were wearing this morning. And that song you were humming when you got home from Vegas tells me you weren't exactly chained up in Chase Ramsey's bed all week, forced to be his love slave against your will. I think," Alandra added, tipping her head to the side, "things between you are starting to get serious."

Elena swallowed past the lump in her throat, her heart pounding like a kettledrum. Once again, she was reminded that she could keep no secrets from a sister who knew her so well. For better or worse, Alandra could see straight through any attempts at subterfuge.

The air shuddered from her lungs. Her shoulders slumped and she let her chin fall to her chest. "I'm in trouble," she admitted, barely loud enough to be heard.

Her sister leaned forward, her expression going serious as she laid a hand on Elena's knee. "You're in love with him?" she asked.

Elena shook her head, slowly, almost as though she couldn't quite believe it herself. "I don't know, but I think I'm close."

She raised her head and met her sister's understanding eyes as her own started to sting and grow damp. "I'm really, really close."

Nine

Between her nerves over meeting Chase's parents and her disturbing conversation with Alandra before leaving, Elena's stomach was in knots. Her palms were sweating, her knees were shaking and every once in a while, her chest tightened so much, she could barely draw a breath.

When Chase pulled up to the house at six on the dot, Elena made her sister stay in her room. The last thing she needed was for Alandra to race down the stairs to catch a glimpse of him or be caught peering around the corner like a child on Christmas morning, trying to catch Santa Claus piling presents under the tree.

But even though Alandra bided by her wishes and stayed out of sight, Elena knew she was watching from the upstairs window as Chase helped her into the car and they pulled away.

On the drive, she tried to make small talk, tried to respond with some modicum of sensibility when Chase spoke. But inside, her blood and muscles and bones felt as though they'd been touched by a live wire. She was surprised he didn't notice a glow in her eyes or sparks shooting from her fingertips.

The Ramsey ranch was on the other side of Gabriel's Crossing, but they still arrived much too soon for Elena's peace of mind. Chase's shiny silver luxury car bumped down a long, rutted dirt driveway, kicking up a cloud of dust behind them.

A dark blue pickup truck was already parked in front of the house. Chase pulled up beside it and cut the engine.

For a moment, they sat there, neither one making a move to get out. Elena stared at the front door, fully expecting it to fly open and the stuff of nightmares to pour out.

Alandra was right; it meant something. Despite her better judgment, she was falling for Chase, and falling hard. And for some reason, whether or not his parents liked her felt like a very big deal.

She wished it didn't. She wished she could convince herself that this was merely another business dinner he'd asked her to attend. Meeting his parents felt entirely too much like something a girlfriend would do.

A girlfriend, not a mistress.

The click of the door latch releasing on Chase's side of the car interrupted her thoughts and she hurried to open her own and climb to her feet. Brushing her hands on the legs of her slacks, she took a deep breath and tried to calm the jumble of anxiety tightening her stomach.

She was his mistress, she reminded herself as brutally

as she could. Not his girlfriend, not his fiancée, not even, really, his lover. This might be his family, but to her, they were simply another group of strangers she needed to entertain and impress to fulfill her part of the bargain.

Chase met her at the front of the car, only steps from the narrow porch that ran the full length of the front of the house.

"Ready?" he asked, seeming to sense her reluctance, even though she was doing her best to tame it.

She swallowed hard and let him take her hand, pasting on a wide smile she didn't quite feel. "Of course."

He led her onto the porch and through the front door. Voices assaulted them as soon as they stepped into the house. Male and female, one on top of the other.

They moved through a wide, homey living room that took up the front of the house, and down a short hallway that opened into a dining room filled with people—the source of all the noise.

Two men sat at one end of a long pine table already set with plates and silverware. One was older, one younger, but Elena could tell right away that they were related. Chase's father and brother, she would guess.

Beside the younger man stood a high chair with a brown-haired little girl seated inside, seemingly content to occupy herself by chewing on the wrong end of a small plastic spoon.

While Elena was taking in her surroundings, a swinging door opened and two women came out, both carrying a bowl or platter in each hand as they smiled and chatted.

"Chase!" the older of the two cried the moment she spotted them standing there. She quickly set sliced pot roast and buttered green beans on the table, then rushed toward them.

"Hi, Mom," Chase said, returning the woman's hug as she threw her arms around him and squeezed.

When they separated, his mother turned to face Elena. "And you must be Elena. Chase told us he might bring you along."

Elena returned her greeting and shook the woman's hand when she offered it, with Chase adding to the introduction.

"Elena, this is my mother, Theresa. And this is everyone else," he said, pointing as he went around the room. "My father, Isaac; my brother, Mitch; his wife, Emma; and their daughter, Amelia. Everyone, this is Elena Sanchez."

They all smiled and said hello, and she felt her anxiety begin to ease as Chase pulled out a chair and waited for her to take a seat, then sat down beside her.

Pot roast, mashed potatoes, green beans and sliced peaches were passed around the table, the room filling once again with noise as everyone started speaking at the same time. Voices and laughter mixing, conversations overlapping and turning on a dime.

Instead of being overwhelmed, Elena found the exuberant atmosphere comforting. It reminded her of some of her own family's gatherings, back before her mother died. She, Alandra and their father still ate meals together as often as possible, but they tended to be quieter, more subdued affairs these days.

Although she didn't take a large part in the interaction, she responded whenever questions were directed at her and found herself laughing several times at one thing or another. And as if the meal itself wasn't delicious enough, Theresa brought out a fresh-from-the-oven pecan pie that nearly made Elena weep.

With everyone stuffed, and little Amelia's eyes drooping, things began to quiet down. Elena helped Theresa clear the table and fill the dishwasher while Emma took the toddler upstairs to sleep and the men moved from the dining room to the living room. A few minutes later, they heard the front door open and then close, and Theresa rolled her eyes.

"Isaac thinks I don't know about those filthy cigars he likes to sneak after dinner. Like I can't smell them on him for hours afterward."

She reached into a cupboard and removed three short-stemmed wineglasses to go with the bottle of chardonnay she'd already set on the counter. Holding the three glasses upside down in one hand and the neck of the bottle in the other, she nudged the kitchen door with her hip and led the way through the house to the sitting room.

"He takes the boys outside with him so he can claim they needed to talk. I won't say anything tonight, though, since it will give us girls a chance to chat, too."

Emma came back downstairs then, to curl up in one corner of the overstuffed sofa. She smiled and thanked Theresa when the older woman passed her a half-full glass of wine.

Elena took a seat on the other end of the sofa, not quite at ease enough to put her feet up. But then, she was a guest here, not a daughter-in-law.

Theresa handed her a glass, too, then sat back in a matching armchair to sip from her own.

"So," Theresa murmured casually, "tell us how you came to be dating my son."

"So what's up with the raven-haired beauty?" Mitch asked, sipping at the three fingers of scotch he'd poured before their father had dragged them outside so he could sneak a few puffs from his cigar before their mother discovered him.

Chase took a sip from his own glass before responding. "Nothing's up. She's a friend, that's all."

"Mm-hmm." Keeping his gaze on the barn and paddock several yards from the house, his brother said, "You haven't brought a woman home to meet Mom and Dad since we were in high school."

"She seems like a nice girl," Isaac put in from farther down the porch railing. "I like her."

Chase elected not to respond to that. Mitch was right about him not bringing a girl home to meet his parents since they were both teenagers, but he didn't want to give anyone ideas.

He couldn't even say for sure why he'd brought Elena along tonight. It wasn't to meet his parents—not to see how she acted around them or what they thought of her.

He'd just…wanted company. He hadn't wanted to show up for yet another family dinner by himself, feeling a bit like an outsider now that his brother was married and so obviously happy with his wife and daughter. Ever since Mitch and Emma had gotten together, his parents—or at least his mother—had focused on seeing him settled down.

She wasn't single-minded about it, thank goodness. Only the occasional question about his personal life or remark about his finding a "good woman" to let him know he was still on her radar.

He'd known that even before asking Elena to accompany him tonight. So why the hell had he gone through with it, anyway?

Because it was part of their agreement. She would go with him to meetings and dinners whenever he needed her, and he'd needed someone with him tonight.

That's all there was to it, nothing more. The fact that his mother and father—and even his brother, apparently—were reading more into it was none of his concern.

Not that he hadn't noticed how well she fit in with the rowdy bunch he called family. She hadn't been overwhelmed by them, as he'd feared. Instead, she'd seemed to enjoy the boisterous camaraderie and had handled the many switches in conversation with ease.

Then again, what did he expect? Ever since he'd started spending time with her again, there wasn't a situation he could think of where she'd been uncomfortable or out of place.

Perhaps he'd been testing her, tossing her into the middle of one of his family's dinner gatherings to see if there was *anything* that caught her off guard. Or maybe he'd simply wanted her with him, wanted to share a part of his life with her that he hadn't before.

Of course, it didn't make him too happy to think that might be the case. If it was, he was in trouble. She was supposed to be his mistress…and only that because he wanted to exact a bit of revenge on her for the way she'd treated him in junior high.

A man didn't usually bring his mistress home to meet his parents. And a man bent on revenge certainly didn't look for ways to incorporate the subject of his vengeance more firmly into his life.

He threw back the last of his scotch at the same time his father stubbed out his cigar.

"She's just a friend," Chase repeated, his tone leaving no room for argument. Heading for the front door, he stopped with his hand on the knob to turn back and fix his brother with a warning glare. "Leave it alone."

As interrogations went, Elena supposed the one with Chase's mother and sister-in-law wasn't so bad. It had started with, "So, tell me how you came to be dating my son," but hadn't gone much farther than that.

Elena had explained that she wasn't dating Chase, that they were really just friends and business acquaintances. And Theresa Ramsey was savvy enough to realize her son wasn't a topic Elena cared to discuss, so she'd quickly moved into less personal, less dangerous territory.

They'd talked about Chase's and her trip to Vegas, but only in the vaguest of terms. About Chase's company, Ramsey Corporation, and how he'd built it from the ground up all on his own. About Elena's family—but again, only in the vaguest of terms—since Elena didn't particularly want to remind Theresa of the Christmas party they had attended where she had been so rude and cruel to Chase. And finally, about how Emma and Mitch had met—as children—and then ended up falling in love and getting married so many years later.

It was a lovely story, one that brought tears to Elena's eyes. For a moment, it almost made her believe true love existed and that fate could take a hand in a person's life, even if things had gotten off to a rocky start.

But what was she thinking? That some unseen force would reach down and bring her and Chase together?

Who was she trying to kid? Even if he found her physically irresistible…even if their current relationship lasted much longer than originally intended…she didn't think he would ever be able to get past what she'd done to him all those years ago.

She didn't blame him, but she did wish things could be different.

If only she hadn't been such a spoiled, arrogant brat as a teenager.

If only they had met again as adults with clean slates and no ugly baggage from their pasts.

Then, maybe they would have actually had a shot at making things work.

But the way it stood now, she knew they didn't. She also knew that when the time came for them to call it quits, a little part of her heart would break off and travel with him wherever he went.

Her chest tightened and her eyes began to dampen again. She quickly swallowed and took a deep breath, hoping her companions wouldn't notice the sudden rush of emotion that threatened to close her throat.

To her left, the front door creaked open and she welcomed the sudden distraction as Chase entered the room, followed by his brother and father.

Chase, she noticed, was carrying an empty tumbler and moved directly to the bar. For a moment, he hesitated, apparently contemplating a refill. But then he set his glass down and walked away.

Moving to the sofa, he took a seat at her side while his brother did the same beside his wife, so that the two women were at the ends with the two men sandwiched between them.

Rather than sit down, Isaac took up position behind his wife's chair. Close enough, Elena noticed, to play the part of the loving husband, but far enough away that Theresa wasn't likely to comment if she noticed the scent of cigar smoke lingering on his breath or clothes. To cover her grin, Elena lifted a hand to her mouth and pretended to cough.

For the next half hour, the six of them made small talk. Thankfully, the conversation completely avoided the topic of Chase's and her relationship.

And then it was time to leave. Chase stood, holding a hand out to her to help her to her feet, and everyone else followed suit.

Theresa and Emma both hugged Elena while Isaac and Mitch shook her hand and wished her well. She was invited to come back any time, and she promised that she would, even though she suspected such an event would never actually take place.

In the car, Elena waited until Chase had started the engine and turned down the driveway before leaning against the headrest and releasing a long breath. The bright headlights created twin streaks of yellow along the dirt lane.

"Tired?" Chase asked, glancing in her direction before returning his attention to the road.

"Not really," she answered honestly. She was, but only because she'd been so nervous and tense about meeting his family to begin with. With the anxiety behind her, she suddenly felt like a blown-up balloon pricked by a pin and allowed to expel its air all at once. "I was just thinking about how nice your family is. Thank you for introducing them to me."

A beat of heavy silence passed, then he said, "They liked you, too."

She smiled in the darkness. "I'm glad."

He turned on the radio and the soft strains of a classical CD filled the space around them. Neither of them spoke another word until they neared her house.

At a stop sign, Chase stopped. Only when they remained there for longer than Elena thought was necessary did she look at him, brows drawn together in an unspoken query. His fingers flexed on the steering wheel and he didn't meet her gaze.

"I can take you home," he said slowly. "Or you can come back to my place with me."

Her stomach jumped and every inch of her skin broke out in gooseflesh, tingling as though she'd just been touched by a live wire.

She licked her lips, her mouth gone dry. "I…can go home with you, I guess," she told him in a soft voice.

His only response was a tight nod. Then, instead of turning right as he would have to drop her off, he went straight, toward his own home.

She'd never given much thought to where he lived. Whenever she pictured him in his own environment, it was his office, behind his desk, as he'd been that first time she'd gone to plead her father's case. Aside from that, she supposed she'd always assumed he lived in an apartment somewhere, perhaps a penthouse on the top floor of the Ramsey Corporation office building.

A man like Chase—single, wealthy, independent— wouldn't need much space. Just a bedroom, bathroom, small kitchen and of course an office where he could work.

So her jaw nearly dropped when he turned into an upscale housing development and stopped in the driveway of a gorgeous, sprawling two-story brick home.

"This is your house?" she asked as he cut the engine, not bothering to hide her awe.

He sat back in his seat, offering a wry smile. "Yeah, why? Did you think I lived at some cheap hotel? Or maybe sleep at my desk at work?"

She flushed at just how close his guess was to what she'd been thinking and was glad it was too dark for him to see.

"No," she denied, "I just didn't realize you owned your own house. It's gorgeous."

"Thank you. Though it's not quite the mansion you grew up in, I know."

He opened his door and stepped out and she followed suit.

"Yes, well, even I admit Pop went a bit overboard when he built it. He was the first member of his family to really make something of himself, and I think he confused the house from *Gone with the Wind* with the average American dream."

That earned her a chuckle and she joined in as he led her up the moonlit path to the front door. Reaching around the jamb, he flipped a switch. Light flooded the foyer and part of the front yard from a massive chandelier hanging in the center of the ceiling where dozens of crystal teardrops twinkled brightly.

"Would you like a tour?"

She nodded eagerly, already fascinated by the little she'd seen.

He showed her the den, kitchen and family room, and stood in front of a set of wide French doors at the back of the house as he described the patio and lawn that she couldn't see much of in the muted illumination from the house. There was also an indoor pool and workout room, two things even her father's sizeable estate couldn't boast.

Then he led her upstairs and pointed out several beautifully decorated guest rooms, as well as a central restroom that didn't look as though it was used very often.

At the end of the hall stood the master bedroom, easily twice as large as any of the others, and done in dark, masculine tones. The bed was a giant four poster made of mahogany and covered with a comforter of forest green and navy blue swirls. On either side of the bed stood two-drawer nightstands carved of the same wood and with the same design as the bedposts, and holding matching wrought iron lamps. A doorway to the right of the bed led to the master bath, with a sunken whirlpool tub, a separate shower and two sinks set into a long marble countertop.

As though she wasn't impressed enough already, he informed her that he'd overseen both the design and decoration of the entire house. The man had great taste, she admitted, more than a little surprised by just how luxurious and tasteful his home was.

It was a shame, though, that he lived there alone. Such a large place seemed wasted on only one person.

"So," he murmured, "would you like a glass of wine, or something else to drink?"

They were still standing in the middle of the bedroom, but while she had felt completely comfortable a moment ago, she was suddenly faced with an attack of nerves. Her reason for being in his home, alone with him, this late at night flashed back to her and her heart gave a tiny flip.

"No, thank you," she said softly with a shake of her head. She'd had two glasses of chardonnay at his parents' house. Any more and her head might start to get fuzzy.

Her fingers worked distractedly on the strap of her purse as she added, "I should call my sister, though. Let her know I'm going to be late."

He nodded, then pointed to the cordless phone charging on one of the nightstands. "Help yourself."

Striding to the walk-in closet at the far side of the room, he shrugged out of his suit jacket and hung it in the jungle of other suit jackets.

"If you'd like," he said as she was dialing, "you can tell her I'll bring you home in the morning." Cocking his head in her direction, he shot her a glance filled with sultry and seductive meaning. "That is, if you'd like to stay the night."

Ten

Elena inhaled deeply and stretched, her toes curling into the soft Egyptian cotton sheets, her arms reaching over her head until her fingers bumped the mahogany headboard.

She couldn't remember the last time she'd slept so well. Of course, she and Chase had worn themselves out pretty well before finally drifting off sometime after midnight.

At the sound of movement in the room, she opened her eyes and sat up, clutching the covers to her chest. Chase wasn't beside her in the gigantic four poster bed, but already up and dressed. With a tray in his hands, he crossed the carpeted floor in bare feet, well-worn jeans and a casual white button-down shirt with the sleeves rolled to his elbows.

The tray held a plate piled high with what looked like French toast and scrambled eggs, two glasses of orange juice and a tall, narrow vase with a single bright purple tulip in full bloom.

"Good morning," he said, his low drawl dripping down her spine like warm honey.

"Good morning," she returned as he rounded the bed and crawled onto the mattress from his side, setting the tray carefully between them. It looked and smelled delicious.

"What time is it?" she asked, turning her head toward the clock on the bedside table.

Before she could see for herself, he said, "A little after nine."

"Nine?" Shock and fear rolled through her as she realized she was late for work. She was never late for work.

She threw back the covers, ready to jump out of bed and dress as quickly as possible. If she hurried, maybe she could get to the office before her boss realized she was late, even if it meant showing up in the same outfit two days in a row.

She would rather put up with gossip about her personal life than gain the reputation of shirking her duties. And if she called Alandra from her cell phone on the way, she might even be able to get her sister to meet her there with a change of clothes.

"Relax," Chase told her, reaching out to grab her wrist before she'd leapt completely off the mattress. "I phoned your sister and asked her to call you in sick from work."

For a moment, Elena wasn't sure she understood what he was telling her. Then, as it began to sink in, she raised a curious brow.

"Although, if you'd like to leave the covers off and eat in the buff," he added with a devilish wink, "I'm all for it."

She looked down and saw that she was, indeed, naked,

the sheet tossed off to her ankles. With a gasp, she grabbed the sheet and yanked it back up to her chin.

He chuckled at the blush that filled her cheeks. "Do you really think there's any part of you I haven't already seen?" he asked, and then added, "And explored quite thoroughly?"

It was true. He was a very thorough man.

"I don't make a habit of sitting around, eating breakfast in the nude," she replied primly, turning her nose up just a little.

Which only earned her another deep laugh.

"And what do you mean you asked my sister to call me in sick to work?" she demanded, pretending to be more annoyed than she really was.

In all honestly, she was relieved. Yes, it was highhanded of him, but then, this was Chase. Chase was nothing if not forceful and commanding.

He shrugged one broad shoulder. "I kept you up pretty late last night, so I figured you'd appreciate a morning to sleep in. I also thought we could spend the day together, since I called and let my secretary know I wouldn't be in, either."

Now, that surprised her. She didn't think Chase Ramsey ever took a day off work, or would know what to do with himself if he did.

Since it seemed like a moot point now, she gave up on worrying about her job and reached for a fork and the plate of French toast.

"What did you have in mind?" she asked.

"Hey, that's for both of us," he complained when she dug in.

"I'll let you have whatever I can't finish," she shot back with a wicked tip to her lips.

He snorted, but let her go. Then he said, "We can do anything you like. Sit by the pool sipping umbrella drinks, or on the back patio doing the same. We can even pack a picnic lunch and go over to my brother's to see if he'll let us take a couple of his horses out for a few hours."

For a man who professed to need her only as his mistress, he seemed awfully accommodating all of a sudden. A picnic lunch? Sipping umbrella drinks by the pool?

She took a bite of French toast and chewed slowly, then washed it down with a sip of juice.

As much as she enjoyed horseback riding, the thought of staying here and spending the day only with Chase held much more appeal. After all, she didn't know how much longer they would have together before he decided he didn't need a mistress anymore…or at least didn't need *her* as his mistress.

"A dip in the pool sounds like fun," she said slowly. "I don't have a suit, though."

"That's all right." He reached out and snagged a slice of French toast from the plate she was holding and lifted it directly to his mouth. "You don't need one."

"You expect me to swim naked?" she asked, somewhat startled.

"Why not?" He took another bite, chewing thought-fully. "I'll be naked, too, and even if you did wear a suit, I'd have you out of it in no time, anyway."

She paused with the fork almost to her mouth, her throat closing suddenly as a jolt of arousal flushed through her system. Lowering her hand, she replaced the fork on the plate and set it all aside. Chase didn't miss a beat in picking it up himself and digging in.

"What do you say?" he asked, mouth half-full of food. "Do you still want to swim?"

The vision of frolicking in the water with him, making love with him there, flashed through her head, and the muscles in her body went lax. She swallowed hard, licked her dry lips and barely managed a breathless, "Okay."

Hours later, Elena was glad she hadn't had to go to work that day. She wasn't sure she'd have the energy to even go in tomorrow.

Chase was stretched out on a lounge chair a few feet from the pool, eyes closed, chest rising and falling with his breathing. She was draped along his side, her head on his shoulder, her palm resting on the flat of his abdomen. And they were both entirely, blissfully naked.

Two colorful drinks, complete with the umbrellas he'd promised, sat on a small glass table beside the chair, practically untouched, and soft music played over the sound system that was piped through the entire house.

"I've got a party to attend tomorrow night," he said, startling her out of her drowsy reverie.

Rolling her head back slightly, she realized his eyes were still closed, but he obviously wasn't asleep as she'd first thought.

"You wanna go with me?"

"Do I have a choice?" she asked, shifting slightly to re-distribute her weight along his chest and thigh.

"You always have a choice. We all do," he replied calmly. Lifting his arm, he thread his fingers through the damp hair at her temple. "But I'm asking you. It's a business gathering, but you don't have to go if you don't want to. I can make it through one black-tie party on my own, I think," he added with a chuckle.

She felt his laughter vibrate through his body, and nearly sighed at the tender, relaxing sensation he was creating along her scalp.

"I'd like you with me, though, if you'd like to go."

Swallowing hard, she tried not to let her emotions tense her muscles or hasten her breathing, but her mind was spinning.

Was this a turning point in their relationship? Was he beginning to see her more as a lover, a girlfriend, than simply a mistress by business arrangement?

She didn't want to get her hopes up, didn't want to read too much into his one small comment, his one tiny shift in attitude. But her heart swelled with the possibilities.

"I would like to," she said softly, relieved when her voice came out steady and self-assured.

"Good. I'll pick you up at eight."

Then, without warning, he rolled over, twisting her beneath him, catching her just before she fell off the edge of the chaise. She gave a little yelp, her eyes going wide in startlement.

"Wear something slinky and sexy that shows off your great breasts and bottom."

He pinched her there and she made a sound that was half-gasp, half-laugh.

"You think I have a nice bottom?" she asked when she'd regained her breath.

"Stellar. Classic. Greek statues weep in envy."

She grinned, letting her head fall back as he nuzzled her throat. His unshaven cheek scratched along her tender flesh, likely leaving a mark that she would later have to explain to her family and co-workers, but she didn't care. Her back arched in pleasure, her hips bumping into his obvious arousal.

His hands slid higher as his mouth moved to her ear. "And make sure it's backless. Something that leaves your smooth, gorgeous back bare to the room. Every other woman there will want to scratch your eyes out," he murmured. "And every man will want you."

"Including you?" she asked, finally getting into the flow of his building passion. She lifted her arms around his neck, her legs around his waist and licked the line of his jaw.

"Especially me. I'll be wanting you even before I pick you up."

He emphasized his point by slipping inside her in one long, steady stroke. Her lungs seized, and for the rest of the afternoon, all the thoughts and concerns jumbling through her mind were pushed aside by the sinful, delicious things Chase did to her.

Ever an agreeable mistress, Elena wore something slinky, sexy and backless that she hoped did an adequate job of highlighting her chest and rear. Chase, she supposed, would be the judge of that.

She couldn't wait to see his reaction when he caught his first glimpse of her. He would be there any minute, and all she had left to do was slip on her necklace and earrings.

Her gown was red and floor-length, with a slit that ran to mid-thigh. The material was struck through with silver threads so that every bit of it shimmered, especially when she moved. The bodice, cut in a deep vee and tied behind her neck, left her shoulders and back completely bare.

She wore high, red heels with a criss-cross design across the top of her foot. Tiny rhinestones sparkled at the junction where each of the straps crossed.

Her jewelry was surprisingly simple—just a diamond pendant at her neck, matching teardrop earrings and an understated tennis bracelet on her right wrist.

According to Alandra, she looked "hot enough to peel the paint off a '57 Mustang." Whatever that meant. But she'd laughed anyway, and taken it as the compliment she was sure her sister meant it to be.

Grabbing her small red clutch, she left her bedroom and headed downstairs. Her foot had just cleared the last step when the doorbell rang. She moved across the foyer, her high heels clicking on the polished parquet floor, and opened the door.

The sun was beginning to set, but it was still light enough to make out every detail of Chase's broad, masculine form. And that form was positively mouthwatering in a tuxedo.

His black hair was slicked back instead of being left in its usual, carefree style, making him look sexier and more sophisticated.

She started to lick her lips, then remembered the recently applied lipstick and forced herself to rein in her roving tongue.

"Wow," he muttered, reading her mind. "You look fabulous."

"Thank you," she said, then did a little pirouette in the doorway. "Does my dress meet with your approval? It's slinky, sexy, shows off my breasts and bottom and is even—" She turned again, flashing the expanse of her back, left completely bare by both the dress and her upswept hair. "—backless."

"Nice. Very nice," he drawled. Reaching out, he ran the knuckle of one index finger along her spine, from the small of her back to the nape of her neck.

She shivered, both from his touch and the low, suggestive tone. If she wasn't careful, they would end up rolling around on the floor of her father's entryway and miss the party altogether.

Slowly, she turned around to face him, placing her hand on her stomach in an attempt to quell the butterflies swooping and swirling inside.

"Should we go?" she asked.

With a heartfelt sigh, he hung his head and let his arm fall back to his side. "If we must."

She smiled, following him onto the front stoop and closing the door behind her.

He helped her into the car, then walked around and took a seat on the driver's side.

It took nearly half an hour to reach the hotel where the fund-raiser was being held. When they arrived, Chase passed his keys to the valet before rounding the hood, opening her door and taking her hand as she stepped out.

With her arm linked at his elbow, they strode through the luxurious hotel's lobby, took the elevator to the fourth floor and crossed to the entrance of the decorated, already packed ballroom. For a minute, they stood at the open double doors, taking in their surroundings.

Just before Chase took a step to lead her inside, Elena tipped her head and glanced up to meet his gaze.

"Oh, I almost forgot," she said in as innocent a tone as she could muster. Then she stood up on tiptoe and leaned close to his ear to whisper, "I'm not wearing panties."

I'm not wearing panties.
I'm not wearing panties.
I'm not wearing panties.

The ballroom was crowded with people, most of whom he knew, many of whom he'd done business with. A hundred voices mingled together, raising the volume to near headache level.

And still, all he heard was those four words Elena had whispered in his ear a split second before they'd stepped into the party.

Stepped. Yeah, right. He'd been so stunned by her erotic admission that he'd been frozen in place. Riveted to the spot, his entire body hot and flaring like a lit match tip with unleashed passion. She'd had to practically drag him the rest of the way into the room. He couldn't have taken a single step on his own if his life depended on it.

And, frankly, he hadn't wanted to. The last thing he'd wanted to do at that point was mingle with business acquaintances and make small talk all night. He'd have rather written a sizeable check to tonight's charity—whatever the heck it was, anyway—and dragged Elena off to the nearest bed. His, hers, one of the hotel's…he honestly didn't care.

But even though she'd prodded him to do the right thing and go through with his plans for the evening, he heard nothing but her voice echoing in his brain.

I'm not wearing panties.

His gaze slipped—not for the first time—to her rear end, which swayed beneath the slithery, shimmery material of her gown when she moved.

If she hadn't told him she was naked beneath, would he have figured it out on his own?

Maybe. Lord knows he's spent his fair share of time staring at her derriere.

Then again, probably not. It wasn't like he was an expert on women's underwear or panty-lines.

But now that he knew...man, now that he knew, he couldn't seem to concentrate on anything else.

People kept coming up to him, Elena kept pulling him from place to place to chat, and he didn't think he'd heard a word any of them had said. She'd thoroughly scrambled his brain and sent every ounce of blood in his body just below the equator.

"Can we leave yet?" he whispered in her ear the first chance he got, pressing himself along her back so she would know exactly *why* he wanted to get out of there.

With a wide smile on her face for everyone else's benefit, she cocked her head in his direction and said, "We just got here. It would be rude to leave so soon."

He took the plate she offered, covered with a little bit of everything from the dinner buffet, while she turned back to get something for herself.

Leaning close, he let his breath stir the hair at her nape. "Then let's find a dark corner somewhere so we can be alone."

She laughed, the sweet tinkling sound going straight to his gut. His fingers clenched so tightly on the plate in his hand, he was surprised it didn't shatter.

"I'm not going to sneak off with you in the middle of this event so you can have your wicked way with me."

Her voice was moderately chastising, but her eyes glimmered with a sensual, teasing light.

"Then you shouldn't have told me about your underwear," he growled.

She blinked a couple of times with supreme innocence, then replied with equal innocence, "But I'm not wearing any."

His teeth snapped together hard enough to crack his molars. "That's what I mean," he hissed through tight lips.

With both their plates filled, she sashayed away from the buffet and toward the large round table where they'd been assigned seats with three other couples he recognized, but barely knew. Chase had no choice but to follow. When they reached the table, Elena set her plate at her place, then took his and did the same.

Still with that overly bright smile on her face, she moved close to him and whispered, "That was just an aperitif. A tiny treat to keep you interested until this little soiree is over, when we can go back to your place and do all of the things I know you're fantasizing about right now."

He studied her for a minute, nostrils flaring as he breathed heavily through his nose. She had no idea how close she was coming to being thrown over his shoulder and hauled out of there like a sack of grain. It would cause a horrified uproar, and their pictures would probably be in the morning paper, but at this point he honestly didn't care.

Then she moved even closer, brushing against him from shoulder to thigh as she took her seat from the side closest to him rather than farthest away.

"I promise it will be worth the wait," she murmured softly before sitting down.

Rather than tempering the desire that thrummed through his veins, her words threw fuel on the fire. But there was something to be said for waiting, wanting, letting arousal build to a near-agonizing level.

And when he finally got her alone, he would hold her to her promise. There were at least sixteen highly evocative images simmering in his brain at this very moment, and he intended to make sure they executed every single one.

He pulled out his own chair and sat down, muttering for her ears only, "It better be."

She smiled at his attempt to pout and patted his knee.

For the next hour, they picked at their meals, sipped champagne and chatted with the people around them. Chase couldn't have cared less about what anyone was saying, but he was well-schooled in the art of schmoozing.

After the food and drink and requisite speeches, everyone got up from their seats and once again began to mingle. This was when he could lean in and say, *We're out of here,* and drag her off the way he'd been dying to all night.

He put his hand on her elbow, prepared to do exactly that, when a small gaggle of tall, willowy, attractive women sidled up to them, their gazes sweeping over him before settling on Elena.

"Elena?" one in a low-cut lavender gown queried. "Elena Sanchez?"

"Yes?" Elena returned, her eyes warm and welcoming, as they'd been all night. Chase was beginning to think of it as her "polite public demeanor," the way she interacted with everyone from his business associates, to the chairwoman of tonight's fund-raiser, to the servers who milled around clearing tables and making sure no one's glass ever became truly empty.

"I thought it was you," the other woman practically squealed, taking Elena's hands in both of her own and giving them a squeeze. "I haven't seen you in years. Since high school."

The other three women in the little clique nodded and smiled just as widely. But when Elena didn't seem to recognize them, the one in lavender clucked her tongue and gave her an admonishing eye roll.

"Tisha Ferguson. We went to school together. Of course, I'm Mrs. Ferguson-McDonald now." She waved her left hand, making sure everyone in a six-foot radius got a glimpse of the huge diamond weighing down her ring finger. "I married very, very well."

To keep from scoffing Chase tightened his jaw until the bones nearly cracked. She'd married well. Well, bully for her. So had every other woman present. A person couldn't spit in this room without hitting a woman who had married very, *very* well.

"Tisha!" Elena said. "Of course. You look wonderful, I barely recognized you."

Leaning in, the two women kissed—that double cheek thing Chase had never understood. Then Elena's glance slid to the other women standing just behind Tisha.

"Leslie. Stephanie. Candy. It's nice to see you again. How have you been?"

The five of them chatted for a few minutes, with Tisha—the obvious spokesperson for the group— monopolizing most of the conversation. Finally, when there was an opening, Elena turned to him and attempted introductions.

"Do you remember Chase Ramsey?" she asked the four of them. "He went to school with us, too, though he was a year or two ahead of us."

The three standing back a bit smiled and nodded, but Tisha tipped her head and studied him more closely through narrowed, heavily painted eyes.

"Chase Ramsey. You're not…" Her glossy pink lips, previously pursed in thought, widened a split second before she broke into a high-pitched, cackling laugh. "Oh, my God! Chase Ramsey. I remember you now. You're that pathetic farmer's son who asked Elena to dance at that Christmas party at her parents' house. You should have seen your face when she turned you down. Oh, it was priceless!"

Eleven

Tisha threw back her head and chortled loudly, the other three joining in on a slightly less obnoxious scale.

Elena felt her heartbeat accelerate and a cold skittering of foreboding snake down her spine. The fingers of both hands curled instinctively as she fought the urge to plow her fist into the stuck-up witch's face.

Horrified, she glanced at Chase and saw the fury spark in his eyes before a mask of indifference dropped into place, hiding his true feelings from the world.

"Chase," she began, desperate to hold on to him. But before she'd even finished breathing his name, he turned on his heel and stalked away.

As she stared at his back, Tisha's laughter grew in both volume and venom.

And suddenly, Elena couldn't take it anymore. She

spun on her former friend, just keeping from reaching out to slap the smug grin off her face.

"How dare you," Elena charged.

Leslie, Stephanie and Candy quieted immediately, their mouths rolling into tiny Os of surprise that anyone would dare speak to their queen in such a tone. It took a moment longer for Tisha to settle, but finally the gleeful expression washed from her face and her eyes narrowed in annoyance.

"Excuse me?" she responded haughtily.

"What gives you the right to talk to people like that? To treat them like they're beneath you?"

Tisha's nose began to tip up, but Elena plowed ahead, not caring a whit that their confrontation was starting to draw a crowd.

"Do you know what you are, Tisha? You're a bitch. An arrogant, selfish, snobbish *bitch*. I'm sorry I ever met you, let alone was a part of your vicious little pack of hyenas back in high school."

Her blood was boiling, her lungs burning with the effort to suck in enough air for all she had to say to this woman.

"*You're* the one who's pathetic, Tisha Ferguson-McDonald." She sneered the hyphenated last name, making it as much of an insult as she could manage. "*You're* the one who should be embarrassed by your up-bringing, your appearance, your very existence, because you aren't half the human being Chase Ramsey is. He's the one who should be looking down his nose at you, not the other way around."

There was so much more she was feeling, so much more she wanted to say, but none of it was worth the time she was losing in following Chase.

Leaving Tisha and her cohorts with their mouths hanging open in shock, she spun around and pushed her way through the crowd, following the path Chase had taken only moments ago. The closer she got to the doors of the ballroom, the faster she moved until she was all but running.

Through the crowd, through the open double doors. In the spacious hallway, she stopped, looked around, but didn't see him.

Racing to the elevator, she elbowed people aside and pushed the down button, punching it over and over again until the doors closed and the compartment began to move.

"Come on, come on," she muttered, wishing belatedly that she had taken the stairs. Even in heels, she was convinced she could have made it to the lobby faster than the elevator was doing the job.

When the doors opened, she burst out, hurrying across the marble floor, glancing right and left for any sign of him. Outside, she scanned the cars coming and going, being both brought up and taken away by the crew of valets. Rushing up to the nearest green-vested worker, she described Chase and his car, and asked if the man had seen him.

"Oh, yeah," the man said, pointing toward the end of the hotel's long, curved driveway. "He just took off."

Elena's gaze followed the direction of the valet's finger. She saw brake lights flash for an instant and then tires squealed as the driver pulled away.

There was no use running after him, no use trying to catch up. He was gone, and Elena didn't know if she would ever get him back.

* * *

It had been two days since the party. Two days since Chase had taken off. Two days he'd refused to speak to her.

She'd taken a taxi to his house straight from the hotel, but either he hadn't gone home, or he simply hadn't answered the doorbell or her desperate knocking.

Although it was the last thing she wanted to do, she'd gone home from there and immediately tried to call him. First at home, then on his cell and even at his office. There'd been no answer, and he hadn't bothered to call her back, even though she'd continued to call several times a day, leaving numerous messages.

Elena suspected he was at work, but whenever she called, his receptionist asked for her name, then quickly told her he was unavailable.

He wasn't unavailable. He was avoiding her, and she knew it.

She could just strangle Tisha Ferguson-McDonald for her rudeness and insensitivity. Forty-eight hours later, she still wanted to track the woman down and slap her silly.

But most of all, she wanted to apologize to Chase and make sure he was all right. Well, he wasn't all right, as she was well aware. Otherwise he wouldn't have stormed out of the charity event, leaving her to find her own way home, and he wouldn't be dodging her calls.

Still, she felt she owed him an explanation, owed it to him to let him know she hadn't stood around and joined in on Tisha's cruel laughter and remarks after he'd left. She'd been a fool to be friends with those girls as a teenager, but she wasn't a fool any longer.

She'd also learned—possibly the hard way—just what

kind of man Chase Ramsey was, and that if she'd been smart, she would have danced with him that night at her parents' Christmas party and left her so-called friends standing there feeling stupid and alone.

Even if he couldn't forgive her, even if Tisha's careless comments had brought back too many old feelings, opened too many old wounds, she needed him to know *she* wasn't like that anymore.

When the phone on her desk rang, she froze, her heart dropping to her stomach. She hadn't been getting much work done, anyway, between praying Chase would call and her many attempts to call him, but she was almost afraid to answer for fear it *wouldn't* be him.

Finally, after four rings, she took a deep breath and picked up the receiver.

"Elena Sanchez," she answered, as she always did her work phone.

"Miss Sanchez, this is Nancy, Chase Ramsey's personal assistant. Mr. Ramsey would like you to meet him this evening at Chez Pierre at seven o'clock. You'll be accompanying him to a business dinner, so please dress appropriately."

Elena went from disappointed, when she realized the caller wasn't Chase, to surprised at the woman's words. With the fast-paced, matter-of-fact delivery, it took a moment for the request to sink in.

"Do you have any questions about these instructions, Miss Sanchez?" the woman prodded.

"No. I mean, yes! Yes." Elena was leaning forward on her desk, her free hand squeezing the phone cord so tightly, she was amazed the reception remained clear. "Is Chase there? Can I please talk to him?"

"I'm sorry," his assistant apologized with a distinct lack of emotion, "Mr. Ramsey isn't available at the moment, but he will see you tonight at Chez Pierre. Don't be late."

And then the line went dead, leaving Elena feeling empty and confused.

He wanted her to meet him tonight for a business dinner. What did that mean? Had he forgiven her for whatever imagined slight she'd committed the other night at the party? Had he gotten over Tisha's rude remarks?

And if so, why hadn't he called her himself? Why had his assistant contacted her and been so cold, when the woman had always been friendly to her before?

She didn't have answers to any of her questions and wouldn't until she saw him tonight. Only five more hours, she thought, glancing at her watch.

Five more hours until she would see Chase again, and could find out how he really felt about her.

From where he was sitting, Chase watched Elena enter the restaurant. She looked gorgeous, as always, in a brown and black animal print skirt and frothy brown blouse that dipped into a deep V in front.

But this time, he wasn't going to let her body or her smile affect him. He'd been crazy to ever let her get under his skin at all.

Convincing her to share his bed and accompany him to a few business dinners had been a bad idea to begin with. What had he been thinking?

Oh, he knew. He'd been thinking he could exact a little revenge for the way she'd treated him when they were kids, and get lucky in the process.

Hmph. Look how well that had turned out.

He took another gulp of the wine he'd been nursing since he'd arrived half an hour ago, glad Elena hadn't spotted him yet and made her way over. It was cruel of him, perhaps, but he wasn't going to lift a hand to draw her attention. He needed as much time as he could get before he had to be close to her again. Smelling her perfume and the fragrant shampoo she used on her hair...seeing her soft skin and remembering how it felt to touch, to stroke, to taste.

Against his will, his body hardened, every muscle going taut with desire.

Damn her. And damn his traitorous soul for still wanting her.

He didn't *want* to want her. He wanted to punish her—for what she'd done twenty years ago and for what had happened the other night.

His gaze narrowed as the rage began to roll through him. Rage, tempered with a modicum of embarrassment and a fair share of good old-fashioned lust.

She was coming toward him now, a tentative smile on her face. He could almost see her mind racing, wondering what she would encounter when she reached him.

Would he stand up, take her hand and kiss her cheek before inviting her to sit beside him? Or would he remain stoic and barely speak to her as she found her own place at the table to await their other guests?

He pushed aside the niggling of guilt that tried to convince him to forgive her, to let go of what had happened the other night at the fund-raiser and allow their relationship to fall back to the way it had been when she'd spent the night at his house. In his arms.

But that ship had definitely sailed and his head was once again on straight.

Elena was his mistress for as long as it took her father to get Sanchez Restaurant Supply back into the black—if he ever could—or until she decided to call things off. In which case, Chase would swoop in and buy out SRS, as originally planned.

But until one or the other of those things occurred, he intended to take full advantage of their arrangement.

She approached the table, still smiling, the maitre d' at her side, ready to hold her chair and see her properly seated beside Chase, leaving the other side open for the other two members of their party. Hiding her small purse beneath the cloth-covered table, she pulled her chair a fraction closer and nodded when the newly arrived waiter offered to fill her glass with the same dark claret Chase was drinking.

Her heart was pounding a mile a minute, and she was grinning so widely she was afraid her face would crack. Chase still hadn't spoken, which only made her stomach tighten all the more.

"Hi," she said brightly. So brightly, it hurt her own ears. She sounded like a puppet on one of those upbeat children's morning shows.

He nodded, taking a sip of his wine.

"I'm glad you called. Or at least had Nancy call for you," she added with a grin.

Leaning in, she lowered her voice and reached out to touch him. Before she could make contact, he once again raised his glass to his lips. She swallowed hard and drew back her hand.

It didn't mean anything, she told herself. Just because he hadn't spoken to her yet and apparently didn't welcome her touch didn't mean he was angry with her or still hurt about the other evening.

Maybe he simply wasn't a fan of participating in public displays of affection, however tame. Or maybe he was afraid his business associates would walk in any minute and get the wrong idea.

"I've been trying to reach you," she went on as though he wasn't acting the least bit peculiar. Folding her hands in her lap, she met his eyes. "Chase, I want to talk to you about—"

"Here they are," he said shortly, cutting her off. "This is a very important business associate and his wife. I'd appreciate if you'd be on your best behavior and try *not* to embarrass me."

Her eyes widened at his sharp warning. In all the time she'd been accompanying him to events and dinners like this one, she'd never done or said anything to embarrass him, nor had he ever felt the need to dictate her behavior before.

She found it more than a little strange. But maybe he was still smarting over Tisha's remarks. She couldn't blame him, and since she still felt she owed him an apology for that, she decided not to hold his apparently lousy mood against him.

He introduced her to the other couple, and Elena did her best to make witty, companionable small talk while they studied the menus, placed their orders and shared another glass of wine. While Chase was polite enough to Mr. and Mrs. Hasslebeck, he remained cold toward her. Which was why she jumped when his hand cupped her knee and started sliding upward.

The wine she was drinking sloshed against the sides of her glass and she gasped as it narrowly missed spilling on her blouse. Every eye at the table turned to her.

She laughed nervously, unnecessarily straightening the items at her place setting and jiggling her leg beneath the table in an attempt to shake off Chase's fingers. They didn't budge.

"I'm sorry," she apologized. "I was afraid I'd spilled wine on my clothes. You know how hard it is to get stains out of silk."

The other woman agreed with a chuckle and launched into a diatribe about some of the more stubborn stains she'd encountered in her lifetime.

Instead of being daunted by the turn in conversation or her attempt to dislodge his hand, Chase seemed even more determined to reach his goal. The hem of her skirt began to bunch as he roamed higher on her thigh.

His fingers skimmed between her legs and she had to bite her tongue to keep from making a sound. She clamped her thighs together, trapping his hand and stopping its maddening ascent.

Thankfully, their meals arrived a second later. He tugged and she reluctantly loosened her grip, knowing he needed his right hand to eat.

At least while he was busy at that, he wouldn't be feeling her up, she thought with distaste.

Not that she was opposed to Chase groping her under the right circumstances. She just didn't think they should be messing around beneath the tablecloth during what was supposed to be a business dinner. After warning her to be on *her* best behavior, shouldn't he be more careful of his own actions?

The meal passed without incident, and with Chase and Mr. Hasslebeck spending a good deal of time discussing business. Elena had just begun to breathe easy again when the coffee and desserts arrived, only to feel that telltale tickling once again.

Glancing over, she found Chase sipping his coffee, which he held in his left hand. His right was beneath the table…and crawling steadily upward.

"Excuse me," she said, pulling the cloth napkin from her lap and setting it beside the small plate holding a delicious-looking chunk of tiramisu as she got to her feet. "I'm just going to run to the restroom."

Without waiting for a response, she retrieved her purse and headed for the rear of the restaurant. Once inside the ladies' room, she rested her hands on the edge of the counter and took several deep breaths, gazing at her reflection in the mirror over the sinks. Behind her, a stall door opened, and the only other person in the restroom smiled as she walked up, washed and dried her hands, then left.

As soon as the door closed behind the woman, Elena shook herself, tore off a piece of paper towel, and wet it with cold water, dabbing her chest, her forehead, the nape of her neck.

She might not approve of what Chase had been trying to do out there, but that didn't mean it had no effect on her. One touch of his hand and she melted like snow on the first day of spring. Even now her knees were as weak as cooked noodles and her nerve endings were fluttering with unfulfilled desire.

The ladies' room door swung open again, and she

quickly straightened, pretending to be just finishing up so no one would think she'd been hiding…even if that's exactly what she was doing.

She smiled and turned to greet the woman who had entered on her way out. Her face fell when—instead of another woman—she found Chase leaning nonchalantly against the closed restroom door. His mouth curved with satisfaction, his eyes burning with devilish intent.

"What are you doing here?" she asked harshly, her fingers tightening on the damp paper towel in her hand.

Reaching behind him, he flipped the bolt on the main door, locking them inside, then took a menacing step forward. "What do you think?"

She took a step back, her hip bumping into the counter-top. "You can't be in here," she told him in what she hoped was a stern voice. "This is the ladies' room."

He kept walking, leaning over to check for feet visible under the stall doors. Then, when he found them all empty, he straightened and turned his attention fully on her. "I know what it is. And I know what I want."

It was clear from his expression that what he wanted was her.

She'd never seen him like this before. Passionate, yes. Eager. Determined. But he'd also always maintained a sense of control that seemed to be missing at the moment. As many times as they'd made love, and as hot as they'd been for each other, he'd never been driven to lock them in a public bathroom and take her while guests—*his* guests—were waiting to finish their dessert.

"Chase…"

She held out her hand, even threw the balled-up paper

towel at his chest. He only chuckled and continued stalking forward, already loosening his belt buckle.

She twisted, intending to leap for the locked door, but he caught her, pulled her around and pushed her against the row of sinks.

"Chase, no. We can't."

"Oh, yes, we can." His mouth covered hers while his fingers made short work of his slacks and then moved to the bottom of her skirt. "We just have to be quick and quiet about it."

He lifted her enough to hike her skirt to her waist, then set her more fully on the counter. His thumbs hooked into the sides of her garter belt and panties, pulling the delicate garments down to her ankles with one swift yank. She thought she heard something tear, but couldn't find it in her to care.

She hardly had time to breathe, let alone think, as he pried her legs apart, then closed the short distance between them and filled her to overflowing.

She gasped, her fingers digging into his shoulders, her thighs clutching at him as tightly as they could from such an awkward angle. He thrust hard and fast, his mouth scouring her face and throat, his hands dancing over her breasts and spine and buttocks—anywhere he could reach.

Her hips tipped to meet him, her need matching his own as they built rapidly toward climax. She'd never been taken so roughly, so spontaneously, before. She'd never *wanted* to be taken that way. But now…oh, now, she knew what she'd been missing.

Everything in the world faded away except Chase and

what he was doing to her. His hands, his mouth, his rigid length…all conspired to drive her over the edge.

With a barely suppressed shriek, she came, her body convulsing, her fingertips digging into his upper arms, her teeth biting down on a mouthful of his expensive Italian suit jacket to muffle the sounds she couldn't help but make. A second later, Chase stiffened, following her over and into the abyss.

His chest rose and fell against hers for several long minutes, then he straightened, took a step back, and began rearranging his clothes.

Startled by his sudden withdrawal, and self-conscious of her disheveled state, she hopped down from the counter and started redressing herself.

"We shouldn't have done that," she said, fighting to get her garter belt and stockings back in place without stripping completely and starting over from scratch. "What will your friends think?"

"They'll think we took a little longer than usual in the bathroom," he told her, rebuckling his belt and tucking in the tail of his shirt. "Either that or they'll think we sneaked off to the coat room for a quickie. Which isn't far from the truth."

He grinned, but there was no warmth in his eyes. A chilling sensation crept through her bones, heightening her senses.

"Chase," she said slowly, running her hands over the front of her blouse and sides of her skirt, checking the buttons and seams and even her jewelry. "Why did you do this?"

"Do what?" he asked distractedly, glancing past her into the mirror at her back and running his fingers through his slightly rumpled hair.

"This." She waved a hand, her voice growing stronger as her suspicions grew. "These strong-arm, neanderthal tactics. Following me to the restroom and locking the door. Having sex on the counter while your dinner guests wait and wonder where you are."

"What about it?" he asked, sounding cockier than ever. He finished fiddling with his hair and clothes and met her gaze. "I wanted you, and since you agreed to be my mistress for the foreseeable future, that means I can pretty much have you any time and anywhere I like."

Without waiting for her to respond, he spun on his heel and marched to the door. He flipped the lock, pulled on the handle, then said over his shoulder, "I'll see you back at the table." The door eased shut behind him.

Elena stared after him, speechless and wondering when her life had begun to spin so far out of control.

Yes, she'd agreed to be his mistress. She'd even enjoyed it after the initial uneasiness had worn off and she'd realized what kind of man Chase Ramsey really was.

But what she'd just seen was *not* the man she'd come to know. It was the side of him she'd met that first day in his office, but hadn't encountered since. She'd thought that part of him was gone, transformed into something more, something different, because of their growing affection for each other.

Apparently, she'd been wrong. Terribly, horribly wrong. And she couldn't pretend it wasn't.

Her hands shook as she picked up her clutch, her fingertips as cold as though she'd been sitting in a walk-in freezer for the last ten minutes.

She couldn't do this anymore. Couldn't play the part of

his mistress when her emotions were so much more involved than that. And she *wouldn't* stick around and be treated like a common whore by the man she'd fallen in love with.

Twelve

From the corner of his eye, Chase saw Elena reappear at the rear of the restaurant, skirt the dining area and march straight out the front door. She didn't glance in his direction or even stop to leave a message with the hostess about her premature exit.

For a minute, he considered going after her. Dragging her back to the table, if necessary, and demanding she fulfill her end of their bargain.

But then, he couldn't really blame her for ducking out early. He hadn't exactly been a gentleman with her in the ladies' room.

And that was as it should be. He refused to feel guilty for doing what they'd agreed upon from the very beginning, especially when he knew damn well she'd been just as hot and eager as he had. The memory of their fierce, frantic coupling still rang through his veins, making him want to track her down and take her all over again.

Which didn't bode well for his decision to put their relationship back on the right track. He was finished being led around by his raging libido. Finished being manipulated by wide eyes and pouting lips.

Elena might be beautiful, and she could certainly be both sweet and seductive, but she wasn't worth losing his soul.

Was she?

He watched until she disappeared from sight, then turned reluctantly back to the couple seated across from him. Creating an excuse for Elena's absence, he told the Hasslebecks she hadn't been feeling well before dinner, and that something she'd eaten must not have agreed with her, so he'd called a cab and sent her home. He wasn't sure they believed him, but he also didn't care.

Then, feigning an interest he didn't quite feel, he wrapped up the evening as quickly as possible, put the amount for the entire meal on his gold card and left a generous tip for the server. Parting company with Mr. and Mrs. Hasslebeck in the lobby, he headed for his car and drove home.

He didn't feel remorse for the way he'd treated Elena. Didn't miss having her near or want to track her down just to hear her voice again.

His fingers tightened on the steering wheel, his knuckles turning white.

He didn't. And he was damn tired of her invading his thoughts twenty-four hours a day.

Pulling into his driveway, he cut the engine, slammed the car door and stalked into the house.

He was better off without her.

First thing in the morning he'd have Nancy call Elena and find out if she was still willing to go along with their bargain. If she was, then he'd have to make it clear that he expected her to be where he wanted, when he wanted. No more of this flitting off just because she got her nose out of joint over something he did or said. As his mistress, she didn't get a say in his behavior.

And if she wanted out, that was fine with him, too. It might even be a better turn of events for both of them.

Of course, if that was the case, then his first order of business would be to put the wheels in motion to buy out Sanchez Restaurant Supply.

Either way, he was bound to win.

Too bad he didn't feel like a winner.

He tromped upstairs, his feet dragging like lead weights at the ends of his legs. He loosened his tie and shrugged out of his jacket, draping both garments over the back of a chair as he entered the master bedroom.

His bedroom, although it didn't feel quite as safe and comfortable as it once had. Before Elena had spent the night there…in his house, in his bed.

Even though she wasn't there, her presence lingered. Her perfume, the sound of her voice. He could smell her in the air, on the towels in the bathroom, on the sheets and pillowcases beneath the heavy comforter. He could hear her husky laughter everywhere he went, inside the house and out.

With a frustrated growl, he finished stripping on his way to the shower. Hot water did nothing to smooth the sharp edges of his lousy mood, and cold water did nothing to calm the arousal building steadily through his system.

What did he have to do to get her out of his head, out of his life?

He slapped his hand against the wet tile, letting beads of water pelt him directly in the face, wishing it could wash away the sick, gnawing ache in his gut as easily as it did dirt and sweat.

Just as he was stepping out of the shower and reaching for a towel, the phone rang. He thought about ignoring it, letting it go to voice mail, but at the last minute wrapped the towel around his hips and lunged for the nightstand.

"Yeah," he answered shortly.

"Chase," came the low, feminine response.

He didn't need the caller to identify herself to know it was Elena. His muscles immediately tensed, every cell in his body alert with physical longing.

"This is Elena," she continued matter-of-factly. "I'm sorry, but I won't be able to continue with our agreement. I—"

Her voice cracked, and deep in his chest he felt something crack, too.

"I just can't. I'd ask you to reconsider your plans to take over my father's business, but I know it wouldn't make much difference, so I guess I'll have to live with that. Goodbye."

Her words were strained and tear-thick until the very end, when they turned firm and confident. Chase sat on the edge of the bed, phone pressed to his ear, listening to the droning of the dial tone long after she'd disconnected.

Well, he had his answer, then, didn't he? It was over. She would finally be well and truly out of his life…out of his bed, out of his blood, out of his head.

Which was exactly what he wanted. The sex had been great, no doubt about it, but he could get good sex elsewhere, without all the strings that came with a woman like Elena Sanchez. The last thing he needed was strings tangling up his life.

Returning the earpiece to its cradle, he stood and made his way stonily back to the bathroom. He finished drying off and pulled on a pair of boxer shorts before climbing back into bed and beneath the covers.

With Elena out of the picture, he would no longer be haunted by the past. Finally, things could get back to normal.

He took a deep breath and closed his eyes, ready for the peace he expected to feel to wash over him. Instead, Elena's scent invaded his lungs. Her hair and skin and perfume, the mix of what made her fragrance so uniquely hers, filled his nostrils and caused his gut to twist.

He could strip the bed, leave the room, but he knew it wouldn't help. It wouldn't help because the smell wasn't in the sheets; the sheets had been washed since she'd last slept there. No, the smell—*Elena*—was in his blood and his brain. And maybe even, he suspected, his heart.

Elena couldn't stop crying. Not because of the way Chase had treated her the night before, but because she'd finally admitted to herself that what they had was not going to work. And she'd finally found the courage to call and tell him it was over.

Maybe, if they hadn't had the bad luck to run into Tisha at that party, things could have been different. At least they'd have had more time to see where the relationship was going.

She hadn't expected forever from him, but she would be lying if she didn't admit she'd been hoping for more. More time, more of a chance, just...*more*.

But now it was done, over, and she had to get on with her life.

Inhaling a ragged breath, she blew her nose, wiped her eyes and did her best to retouch the makeup she'd been attempting to apply for the last half hour.

With another sniff, she realized it was about as good as it was going to get. She didn't even bother with mascara, knowing she would simply cry it off in a matter of minutes and be left with black streaks running down her cheeks.

Fighting to get her emotions under control, she left the house and drove to her father's office, glad her sister wasn't around to chastise her for continuing to weep over a man Alandra now considered to be the scum of the earth.

It didn't help, either, that because of her decision to break things off with Chase, Elena now had to sit down with her father and explain that it was entirely possible he was going to lose his business because the extra time he'd been given to collect funds and backers was gone.

Pulling into the first parking spot she found on the street in front of the SRS building, she grabbed her purse, locked the car and headed inside.

The door of her father's office stood open, as usual. She tapped lightly, feeling her spirits lift when he raised his head and smiled widely at her.

"Elena, *querida,*" he said, getting to his feet and moving around his desk toward her. "You look lovely today. I'm so happy you came to visit me."

Only her father could make a positive comment about her appearance on a day like today, when both her eyes and nose were red and puffy from crying for the last twelve hours.

Victor Sanchez was on the short side, with a thick,

stocky frame and a generous portion of gray in the otherwise black hair forming a crown around his balding head. He stood two inches shorter than Elena, but that didn't keep him from wrapping his arms around her and lifting her off her feet as he hugged her close.

Elena laughed, as she always did when her father showed such affection for his girls, even as regret poured through her at the pain she was about to cause him.

"Papa," she said reluctantly when he pulled away, tears once again stinging her eyes, "I need to talk to you."

The joy on his face faded slightly as he sensed her inner turmoil. "Of course, of course."

He led her to a couple of chairs in front of his desk and sat down, urging her to do the same, still holding one of her hands. "Now tell me, *hija,* what has stripped the sunshine from your eyes."

"I have some bad news, Pop."

His salt-and-pepper brows met, his fingers tightening around her own. "What is it, *querida?* You know you can tell me anything."

She nodded, swallowing hard before continuing. "I know I told you everything would be all right with the company, that I worked out a deal with Chase Ramsey to give you some time to get together the money and backers you need to keep SRS afloat, but—"

She swallowed again, what she needed to say sitting in her chest like an anchor, pressing down on her heart.

"The…agreement…fell through." Her throat closed and the tears brimming in her eyes finally spilled over. "I'm so sorry, Papa. So, so sorry. I really did try."

For a few moments, her father sat in stunned silence.

Then he opened his mouth, but before he could speak, another voice cut him off.

"Victor, there you are."

Elena spun around in her seat, both her and her father's gazes whipping to the doorway, where Chase stood with his hands on either side of the jamb.

Her heart went from feeling like a stone in her chest to speeding like a racecar at the Indy 500.

What was he doing here? Especially looking like that.

She'd never seen him so rumpled. His expensive, tailored suit was a mass of wrinkles—and if she wasn't mistaken, it was the same one he'd been wearing last night at dinner, right down to the hastily knotted tie. His jaw carried a day's worth of dark beard stubble and his hair didn't seem to have been combed by anything more than his fingers.

"Chase Ramsey," he said by way of introduction. "I know we haven't met in several years, but I've been meaning to talk to you about Sanchez Restaurant Supply."

He directed his words to Victor, but his glance strayed more toward her.

"I'm no longer interested in acquiring your company for the Ramsey Corporation. I know you still have a ways to go before SRS is in the black again, and if you'd like some assistance in that area, I'd be happy to offer my expertise, maybe even some financial backing."

This time she and her father were both at a loss for words. She stared at Chase, wondering why he had changed his mind, even as she realized she didn't really care.

"I… *Gracias,*" Victor managed to stammer. "Thank you. I appreciate that, Señor Ramsey."

Chase nodded brusquely, as though the announcement about her father's business was merely an afterthought, then turned his intense sapphire gaze on her. "Elena, can I talk to you for a minute? Alone."

Dropping his arms, he took a step back from the open doorway, inviting her into the hall. His expression was both wary and hopeful.

Curious and confused, she stood, sparing a quick glance at her father, who looked almost ready to burst with happiness at having the family business out from under the oppressive threat of a takeover. Not to mention the possible assistance of a corporate tycoon who seemed capable of turning straw into gold.

"I'll be right back," she said shakily, then smiled at her father—whether to reassure him or herself, she wasn't sure.

Leaving her purse on the seat of her chair, she crossed the room, her heels clicking a staccato rhythm that matched the erratic beat of her heart.

She kept her eyes averted as she slipped past Chase, who towered in the doorway, and waited while he pulled the door closed. He wrapped a hand around her elbow and guided her a little ways away, sending a shock of sensations up her arm.

It was sad, she thought, that he could still have such an effect on her when she'd decided just yesterday to be finished with him. She should be immune to him already, shouldn't she? She should have cut off any feelings for him and built an impenetrable wall around her heart.

And maybe, if he hadn't waltzed into her father's office thirty seconds ago and done something so sweet, so generous, so completely out of character, she could have *stayed* mad at him.

Clearing her throat, she lifted her head and met his gaze. "That was very kind of you, thank you." And then, because she had to know, "What made you change your mind?"

"You did," he said, his fingers tightening where they still held her elbow before suddenly releasing her and letting his arms fall to his sides.

"After you left the restaurant last night, I went home, thinking everything was fine. Better than fine. I knew you were through with our agreement, through with me, and I was *relieved,* because ever since we started spending time together, I haven't felt like myself."

Running his hands through his hair, he blew out a harsh breath. "When you first walked into my office, I wanted to hate you, Elena. I relished the opportunity to punish you for how you made me feel twenty years ago in front of your friends."

"I'm sorry about that," she told him solemnly. "I've already tried to apologize—"

He shook his head, waving off her words. "I know. It doesn't matter. See that's the thing—I thought it did. For twenty years, I couldn't get the night of that Christmas party out of my head, and when you came to me with the request to help save your father's business, I reveled in the possibility of finally getting back at you."

She opened her mouth to speak again, but he cut her off.

"Then there was last night. I treated you with less than a hundred percent respect at dinner, pushing you, trying to put what was between us back on an even keel. What I considered an even keel, anyway," he added with a shrug. "You didn't appreciate my behavior and walked out— which is exactly what you should have done, and no less than I deserved. And after you called, told me our deal was off, I thought I'd feel better. I expected this weight to lift from my chest and my world to right itself again. Instead, I couldn't sleep. I could barely breathe."

Reaching down, he caught her hands, folding them within his own and giving her fingers a squeeze. "I could smell you in the room, hear your voice whispering in my ear. And despite everything I'd told myself, everything I *thought* I felt, *thought* I believed, *thought* I wanted, I suddenly realized what an idiot I've been. Because what I really wanted was for you to be right there beside me, in my arms. That's what I *want*. Now and forever."

Elena blinked, almost feeling the need to clean her ears and ask him to repeat what he'd just said. Her insides were quaking. She was moved and yet extremely wary.

Last night, he'd treated her as nothing more than his paid companion—albeit paid with a favor to her father rather than money. Now, he seemed to want more, he seemed to be saying he cared for her.

But how could she be sure? How could she know that he wouldn't change his mind the next time they ran into Tisha Ferguson-McDonald or someone just like her?

Her brain was telling her to be careful, to proceed with caution and maybe even make him suffer a little bit, make him earn her forgiveness.

Her heart was telling her to throw her arms around him, hug him tight and never let go.

She decided to opt for a reaction somewhere in between.

Ignoring the flutter of nerves in her belly, she steeled her voice and asked, "What are you saying, Chase?"

His hands tightened on hers as he readjusted his hold, linking their fingers together. He yanked her a step closer, staring down at her with the most intense, sincère expression she'd ever seen on his face.

"I'm saying I love you. I think I have since junior high. Even after you turned me down at your family's Christmas party, I don't think I could have been so hurt and angry for so long if you hadn't meant more to me than I cared to admit."

Hearing the words *I love you* on his lips made her pulse pound and her whole body flush warm with affection. She loved him, too. Her feelings hadn't blossomed quite as early on as he claimed his had, but she'd certainly admitted to them sooner.

"But what about what happened the other night with Tisha Ferguson-McDonald? I didn't have anything to do with what she said, Chase, I swear I didn't. And I don't share her opinions or her views. She's an arrogant, ignorant snob."

Her blood was running hot now with remembered fury and indignation. But instead of turning cold and shutting down the way she would have expected—the way she'd seen him respond before—he chuckled. Lifting their locked hands, he pressed the back of his index finger to her lips to postpone the rest of her Tisha-is-the-devil tirade.

"I told you," he said slowly, his tone low and lulling, "it doesn't matter. Yeah, it pissed me off and brought up a hornet's nest of ugly memories I didn't want to deal with and had been hoping were behind me. But it also helped me to realize—a little late in the game, I know," he said, his cheekbones turning pink for a split second as he glanced away sheepishly, then returned his gaze to hers, "that you're nothing like her. Nothing like the women who were with her. Maybe you were at one time, trying to fit in, just as you told me back in Las Vegas. But we all try to fit in when we're kids—even more so as teenagers— and we all do stupid, insensitive things, usually on and off throughout our lives."

He leaned in and pressed a soft kiss to the corner of her mouth. "I can forgive you for what you did when you were fourteen, if you can forgive me for what I did last night. I thought that by pushing you away, I could regain control of my emotions, relegate you to the status of a business arrangement where you belonged. I didn't understand at the time that you were so much more than that."

His voice lowered, seeping into her pores like warm honey.

"That you had gotten under my skin and into my heart. I had to almost lose you before my head cleared and I came to my senses."

Letting her arms fall limply to her sides, he cupped her face and tilted her chin up a fraction. Elena hoped her eyes weren't bright with tears and that her lips weren't quivering with the elation getting ready to spill over from her rapidly swelling heart.

"Tell me I'm not too late, Elena." He whispered the request, his breath dusting her cheeks and fluttering the hair at her temples. "Tell me you feel the same, and that I haven't completely screwed things up with my thick skull and obstinate nature."

For a moment, all she could do was blink. If she closed her eyes, she thought she might faint from such pure, undiluted joy. It all sounded so wonderful, so promising, like everything she'd ever wanted and more.

But she was afraid of getting her heart broken. Of opening herself up to him again, only to be hurt again—and possibly be hurt much worse the second time around.

"What about what Tisha said? What if we run into her—or someone like her—and she acts the way she did the other night? Are you going to hold that against me? Are we going to have to go through this every time someone says something you don't like?"

His lips thinned for a brief moment, but he answered easily enough. "I can't promise I'll be happy about it, or that it won't put me in a bad mood for a couple of days. But I won't take my frustrations out on you; I'll only ask that you put up with me and listen to my complaints until I get over it. I know who I am, though, and I don't need anyone's approval or reassurance."

He ran his fingers through her hair, tucking a few strands behind one ear. "It might have taken me twenty years to figure that out, but I know it now and I'm not going to forget. All I'm asking is for you to give me a chance to prove that. I do love you, Elena. I want you to stay with me. Not as my mistress, but as my wife and partner for the rest of our lives."

A beat passed while Chase studied her face, his eyes blazing like chips of blue ice.

"What do you say, sweetheart? Am I worth the risk?"

He was. Their relationship might not always be easy, but as long as they loved each other and agreed to talk things out, she believed it could work.

"You're a hard man to say no to," she said softly, blinking back tears and sucking air into lungs that felt as if they hadn't been filled for years. "And I do love you, so my answer is yes."

A grin as bright as the sun spread across his face. His happiness spilled onto her until they were both smiling and laughing.

He kissed her, as thoroughly as she could ever remember, and she let herself sink into him. With a sigh, she wrapped her arms around his neck and just barely resisted the urge to pick up one foot the way women did in those old black-and-white movies when every cell in their bodies was being seductively devastated by a man's passionate embrace.

They pulled apart, panting and quickly heading toward overheated.

"So is that a yes?" he asked. "Will you marry me?"

"That's a yes," she said, unable to keep the smile of contentment from her face. Then she reached out and pinched him in the stomach, hard.

He yelped, rocking back on his heels and rubbing at the abused area.

"But I reserve the right to slap you upside the head if you start acting all pouty and rude the way you did the other night."

"Agreed," he said, giving his rumpled shirt a final pat before returning his hands to her waist. "Absolutely agreed. Slap me, kick me, douse me with ice water. But I promise never again to do what I did to you at that restaurant."

She cocked her head and arched a brow. "Oh, I don't know. It wasn't *all* bad. I'll certainly never be able to wash my hands in a public restroom again without having flashbacks."

His grin widened. "Why, soon-to-be Mrs. Ramsey, I think you're a little bit naughty."

Tossing her hair over one shoulder, she smiled back at him and pressed the front of her body against the long, solid warmth of his.

"What can I say?" she returned with all the mischief she could muster. "I've had a lot of practice recently. And I learned from the best."

Epilogue

Christmas music played softly in the background while approximately fifty guests, family and friends, drank and laughed and mingled. The elegant ballroom was decorated with golden ornaments, silver snowflakes and garlands of holly strung across the top of every window and doorway. In one corner a giant Douglas fir twinkled with a thousand tiny yellow lights.

Off to the side, near a long table set with a punch bowl and platters of colorful cookies, Elena stood with her hand clasped in Chase's. She wore a simple white dress that fell to mid-calf, and carried her bouquet of white roses with a single bright red poinsettia in the center. On her left hand, a princess-cut diamond and brand-new gold band sparkled.

It was her wedding day, and she'd never been happier.

She'd never seen Chase look more handsome or content, either.

He'd been the one to suggest they get married on Christmas Day, and hold both the ceremony and reception at her father's house—in the same room as the Christmas party he'd attended all those years ago.

She'd argued strenuously against it, afraid it would tear open too many wounds, stir up too many old feelings they were just starting to put behind them. But he'd been adamant and she'd finally given in.

She was still surprised the day had gone off without a hitch—and that Chase hadn't gotten cold feet at the last minute. But then she felt guilty for even thinking that way.

Tipping her head to the side, she glanced up at her new husband and smiled when he turned to meet her gaze. He leaned down and pressed a kiss to her mouth—something he'd been doing on a regular basis since the minister had said "You may now kiss the bride" only a few hours ago.

"Merry Christmas, Mrs. Ramsey," he murmured as he straightened.

"Merry Christmas, Mr. Ramsey," she returned.

He wrapped his arm around her waist and tugged her close to his side. She leaned her head back on his shoulder, watching their friends and relatives enjoying themselves, even though they'd sacrificed their own holiday plans to be with her and Chase on their special day.

Her father was dancing with Chase's mother? His brother and sister-in-law were standing close, their arms wrapped around each other in an imitation of slow dancing, but they seemed to Elena to merely be swaying back and forth while they exchanged soft, intimate kisses. Chase's father was doing a two-step with a few exaggerated bounces to amuse baby Amelia, who giggled and cooed in delight. And Alandra, of course, was moving around the room, dancing with the eligible bachelors who caught her eye.

Their families got along stupendously, much to Elena's relief. And thanks to Chase not only offering advice to her father on how to rescue SRS from certain doom, but jumping in with both feet and actually becoming a partner in the business, Sanchez Restaurant Supply was doing almost better than it had in its heyday.

"We should probably be dancing ourselves," Chase said above her ear. "People will start to talk if all we do all night is stand here looking stiff and dopey."

She chuckled, then twisted around and began to walk backward onto the dance floor. "I suppose you're right. Christmas carols are an odd choice for a wedding reception, but then, so is a Christmas wedding."

When they reached an open area, he pulled her into his arms, holding her tight as they moved to the more energetic beat of "Jingle Bell Rock."

"It's not odd, it's romantic. And think of it this way— I'll never forget our anniversary. If I do, you have my permission to divorce me and demand I give you everything I own as alimony."

"You're darn right you better not forget our anniversary," she told him, poking him none too gently in the chest. "Especially when all of this was your idea."

When he didn't say anything more for several seconds, she asked, "You aren't sorry, are you? That we had the wedding here, at this time of year? You know, considering."

"What? You mean because this is the site of my abject

humiliation back when I was a sensitive, impressionable teenager?"

He looked down at her for a moment, his expression so serious, she was sure they were about to have the first blow-up of their married lives. Then he grinned and relief washed over her.

"No, I'm not sorry. I wanted to marry you here, on Christmas Day, so that you would know I've well and truly put the past behind me. Besides, if it hadn't been for what you said to me that day, I wouldn't have spent the next twenty years hating you."

She rolled her eyes at that, but he ignored her and continued.

"And I wouldn't have blackmailed you into going to bed with me, and we wouldn't have fallen in love. If anything, I should be thanking you for being a conceited, snobbish little prima donna, trying to impress her friends by stomping on my tender, youthful heart."

He said it with such suppressed glee that she almost reached out to smack him on the back of the head. And wouldn't that be a lovely thing for their guests to witness on their wedding day? Not to mention the photographer, who—while circumspect—seemed to be catching on film everything that happened in the room.

"I thought you said you forgave me for that," she pointed out, taking the opportunity to step on his foot "accidentally on purpose" as they made a semi-difficult turn.

His eyes glittered in the dim lighting, letting her know just what a wicked, dangerous man she'd married.

"Oh, I do forgive you," he said. "That doesn't mean I won't rub it in for a while, though."

She gave a low snort. "Fine. But I'm only going to put up with it for twenty years or so, so you'd better get it out of your system while you've got the chance."

The corners of his mouth curved and he leaned in until his lips brushed hers. "Sounds fair to me."

* * * * *

Celebrate 100 years of pure reading pleasure with Mills & Boon®

To mark our centenary, each month we're publishing a special 100th Birthday Edition. These celebratory editions are packed with extra features and include a FREE bonus story.

Plus, starting in February you'll have the chance to enter a fabulous monthly prize draw. See 100th Birthday Edition books for details.

Now that's worth celebrating!

15th February 2008

Raintree: Inferno by Linda Howard
Includes FREE bonus story Loving Evangeline
A double dose of Linda Howard's heady mix of passion and adventure

4th April 2008

The Guardian's Forbidden Mistress by Miranda Lee
Includes FREE bonus story The Magnate's Mistress
Two glamorous and sensual reads from favourite author Miranda Lee!

2nd May 2008

The Last Rake in London by Nicola Cornick
Includes FREE bonus story The Notorious Lord
Lose yourself in two tales of high society and rakish seduction!

Look for Mills & Boon 100th Birthday Editions at your favourite bookseller or visit www.millsandboon.co.uk

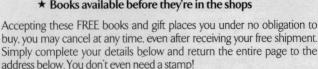